AF084601

PapRise
A story of Growth and Betrayal or How PapCorp came to rule the world
by
Adam R. Mathews
ISBN: 978-1-9161066-3-5

© Adam R. Mathews, 2019

The right of Adam R. Mathews to be identified as the author of this book has been asserted in accordance with the Copyright, Designs and Patents Act 1988.

All Rights Reserved.

No reproduction, copy or transmission of the publication may be may be made without written permission. No paragraph or section of this publication may be reproduced copied or transmitted save with the written permission or in accordance with the provisions of the Copyright Act 1956 (as amended)

A copy of this book is deposited with the British Library

Disclaimer:

This is a work of fiction. Names, characters, businesses, places, events, locations, and incidents are either the products of the author's imagination or used in a fictitious manner. Any resemblance to actual persons, living or dead, or actual events is purely coincidental. Historical details should not always be taken as accurate.

Published by

i2i
PUBLISHING

i2i Publishing. Manchester.
www.i2ipublishing.co.uk

Contents

Chronological Timeline	iv
List of main characters with birthdays	v
Notes on pronunciation	vii
1. Exile	1
2. The Tower	17
3. The Meeting	37
4. Up and Out	53
5. Lemonade	70
6. Rascals	84
7. Bio-dome 1	98
8. Bio-dome 2	114
9. Flowering	126
10. Action	144
11. Revolution	159
12. Consequences	173
13. Enclosure	192
14. Carrascoy	209
15. The Referendum	225
16. Business	234
17. Going Back	249
18. Moving Forwards	269
19. Power	283
20. Home	298
21. Lies	315
22. Growth	329
23. Pressure	342
24. Pop	357
25. The Ides of March	373
26. Truth	393
27. Exile Again	404
Credits	422

Chronological Timeline

Day	Year	Chapter
22nd/23rd November	1956	1. Exile
13th June	1957	5. Lemonade
21st August	1958	9. Flowering
17th September	1959	16. Business
27th October	1961	22. Growth
15th March	1962	25. The Ides of March
23rd August	2030	3. The Meeting
22nd September	2032	6. Rascals
15th May	2035	10. Action
13th October	2035	12. Consequences
6th November	2036	21. Lies
9th December	2037	26. Truth
18th March	2042	4. Up and Out
5th May	2045	11. Revolution
26th October	2045	7. Bio-dome 1
26th October	2045	8. Bio-dome 2
10th February	2048	19. Power
26th November	2050	13. Enclosure
1st June	2053	15. The Referendum
24th May	2055	14. Carrascoy
8th December	2057	2. The Tower
17th September	2059	17. Going Back
17th September	2059	18. Moving Forwards
18th September	2059	20. Home
16th July	2061	23. Pressure
16th July	2061	24. Pop
2nd April	2063	27. Exile Again

List of main characters with Birthdays

(In order of first named appearance)

Name	Place of Birth	Date of Birth
Zoltán Papp	Budapest, Hungary	8th Dec 1932
Attila Bacsik	Budapest	1926
Gábor Bacsik	Budapest	1932
Nóra Weissmann	Székesfehérvár, Hungary	1940
Vincent Humbolt	Whitby, England	2033
Zoltan O'Dillon	Manchester, England	2011
(Lord) Michael O'Dillon	Manchester	1983
Francis Atkins	Sandringham, England	1994
Larry Pickering	Harrogate, England	1987
Jemima Kemel	Adana, Turkey	2026
Minnie Brownlow	Manchester	2025
Brian Brownlow	Manchester	2022
Ruth Brownlow	Manchester	2047
Naomi Brownlow	Manchester	2042
Helen Humbolt	Whitby	2008
Rebecca Kingston	Middlesbrough, England	2008
Winston Humbolt	Manchester	2001
Tariq Emami / Panjit Agarwal	Middlesbrough	2001
Paul Broddle	Scarborough, England	2005
Henry Gritton	Knighton, Shropshire, England	1913
Molly Gritton	Wolverhampton, England	1920
Harry Lanker	London, England	1992
Bernie Douglas-FitzAllan	Glamis, Scotland	2011
Samuel Dietrich	Manchester	2001
Éamon O'Dillon	Manchester	1922
Callum O'Dillon	Manchester	1937
Aliyá Talavera	Murcia, Spain	2038
Dolores Talavera	Murcia	2009

Oscar Talavera	Murcia	2009
Paco Rufián Senior	Murcia	2016
Paco Rufián Junior	Murcia	2038
Jaap De Waal	Colesburg, South Africa	2027
Benjamin Humbolt	Whitby	2038

Notes on pronunciation

PapRise includes a number of characters whose first language is not English. Some terms show the foreignness of conversation to characters and readers alike. Others are to give their language more flavour. Below are a selection of important words, with pronunciations by the author.

Aguardiente: Spanish for 'firewater' or strong liquor, the A is open like in bad not bade, guar is from jaguar, di is more like in dig than in dirt, ente are the first sounds of entertain
Alcalde: Meaning Mayor in Spanish, where Al in is Alex not final, cal is like calorie not call, and de is from Denmark but not from deliver
Anyám: Meaning my mother in Hungarian. An is pretty much how the English say on, while yám is a sort of sweet potato
ÁVO: Although an acronym, this is said as one word, where ÁV sounds like a Cockney saying have, and the O is like the beginning of ought
Bacsik: Bacs is pronounced 'botch', as in to do a bad job, ik is like sick with no 's'
Baszd meg: A common Hungarian curse word. Baszd is basically the same as 'bossed' in English, although the last letter is a firm 'd' not a 't'. Meg is short for Megan
Cabrón: Cab is like taxi, rón is the name of a ginger wizard
Chucho/Chuchi: A Spanish nickname for men called Jesús, chu is more like in chutzpah than churlish, cho is from chomp not choke, and tai chi is a bit like kung fu
Csepel: A working-class district of Budapest. Cse sounds like 'che' as in Chelsea, pel is like spell with no 's'
Coño: A vulgar Spanish term for female genitalia, it is more accepted in Spain than in Britain. Co is from comment not comb, like the ñ is from new but not known. The o is from honour not throne
Fiúk: Literally 'boys' in Hungarian, Fi sounds like a fee you have to pay, úk is like the end of hook
Fröccs: An important drink in Hungarian culture, white wine and soda water, the Fr is like in freedom but slightly rolled if you can, while öccs is pretty much church without the first ch
Fuego: Pronounce all the letters, as in kung 'fu', and ego rhymes with 'may go'
Grüß Gott: An Austrian greeting meaning 'greet God', where Grü is like in gruesome, ß is a sharp German 's' as in Simon not Sherlock, Gott as in forgotten

Guiri: A Spanish term for white foreigners. Gui is written in English as 'gi' in give, ri is a rolling 'ring'
Győző: Győ is a soft Ger, like a Brummie saying German, ző rhymes but with a 'z'
Hija/Hijo (also spelt mee-khá): Meaning (my) daughter or son. The h is silent and the j (or kh) is a guttural sound like the end of a Scottish loch, hence 'ee-khá'
Hostia: Literally sacramental bread, the word is used often in Spanish for various reasons. The h is silent, so it's pronounced 'os-tear', as in crying not to rip
Jaap: J is said like an English 'y', while aap is something like the end of harp
Kurva: Meaning 'whore' in Hungarian, it's often used as an adjective. Kur is like core in English with a rolled 'r', while va sounds like the 'vo' in volunteer
Mogollón: Colloquial Spanish for 'a lot'. Mog rhymes with fog, the o sounds the same, while llón is like a Frenchie saying Jon
Murciano: The slurred dialect of Murcia or the name for its inhabitants. Mur rhymes with a Scottish person saying 'sure', ci is the 'thi' in atheist, a is open like in amber, no is more knot than know
Na: A highly versatile Hungarian word, the sound is approximately written in English as the 'no' in nob but not nobility
Persze: Meaning 'of course' in Hungarian, per is like pair or pear, the r should be rolled, and sze is the start of sense
Petőfi: Hungary's national poet, the Pe is like in pet, tő is basically turn with no 'n', and fi is the same as in 'fiúk'
Qué dices?: Literally 'what are you saying?' Qué is the typical Spanish, like someone you can't say the last two letters in 'Kent', di is more River Dee than Lady Di, ces is 'thes' as in thespian
Szabad Magyar: (often spelt So-bod Mod-jar) Sza/So is from sorry not solar, bad/bod like in bod, not bode. Magyar is a
combination of mod, from modest not modal, and jar which is where you keep jam
Szia: Almost 'see ya' in English, it means both hi and bye. The 'ya' is like the 'yo' in yob
Szóda: Similar to the English 'soda' the ó is elongated to sound like the 'ou' in pour
Tío: Literally uncle in Spanish, it's used more like mate. Tí is very like 'tea' which you drink, o is more from than old
Venga: Meaning come on, the Spanish v is somewhere between an English 'v' and 'b', en is the same as enable and ga is like gap with no 'p'
Zoltán: Differs from 'Zoltan' as the á is strong like in apple, not in orange

To mum,

Without your help and support,

None of this would've been possible

1. Exile

22nd November 1956
Győr-Moson-Sopron County, north-west Hungary

Yellow mud clung to Zoltán Papp's boots. He kicked the air and the leather sole of his standing foot almost slipped from under him, but the clay hung on. It was as if the soil of Hungary was making one last grab for its children before the Red Army could drive them away.

It was one of those winter days when the mist dulled the senses, mixed with wood smoke and drifted like watercolour over bare branches. The freezing air bit at Zoltán's face and he tucked his chin into his scarf, felt the wool graze his stubble. Hunger gnawed at his stomach, while his deep-set eyes had sunk further behind his cheekbones. And although he hadn't dared to look at his feet since fleeing the capital, the blisters made him wince at every step.

Despite it all, Papp was as alert as ever and far from alone. Before him, along the boundary between marshland and forest, trudged a line of similar refugees. From his place at the rear, Zoltán couldn't see those out front – they were already hidden amongst the trunks of the next copse.

Right before him plodded a couple with a child between them. Gloved hands in theirs, the boy was tugging at the two adults to swing him along but neither lifted an arm. Zoltán watched the mother bend down to speak to him but couldn't make out what she said.

Whatever it was, it didn't work, because the boy grabbed both his parents' sleeves and jumped into the air, kicking up a spray of earth. At his highest point, he lost hold of the fabric and fell to the muddy path. He slid to a halt on his backside, looked up at his mother with his arms upstretched and cried out, "anyám!"

"What did you expect, Győző?" his mother replied. "I told you not to do that. This isn't the time for fun and games. No one's enjoying this walk, but we have to keep going. We mustn't get left behind."

Zoltán Papp heard the latter part of the conversation and he stopped beside the family. "I can take him for a while," he said, "if it'll help. As you say, we don't want to get too far behind. Do you want to ride on my shoulders, little man?"

Zoltán bent down to lift the boy but found Győző already on his feet, smiling up at him. "He's terribly dirty," said his mother, her head wrapped in a muddied shawl. "And he's not as light as he looks. Are you sure you want to do this?"

"We need to keep moving," Zoltán replied, "and this is the quickest way. We're almost a whole field behind the others now and trailing off like this isn't a good idea."

"I agree," said Győző's father, peering through a slit between his scarf and flat cap. "Do you know where we're going?"

"One of the guys up front has family around here," said Zoltán. "We're going to their farm and they'll lead us to the border."

"Who is he?" said the father. "Can we trust him?"

"I know him from university," Zoltán replied. "We studied chemistry together at the BME."

"And you've walked the whole way from Budapest together?" the man continued.

"Sure. It was far too risky to get on a train." Zoltán glanced upwards. "Come on," he said, "we need to go. It'll be night soon." The boy climbed onto his shoulders.

But the father kept talking. "You were right about the trains," he said. "We managed to get one of the last out of the Eastern terminus. The carriages were so full we barely had room to stand. Just before Győr, we heard a rumour that the ÁVO were waiting at the station, so when the train slowed down, we jumped out of the window. We left most of our luggage inside. We've been walking two days since then. I lost half the sole of my boot yesterday and the rest is just tied on with string." The man showed off the underside of his shoe.

Zoltán nodded, secured Győző on his shoulders, and strode off in spite of his blisters. The boy's parents trotted on behind, unable to continue their chitter-chatter.

But taking after his father, the boy nattered on the whole way. "Do you know anything about Austria?" he asked. "Are there going to be other children there?"

"Of course there are," Zoltán chuckled, "there are lots of children, and good schools. You'll make loads of new friends, I'm sure."

"Do they speak Hungarian?"

"No, in Austria they speak German."

"But I don't know German," said Győző.

"Me neither," said Zoltán, "but we'll learn."

"I don't want to learn German. I want to stay in Hungary."

"So do I, Győző. So do we all. But we don't have a choice. If I don't leave, they'll send me to Siberia, if I'm lucky."

"Where's that?"

"Far, far away."

"And what if you're not lucky?"

"I don't want to find out. The ÁVO are evil people, they do horrible things."

"Like what?"

"Let's just hope we never find out."

"What do they do, Zoltán? Tell me, I want to know!" The boy kicked his heels against the young man's chest.

Zoltán grabbed Győző's ankles. "If you don't stop that, you'll have to walk. Do you want that?"

"No," said the boy, gazing into the shadows of the forest. He kicked no more.

In the last months of 1956, some quarter of a million of Zoltán Papp's countrymen made that same trip westward. Only weeks earlier, in the heat of revolution, they'd dared to believe they'd thrown off their Soviet shackles for good. But then the tanks rolled into Budapest and the ÁVO secret police came out of hiding to take revenge.

Which is why the group avoided the main roads; it was obvious to anyone that saw them where they were coming from, where they were heading. Class traitors all, wanted for crimes against the state. The threat of repercussions was so severe as to force so many from the only country they'd ever known, had ever wanted to know.

As the afternoon wore on, the light faded through the misty maze of tree trunks. From his perch on Zoltán's shoulders, Győző ducked around the bare branches. Yet the boy barely stopped for breath as they ghosted through the forest. Which is how Zoltán Papp learned which girls and boys at school his young friend liked the most, and the least; his favourite walks in the Buda hills; a bicycle he'd seen in a shop window. Eventually, his ramblings turned to questions. "Where is your family, Zoltán?" he asked.
"They're still at home in Budapest."
"Didn't they want to come too? Aren't they worried about you?"
"I'm sure my mum's worried," said Zoltán, "but my dad works at the telephone exchange and he won't leave. He says he's a good worker so he's safe. I tried to persuade them they were in danger, but it was no use. My father's a very stubborn man."
"What will happen to them?"
"I don't know Győző, I really don't know..."

Winter nights come early in Hungary. Even though it was still not six in the evening, it had already been dark for some time when the outline of a barn materialised in a clearing. Light flickered through the gaps in the wooden-plank walls, and the murmur of conversation grew louder as they approached. Zoltán lifted young Győző from his shoulders and placed him on the ground, then stretched his arms out wide and rotated his shoulders.
Papp nudged open the door and peered inside. There must have been two dozen people in that candle-lit cowshed, but

after searching every one Zoltán couldn't find his university mates. He noticed a pile of hay bales at one end of the barn and clambered up to get a better look. But still he couldn't see anyone he recognised.

Papp found he wasn't alone at the top of the stack. Beside him, three other souls slouched between the wooden rafters, wrapped up in scarves and hats and shrouded in the stench of gasoline. Zoltán turned to the closest of the three. "Have you seen Peti and Krisztina?" he asked.

"Who the cock are you talking about?" the man growled back.

"The leaders of the group," Zoltán replied, "the ones we've been following."

"We've not been following no one," said the man, "we've got here on our own."

"Then what are you doing here?"

The farthest set of rags twitched. "We've been looking for the border for two days," said a young woman. "We heard they blew up the bridge so we're looking for a way across, just like everyone else."

"Baszd meg," Zoltán cursed. "I wish I had my rifle with me."

"You?" his neighbour sneered. "You're saying you actually fought? I thought all you students did was march around the campus with posters and lists of demands."

"I was at the hospital on Rákóczi Street," Papp replied. "I was firing at the tanks from the second floor."

"A rifle against a tank?" jibed the man in the middle. "That wasn't much use. Did you even hit anyone?"

"I didn't have many bullets."

"So, no then?"

"No."

The man huffed, crossed his arms and sat back on the haystack. They said not another word to each other. But neither could any of them sleep.

It was late into the night when a man came into the barn to herd the group outside. Zoltán Papp was among the last to gather, and when he joined the others, he found the temperature had plummeted yet further and the fog was thicker than ever. Zoltán scoured the faces and hunched backs for someone he knew. But the amounts of clothes people were wearing, as much as the breath steaming before their faces, hid their identities and muffled his voice so he couldn't see them and they were unable to hear him.

There was a muted shout of "Zoltán!" and a pair of little arms wrapped around his leg.

"Be quiet, Győző," said his mother, "remember that there's no speaking now, okay?"

"Next stop Austria!" said the father.

"I'm not happy about this," said Papp, shaking his head. "I don't know where my friends are, and I don't know who this guy is."

"He seems okay," said the father. "He said he'd post the letter to my mother."

"And charged you two whole forints for the stamp," said his wife.

"So?" said her husband. "What am I going to do with forints in the West? They're worth nothing as it is. And I'm happy to tip this guy well, if it means we'll be any safer."

The guide led the way for the group to waddle after him; wearing four or five pairs of trousers they walked with legs straight like debreceni sausages. But Zoltán Papp had only the scarf, overcoat and grey flat cap he'd been wearing since he fled. He shivered. The night air stung his nostrils and he pulled his scarf up over his nose to warm himself on his breath. He rammed his gloves into his jacket pockets and walked alongside Győző and his parents.

The night held a kind of silence that the city dwellers had rarely heard. As their guide took them along a roadway raised above the swamps, the only noises were the crackle of frozen reeds to either side and the scuffing of boots on dirt.

Zoltán turned to Győző's father. "I don't like it," he whispered. "We're such an easy target here. If any patrols come along, we're done for. We should get off the road."

"I'd prefer to stay with the guide," said the father. "I mean, the fog will hide us pretty well, thank the Lord. But I have no idea where we are, and I really don't want to get lost in those freezing marshes."

"Okay," Zoltán replied, "that's your decision. I'll stay with you all, but I'm going to do it from down there."

Zoltán Papp slowed his pace. When there was no one behind him, he darted down the bank and slid to a stop just before the reeds. He glanced up at the roadway and saw the group walking on like ghosts in the fog.

Papp picked his way along the edge of the marsh, watching only the procession of shadows above him. With a hand on the bank to balance himself, he continued on for what felt like hours. Even wearing both his pairs of gloves, the frost soon seeped through the wool and numbed his fingers. But his mind was sharp on adrenaline, and he froze at the first rumbling of a motor. Only then did he notice he was shivering from cold or from fear.

A pair of headlights appeared through the mist. Zoltán held his breath, could hear his own heart thump through his shaking body, felt the pressure building in his gut. He watched a canvas-sided van stop before the group, heard the squad of soldiers jump from its rear and he threw himself face up onto the bank. He took a few breaths before lifting his head to see what was happening. But all he could make out was the refracting light of the headlamps and an eerie waltz of shadows.

Up on the road, some metres ahead, Győző held tight to his mother's glove. "I'm scared mummy," he said.

"Me too, my son," she replied, "but we have to be brave now and do what they tell us."

"These are bad people, mummy, we have to run away, or they'll turtle us."

His mother smiled into her shawl. "You stay with me, Győző, and you'll be fine. They won't turtle you or torture you, you're only four-years-old."

"These are bad people, mummy. I know who the ÁVO are and what they do. I wish we could hang them all like the ones I saw in Moscow Square." The boy's hand slipped out of his mother's. "I love you," he said.

His mother had no time to react as the boy turned a right angle and darted towards the swamp. "Győző!" she shouted.

But it was too late. A rattle of gunshot broke the stillness and the young boy splashed into the reeds.

Zoltán saw it all. The pressure in his stomach shot up through his chest and out of his mouth. "Nem!" he yelled, jumping up and running towards his young friend. But the ratter-tat-tat of a machine-gun stopped him and sent him reeling into the frozen fen.

23rd November 1956

When Zoltán Papp blinked his eyes open, he found the pale winter sun hanging low in the sky. He tried to stretch out his legs and arms, only to find his whole body cocooned in a pile of straw. He wormed himself free, pulled out the hay he found in his boots and eased his feet into them. They were damp, chilly, but the grass had absorbed most of the moisture from both his clothes and his shoes, and when he glanced at his shoulder, he found it bandaged in bright white cloth. He sniffed, recognised the smell of petrol and looked up to see the group of three from the barn.

"Oh, here's the son of a bitch," said the younger of the two men. "We thought you'd had it, we were just discussing leaving you here."

"No, we weren't," said the woman. "Ignore him. How are you feeling?"

"I'm okay, I think," said Zoltán as he poked the bandaging around his shoulder.

"You were lucky," the woman continued. "It was just a scratch. And we weren't far behind you to help. My name's Nóra Weissmann, these two are the Bacsik brothers, Attila and Gábor." This was the first time Zoltán had seen any of the group's faces, and he noticed immediately how young the woman was. She must have been sixteen at most, cheeks rosy with youth, her green eyes sparkled, and her hair fell in thick red strands from a Russian-style hat that she wore slanted over her right ear. Of the two brothers, Attila was the older and the gruffer. Bags drooped down his cheekbones and he held the distant stare of a man who'd seen more action than he'd ever wanted. He and his younger brother were dressed in matching grey overcoats, with camo-green field caps pushed identically back over their foreheads. But while Gábor's flawless complexion and darting stare carried the look of youthful innocence, their appearances were deceiving; young Nóra and Gábor had each killed twice as many Russians as Zoltán and Attila combined.

Zoltán shook hands with them all. "What happened to the kid?" he asked.

"What kid?" Attila replied.

"The one they shot."

The three looked at each other, but it was Nóra who answered. "Oh, that kid," she said. "They missed. He went crying back to his mother just after they hit you."

Zoltán stared at the young woman, unsure of whether she was telling the truth or lying to make him feel better. He nodded to himself. "And are you all from Budapest?" he asked.

"We're from Csepel Island," Attila growled. "I was an engineer at the locomotive factory and my brother was in the fifth year of his apprenticeship there."

"You Csepel boys," said Zoltán, shaking his head. "We always thought you were with them. You were Commie celebrities, 'The Heroic Workers of Csepel island'."

"We don't care who's in charge as long as they pay us right," said Gábor.

"But you fought, didn't you?" asked Zoltán.

"Sure," said Attila, "we pulled down the statue of Stalin in City Park."

"Really?" Zoltán asked.

"Yeah, really," said Gábor, "we commandeered a works' van and we were driving around listening to the radio for ways we could help. We heard the sixteen-point plan, which included tearing down the statue, and as we were already in Zugló we figured we'd go and have a look. When we got to the edge of the park, we found a crowd of people hacking at it with hammers. Well, we had ropes in the back, so we gave them a hand. And you know the rest, I'm sure."

"That's where we met," said Nóra. "I was so in awe of these guys. I guess I must've been high on the air of freedom because I went up to Gábor and kissed him on the lips right there. We've not left each other's side since." She smiled at her partner. "All the guys I know are such wimps," she continued. "They just wanted to sit around and talk, but none of them was actually brave enough to be there on the front line."

"We lost a lot of friends," Attila added. "The air of freedom wasn't so fresh where we were." The three stared at each other in turn.

Again, it fell to Nóra to explain. "We joined the Széna Square group," she said. "Uncle Szabó wanted to send me home at first, he said I was too young. But I refused to leave and Gábor wouldn't let them throw me out. So, I stayed. It was peaceful for a while, when we really thought we were going to win. But those last few days in the Bem barracks, all we did was fill bottles with petrol for hours on end. Then the shells started to hit the building and we heard Uncle Szabó had escaped with a messenger, and we ran for our lives."

"Only God knows how we made it," said Attila. "We haven't seen anyone from there since, so we might be some of the very few to have got out."

They stood, lost in their thoughts, staring at the sun hanging dull and low in the winter sky.

Gábor inhaled a cigarette and pointed at the sunrise. "So that's west then," he said.

"It might be the last sunrise we ever see over Hungarian soil," Nóra replied. "But like all the ones before, that's east and it always will be. You can go that way if you want, Gábor, but the border's the other way."

Gábor shrugged, threw his cigarette butt to the ground and snuffed it out with the toe of his boot.

The four Hungarians picked their way through the forests all morning, listening for cracks of branches or the rumbling of engines. At first, the slightest squeak would bring them to a halt. They grew more assured as the day wore on, but Zoltán's heart still skipped a beat when a twig snapped close beside him. He jerked his head to find Nóra next to him. "I didn't see you there," he said.

"I know," she responded, "but I saw you. So, what does that say?"

Zoltán stared at her face, searching for a clue. "I don't know," he said eventually.

She tutted back at him. "So, will you keep studying in Austria?" she asked.

"I don't know," Zoltán responded, staring at the yellowed leaves on the ground, "I'd like to, but I'm going to have to learn German before I go any further."

"We might not even end up in Austria, you know. Maybe we'll go somewhere like the United States where my German will be no use at all."

"So, you speak German?"

"Of course."

"Then you didn't work at the Csepel factory?"

"Me?" Nóra chuckled. "I haven't even finished high school. I'm from the seventh district. I was born in the ghetto."

"Oh," said Zoltán, "so you're Jewish then?"

"Yes," Nóra replied. "Is that a problem?"

"No, not at all, I was only asking. But don't your parents mind you being with Gábor?"

"They would mind, I'm sure, if they were still alive."

"I'm sorry."

"Don't be, that was a long time ago and we've got other things to worry about now. Besides, between you and me, I'm not sure how long I can really stay with Gábor. I mean, he's a good man. He's as honest as anyone I've ever met, and I know I can trust him with my life. But he's completely fallen in love with me and he's talking about starting a family, about us getting married. I'm too young for all that. It won't last, I know that. I was just caught up in the moment. But we're not on the same level, you see, we have nothing to talk about. He might be eight years older than me, but he's like a little kid."

"Then why are you still with him?"

"We've come a long way together," said Nóra. "So much has happened in such a short time. And I don't want to break his heart. Not at the moment anyway. Right now, I need him to get me away from this fucked out country. But I have ambitions, I want to do something that isn't just being the wife of a factory worker. My father was a book publisher before the war. I want to go to university and study literature, and then I want to go and explore the world."

"Well, let's hope you're about to get the chance," said Zoltán, kicking the leaves.

They walked through the day, pushing themselves around fens and through forests until the sun had set and the Milky Way was stretching bright over the frozen sky. A near-full moon shone its cold, reflected light over the crackling reeds, and again the temperature tumbled. Droplets of ice on their eyelashes, they shuffled on towards a line of trees whose bare branches whistled in the wind.

Those silver birches turned out to be lining a canal, its water so still that it shone like a pearl pavement in the moonlight. On the far side, the forests had been cut back from the bank some fifty metres. And in the middle of the clearing stood a figure. It was waving at them.

"Look," said Gábor, nudging Attila, "there's someone on the other side over there. Do you think it's an ÁVO?"

"I don't know," said Attila. "Is he waving at us?" He cupped his lips. "Tudsz hol a határ?" he shouted. 'Do you know where the border is?'

The man on the other side shouted something back.

"What the cock did he say?" asked Attila.

"I don't know," Zoltán replied.

Nóra stepped in front of the men. "Ist das die Grenze?" she shouted.

"Genau," the man replied. "Hier ist Österreich. Das ist die Grenze."

Nóra translated the words into Hungarian so the men could understand. "This is the border," she told them. "Austria's on the other side of the canal."

"How do we know we can trust him?" Attila asked.

Nóra looked up and shouted in German, "Who are you?"

"I'm a fourth-year physics student from Vienna," the Austrian replied. "I'm here with my friends. We have a camp with a fire on the other side of the forest, and we can call a bus to pick you up and take you to the nearest village."

"He speaks with a pure Viennese accent," Nóra said to the boys. "There's no doubt he's Austrian, and I've been around enough to know. He's not an ÁVO, that's for sure."

Rifle shot cracked the night. The three men threw themselves down, even the Austrian fell to the ground. Only Nóra remained standing.

"Get down!" Gábor hissed.

"It was far away," Nóra replied.

But at a second volley of shot she ducked her head to join them. "What are we going to do?" she asked.

"Ask him how we get across," said Attila.

Nóra waited for the next rally of gunfire, one that seemed no closer, and she shouted as loud as she dared.

The Austrian replied and she translated for the three men.

"He says the army blew up the bridge two nights ago."

"Baszd meg!" Zoltán cursed. "Looks like we have no option but to swim."

"I can't swim," said Nóra.

"And that water looks cold enough to freeze hell," Attila added. "We'll have to find another way. Build a raft or something."

"Okay," said Zoltán. "Then we need to find some wood."

"It shouldn't be too difficult," said Nóra. "Why don't we split into two groups and go either way to see what we can find?"

"All right," Gábor agreed. "I'll go with you. Attila, you can go the other way with the student."

Attila nodded. "We'll need a mixture of sticks and sturdy pieces that are long enough for us to sit on," he said. "Then we'll need some rope to tie them together. Can you see if your Austrian friend can find us some?"

Nóra nodded, did as Attila asked and the man over the border ran off into the forests to get help.

On the Hungarian side, the group split up. Nóra produced a knife from her backpack and used it to point out scraps of wood for Gábor to collect in his arms. By the time they'd gone fifty metres or so, the young man could carry no more. "Put them down here," Nóra instructed.

"Why here?" Gábor asked.

"You'll see. Just do it."

He did what she said.

Nóra grabbed a low branch with one hand and swung the knife with her other. It came loose with a single blow, and she ran the sharp edge along its surface to remove the twigs and knots. "Do you know any poetry, Gábor?" she asked.

"Me?" he said. "Of course not. Why are you thinking about these things right now?"

She felt for his hand and found it as cold as hers. She placed it on the stick, and they held it out between them. "There's a verse I keep thinking about," she said, "from an Endre Ady poem." She closed her eyes and recited the stanza:

"I'll cut a staff at the border, My rabid nation's ground
Will drink no more of my blood: And I'll never turn around."

She looked up at him and his head tilted into hers. Their frozen lips warmed in the embrace.

When Nóra and Gábor got back, with arms full of sticks, Attila and Zoltán were waiting for them. "Look what we found," said Attila, walking them not five metres the other way. There, propped up against a tree, was a trunk at least as tall as the canal was wide.

"What are we going to do with that?" asked Gábor.

"We're going to use it as a bridge," Zoltán Papp replied.

"Are you sure it's long enough?" asked Nóra.

"We think so," said Attila, "but we were waiting for you so we could let it down gently on the other side. We don't want it to snap in half."

The four arranged themselves around the log. They worked it free of the tree's branches and lowered it as gently as they could towards the three Austrians who now stood on the far side to help.

But the weight turned out to be more than anyone had imagined, and the momentum of their improvised bridge took it away from their hands. The standing end slipped. The far end missed the bank and splashed into the water, shattering the night like breaking glass.

Gunshot rang back at them.

"Baszd meg!" Zoltán cursed as the shots released a shower of sticks from the treetops. He saw his comrades trying to pull the sunken bridge up at one end. "Baszd meg!" he cursed again.

Zoltán Papp saw no alternative. He removed his overcoat, scarf and cap, handed them to Nóra, and jumped into the canal without another thought.

The icy water stabbed at his body like a thousand knives, filling his boots and dragging him down. He managed one stroke, two strokes, and he came up for air. The chill pressed on his chest and he was barely able to breathe, but he saw he was only feet from the other side. So, he went down again, groping for the log.

He found it dug into the canal bed. Holding his breath, Zoltán planted his boots on the silt floor and heaved the log upwards. He found it buoyant under the water. Only when his arms were at full stretch, with the air biting his fingertips, did he feel the full weight of the log. But the load was fast relieved.

Yet when Zoltán tried to kick himself up from the canal bed, he found the sand and water had formed a vacuum around his boots and he couldn't get himself free. He wailed his arms in panic and got a noseful of icy water. 'Surely this can't be it?' he thought to himself.

Leather gloves reached down, grabbed Zoltán's wrists and yanked him up onto the shore. He coughed, spluttered, opened his eyes. He found he couldn't speak, that he was shivering uncontrollably and needed desperately to vomit.

People were running here and there around him. And above him stood a man in a black peaked cap. Zoltán's immediate thought was that he must have been a member of the ÁVO Secret Police. He crunched closed his eyes and rolled himself into a ball.

Only when the man addressed him with an Austrian "grüß Gott!" did Zoltán Papp dare to look up.

2. The Tower

8th December 2057
Manchester, England

Below a bush of curly hair, the anchorman's smile sparkled from his soft-brown face. "You're watching PapNews," he said. "I'm Vincent Humbolt, and I'll be with you all day as we bring you uninterrupted coverage of the opening of the Zoltán Papp Tower."

The pictures skipped from the studio to a view high above Manchester. Way below, the sun glinted off the curved Bio-dome roofs as the shot panned towards a tapering column. The tower stretched up even higher into the cloudless sky, stripes of red and white winding around its surface which flashed with the words 'Come and see the lights at the Blackpool Pleasure Dome!' wherever the viewer looked.

"And there's the highest rock this side of the Caucuses!" said the presenter, reading a joke that would be mis-translated into a hundred languages. "At over five kilometres high, it's the tallest structure humanity has ever conceived. This is the first building in history to have more than a thousand floors. And the world's highest pressurised room, at the very top, will today be the venue for the first of what will surely be many special occasions. That said, it'll be difficult ever to match the scale of today's ceremony."

The pictures dropped a few miles, to nestle below the criss-crossed steel rafters that made up the Bio-dome ceiling. Billions of screens, from Kidderminster to Kazakhstan, showed a bird's-eye image that floated above ten lanes of PapWay. Cylindrical PapHome towers lined the road, today all done out with a continuous tribute to the Blackpool Pleasure Dome. But on the asphalt surface that used to be Rochdale Road there was not a single car. People walked the sunlit roadway or gathered in groups to marvel at the red-and-white-striped tower that stretched up and out through the Bio-dome.

Despite all the architectural awards it had won, the records it had broken, the Zoltán Papp Tower was really just a uniform yellow cone that tapered gently up into the Manchester winter. It was only the augmented vision of screens or PapDrive implants that gave the tower its helter-skelter skin, that stripped away the churning clouds and left the sky a brilliant blue.

In the augmented sunshine at the foot of the tower, PapSec soldiers formed a solid line to keep the riff-raff from the dignitaries. But in their all-yellow graphene armour and beach-ball-like helmets, the troops were completely augmented out of view to anyone wearing PapDrive lenses, glasses, or implants, or watching an enhanced broadcast, which was everyone, pretty much.

Between the hidden cordon and the tower, a black limo pulled up behind a dozen similar models. Zoltan O'Dillon was the first to get out, followed by a tall grey man with a back as straight as a pillar and a short woman in a bright orange dress. Zoltan waited for her.

Jemima Kemal was a good foot shorter than Zoltan and at least half his weight, her big brown eyes sparkling many-colours through her PapDrive lenses. She pointed at the projections over the wall of the tower. "There must be millions of people here," she said, "and I can't imagine how many others watching elsewhere. You should at least try to look happy."

"How can I be happy?" asked Zoltan, "after what you just told me. I thought we'd be together forever, you and me." He reached for her hand, but she pulled away.

"Don't," she said. "That's one of the problems. You can't keep touching me in public, people notice. We need to have more distance and more discretion if we're going to continue."

"But you're my number one lady," said Zoltan. "I don't know what I'll do without you."

"You'll find someone," said Jemima. "And there's always Francis. He's a good man. He's got your back. Besides, we'll still be working together. Just think how useful it'll be having me running PapNews." She nodded towards the tower. "I'd never do that to you, for example."

When Zoltan O'Dillon followed her gaze, he found the broadcast was now showing the back of his head amplified a thousand times above them. The rolls of fat down his neck didn't concern him as much as the blown-up bald spot at his crown. He turned to the crowds, waved, and the shot focussed on his bloodshot cheeks. People cheered. Zoltan clapped his hands above his head and thousands did likewise.

"And there's Zoltan O'Dillon," said the commentator. "Just look at the reception the CEO of PapCorp is receiving from the crowds. He's wearing a suit hand-stitched by Gasparo de la Rey, and is accompanied as always by his two advisors, Brigadier Francis Atkins and Jemima Kemal. In a moment, he'll be joining his father the Prime Minster in a liftpod that will spin them up five thousand metres in just ninety seconds. But before then, let's take a moment to enjoy the crowds, some of whom have been queuing for days for their spot. For those who get to see these great men up close, it will surely have been time well spent."

Rusholme Township, Manchester

Just two miles south of Manchester city centre, without the mesh roof of a Bio-dome or implants to augment her vision, Minnie Brownlow couldn't see the tower behind a ceiling of churning clouds. Drizzle splattered into puddles and dropped from the shoulder-length tips of her hair. She was completely grey, despite being only thirty-two, and deep grooves wrinkled her forehead. She'd never been tall, but the weight of life, as much as the bags of vegetables she was hauling and the secret she was carrying, meant she walked with shoulders stooped.

There was no traffic between the mirror-image rows of brick terraces; these streets barely saw cars anymore. But as Minnie approached her house at the end of Welwyn Street, she saw a lanky man in an anorak crossing the road in front of her. Despite her load, she skipped from one patch of tarmac to the next, like stepping stones along the cobble lake. She grabbed the man's arm and hurried him to the bare-brick wall around the end of the row. "What are you doing here, Neville?" she asked.

"I can't stop thinking about what you told me," Neville replied. "I'd like you to reconsider."

"I knew you would," said Minnie. "But I've told you how it is. I can't have this baby of ours, Nev, much as I'd like to. You know I can't leave Brian and the girls, it'd tear them all apart. Without me, they'd most likely starve."

"But it's so dangerous…" said Neville, his thoughts cut short by Minnie's stare.

"I'm the one having this abortion," said Minnie. "It's not you putting your life on the line."

"I just want you to be safe. You still love me, don't you?"

Minnie smiled through the drops of rain and tears that fell down her cheeks. "Of course, Nev," she said. "You're the one and only light in my life. You know I'd change things if I could. In a way, it's a miracle this hasn't happened before. We've not been very careful, have we?" She reached up and kissed him on the cheek. "I've got to go," she said. "Them lot in there will be expecting dinner."

Neville Jennings watched his lover skip away around the corner. He dug his hands into the plastic pockets of his cagoule and stared for some minutes at the spot where she'd been, wishing beyond everything that things could be different.

The Zoltán Papp Tower

Lord Michael O'Dillon was even more obese than his son. He wore the same standard suit and bright yellow tie. But the elder man's eyes were riddled with blood vessels and drooped from a lifetime of too little sleep.

The liftpod doors were closing out the cheering crowds when Zoltan greeted his father. "Don't you think this PapBreaks advertising campaign's really something?" said Zoltan, nodding at the augmented projections over the pod's walls. Their PapDrive corneal implants showed them flying over a sandy beach beside a quaint promenade. A sea breeze blew over their cheeks, carrying on it the smells of candy floss and donkey droppings, the sounds of squawking seagulls, rattling trams and a distant brass band playing, *'Oh I do like to be beside the seaside'*. "Jemima oversaw the whole project," Zoltan explained. "Hasn't she done a good job?"

"Yes," said Lord Michael. "Well done young lady, you're a real gem. He's certainly going to miss you."

"Miss her?" said Zoltan. "What do you mean by that?"

"She's leaving you, isn't she?" said Zoltan's father. "Just like every other woman in your life."

Zoltan O'Dillon wanted to punch his father in the face. Instead, he clenched his fingernails into his palms and spoke as calmly as he could. "How do you know that?"

"Do you need to ask?" said Lord Michael, before turning his attention to Jemima. "I'm sure you'll be a great addition to PapNews," he said. "But I hope my son can find a decent replacement for you. Francis is always here to sort out the more technical side of his job, like Larry used to. But he's had so many wasters at his ear over the years, none of whom could keep him sober. Until you."

"Get lost!" Zoltan responded. "I'm not some kid anymore, Mike. I'm quite capable of keeping myself on the straight and narrow."

His father chuckled. "I'd dare say there's so much in your system that it'll take years to flush it all out."

Michael O'Dillon's advisors outnumbered Zoltan's by five to one, and all ten men chortled along with their boss. But of Lord Michael's crew, none laughed louder or longer than the thin grey man at his shoulder.

Zoltan huffed. His hands whirled, selecting icon after icon on his personal PapDrive interface until the image of a padlock appeared in the bottom left-hand corner of his vision. Everything went dark but his father's face.

Lord Michael responded with his own hand jive and reversed his son's actions. The padlocks vanished, visions restored. "We're not speaking privately in here," he said, "if you have something to say, you can say it to everyone."

"Yeah?" Zoltan replied. He felt Jemima's hand on his, knew she was trying to calm him down. He continued nonetheless. "So what does this say about Lord Michael, eh? That his enduring legacy will be the world's largest erection?"

"It must be difficult for you, son," Michael O'Dillon responded, "to see what hard work and a bit of consideration can achieve. This tower was the most complicated project PapEng has ever undertaken. Compared to this, laying a few sheets of laminate in the desert should've been a walk in the park. But where is your ridiculous advert for the aliens? Nowhere, that's where."

"That's a lie!" Zoltan screeched. "It's well under way, as you know. It'll be ready in time for PapCorp's centenary. And in any case, you can't compare the two. This is Manchester, in England, where you can just issue local residents with a compulsory purchase order, bung them a few PapPounds and they're gone. How many people had to move for you to build this tower? Five? Fifty? The PapPop ad is over a million acres of foreign land, where we both know millions of people used to live. In case you don't remember, we had to clear them out before we could get on with the construction, and it turned out they couldn't be bribed with PapPounds and cheap holidays. But we're on schedule. Don't you worry."

"We're not worried," said his father's tall advisor. "If it goes to shit, its got your name all over it. I for one told you to quit long before things got nasty. But you wouldn't listen, would you? Just as always, Zoltan knows best."

"Don't you dare, Larry Pickering!" Zoltan shouted. "You filthy, backscratching, two-faced pen pusher. Why, I'll…" He felt Jemima's fingers work their way into his and paused a moment to see her eyes sparkling up from below her jet-black fringe.

"Breathe," she whispered. "Don't let him wind you up."

Zoltan smiled back at her and said nothing more.

Rusholme

Minnie put all her grocery bags in one hand and rummaged in her jacket pocket for the key. She tried to ignore the lines of peeling green paint in the door to number 56, but she never could.

One step up and she was inside, straight into a living room just as cold, and almost as damp, as the street. She found the television screen flashing out pictures of children playing in a turquoise sea below a Bio-dome sky. A woman narrated in a Lancashire accent: "When me and my family took the PapTrans HyperLink to Blackpool," she was saying, "it was the best holiday of us lives. It's like 'eaven – a hundred miles of sandy beaches where the temperature's always thirty degrees and the sun never burns your skin. We're going for Christmas. Why don't you join us?"

Minnie's husband Brian was taking up his usual position on the sofa, tucked up in an extra-large sleeping bag from which his head poked out, like a tortoise. Their eldest daughter sat beside him under her own blanket, and both were watching the main light in the room.

"Hello," said Minnie. But she got no reply from the couch.

The only person who noticed her arrival was Minnie's ten-year-old daughter, Ruth. She was sitting cross-legged on the carpet, balancing an ancient laptop computer on her knees. Ruth glanced up from her machine. "Hello mum," she said, before returning her gaze to her own screen. "Hello Ruthie, love," Minnie replied. "It's blowing a gale out there. And it ain't much better in here. Why didn't you light the fire?"

"We were waiting for you," said Ruth.

"Well, it's blooming freezing," said Minnie. "I'll get the fire going. Does anyone fancy a cup of tea?"

Her husband grunted. "I wish we could go to the Blackpool Bio-dome," he said.

Minnie tutted. She knelt on the tiles before the hearth, arranged a pile of sticks and struck a match. "I heard a real tough one today," she said, holding the flame to the kindling.

"In the queue at the food centre, the woman in front of me has been squatting in one of them condemned houses on Langley Road. She told me about a boy not much older than Ruth. He was in the room next to hers. His parents had gone out and left bags of MX75 within the kid's reach. I imagine he knew what to do from watching the adults getting off their faces, but he didn't know how much to take. Luckily the woman heard him throwing his guts up and saved him. If she hadn't got to him in time he could've been lying there dead for days. Makes you think, doesn't it?"

"That's dreadful, mum," said little Ruth, gazing at her computer. Neither of the others said a word.

The flame caught. After a bit of fanning and blowing, Minnie filled a blackened kettle from the tap in the kitchen, hooked it over the fireplace and sat herself on the arm of the sofa beside her husband. She gazed at the side of his face. She knew the rolls of fat started just under the sleeping bag and extended out over his midriff, making his head seem so small. She contemplated his mouth hanging open, wondered how she'd ever found his goofy expression so charming. Now he disgusted her. "What's on?" she asked.

"The opening of the Zoltán Papp Tower, of course," her husband replied, staring at the screen. "What else is there?"

"It looks like adverts to me," said Minnie. "They never mention all those poor people who were forced out of their homes in Blackpool, do they? All so PapCorp could make the town into some Victorian theme park."

"You know they got paid to move," said Brian. "They're probably living the life of Riley now on all them PapPounds."

"I wouldn't be so sure," said Minnie. "I heard those compulsory purchase orders were barely enough for six months' rent."

"Whatever," Brian retorted. "You can't halt progress."

"This isn't what I call progress," said Minnie. "It won't be long till they come for this house, either, you mark my words. But we'll be waiting for them. In Longsight they've managed to delay construction of the Bio-dome for five years already, through the courts and on the streets. When it's our turn, we'll be prepared."

"It can't come soon enough, if you ask me," said her elder daughter. "I've already spent too much of my life living outside, exposing my skin to the elements. I say bring on the Rusholme Bio-dome, and make it snappy."

"If only you realised, Naomi," her mother sighed. "There's nothing real under those Bio-domes, just a PapCorp illusion to make people spend more of PapCorp's money on more of PapCorp's products. Those places are nothing but pap, pap, pap."

"And how do you know?" Naomi retorted. "Have you ever been in one?"

"Of course I have. We went together."

"I'm not talking about that. Have you been since?"

"Listen young lady, I don't need to visit those places to know what they're like. I've seen it on TV enough times, I've heard from enough people to know how it is."

"And do you really expect me to live in this slum for the rest of my life?" asked Naomi. "Working the gardens every day, picking bloody turnips? I weren't made for hard labour, mum. If the Bio-dome doesn't hurry up and get to me, I'll just have to get myself into a Bio-dome."

"One of these days you'll realise," said her mother, "when you're making the room of some fat, rich man, picking up his soiled underwear and battering off his approaches. Then you'll see just how good life is here in this township."

"Mum!" Naomi screeched, getting to her feet. "How dare you say things like that? Saying I'm only good enough to be a cleaner! I'm going to be a pop star. You know that."

"I know that's what you want, Naomi. I'm just trying to prepare you for what happens when that doesn't work out."

"Will you two put a sock in it?" said the father of the family, his eyes transfixed on the screen. "Lord Michael's about to speak."

The teenage Naomi looked at her father and mother in disgust. She huffed, threw her arms in the air, whipped her blonde hair around her head and stormed off upstairs.

The Zoltán Papp Tower

Millions of tiles made up the top-most floor of the Zoltán Papp Tower, each attached to its own tiny hydraulic pump which allowed the auditorium to be arranged in any number of ways. For today, Lord Michael had ordered a theatre in the round. But rather than descending from outside in, the seating went the other way; each inner row was higher than the last until they peaked at the stage.

Lord O'Dillon made his entrance on a platform which rose up in the middle of everybody until he towered above all. He let the ovation go on till he felt it sufficient, then he lowered his palms and the plaudits rescinded. "Thank you!" he boomed from his belly. "Thank you, ladies and gentlemen. And let me tell you what a pleasure it is to be back in Manchester on such a fine day as this." He gestured at the clear winter sky beyond the mini-domed ceiling.

The stage rotated slowly for all to see Prime Minister O'Dillon, but the broadcasts remained fixed on his face. "A hundred years ago today," he continued, "Zoltán Papp was celebrating his first birthday in England, on a farm in the Welsh Marches. Little did anyone know then that the drink that refugee labourer carried in his head would make him the most famous Hungarian ever to walk the Earth. He remains, to this day, a guiding light for all in this great company and nation to follow. Which is why we have built this tower in his honour, to shine out like a beacon for Western superiority. So please, I ask you again, put your hands together for Zoltán Papp, and the people at PapEng who have built his great monument."

Lord Michael let the applause last just a few seconds before again bringing it down with his palms. "When I took over PapCorp, long long ago," he continued, "it was still known as Papp Beverages Limited. My father and my uncle, God rest their souls, laid the foundations for me to take this enterprise from the country's favourite drinks makers to the most powerful company the world has ever seen."

The Prime Minister glanced outside. "While great cities falter and fall," he said, "PapCorp has made Manchester into the most modern, fastest-growing metropolis on the globe. The PapWay network and PapTrans HyperLink make it the model of a 21st century city. We all know that others are trying to catch up; London and Leeds, New Delhi and Mumbai all have areas of PapEng Bio-dome coverage. But nowhere in the world can compete with England's North West. When the Liverpool Coverage Network and the Blackpool Pleasure Dome are incorporated into Manchester's Bio-domes next year, it'll create a sunbelt from the North Sea to the Pennines, the largest covered area ever imagined."

He paused to take a sip of PapAqua before his speech changed tack. "There have been many doubters along the way," he said, "many who have questioned my methods and my goals. But I ask you this – would outdated concepts like liberal democracy have produced a modern wonder like Manchester? Would this tower have got built if we'd had to ask for everyone's permission first? Of course not. What is clear to all, is the power and capacity that my leadership has brought to this city and this country. And what better sign could anyone need but this very tower, and the magnificent megalopolis over which it stands, to display the glory of modern Britain? I am speaking to you from the centre of PapCorp's solar system, the beating heart of a global empire from which we all benefit. This is the very embodiment of the old mantra, truer today than it has ever been. What is good for PapCorp is good for Britain, and what is good for Britain is good for PapCorp!"

Rusholme

Minnie Brownlow shuffled her buttocks. "What's good for the O'Dillons is good for the O'Dillons, more like," she said.

Her husband sighed. "How can you sit there and cast doubt on good Lord Michael and his son?" he replied. "They're two of the greatest, most upstanding men this country has ever produced. What they've done for this city, and the world, is beyond compare."

Minnie shook her head. "Everywhere's a dictatorship of some sort these days," she murmured. "Lord Michael's PapState is no better than any of the others."

"Please, Minnie, will you give it a break for once? The Prime Minister's talking and I want to listen."

Minnie nodded to herself. "Of course you do," she said, as their eldest daughter belted out an Aretha Franklin number in the upstairs bathroom.

"Would you shut up, Naomi!?" Brian yelled. "I'm trying to watch the telly!"

The Zoltán Papp Tower

He may have been a vain and grudge-laden old man, but Lord Michael O'Dillon had a great understanding of people. He knew well the laziness of journalists, understood that many would snooze through his speeches or be watching clips of other things as he spoke.

So although Lord Michael would go on to fill another hour with boasts of his achievements or jibes against anyone who'd ever opposed him, the real juice of his talk was kept for the end. Selected journalists had received their questions before Lord Michael arrived, so they'd had the chance to practise them in their heads a few times and add the odd personal touch.

When the Prime Minister brought down yet another ovation, the first question went to a young man with a head like an bush-topped olive who was fast becoming the face of PapNews. "Lord Prime Minister," said Vincent Humbolt in his Yorkshire twang. "Thank you for giving me the opportunity to congratulate you on this magnificent achievement. Manchester has always been a lively city, but I've never known her to be as alive as she is right now. The place is buzzing like the bees on her flag. And yet, as we all know, this great city is not without its problems. Drug abuse is rife, both under but especially outside the protective cover of the Bio-domes, and many are claiming that public order is under threat. What are you, as Mayor of this city and Prime Minister of this country, going to do about these issues?"

Lord Michael smiled down at his questioner. "Thank you for your kind words, Vincent," he said. "It's good to see PapCorp's news channel keeping up the high standards and tough line we all expect from the British press. You're right, of course, that the MX75 problem has reached epidemic proportions, especially in the slums that have developed around the Bio-domes where PapSec have yet to establish full control. However," he said straight to the camera lens, "to all those families affected by this plague, I can promise you this. We are today taking unprecedented action against the drug gangs that terrorise your communities. Which is why, from tomorrow, PapSec will be recruiting another ten thousand community crime prevention officers to combat the criminal gangs and bring their members to justice. It's not right that a few bad apples should be allowed to ruin the lives of millions."

Rusholme

"You see," said Brian Brownlow on the sofa, "I told you not to doubt Lord O'Dillon. Like he always says, he knows the British people better than we know ourselves. He knows there's a drug problem, and he's going to sort it out. You don't need to worry now that PapSec are getting involved."

Minnie shook her head. "If Lord Michael O'Dillon wanted to do something about the drug problem, he would," she said. "He claims to have eyes all over the country. He can see every single transaction made in PapPounds, so he must know where that stuff's coming from. How could PapSec ever help someone like that kid I was talking about? He doesn't need military intervention, he needs caring for. PapSec would probably take him away and sell him."

"Have some common sense would you, Minnie?" said Brian. "PapCorp don't sell children."

"I wouldn't be so sure," said Ruth, from her cross-legged seat in front of her laptop. "I read there are networks of slaves in the Bio-domes, that nothing would work without them. Probably he'd end up there."

"Ruth!" her father scolded, "you're ten-years-old. You shouldn't be reading the dark web, and you certainly shouldn't believe the lies they tell. If you're not careful you'll end up a brainwashed radical like that Harry Lanker, and we all know what happened to him."

Minnie inhaled, crossed her arms and her legs. She and her daughter said nothing more.

The Zoltán Papp Tower

Lord Michael O'Dillon's audience was a selection of friends and allies, all of whom wanted to congratulate the man in person, to shake his hand, to have a selfie with him. All, that is, except his son Zoltan, who skulked around the edge of the theatre exchanging pleasantries with dignitaries and family friends, biding his time before he could talk to his father.

The room was nearly empty when Zoltan found his moment. Seeing Lord Michael alone on the stage, he bounded upwards as fast as he could. When he came face-to-face with the elder O'Dillon, Zoltan was quite out of breath. "When did you think..." he heaved. "When were you going to tell me about this?"

"Calm down, Zoltan," said his father, "don't give yourself a heart attack. Here, would you like some PapAqua?"

"No, answer the question. How much is this going to cost?"

Lord Michael's hands whirred until the background grew dark and a padlock appeared in the bottom corner of their visions. "Don't talk about private PapCorp business in public, Zoltan. Anyone could hear you."

"Oh that's right," said the younger man, "we talk openly when Larry Pickering's around but not if it's just the two of us."

"We're not having another argument about Pickering," said Lord Michael. "He served you well for the best part of two decades. He helped me get you out of some pretty sticky situations, so it's only natural I have him in my Cabinet these days."

"Whatever," Zoltan shrugged. "That's not my question."

"Well I have a question for you," said the Prime Minister. "When are you going to congratulate me on my great achievement?"

"Whose great achievement?" Zoltan sneered. "What did you do to build this tower except announce it and take all the credit? This is the first time we've met since the deal to buy Xi-fan Corporation went through and you haven't even mentioned a word."

"I just think you paid over the odds. You know that."

"Five years ago, her market value was twenty times what we paid."

"Well this isn't five years ago, is it?" said Lord O'Dillon. "This is now. If you'd waited another six months you could've knocked another nought off that figure. I just think you didn't hold your nerve long enough, Zoltan. And you've cost us as a result."

"You have no idea what you're talking about!" Zoltan screamed. "Me costing PapCorp money? It's you that's just announced we'll recruit another ten thousand PapSec Community Crime Prevention Officers! I tell you this, if I'd waited any longer, the Indians would've snatched Xi-fan from under our noses. And then who'd be the largest company in the world?"

"That wouldn't have happened…"

"Gooda-bloody-Industries, that's who. You're not CEO anymore, Mick, you're not up to date with the market. You seem quite happy to load PapCorp with more and more responsibility, but you can't see what's good for the company anymore. How could you launch a new drug war on our behalf without consulting me first?"

"I don't get what you're saying, Zoltan. Is PapCorp refusing to take on this project?"

"Don't be daft, I'm just..."

"Because if they are, then maybe it's time to open up competitive tendering again. I dare say Gooda Industries could undercut PapCorp on most government contracts, especially given their labour practices."

"You can't give state contracts to users of slave labour, that'd be morally wrong."

"Because PapCorp doesn't use slaves, of course."

"No," said Zoltan. "Well, not really... that's different. I'm just saying you should consult me before making these kinds of announcements."

"And what were you going to say? No? I have no choice in my role as Prime Minister but to act on the worries and fears of my constituents."

"You have no constituents, father. You're not elected."

"I am! And I consider every person on this island to be one of my constituents, the five million that didn't vote for me just as much as the thirty-seven million that did."

"And what about my worries and fears?" Zoltan shouted. "Those of your son, the CEO of the family company? PapCorp isn't your plaything anymore, father dear. The amount of projects you're committing us to without my permission is unacceptable. Not only are we footing the bill for your Papp-damned tower, now we have to train and employ thousands more PapSec lackeys just to stop a few poor people from having some fun. And that's not even mentioning the bill for the compulsory purchase orders. Do you have any idea what that's standing at right now, by the way?"

"I don't know and it doesn't matter," said Lord Michael.

"How can you possibly say that?" Zoltan squealed. "You're spending more buying up farms in the middle of the countryside than I paid for Xi-fan, and to think of the shit you give me for that..."

"We pay the compulsory purchase orders in PapPounds, Zoltan. You paid the Chinese in gold."

"What's the difference? That deal led the PapPound to jump ten per cent in one day, which means we could buy ten per cent more gold than I gave them."

"Zoltan, my son. Are you really telling me that you're in control of the largest company the world has ever known, and you don't understand what money is?"

"Of course I know what money is, don't be daft. There was a module on it at university, I think."

"You think, but you don't know because you could never be bothered to go to any of the lectures. Am I right? You were too busy molesting young women with Bernie the Earl to do any actual studying. If you weren't my only son you'd probably be lying face down in a ditch by now. As it is, you're just going to have to take my word for it. Money's a con trick, a sleight of hand. As long as people have faith in a currency, anything can be money. It doesn't matter if it's dollars or cigarettes or PapPounds, they're all fictions, they have no real value unless people believe they do, and therefore want them. You, as CEO of PapCorp, can magic up PapPounds from nowhere at the flick of an icon. That's what gives PapCorp limitless access to resources. But gold, everyone wants gold, always. Which means it's the closest thing we have to actually being worth something. You gave away half of this country's gold reserve in that deal and we're never going to get that back. On the other hand, you can magic up PapPounds for compulsory purchase orders at the flick of your hand. And in return we exchange digits for something real. Land."

"I get that," said Zoltan. "I just don't know what you're planning to do with all that land."

Lord Michael flicked his fingers and the padlocks disappeared, again the two men were visible to others. "You'll find out soon enough," he said, and bounded off down the stairs.

Glaisdale, North Yorkshire

In the belly of the North York Moors, 120 miles to the north east of Manchester, an elderly woman sat cross-legged on her single bed. She was dragging a brush through streaks of grey hair, recalling how thick her locks once were. She was staring at a poster, meditating on the faded-brown cheeks of her girlhood crush. She reached forward, stroked her fingertips over the lines she'd worn in the image. After so many years dreaming of Marvin Percy's embrace, when she closed her eyes, she was sure she could smell his earthy skin.

She knew it was madness, but she found this a much happier place than all those years she'd spent wondering how things had ever got to this. She looked at her fingers, like knobbly twigs. If it weren't for the food parcels that arrived on her doorstep every week, she'd have starved long ago. And only today would they have found her body.

Helen Humbolt was expecting the knock at the door. When it came, she struggled to her feet, hobbled over to the bedside table and opened the top drawer. It was empty but for a little box, which she took out and opened, gazing at the gold ring inside. She removed it, felt its surface between her fingertips, slipped it onto where it had lived. But it wouldn't stay there anymore.

There was another knock at the door, and this time the letterbox rattled. "Mrs Humbolt," shouted a man. "Helen Humbolt? Are you in there? Are you okay?"

"Yes," she replied in a high-pitched squeak. She coughed. "Yes," she repeated, louder. "I'm coming now." Her voice wasn't used to talking.

She dropped the ring into her pocket and walked gingerly down the stairs, hands on both bannisters. There was another knock. "I'm coming!" she croaked.

Outside, she found two young men in yellow suits with lemon-peaked caps square on their heads. "Mrs Humbolt," said the shorter of the two, "my name's Mark and this is David.

We're PapSec Community Crime Prevention Officers and we've come to take you to your new home."

"I'm all right here," said Helen. "Thank you very much, but I'd prefer to stay."

"I'm afraid you have no choice, ma'am," said the taller officer, David. "As you presumably know, there's a compulsory purchase order for this whole area, which has been signed by Prime Minister Lord O'Dillon himself. You're pretty much the only person left living in the village right now; everyone else's gone save a couple of farmers who are threatening to shoot anyone that tries to take their land. But they too are gonna have to give it up sooner rather than later, even if it takes a few PapSec fighting platoons to smoke 'em out."

"You don't have to worry about anything though," said the shorter man. "We're here to take care of you, to get you all settled in to your new place. Do you have any luggage?"

"I don't want to go," Helen Humbolt repeated as if in a trance. "Just leave me be, please. I just want to be alone. I'm all right on my own."

She went to shut the door but the shorter officer stuck his boot in the frame. "You can be alone at your new place, Mrs Humbolt," he said. "Don't you worry about that. Your food parcels will be delivered there from now on."

"You know about the food parcels?" she asked, reopening the door. "What do you know about them? Who are they from?"

"That's I can't say, ma'am. All I'm authorised to tell you is that they'll keep coming without fail. Now come along, we've got lots on today. Where's your luggage?"

With cases in both hands, the PapSec Officers had Mrs Humbolt out of her house before she could think what was happening. The door slammed behind her and she reached into a pocket for her keys. She took them out and held them to the lock.

"There's no need for that," said the taller officer, "this house will be demolished in a few days. Why don't you leave the key with me?"

Helen Humbolt nodded, jangled the metal bunch into the man's outstretched palm. "Will you do me a favour?" she asked. "Would you make sure my sons know where I am? They never come and visit, you see. So I was thinking, they probably don't even know where I'm going. Would you do that for me, son? Would you tell them where to find me?"

"I'll do my best, Mrs Humbolt," said the officer. "I'll do my best."

3. The Meeting

23rd August 2030
Glaisdale, North Yorkshire

Helen Whitman ran a stubby finger through her hair. She pinched a strand of strawberry blonde between two fingers and worked it into her plait, then repeated the action with her other hand. Again and again she alternated sides until there was no more hair to knit. Then she tied up the end in an elastic band and gazed into the full-length mirror, admiring how the black hoops she'd knitted into her beige dress knotted their way around her curves. She flung her braid over her shoulder and turned to her bedroom. "What do you reckon?" she asked.

One of her friends was sitting with her legs stretched out over Helen's bed, a flower-print skirt riding up her tanned thighs. She looked up from the square sheet of plastic she held in both hands. "Aren't you going to put a bra on?" she asked. "I mean, I know we're only going to Whitby, but still. I can see your nipples."

"I don't know if I even own a bra," Helen replied.

"You don't own a bra!…"

"Leave it out, Melinda," said a third friend, in a polka dot dress as red as her lipstick, her blonde hair standing up like straw. "I think she looks lovely."

"Thanks Rebecca," said Helen, "I know we're only going into Whitby, but I almost never get to leave the village these days. I spend every minute of daylight with mum and dad on the allotments, and when we get home there's nothing to do but sit around and watch telly. It's so depressing. Just look at my hands." She splayed out her fingers. "I can't grow fingernails anymore, they break off when I'm working. And before you ask, Melinda, there's no way I could afford fake ones even if there were any shops left to buy them in. I'm stuck at the arse end of a village which is dead on its feet. Since the pub closed there's not a single place to go out, and now the trains don't even stop here on the way to Whitby. All that's left is that shitty little PapMart where the Post Office used to be."

"Then get a job," said Melinda. "Then you can move out. My Dave says people like you need to get off your backsides and find work."

"And does your Dave realise what that's like if you don't have his connections?" asked Rebecca. "I must've applied for hundreds of jobs and never even got an interview."

"That'll be the immigrants for you," Melinda continued. "My Dave says they'll work for nothing, just food and lodgings. So how are you ever supposed to compete?"

Helen tutted. "If the police upheld the law on illegal labour, then maybe we could find something," she said. "But I'd never blame the people themselves. They're just like the rest of us, just trying to survive."

"Well I'm bored of surviving," said Rebecca, "I'd like a bit of action, some excitement for once. Helen's right, all we get is the daily grind. I've been looking forward to tonight for ages."

"Having a job's not everything it's cracked up to be, you know," said Melinda without taking her eyes from the paper-thin plastic Xi-fan sheet in her hands.

"Oh come off it," said Helen, "at least you have security and independence."

"And healthcare," Rebecca added. "My mum's so scared I'll catch a super-bug that she didn't let me out of the house at all last winter. Me and my sisters spent five long months cooped up inside, and this year'll most likely be the same. I guess it's understandable, you know, since dad died and everything. But it's no way to live. I even had to lie about coming out tonight. I said we were having a sleepover, like when we were kids."

"Well I've made us apple strudel," said Helen, "like my gran used to do. Help yourselves, by the way." She pointed at a plate on the bedside table.

"Not for me," said Melinda, "I have to watch my weight."

"Do you?" said Rebecca, helping herself to a fruit-filled pastry. "You're the thinnest of us all by a mile."

"Exactly," said Melinda. "And it's little wonder why, isn't it? I'm the same weight now as I was when I was fourteen. I bet you two can't say the same."

"Get lost!" said Rebecca. "I'm perfectly happy with how I look, and Helen should be too. We're trying to have a nice night, like in the old days. So could you please stop it with the wisecracks?"

"All right," said Melinda, "let's have a night like we used to have on condition you don't make us listen to any more flamin' Marvin Percy. He's so early-2020s. Helen. When are you going to take those posters off your wall?"

"When I'm ready," Helen replied. "I like having them up, they remind me of happier times. When things get better I'll redecorate, but I'm not in that state of mind right now."

"What chance have you got of meeting a real man if you're still carrying around childhood crushes?" Melinda sneered. "You need to get out more."

"Which is precisely what we're doing," said Rebecca. "What time's your Dave coming to pick us up?"

"Seven," Melinda replied, "and we shouldn't be late, he doesn't like waiting."

Helen was doing up the buckles of her closed-toe sandals when an outside burst of car horn announced Dave's arrival. Melinda was out in a flash, but the other two women held back. "Is my makeup okay?" asked Helen. "It doesn't hide too many of my freckles, does it?"

"I think you look lovely," said Rebecca. "Come on, let's not keep Melinda's Dave waiting too long."

Helen grinned at her friend, shouted "bye" to her parents, and closed the front door behind her. They dawdled down the driveway, taking their time getting into Dave's car. But as soon as they'd closed both rear doors, they were away, screeching up Park View as if the driver were late for his next meeting.

Out of the village, twin beams of brilliant white lit the lane through the forests. Dave kept accelerating down the hill, so that when they crossed the humpback bridge all were thrown a little into the air. Then up the other side of the valley they went, the engine squealing to a musical accompaniment of bass beats and electronic crashes.

In the back, Helen leaned towards Rebecca. "I know Marvin Percy isn't cool these days," she said, "but at least he could hold a tune. This music sounds like someone smashing plates."

Whitby, North Yorkshire

The rhythmical breaking of crockery continued all the way into town. Dave slowed to precisely the speed limit, but only turned down the music when they pulled up outside a whitewashed pub on the corner of a one-way street. "You lot just be careful," he said. "Whitby's not as safe as it used to be. Do me a favour and stay indoors, okay?"

"Of course, honey," said Melinda. "We're only going for a few in the Nelson, and if the girls can hack it we might end up in a club. I'll message you when we're done."

"You do that," said Dave, kissing his wife on both cheeks. "Just be careful who you talk to, there are a lot of undesirables around these days, if you know what I mean."

The instant Helen got out of the car, Rebecca grabbed her by the arm and pulled her towards the pub. "We'll talk to whoever the heck we like," she said.

Helen grinned back.

They pushed open the oaken door to face a wooden bar along the far wall, with leather-topped stools tucked in at equal distances. The rose paint of the walls matched the carpets, and were separated by green leather benches beside an assortment of round pub tables that formed into alcoves at either end. Pretty much all of which were empty.

Rebecca gazed around. "It's dead in here," she said. "Apart from those men playing cards, we're the only people here. Why don't we go somewhere with more life?"

"Because this is my favourite place," said Melinda. "Remember when we had my eighteenth birthday in here?"

"That was probably the last time I went out," said Helen. "It was a lot busier that night, though."

"You're right," Melinda said. "It's Friday night, this place should be heaving."

A barman approached in a black waistcoat and bow-tie. "What can I get you, ladies?" he asked.

"It's very quiet for a Friday night," said Rebecca. "Where is everyone?"

"It'll liven up later," he replied, "when the meeting finishes."

"What meeting?" asked Helen.

"What meeting…" the barman repeated, smiling. "The Citizens' Forum, of course. It is Friday. They're so popular these days that they've had to move to the beach to find space. No one'll be here till after the tide comes in. I'd be down there myself if I didn't have to work."

"We'll have three so-bod mod-jars then," said Melinda. "And make them big ones."

"Hang on," said Rebecca, "shouldn't we talk about this first?"

"What's there to talk about?" said Melinda. "We just told my Dave that we'd be in here all night, and that's precisely what we're going to do. Any change of plan could be dangerous, and I don't want him worrying about me, okay?"

"You told your Dave we'd stay here," said Helen, "me and Rebecca didn't say a thing."

"Come on Mel," said Rebecca, "we want to live a bit for once. We could stay in here and play dominoes with the granddads, or go down to the beach and see what's happening."

"Absolutely not," said Melinda. "Look at us, we're all dressed up for town, not the beach. And anyway, you heard what my Dave said about undesirables. He says those meetings are full of hooligans and violent radicals."

"What does your Dave know?" Rebecca responded. "Going to the beach can't be any more risky than getting in the back of his car."

"Quite right," said Helen. "He drives like a lunatic. In any case, you heard what the barman said, he looks normal enough. And seeing as how most of the town seems to be there, it can't be that bad."

"Well, I don't want to go," Melinda insisted.

"Fine," said Rebecca. "Then stay here. Helen, what do you say?"

Helen glanced left and right down the bar. "Well it sounds a lot better than this place," she said. "Come on, it's a nice enough night. Let's go and have a look from the cliffs at least."

It may have been years since they'd last been in town, but the girls could still pick their way through Whitby's maze of alleys.

Melinda trotted a couple of paces behind, doing her best to balance her heels on the uneven paving. "Hey!" she said as they turned into another narrow lane between pink- or white-brick cottages. "I don't like it down here. Can't we go somewhere with more light? It might be dangerous."

"Then keep up," said Rebecca. "You've seen the films, it's always the one who lags behind that gets caught. As long as the three of us stick together, we'll be fine."

"All right," said Melinda, bending a knee to unbuckle her shoe. "But we're just going to the cliffs, okay? No further."

"Yeah, okay," said Rebecca, turning on her flat feet and trotting away. A gust of wind blew her skirt up over her hips.

Around a corner, the ruins of the abbey appeared on the far hill, black against the evening sky. They crossed the road in silence, to walk along the rolling crest of the river bank. Opposite cast-iron railings and a line of three-storey townhouses, the pathway led under a row of street lamps which came on in turn as they walked past.

"You see that?" said Melinda. "That's my Xi-fan sheet. It's programmed to synchronise with all the streetlights in Whitby." She retrieved a stamp-sized square of plastic from her bag and pulled at the corners to stretch it out to the size of a letter. She showed off the illuminated screen but the other women simply nodded, neither could've cared less.

Above the mouth of the River Esk, where salt water mixed with fresh through the offset harbour wall, the streetlights stopped at the whalebone arch. Despite the darkness beyond,

Rebecca went straight past. She stopped at a line of tape which flapped in the wind where a fence used to be.

When Melinda and Helen joined Rebecca, they could hear shouting from below.

"These things have been on the news," Melinda said, touching Helen's arm. "There was one of these illegal gatherings in Kings Lynn which ended in a riot. The police had to come and break it up. I think we should go back into town. Come on, let's go." She started back towards the streetlights.

Helen paused. "Well?" she asked Rebecca. "I guess we shouldn't leave Mel on her own."

But Rebecca didn't budge. "Listen to it," she said. "It's like they're talking about you and me."

Helen paused to hear the repeated chants wafting up from the beach.

"All I want is a future," someone said.

"All I want is a future," dozens repeated.

"Just a job so I can live."

"Just a job so I can live."

"And a roof over my head,"

"And a roof…"

Although the girls couldn't see it, a sea of waving hands went up in support of the words. "Let's go and see what it's all about," said Rebecca.

"But what about Melinda?"

"Sod Melinda and her opinions."

"Her Dave's opinions," Helen chuckled.

"Exactly," said Rebecca. "Come on, let's go."

"Mel!" Helen hollered. "We're going down to the beach."

Melinda had stopped at the stone pedestal of the statue to Captain Cook. She turned to see her friends disappear down a cliff-side path "Hey," she shouted. "I said I didn't want to go down there. Didn't you hear me? They're dangerous those places. You said we'd stay on the cliffs." But seeing that she was on her own, rather than being left behind, Melinda followed them down in a huff.

At the bottom of the steps, Rebecca and Helen took off their shoes and walked out onto the chilly sand. People were sitting on jumpers or blankets, many with picnics strewn around them. But all sat listening intently to the man on the ledge at the base of the cliffs.

"I work at Whitby General," the man was saying.

"I work at Whitby General," others repeated.

"I won't say who I am or what I do,"

"I won't say who I am…"

"But every day I turn patients away,"

"Because they can't afford Monogon's fees,"

"We need to reclaim our hospital!"

Melinda joined her friends but wasn't impressed. "There's nothing wrong with Whitby Hospital," she sneered. "My Dave was in there last year to have an ingrowing toenail out. He said it was great, that he'd never had such attention. It's like a hotel, apparently."

"Will you shut up about your Dave?" Rebecca said under her breath. "That guy's not talking about minor operations for people with five-star company health insurance, is he? He's talking about everyone else, like me and my family. If we'd been able to get him treatment, my dad would probably be alive now. I and everyone else want to hear what this guy has to say. So just give it a rest. Okay?"

The meeting went on until the tide came in and gobbled up the beach. As wave followed inevitable wave, the moon lit up the footpaths and handholds for people to scramble up the sandstone cliff-face.

But the girls lingered. "What are you waiting for?" asked Melinda, rubbing her shoulders and stamping her feet. "It's finished now. Let's go."

"I want to speak to that guy from the hospital," said Rebecca. "I've been watching him all evening and I'm not sure I've ever seen anyone so beautiful in all my life."

"Him?" Melinda sneered. "But he's a Paki."

"Melinda!" Rebecca scolded. "I can't believe you'd say a thing like that."

"Yeah, well, he is though, isn't he?"

"Maybe his great grandparents were from India or somewhere," said Rebecca. "I don't know and I don't care. You heard him speak. He's as Yorkshire as you and me."

"Then why don't you go and talk to him?" said Helen.

"I can't," said Rebecca. "He's with all his friends."

"I'll go with you," said Helen. "Come on, let's go."

"Are you joking me?" asked Melinda. But by then the other two were already striding away.

The women found a group deep in discussion. "We should've been braver tonight," Rebecca's fancy man was saying. "We should've occupied the hospital. With all those people, we could've taken the place over and reclaimed what is rightfully ours. But no one was willing to support me. I just think it was a missed opportunity."

A young black man in spectacles spoke up. "And can you imagine what would've happened if we'd done that?" he asked. "The police would've been round in a flash. According to the law, that's private property and we'd have been trespassing on Monogon's land. Rest assured that anything had got broken would've been criminal damage, even if the police did it. They'd have found a way to send half of us to prison."

"Still though, Paul," said a third man, taller than the rest, the moon reflecting off his bald brown temples. "Tariq's right that we have to make use of this momentum. We just need to consider our actions beforehand, to plan what we're going to do and not let this movement die away or be overtaken by mob justice."

"Well said, Winston," said a red-headed woman with an Edinburgh accent. "Now do you think we can go and get that beer? I'm freezing my tits off out here."

It was only as the group turned to go that they noticed the three women lingering. "Hi," said Helen. "Is it an open invitation for that drink?"

"Absolutely," said the tall man with the shiny head. "The more the merrier."

"Aye," the Scottish girl added, "you're more than welcome. As long as you're not infiltrators or nothing."

"Infiltrators?" asked Rebecca. "Infiltrators from where?"

"Could be from anywhere," the big man replied. "You can never be too careful. But you look okay. I think you can join us. Do we all agree?"

"I'm with you, Winston," said the Edinburgher, "just as long as we can get somewhere warm."

They made their way off the beach, wiped the sand from their soles and put their shoes back on before climbing the concrete steps to the pier. Rebecca waited for her man, and walked alongside him for a minute or so before asking as casually as she could "do you really work at the hospital?"

"I do," he replied.

"Are you a doctor?"

"I'm a surgeon."

"Wow," said Rebecca. "I'm not sure I've ever met a surgeon before."

"I meet them all the time."

Rebecca slapped his arm, glimpsed the man smiling at her and glanced away to find her old schoolfriend on her other side.

"So when are you going home to Pakistan?" asked Melinda.

Rebecca's jaw dropped as she tried to think what to say.

But the man chuckled. "Would you believe that I've never even been to Pakistan?" he said. "I've spent my whole life being called a Paki, or worse, much worse. But actually, I am home, pretty much. I was born in the James Cook in Middlesbrough."

"Were you?" said Rebecca. "Me too."

"That's also a Monogon Hospital now," said the surgeon. "Just like Whitby General. Their maternal and infant death rates have gone through the roof, even worse than here. Of course, no one knows for sure because the company will never release that kind of information, but I've heard there's at least two deaths every day at the moment, and with winter coming on it's only going to get worse."

"That's awful," Rebecca sighed. "There's so much injustice in this world. So much that needs fixing. What's your name?"

"I'm Tariq Emami," he replied.

"It's a pleasure to meet you, Tariq Emami. I'm Rebecca Kingston."

The group walked into town at river level, past cockle-and whelk-shacks shut up for the night. On the opposite side of the street, the windows of the old amusement arcades were all boarded up. The Wharf Inn stood between those empty buildings, set back a little from the road with its whitewashed walls and low doorway squeezed in between bay windows.

The group filed inside and Melinda sighed at the warmth. "Finally, I can have a drink," she said. "I'm not like you lot. I work all week and I like to have a nice time on a Friday evening, not get involved in some pointless political demonstration. So-bod mod-jars all round, girls. And don't worry, I'll get them in."

Although now a cosy place, it wasn't hard to imagine smugglers once conspiring in the alcoves and cubby holes of the Wharf. But even tonight, a Friday, the pub was far from full and they were able to find a nook that seated all ten of them.

"Cheers," said Winston when all had sat down. "To old friends and new."

Helen thought she caught the man's gaze when he spoke of new friends, but soon she was sure she was mistaken. He spent ages in conversation with the ginger Scottish woman, whose name it turned out was Fiona McIntyre.

"I just can't believe how blatant it all is," said Fiona. "I mean, the corruption's obvious for all to see. They openly shove it in our faces. What was today's headline? PapCorp CEO Michael O'Dillon made a Lord? Seriously? That was the most important thing the State Broadcaster could find to talk about? All so he can advise on trade strategy, apparently. But whose interest is he acting in? That of the British people or that of his company?"

"Exactly," said Paul Broddle, in his round glasses and hair shorn around back and sides to leave an angle in his afro. "It's like one big rich man's clique and I'm sick of it. This attitude is invading society. I got a formal warning last week for teaching my kids about Steve Biko. Can you imagine that? I'm a history teacher who's only allowed to mention the bits that Griffin

Educational approve. We're doing African colonisation at the moment and I'm forbidden from discussing the Mau Mau or the slave trade. It's mad that a foreign private company can dictate what this country's kids learn at school."

"It's not just Griffin Educational though, Paul," said Winston. "It's all of Spokane. That single American conglomeration is responsible for Monogon Medical and Greyskies Security, as much as they are Bridgeford Asset Management and Whistle Non-stop transport or Moon Burger, or so many other brands. You can say what you like about Lord O'Dillon and PapCorp, but at least they're British."

"And what's that got to do with anything?" Paul asked.

"I mean, they pay taxes here, don't they?" said Winston. "That's something at least. The North-West economy would collapse without PapCorp. They also employ millions of British workers, in one way or another."

"And Spokane don't employ anyone?" asked Paul.

"I'm saying first we need to deal with the external problem," said Winston, "and then deal with our own, one foe at a time. But we need to go after every division of Spokane all at once. Only that way will we be able to make a difference."

"Yeah, right," sneered a white man with dull eyes and hair cropped to hide his baldness. "Like a couple of marches in Whitby are going to make any difference."

"You'd be surprised, Kyle," said Winston. "We're not alone. People are saying the same things all over the country. The movement in Leeds is fifty times what we are here, and just look what they've achieved. And then there are all the things Harry Lanker's doing at national level. We're part of a bigger whole, that's what I'm saying. And if we're strong enough, and stick together, we can make a real difference."

"Well PapCorp or Spokane," said Dr Tariq, "they're both the same to me. Like Marx said, wealth accumulation at one pole leads to misery at the other."

"Mark's who?" asked Rebecca.

"Karl Marx," Tariq chuckled. "You know, the Communist Manifesto and all that."

Rebecca shook her head.

"Really?" the doctor smiled. "You should know about him. I could teach you if you want."

Rebecca grinned through her eyes and touched the tips of her hair. "I'd like that," she said.

The conversation flowed, but at some point Helen lost the drift. It was partly the glasses of bittersweet cocktail that kept being placed before her. But mostly it was Winston. Having been so vocal at the beginning of the night, he now seemed interested only in making eyes at her. She caught his deep-brown gaze and her heart beat faster. She glanced away, ran her fingers over her French plait, and when she looked again he was still staring at her. She smiled to herself and turned to Melinda on her far side.

But Melinda wasn't there. "Hey!" said Helen. "Rebecca, have you seen Melinda?"

"No," Rebecca replied, breaking her gaze and conversation with the surgeon. "The last I saw she was sat next to you."

"She's been gone a while," said Fiona. "A good twenty minutes I'd say. She was playing with that Xi-fan sheet of hers, and got up and left with Dave Spooner. Do you remember him, Kyle? From school?"

"Of course," Kyle replied. "He flushed my head down the toilet almost every week. He was a real twat."

"He still is," said Helen. "But he was also supposed to be giving us a lift home."

"Looks like plans have changed," said Rebecca. "We'll either have to find another way back to Glaisdale or somewhere to crash for the night. Think of it as an adventure. Anyway, we'll have a much better time now she's gone. We can relax without worrying she'll make some silly wisecrack. I mean, that joke she made about Jews. Who on earth could find that funny?"

"I didn't like to say," said Fiona. "But I didn't find her very appropriate. How do you know her?"

"I guess we don't anymore," said Helen, "not on tonight's performance. We three were best mates all through High School, but she got married to that twat Dave. He works for

Whistle Non-stop now, drives a sports car and buys her the latest gadgets. She seems to think she's better than us."

"That was obvious," said Winston. "I'll get the drinks in. Same again for everyone?" he asked the table while staring at Helen.

Helen glanced at Rebecca, who understood her friend's question and smiled back, nudging her head to say 'go for it'.

"I'll come and help," said Helen.

"That'd be great," Winston replied.

There were a handful of people waiting at the bar, but only one man working it. He was pouring pints or leaving them to settle, mixing cocktails, taking in notes and handing out change.

Winston perched himself on a bar stool and Helen did likewise. She wanted to say something, but she couldn't stop staring at the man. She watched him take a square of plastic from his pocket and pull the opposite corners of his Xi-fan sheet to the size of a beer mat. He tapped the surface a couple of times and looked up at Helen. "So?" he asked. "What will you have?"

"I, er, I've, I've, been on those Sow-bodge mow-jars things, or whatever they're called."

"So-bod mod-jar," he corrected her. "where the 'o's are like in orange."

"So-bod mow-jar," Helen repeated.

"That's better," he smiled. "Do you know what it means?"

"Not a clue."

"It means Free Hungarian. It's named after Zoltán Papp."

"That's very interesting," she said, swaying on the stool. "So where are you from then? Did you say Leeds? You don't sound too Yorkshire t' me."

"No, well, I was brought up north of Manchester, but I moved around a lot since then."

"Have you travelled?"

"Not exactly," said Winston. "Not for fun at least. I was drafted into the army for a while. It taught me a lot but I hated it. I've seen some horrible things. You could say that's one of the reasons I'm here doing this."

"It must've been awful," said Helen. "So what brought you to Whitby then? Wife and kids I suppose."

The man chuckled from deep in his belly. "No," he said. "None of that. I don't even have a girlfriend. I got involved with lots of stuff in Leeds. You know, we managed to occupy over ten thousand homes that were being kept empty by this company called Bridgeford Asset Management. We took them over and redistributed them to homeless families. I'm good with locks, you see. But then the muscle men tried to take over and I got a bit scared, thought it might be time to move on. Whitby seemed a good choice, especially after I met a guy that was selling his odd-jobs business. There's plenty of work here and I like the air, it's nice and fresh."

"Bracing, more like it."

"Yeah, the wind does blow a bit, but I'd rather that than the city. Leeds is so polluted that sometimes you can hardly breathe. But if the army taught me anything, it was the ability to turn my hand to pretty much whatever I want. So I can live basically anywhere. There was no movement here when I arrived, so I've helped build all that you saw at the beach today. Along with these people of course." He waved towards his group of friends.

"That's impressive," said Helen.

"I do what I can," he said. "I haven't seen you before, though. Was this your first Forum?"

"Yep."

"So what brought you out tonight of all nights?"

"It was an accident really. Me and my friends were going for a few drinks and a bit of a dance. Tonight's mine and Rebecca's first night out in years, and it's kind of different to the last times we were in Whitby. We live in a village in the countryside you see, and don't get out too much. My life's nowhere as exciting as yours. Breaking in and occupying buildings. You must be really brave."

"Brave or stupid," he replied.

The drinks arrived, and Winston pushed Helen's glass towards her before picking up his own. "Well, cheers," he said.

"I'm glad you picked tonight to come out. It's very nice to meet you…" He paused a moment. "I'm very sorry, I completely forgot to ask your name."

"I'm Helen," she replied. "Helen Whitman."

"It's a pleasure to meet you, Helen Whitman." He held out a hand the size of a bear's paw. "My name's Winston Humbolt."

4. Up and Out

18th March 2042
Rusholme

The clock on the bedside table was an ancient plastic affair. The radio now picked up only static, but when the red digits flashed to 07:15, an electric horn blew through the room.

Minnie reached out a hand from the bedsheets, found the button and silenced the alarm. She glanced over to see her boyfriend snoring through his open mouth. She kissed his forehead and crept out of her side of the bed. She gathered up the pile of folded clothes from the stool and, without turning on the light, she dressed herself in ripped jeans and a faded t-shirt, did up an old cardigan around her belly, and left the bedroom in silence.

It was nearly five months since Minnie had moved in with Brian Brownlow, since her parents had found out she was pregnant and she'd defied her father's orders for an abortion. "We've got little enough on our plates as it is," he had said, "without an extra mouth to feed." And he'd been right, times were hard.

But abortions these days were more dangerous even than giving birth. It wasn't illegal, just too expensive to go to a PapMed clinic and Minnie was too scared to visit the back-alleys around Strangeways.

Without a car or money, she'd walked two hours from her parents' flat in Pendleton, to the only place she thought she'd be welcome. But while Brian himself was delighted to have Minnie living with him, the house very much belonged to his mother. And she was not one for being woken up early.

Which is why Minnie tip-toed downstairs to the kitchen, where she wiped a layer of grease over a slice of stale bread. She took a bite as she buttoned up her duffle coat, pulled a satchel around her shoulder and let herself out the front door, clicking it to as quietly as she could. She finished her breakfast before she was even half way to the school at the bottom of Welwyn Street.

Seventeen-years-old and seven months pregnant, Minnie's crab-apple cheeks shone pink in the morning chill. Her hair was as black as coal, and it bobbed up and down as she walked.

She'd found work at a food exchange, in an old brick supermarket on the corner of Moss Lane East. When the weather was nice, they'd bring their stalls and produce out onto the asphalt carpark. But those days were rare and today was not one of them.

When Minnie got to her stall inside, she found four other women already picking onions from the baskets on the floor, piling them up onto a desk. Minnie bent down to grab a few in each hand, only for a man to say, "Here, let me do that."

Minnie glared at the lanky youth. "I'm pregnant, Neville," she said, "not ill. I'm still quite capable of lifting a few bags of onions."

"Okay," he said. "Sorry. I was only trying to help."

Minnie saw young Neville shuffle away. She lifted as many onions as she could between her hands and her belly, then dropped them into a pile on the table.

As Minnie arranged the vegetables, another woman stood watching. Dahlia was a mixed-race girl, about Minnie's age, with tight-curled hair that seemed to pile up out her head and teeth skewed at every angle. "I think he likes you, you know?" she said.

"What? Neville?" said Minnie. "You reckon? What kind of weirdo would be attracted to a heavily pregnant woman? I look like an apple!"

"Maybe he wants a bit of forbidden fruit," said Dahlia. "He must be as sick of onions as the rest of us."

Minnie chuckled. "I'm sure it can't be healthy for the baby to have a mostly onion diet."

"Probably not," Dahlia mused. "But surely that's the least of your worries. Have you given any more thought to where you're giving birth?"

"It's going to have to be at Brian's house. Remember I told you about his mother's friend who used to be a midwife? She must be ninety if she's a day. I'll be more worried about her welfare than mine."

"So you're not going to St Mary's then?"

"If only!" said Minnie. "But as all the hospitals in Manchester are now run by PapMed, we'd have to sell the house to give birth in one."

"I've heard of people that do," said Dahlia.

"Me too," said Minnie. "But not old Mrs Brownlow."

Her colleague chuckled. "No," she said, "of course not."

Whitby

Helen Humbolt had no need for an alarm clock. She woke every morning at four when the PapMart delivery van rumbled past her window. But while she was alone and wouldn't disturb anyone, she still didn't turn on the lights. She'd calculated just how much electricity she had left on the meter and the oven would need all she had.

She got up, rolled away her mattress and stashed it under one of the benches on the mezzanine floor. She creaked her way down the wooden staircase and went straight for the kitchen behind the counter. She flicked on the oven, and as it pre-heated she washed herself in the stainless-steel sink. Then she took an off-white uniform from the hangers above, worked herself into it and tied up her hair so it'd fit into her baker's cap. She tied an apron over her head and cut off another red thread that had come lose from the chest, from what had once been the embroidered name of her bakery but was now just a mess of red strings. As was her routine, she then opened all the windows, partly to let out the stale air of sleep but mostly to tell the world she was baking.

Back in the kitchen, Helen Humbolt lined up the day's ingredients beside their moulds or cutters. Today she was making nine types of cake, biscuit or pie, the kinds of things she found were still popular. With the PapMart next door offering bread for a quarter of what it cost her to make, she'd given up on the loaves and buns. But sometimes people still bought her cakes, and she always knew that, even if something didn't sell, she'd at least have plenty for dinner.

Which is why she'd ballooned. Helen had never been a slight woman, but as her business followed the rest of her life, she found herself with surpluses that were really far too much for one person. She'd eaten it all regardless.

With the sun glinting through the windows and the kitchen steaming hot, Helen placed a dozen currant-filled Eccles cakes onto one plate, and an equal number of jam doughnuts onto another. She arranged the Viennese whirls around the slabs of ginger shortbread, lining up iced buns in between. Then she cut slices from the Bakewell pudding, the carrot cake, the Victoria sponge, and arranged them so her customers could see their moist insides. It was only when all that was done that she returned to her speciality Flodni layer cake. She scraped out the last of the plum jam and spread it over the top, then finished it off with a thin slice of nut pasty, just as her grandmother had taught her.

Helen was so calm that no one watching would have suspected that she knew exactly what was about to happen.

Foston Village, Derbyshire

It was gone ten by the time Zoltan O'Dillon rolled out of bed. His first action of the day was to stumble into the living room of his stately home, sit himself at an ebony table and pull a bag of white powder from a drawer. He poured out a mound of dust and arranged it into a line. Then he produced a plastic straw from the same drawer and sucked it all up through his nostril.

It was only as his head was jerking and he was wiping his nose that he noticed the snoring mass on the sofa. Zoltan picked an ashtray from the middle of the table and lobbed it at the mound of sheets, hitting somewhere in the middle and throwing up a cloud of cigarette butts. "Wake up Bernie!" he shouted.

The pile of blankets stirred and a head appeared from one end. "Did you throw something?" Bernie asked, rubbing his head. "What am I even doing here? What happened last night?"

Bernie Douglas-FitzAllan, the Earl of Angus, had been Zoltan's closest friend since school. His cheeks were permanently ruddy, man-breasts rested on his stomach and patches of sweat spread from his armpits. That, and the wiry clump of blond hair on his head, gave him the appearance of a man closer to Zoltan's father's age than his former classmate's thirty-one years. And to compound matters today, Bernie's cheeks were smothered in blood.

"For Papp's sake, Bernie!" Zoltan exclaimed at the sight of his advisor's face. "Are you all right? You've got claret all over you."

Bernie wiped a chubby hand over his cheeks and looked down to where he'd been sleeping to find a puddle of red for his pillow. "It's okay," he said. "It's just a nosebleed, I get them sometimes after too much cocaine. Do you remember what happened last night?"

"Not really," said Zoltan. "I remember there was a tractor… Do you want a line? It's great for hangovers."

"Better not," said Bernie, fingering his crusty nostrils.

The double doors behind Zoltan burst open and in marched Sir Larry Pickering. He was a thin man, wearing a pin-striped suit and standard yellow tie, with badger hair swept neatly around back and sides, and square glasses that matched the ordered dullness of his face. He slammed the doors behind him. "What in Papp's name did you pair get up to last night?" he shouted. "We've only been here two weeks! After you got barred from both the pubs, I thought we'd seen the last of this. But now…"

"What do you expect?" asked Zoltan, "sending me into exile in this shit-tip? I have a very active mind, Larry. Brilliant, some would say. And I need more stimulus than some Staffordshire backwater could ever provide."

"Derbyshire," Bernie corrected his boss.

"Same difference," Zoltan continued. "I mean, this is the only PapCorp division without a home on either of the Manchester Campuses."

"You could hardly have an agricultural company based in the middle of a city, could you?" replied Pickering. "You know full well that part of PapCorp's bankruptcy deal with Thornhill Agricultural was that Foston would become the headquarters of PapAgri worldwide. You're in charge of the fifth largest constituent company in the PapSie25. This is a promotion your father's given you, and you should respect that."

"As always," Zoltan sneered, pouring out more cocaine. "This is all down to my father. We're so far away from Manchester, he might as well have sent us to Siberia. It was inevitable there'd be a reaction."

"So your father told you to get high and steal a tractor? Do you even know what you did with it?"

Zoltan shrugged his broad shoulders, put the pipe to his nostril and snorted the line.

Pickering tutted. "After stealing that tractor," he explained, "and running over someone's dog, you damaged a dozen cars and almost killed at least three people. Then you crashed into the security gate of the PapAgri complex and legged it inside."

"So? We didn't hurt anyone," said Zoltan.

"No, but…"

"Then what's the fuss all about?"

"People are angry, Zoltan," said Pickering. "They think you're above the law. And this is just the kind of thing our political opponents love. By the time I arrived this morning, the entire bloody vehicle was covered in these."

Sir Larry unfolded a poster from his jacket pocket and held it out for them to see. 'Enough is Enough' it declared at the top, above a photo of a man with shoulder-length hair, a raggedy beard and an easy smile. Below the portrait was written, 'The Time has Come. Vote RASCAL for Harry Lanker'.

"Bleugh!" Bernie spat. "Who in their right minds would vote for that hairy wanker? Just look at him trying to smile through that ridiculous beard. He looks like some kind of mad mullah."

"He's popular with the poor," said Larry.

"The poor?" Zoltan sneered. "Who gives a toss about the poor? He's only popular with them because they're too thick to know what's good for them. That's why he'll never get anywhere in Manchester. People there understand the modern world like these peasants never could."

"Their votes are worth the same as anyone's," said Pickering, "same as yours and mine. That's how the system works."

"Then the system's broken," said Zoltan. "But I still don't think it's broken enough to bring someone like Harry Lanker to power."

"Exactly," said Bernie. "His brand of neo-Marxism will bring this country to its knees."

Zoltan nodded with rather too much enthusiasm. "You're telling me!" he exclaimed. "I wouldn't put it past him to try and kill off PapCorp. You know what his lot are like, all herbal tea and 'direct democracy', hippies who think they're Robin Hood. I just hope he doesn't manage to steal power while I'm stuck here, out in the sticks. If I was in charge of PapCorp, I'd know how to deal with him. I'm a man of action. But I'm not sure my father's properly prepared."

"Whatever happens," said Pickering, "you can bet Lord Michael will only act in the best interests of PapCorp. I'm sure he won't let some weaselly socialist grind down your inheritance before it's your turn at the top."

"It won't be long," said Zoltan. "You'll see. In five years' time I'll be CEO of PapCorp."

"Will you now?" Pickering mocked. "I think your father might have something to say about that."

"Lord Mike's had his day," said Zoltan. "He'll be sixty next year, it's only a matter of time before his health starts to fail him. Do you know how much he weighs? Over thirty stone!"

"I bet you're catching up fast!" Bernie quipped.

"You can talk, lardarse!" O'Dillon sneered back. "You're probably the fattest person I know. If ever there was a man built to be an Earl, it's you, Bernie Douglas-FitzAllan, Major

Stinkovitch! Now come over here and have some cocaine. It's no fun getting high on my own."

Rusholme

Side-by-side, Minnie and Dahlia worked through the morning. They paid no attention to the posters of Harry Lanker that decorated every wall of the Rusholme Food Exchange, but they knew they were there. They themselves had hung a few.

Half the other stalls likewise stocked only onions, maybe a few potatoes and the odd manky carrot here and there. There was a bakery at the far end of that old supermarket, a butcher's and a fishmonger's as well, although all too often these days their displays were stacked with packets of produce rather than anything fresh.

"What's half of two MancPounds fifty?" asked Dahlia.

Minnie smiled. "Are you joking?" she asked.

"Not at all. I'm no good at maths, you know that."

"It's one MancPound twenty-five," said Minnie, handing a bag of veg to an elderly man with a white moustache and yellow wrinkles around his eyes.

"It'll be PapPounds soon enough," said her customer in a southern Irish drawl.

"Don't remind me, Nigel," said Minnie. "It's like that bloody company's taking over everything. I heard we might be going back to the barter market this place used to be, rather than soil ourselves with more Pap-crap."

"Good on you," said Nigel. "I'm sure everyone round here will welcome that, not that many of us have much to offer, mind. But still. How's that boyfriend of yours doing? His knee recovered yet?"

"I don't think his knee'll ever be good enough to play football again," said Minnie. "They've stopped his treatment, so he mostly sits around watching telly. He's not at his best. Still, at least his mother has finally stopped accusing me of being a hanger-on. She no longer says I'm only with him for his fame."

"It's a dreadful shame when a footballer's career comes to a premature end because of injury," the man went on. "He had real potential, your Brian. People were talking him up as the new Giggsy. And I bet this whole PapManchester FC thing hasn't helped."

"Not a jot," said Minnie, searching out her next customer. "United going bankrupt means they've not only stopped his treatment but also his insurance claim. In two months' time I'll be giving birth, and I'll be off work for who knows how long. Which means he's going to have to find a way to support us."

"You know you'll always get help from the community," said the man, lowering his onions into a cloth trolley before standing back straight and leaning towards the young woman. "You know what I heard?" he said. "I heard United weren't really bankrupt at all. It's just PapBank decided to call in all their loans at once, so PapCorp could force out the owners and take over themselves."

"That doesn't surprise me," said Minnie. "I guess the O'Dillons can see what's about to happen just like we all can. Things are going to change when Harry Lanker gets into power."

"Can't come soon enough," said Nigel. "But of course in the meantime, PapCorp are doing everything they can. Did you see Lord O'Dillon's awarded himself permission for another six Bio-domes? As if that monstrosity they're building over the city centre wasn't bad enough, soon there'll be seven of them. Three thousand acres of central Manchester, all owned by a private company and all full of identical yellow towers."

"I know," said Minnie, "I used to love those old buildings in the city centre, but now they'll just be the first floors of a PapHome. It's a real disgrace what's happening to our city. I just pray Harry Lanker can become Prime Minister in time to put a stop to all this."

The two shared a knowing glance, and nodded to themselves.

Whitehall, London

Lord Michael O'Dillon reclined into a brilliant-white sofa in the Ministry of Health. From a matching couch, on the opposite side of a walnut coffee table, the Minister himself was in the middle of a tirade. "We have to do everything we can to hold on to power," he was saying. "Harry Lanker and his bunch of RASCALs will be a serious threat to our majority when we next have to go to the country."

"He's a threat to more than simply your government's hold on power," said Lord O'Dillon. "He has the potential to jeopardise the entire nation's well-being. His neo-Marxist ideals will bring this country to its knees."

The Health Minister nodded. "I'm sure we can find a way to work together," he said. "On this matter at least, our interests our identical. Now is that why you've come to see me?"

"Not at all, Minister," said Lord O'Dillon, straightening his flabby back against the cushions. "As we both know, the sad demise of Monogon Healthcare has left large areas of this country without a hospital for fifty miles or more. PapMed are doing their best to fill the gaps, but every day the news carries stories about quacks opening their own surgeries in their back rooms, performing C-sections with rusty knives and the like. It's little wonder child mortality's going through the roof."

"I know," said the Minister, "but what can we do? The country's bankrupt, so we can hardly afford to build a hundred new hospitals, can we?"

"That's just my point," said Lord Michael. "The country can't afford it, so PapCorp have to step in."

"Right," said the Minister. "Since PapMed took over Monogon, you now run eighty-odd percent of the hospitals in Britain. What else can I do to aid PapMed's progress?"

"You need to impose strict regulations," said O'Dillon. "Those unlicensed clinics are unhygienic at best, and if they're allowed to fester we'll have a genuine public health catastrophe on our hands. Your government needs to act fast. Give us the regulation we advise and you'll get your new hospitals. Before

PapCorp make their investments, we need some safeguards. If people are able to get cheaper, lower quality service elsewhere, well, it would impinge on profits."

"I'm not sure," said the Minister. "I think it'd be difficult to sell it to the electorate."

"Listen, Minister," said Lord Michael. "Don't you worry about the electorate, we'll look after them. Plant a few well-placed seeds in people's brains and they can be made to believe whatever we want. If you get PapCorp to sprinkle a bit of our magic into your next campaign, your constituents will be begging you for a new PapMed hospital. Now as you know, a recent independent report has made some recommendations."

"An independent report which PapMed wrote," said the Minister. "Listen, Lord Michael, we're not here to discuss some report or other. I want to know exactly what the endgame is here."

"The endgame, Minister, is to prevent the kinds of outbreaks of disease which have come from the fragmented healthcare system advocated by successive British governments. In the cities as much as the villages, plagues we thought went out with the dark ages have come back to haunt this great nation, in ways we thought we'd never see again. What is needed is a co-ordinated approach by the market leader in for-profit healthcare."

"You can wrap it up however you like, Lord O'Dillon. But my question to you is simple. If I were to give such a thing my backing, what could I expect in return?"

"Besides getting you re-elected with a record majority?"

"Yes."

Lord Michael leaned forward with his hands on his knees. He smiled. "Now we're talking the same language," he said.

Whitby

On the ninth chime of the church bell, Helen Humbolt jingled open the door. She turned around the cardboard sign in the window and returned to her stance behind the counter.

There had been days of late when no one would walk through that door at all, but today at five past nine in marched a dozen large men, all in tight-fitting body suits that matched their yellow-peaked caps.

Helen smiled as if it were nothing unusual. "Good morning, gentlemen," she greeted them. "Lovely day for it, isn't it? Now what can I get for you? These iced buns are straight out of the oven, and I'll bet you've never tried anything like my Flodni layered cake."

"Mrs Humbolt," said the officer nearest her. "We are not here to buy any of your iced buns. We were under the impression you'd been informed we would be arriving today at 09-05 hours."

"I know why you're here, son," said Helen. "Just please, try to humour me for a moment. I don't get many customers these days, not since you put up that bloody PapMart next door and undercut me on everything I produce. This was the last independent bakery in Whitby and people used to like it here. Until your company started their stupid price war I was doing all right. And now you're throwing me out. All because I stopped selling PapPop in my shop and refused to buy their shitty ingredients."

"We're not here to discuss the details of your predicament, Mrs Humbolt," that same officer continued. "We are here to repossess the property that lawfully belongs to PapBank. You are the first of five jobs we have today, Whitely's the butcher is next. So if you don't mind, please vacate the premises and let us get on with our jobs."

Helen splayed her palms out before her. "Look," she said. "I've baked all this. I knew you were coming and I've planned ahead. It feels so long since anyone's actually enjoyed my cakes, I'd just like you all to try a bit. I won't charge you, of course, you can have everything for free. Just don't tell me you're only doing your jobs. Believe you me, I've come to understand the meaning of those words. Go on, help yourselves. They're very good."

"I'm afraid that's not going to happen, Mrs Humbolt. It's against protocol to consume anything offered by someone convicted of a crime."

"A crime?" said Helen. "All I did was try to run a business. It was going fine until your rotten PapCorp drove me to bankruptcy. This was my entire life, you understand. All I had left. A nice happy family and this little shop, that's all I ever wanted. And now I've lost the lot. This place has seen me through the worst of times. Take my word for it, the company you work for have done things you wouldn't believe, spiteful, horrible things. And now, now they're taking away the last piece of my life." She took a moment to watch every face in turn and shook her head. "Don't believe a thing PapCorp tell you, lads. They'll lie to your faces and leave you picking up the pieces. I've tried everything to be allowed to do what I want to, but it's no good, there's…"

"Are you finished?" the officer interrupted.

Helen blinked at the man. "Yes," she said. "I guess I am finished. I guess…" her words faded away. She took a couple of Eccles cakes and stuffed them into her handbag.

"You have to leave those here," said the officer. "Everything in this shop now belongs to PapBank. We should technically take your handbag too, but we know there's nothing in it. We're also letting you keep your clothes, of course. So leave the produce and kindly make your way outside."

"Sod you!" said Helen. "It's not like you lot are going to have as much as a bite. It'll either end up in an incinerator or just left to go stale. So what's it to you if I take a couple for the road? In fact, I should take the lot." She seized the Bakewell pudding and stuffed it into her bag, did the same with all the iced buns then picked up her beloved Flodni cake.

"Mrs Humbolt," said the officer. "Please stop that. I can't allow you to leave with all that stolen produce. Please, we're only doing our jobs."

"Screw your jobs," she said, lobbing a v-sign at the young man and barging past him out the front door.

"Hey!" he yelled. He was about to run after her when a hand on his shoulder stopped him.

"Nothing in public, remember?" said a fellow officer. "It's not the look PapMart want, is it? Having their security guards beat up some old lady for taking a few biscuits from her own shop."

"We're not PapMart security guards," said the first man, "we're PapSec Community Crime Prevention Officers."

"Same difference," said a third officer.

"Same pay grade," said another.

In the street, Helen Humbolt flung her handbag over her shoulder and kicked a can against a wall. It bounced off a poster of Harry Lanker which flapped in the wind. "Well you weren't much use, were you?" she said.

Helen balanced the layer cake against the white of her apron, fixed her eyes on the road and took her first steps up Skinner Street. She didn't look back.

Rusholme

When Minnie got home that day, she was carrying ten kilos of onions. Some were in her satchel, most were in the carrier bags she held in either hand. She shut the door behind her and found Brian on the sofa watching their Xi-fan widescreen TV.

"Have you seen this?" asked Brian, pointing at the screen. "PapBank have agreed to rescue the Manchester Pound."

"I know," Minnie sighed. "But I'm surprised it's only news now. We've known about this for weeks at the market. One thing no one's been able to explain to me though, is why the Manchester Pound needs rescuing at all? We use them at the stall all the time, and it's fine."

"Well, I don't know," said Brian. "Apparently there are too many debts or something. Anyway, PapCorp's come to the rescue yet again. We'll be paying for our dinner in PapPounds from now on."

"PapPound!" Minnie declared, imitating the seriousness of the announcer's voice. "It sounds like a refuge for stray dogs.

Will this bloody PapCorp ever stop? The sooner we have elections and vote in Harry Lanker's RASCALS, the better."

"Harry Lanker?" Brian sneered. "Look Minnie, I know you think PapCorp are some big enemy, but that hairy wanker isn't the answer. Let me tell you this, his neo-Marxist ideals will bring this country to its knees. I think the PapPound's a great idea. Tying the MancPound to this city's most successful enterprise ensures the future for all who have invested in the currency."

"What are you talking about?" asked Minnie. "Did you hear all that on the telly?"

"Of course I did!" said Brian. "How else do you think I'd know complicated words like enterprise?"

Minnie smiled to herself. "Well you can always learn," she replied.

Brian grinned back. "You see," he said, "that's why it's good to watch TV. And not just for the footie. It helps me to think clearly. You know what I decided today?"

But before Minnie could respond, Brian's mother stormed into the room. "What have I told you about wearing shoes in the house?" the old woman screamed. "You swan in here like you own the place. Let me remind you, young lady, this is my house. And while you're under this roof you will abide by my rules."

"My shoes are clean, I'll have you know!" Minnie screamed back. "I've been in the market all day, haven't gone anywhere else. Grafting, that's what I've been doing, so you and your son have something to eat. If it weren't for me, you two would be gobbling dirt by now." She tipped up her satchel and onions thumped onto the carpet. "There!" she yelled. "Pick them up. That's where you'd be eating from if it weren't for me, you ungrateful old cowbag."

"How dare you call me un..."

"Stop it!" Brian yelled. "Please, for Papp's sake, could you two just stop going at each other for one minute? I was trying to tell you something, something important. I've made a decision." Brian watched the silenced women a moment before continuing. "I'm going to get a job," he said. "I saw an advert. They're looking to recruit people like me, injured sports players and the like. That's what they said."

"That's what who said?" asked Minnie.

"The PapSec Community Crime Prevention Unit."

The two women gawped first at young Brian and then at each other.

"How do you mean?" asked Minnie, finally. "Are you planning on bringing down PapCorp from the inside? There are easier ways to win back your insurance money, you know."

"We have to face facts," said Brian. "There's never going to be any insurance money, is there? In two months, I'm going to be a father, and I'm going to need to support this family. I don't know what you have against PapCorp, they're good employers. The best in fact. And they pay in PapPounds, not onions! I'm going to make you both proud of me, and then maybe you'll stop bickering and we can live together as a nice family of four."

North York Moors

With nowhere else to go, no friends to put her up and no money even for a phone call, Helen Humbolt walked the seventeen miles to her parents' house in Glaisdale. She tracked the River Esk up and out of Whitby, then followed a train line which rumbled every so often with coupling after coupling of yellow PapTrans containers.

Down tracks and up footpaths she traipsed, her bottom caked in mud like the left side of her overalls. Twice the path led her close by the riverside, and both times she had slipped over. On the first occasion she'd managed to keep her Flodni balanced, the second time she wasn't so lucky and she'd watched it float away downstream.

The route led her through a forest of birch, hazel and holly. Many of their trunks bore carvings of jumping fish that marked a route for people who used to walk for fun. It might've been decades since anyone followed the Esk Valley Trail into Glaisdale, but when the forest broke at the river's edge and

Helen found herself staring at a humpback footbridge, she knew she was almost home. Past the roofless stone shell of the railway station she went, up along the battered old roadway, past trees and white-washed houses. At a stone-built hamlet, the floodplain gave out and the last few hundred metres were a steep climb into Glaisdale village.

Panting heavily, Helen scrambled up a grass bank towards a brick wall covered in ivy. She pulled back the plants to reveal a doorway. From that hidden shortcut, she was only a hop and a skip from her parents' driveway. She took off her muddy whites and left them in the porch, then let herself in with the only key she still possessed.

She heard the television in the living room, going on about PapPounds. "Hello?" asked her mother. "Who's there? Is that you Hells?"

"Yes mum, it's me," she said, heading straight for her old room. "Don't worry!" She slammed her bedroom door.

"Oh Helen," said her mother from the landing. "What's happened now?"

"Just leave me alone, mum, I just need to be left on my own."

Helen collapsed face first onto her bed and buried her eyes in her arms. When she lifted her head again, she looked directly into the deep browns of Marvin Percy's eyes. She saw the poster had come unstuck at one corner, and she got to her feet to re-attach it. She brushed off the dust, stared at the dark-chocolate face and ran her fingers over his cheeks.

5. Lemonade

Tis a long way further than Knighton,
A quieter place than Clun,
Where doomsday may thunder and lighten
And little 'twill matter to one.

13th June 1957
Clun, Shropshire, England

Just as he did every morning at eight, Henry Gritton walked out of his stone farmhouse with a cup of tea in either hand. He closed the door with the heel of his boot and headed towards the cowsheds across Diddim Lawr Lane. He found his brother Tommy standing, staring off down the valley and listening to the choruses of birdsong. Tommy was a slightly smaller version of Henry; both wore bulbous beards and tweed caps, their bellies covered under woven-wool coats, their feet in rubber boots.

Henry held out a mug. "'Ow bist, Tommy?" he boomed.

His little brother wrapped the cup in his fingers to warm them. "I'm going to have to call out the farrier again," he said, still gazing down the valley. "It's that same filly. She threw another shoe in the night, the third this month. I was hoping to take her down Burwarton and a couple of other shows this summer, but I'm starting to think she ain't got the temperament."

"That's bad luck is that," mused Henry. "You had high hopes for that one, I remember."

The two men sipped their milky brews, staring off down the hedged-in trackway at the solitary oak and the Black Hill that rose up beyond. The morning sky was a pale-blue canvas with just the odd brushstroke of white.

"Better be off then," said Henry.

"Ay," said his brother. "Same here."

In this way, the two Gritton men would start every morning.

The Gritton family had worked Diddim Lawr Farm for generations before they got to purchase the land. Their ancestors had come from the deforested wastelands of Castile to seed and plough the soils of England. But while the identities of their forefathers were lost in the folds of history, the family name endured. It was a long-forgotten anglicisation of a Spanish nickname which had applied to one son after another, gritón, shouter.

Because like their father, grandfather and all the rest before them, Henry and Thomas were large men of few words. But when they did speak, their voices could carry for miles.

With his brother's cuppa delivered, Henry Gritton crossed back over the lane to inspect his half of their inheritance, the orchards. At this moment, his workforce numbered just six. Three were local men who spent winters with their wives in Shropshire, but were now preparing for their upcoming months of berry picking on the south coast, and all the freedoms that entailed. The others were a young man and two brothers, refugees from eastern Europe with only a broken command of English. Locals and foreigners alike wore grey overalls, and each had a bucket strapped to his breast.

Clinging to the top rung of his ladder, Zoltán Papp reached out his free hand to grab an apple from a far branch. But in so doing, his basket tipped. The 'thud, thud, thuds' told him he'd lost half a dozen fruits to the orchard floor. "Baszd meg!" he cursed.

The farmer rounded the far end of their row at the very moment Zoltán had overstretched. "Are you going to pay for them, Papp?" he boomed. "Or should I just deduct them from your wages?"

By the time Gritton got to Zoltán's tree, the young Hungarian had climbed down and was checking through the fallen fruit.

"Leave them," said the farmer as he picked an apple from the ground, polished it on his tweed jacket and took a bite. "They'll be all bruised now so we can't send them out. When I said you could have the windfalls, old chap, I didn't mean you should be making your own."

"Yes, Mr Grrit-ton. I sorrr-y."

"It's okay Zoltán, just be careful, that's all. Are we still on for tonight?"

"Yes sirr, of course sirr."

"Good show. Listen, I was thinking, I'm not sure I much fancy coming down to south field. The cattle are grazing down there right now, and I wouldn't like to risk it if I can't see where I'm stepping, if you know what I mean. And in any case, Mrs Gritton's really keen to try whatever it is you've been cooking up down there. She's offered to make you dinner too, if you want. So why don't you come up to the farmhouse?"

"Yes sir. Very good would be that. Thank you. Good woman, your wife. She very good cook, she taking very care for us in Christmas."

The farmer smiled, nodded and walked on past the Hungarians. The migrants were already two whole trees ahead of their local colleagues on the opposite row. And one of them was climbing down his ladder. "Morning, Mr Gritton," said the man.

"Ow bist, Frazier?" Henry replied. "Lovely day for it, isn't it?"

"It certainly is that."

"Mr Gritton," said the worker. "Do you mind if I ask you something?"

"Sure, fire away."

"Are you really going to let that stinking Jew into your house?"

Gritton chuckled. "Well I've seen no signs of him being Jewish," he said. "But yes, Zoltán's coming for dinner, if that's what you're asking. He's going to show Mrs Gritton and I his new drink."

"You're a brave man if you ask me," said Frazier, spitting onto the grass. "I wouldn't go inviting them Hungarians into my house, let alone feed my wife with their concoctions. I don't trust any of them for a start, sir, and I'll bet that shed of his is full of cow shit. Do you really want to risk it?"

"You're forgetting, Dave, that I've been down to south field. I've seen what it's like now in that old barn. And I tell you this, I've never seen a cleaner workspace in my entire life. Puts my brother's milk plant to shame, that's for sure. They're good boys, those Hungarians."

"Good isn't what I'd call them, sir. You don't see 'em like what we do. They're always up to something, plotting away in that horrible foreign tongue of theirs. And it ain't like there's no one round here what could do their jobs. There's plenty of kids in the village looking for work."

"I know," said Henry. "And my best local workers vanish off to swan around on the south coast every summer, right at my peak season."

"Well, if you paid us more…"

Henry huffed. "Not this again," he said. "I'd have to employ a dozen locals to do the jobs which I now get out of those three. The two brothers are magicians with engines, and that Zoltán has quite the entrepreneurial spirit. They're like a breath of fresh air. There's too much damned Bolshevism around here these days."

"You're right there," nodded Mr Frazier, "from the ones too young to have fought, that is. Still though, even those young layabouts need work, and there are millions more in the colonies. They might be coloured, but at least those people know our way of life and could help us find a decent fast bowler for the village team. Those Hungarians don't have the slightest interest in cricket."

"The Empire's had it," said Henry, kicking the ground. "If that Suez business wasn't enough, and all the problems in India, now the African colonies are going too. We're giving away whole continents. The Gold Coast got independence not three months back, and it looks like Malaya's going to be next."

"I still believe in the Empire, sir," said Frazier. "She's a steady old girl. She'll out-see the likes of you and me, I tell you that."

"Ah, Dave, but that you were right."

Between the lines of apples trees, Gábor Bacsik heaved his bucket onto the trailer. He picked up handfuls of fruit and placed each with care into a wooden box. "De kurva hideg van," he moaned, rubbing his hands together. 'It's whoring cold.' "Does summer never come in this lousy country?"

"Little brother," Attila growled from atop his ladder. "Quit your moping and get on with some work. If you're cold then stop playing around with your itsy-pitsy dick and pick some apples."

Zoltán Papp climbed down his ladder and emptied his bucket into the same box.

"Are you coming to the cider night at the Black Stag?" asked Gábor. "It should be pretty crazy."

"Crazy?" Zoltán chuckled. "In Clun? I tell you, the only thing that's crazy here is you two. That cider's dreadful, it gives you a whoring hangover. I still remember the last time I went for a few glasses of that stuff with you two. I was on the toilet for the next three days."

Attila joined the others in emptying out his own bucket of fruit, one of which he polished on his overalls. "There's nothing wrong with these apples," he said, taking a bite. "And there'll be plenty of women tonight. They go weak at the knees when they hear a foreign accent. Gábor here has his own little fan club. Not that he's interested of course, he's still pining for that girl."

"I'm not pining," Gábor spat. "I'm just getting used to a new life, that's all. And it wasn't like there was any room for her here, was there?"

"Yeah, that's what you always say," his elder brother continued. "You're missing a good Hungarian girl to keep you warm at night."

"Aren't we all?" said Zoltán. "Any girl to be honest, I'm not picky about nationalities. Have you ever wondered what it's like to wake up being hugged by you pair? When I finally move out of that stinking caravan, I'm planning on finding myself a nice English girl that smells good and doesn't snore like a Bacsik."

"Good luck with that," said Gábor. "I can't imagine it happening any time soon though."

"You'll be surprised how much you can save," said Zoltán, "if you don't piss it all away against a pub wall. It won't be long till I've got my own place, my own little shop in the village where I can sell my lemonade. If you're lucky, I might even take one of you on as my assistant."

"A horse's cock up your ass!" replied Gábor. "Who says we'll want to work for you? Maybe you'll want to work for us."

"It all depends on what you're willing to pay for our labour," said Attila, taking another bite from his apple. "We're unionised, after all."

The Hungarians' meeting hadn't gone unnoticed by their colleagues. His basket only half full, Dave Frazier had come down from his tree and was making his way over to them. "Oi, Huns!" he shouted. "Quit your plotting and get on with some graft. If Mr Gritton finds out you've been stealing his produce, you'll be out on your ear in no time. And your job'll go to someone who deserves it."

"We no plotting," Zoltán shouted back. "We wait you catch up us. You so slow, you English."

The labourer flared his nostrils as he sized up the three of them. "Careful," he said. "Careful is what we are. We're being paid by the hour, so no point rushing, eh?"

"Typical for a peasant like you," said Gábor.

"What did you call me?"

"I called you peasant," said Gábor. "Because you are one. You, here, you talking the heroes of Europe. Is no wonder you womans loving us. You need show us respect."

"Us show you respect?" Frazier yelled. "Pull the other one. Remember whose village you're in, lads, whose country this is. We might have equal numbers now, but it'll be different tonight at the Stag. There'll be men there what have fought a real war, and won."

"We know," said Attila. "We talk them. They our friend."

"You don't know 'em like what we does," said Frazier. "They're like family to us. If they have to, they'll come down on our side every time. So you'd better quit showing us up."

"We no show up you," said Zoltán. "We just more good than you. Let's we have a race, Hungary and England. We show you who the boss. Like Puskás and Hidegkuti in Wembley and in Budapest."

"Yeah, well, that team's gone now, haven't they?" replied the Englishman. "Puskás will never go home and neither will you three. You'll be relying on Mr Gritton's charity for the rest of your lives. And one day he won't be as generous as he is now!"

Although the English hadn't agreed to the challenge, the Hungarians still picked up their pace. By the time Henry Gritton came back in the mid-afternoon, they were on their third row of the day, at least a dozen trees ahead of the locals.

"Okay lads," Gritton yelled to Zoltán, Attila and Gábor. "When you're done with those trees you can finish for the day. We have to leave something for tomorrow."

Free before four p.m., the Hungarian trio bounded down the lane between the two halves of the farm. They tumbled one after another over an oak stile, in a hedgerow that fizzed with insects. They ran through the pastures, dodging the splatters of hardening manure, imagining themselves passing a sewn-leather football across the lush green turf of Wembley.

They all knew their parts. Zoltán Papp was running towards an imaginary by-line, as his namesake Czibor had done. He passed the invisible ball to Gábor, who dragged his right foot back like Ferenc Puskás, eluded a flailing defender played by his brother Attila, and smashed the ball into the roof of the English net. The three men celebrated like it was real. For a moment they forgot the weariness of labour and the melancholies of exile, losing themselves in memories of home and how happy they'd been that day. They linked arms around shoulders and skipped over the clumpy grass, shouting "Hajra Magyarok!" 'come on Hungarians!' as loud as they could.

Their caravan was a 1940s bubble, with goggle-eyed windows and a two-foot step up to the door. It was lodged on two flat tyres, in a hedgerow of buzzing blossom.

Fitting three men into such a small space meant everything had to fold away or have various uses. The table, which took up the front of the van, would come down at night and the men would cover it in blankets and cushions, then wrap themselves up and sleep head-tail-head beside each other.

But that was for later. Now, the brothers squeezed onto opposite benches. Attila reached under his seat and pulled out a thin deck of cards then shuffled them between his fingers. "Come on Zoli," he said. "Sit down. Let's have a game of Ulti."

"Not now, guys," said Zoltán, unlatching all the windows to get some air moving. "I've got to prepare for this evening."

"You've always got another programme!" said Gábor. "Come on, sit down for a minute. We can't play Ulti with just two of us."

"Then play something else," said Papp, stepping out of his overalls and pulling on a long-sleeved shirt and trousers. He glanced into a nicotine-yellowed mirror on the wall, licked his fingers and patted down his hair. "I'm going to the shed," he said. "Today's a big day."

"Nonsense!" said Gábor. "Stay for one game at least."

"Ignore him," said Attila. "You go and do what you need to. I hope it goes well and Gritton likes it."

"He will," said Zoltán. "You know what Gritton's like, he'll love my drink no matter what. And even if he doesn't, he's too English to say otherwise. But his wife, she seems a straight up person. I'm sure she'll be honest with me."

His hair would not sit down, so Zoltán grabbed a cloth cap and fitted it on his head before heading on down to south field.

Zoltán's workshed was on the far side of a pasture dotted with black and white cows. He eyed them with suspicion and gave the animals a wide berth; having grown up in Budapest, he'd never learn to be comfortable around livestock.

His workshop was at the end of a stone-walled barn in which the cows still slept. To keep them out of his end, the three

Hungarians had hammered together a fence from scraps of wood. That dividing wall was the first thing Zoltán saw every time he unbolted the barn door, which he left to swing open as his only source of natural light; the windows were just a few high-up slits that barely let in any of the daytime. He picked a gas-lamp from its hook on the wall, lit the burner with a match and screwed on the teardrop lid until it flooded with light and illuminated something more of the space. But it brought no heat, and the bare-stone walls left a constant chill in the air.

The floor was dotted with muddy puddles from rain that had leaked through the spots of rust in the corrugated roof. But in the dry areas, it turned out that this natural refrigerator was the perfect temperature for keeping his drink fresh.

Henry Gritton had provided all the equipment, including the wooden kitchen table against the right-hand wall and the chemistry set which Zoltán had assembled on its surface. From asking around, the farmer had managed to find a selection of pans, stirrers and knives which hung from nails knocked in between the stones. A trip to the local scrapyard had yielded a metal sink and cast-iron stove, but Gritton had generously splashed out for the tanks of gas against the wall and the system of shiny Bunsen burners on the desk.

Zoltán kept his ingredients on a two-shelf cabinet in the opposite corner. On the floor beside it was a copper bucket covered with a white tea-towel. He picked it up by the handles and carried it over to the desktop. There, he removed the cloth and ladled out yellow liquid into a large beaker, before pouring that in turn through his miniature laboratory. His hands danced, opening valves and lighting burners until splashes of carbonated liquid dripped into the first bottle.

By the time Zoltán left the barn, the sun was creeping towards the hillcrest that met the western sky. His shadow lengthening, he picked his way through the cow pats, dangling four bottles of yellow liquid from his fingers.

The Gritton farmhouse was really just a tarted-up version of one of their barns. All were crafted from the same grey stone, but the sash windows, chimneys and covering of reddened ivy lent the house a familiar cosiness.

Zoltán knocked once at the front door and it swung open, releasing a wave of heat and cooking smells. There stood Marjorie Gritton, her blonde hair curled in the latest fashion, flower-print dress under her apron. "Come in, Zoltán, please," she said. "Leave your hat on the rack and don't forget to wipe your feet, we don't want you bringing half of south field in with you."

"Thank you, Mrs Gritton."

"Please, call me Marjorie."

He nodded, wiped his shoes as he'd been told. Then he followed the woman along the wood-chipped hallway with its ceramic-tiled floor. She lifted the latch on the kitchen door and Zoltán got a second waft of roasting chicken.

At the oak wood table, Henry was reading the day's news. "Here he is," he exclaimed, folding away the paper and getting up from his seat. He glanced at the clock above the Aga, "right on time as well," he said. "That's what I like to see. Is that the stuff?"

"Yes, Mr Gritton."

"Well don't stand on ceremony, son. Let's see what it's like."

Marjorie pulled three glasses roughly the same size from a cupboard above the sink. She placed them on the table, then took three of the bottles from Zoltán's hands. "I'll put these in the pantry to keep them cool," she said, and popped outside for just a moment. In which time, Henry peeled open the foil cap and poured equal amounts into each glass.

Mrs Gritton returned to find her drink waiting for her. She picked up the cup and inspected the contents – a liquid so yellow it seemed almost to glow. She looked to her husband, who was watching the bubbles burst as they met the surface.

Henry caught his wife's glance, shrugged his shoulders, held up the glass and said, "cheers."

"How do you say that in Hungarian?" Marjorie asked.

"Egészségedre."

"What?"

"Egészségedre," Zoltán repeated, smiling.

She grinned back. "Well that," she said, and they all took a sip.

The liquid tingled against Marjorie Gritton's cheeks. Tiny bubbles popped and crackled over her tongue, leaving behind a taste that was both sweet and bitter at the same time. She blinked as she swallowed, feeling the liquid cascade down her gullet and filling her insides with a satisfying glow.

Henry downed the drink and slammed the glass onto the table. "I love it, lad," he said. "It's blooming marvellous. I'll order twenty bottles from you right this moment. And I'll get on to the neighbours. Let's see if we can't start making back some of my investment."

His wife stood in thought as the liquid radiated through her body. "I don't know what to say," was all she finally said.

"You no like?" asked Zoltán.

She shook her head at the young man. "I think it's the most amazing thing I've ever tasted," she said, putting down the glass. "So much better than those horrible colas the Americans are so obsessed with. It tastes fresh and sweet and sour all at the same time. It's brilliant. Did you come up with the recipe yourself?"

"My grandmother make-ed it, before the war."

"A family recipe," said Henry. "So I guess you own the rights."

"Yes, sir, I guess I do."

Mr Gritton glanced up at his wife. "So how about dinner then, love?" he asked.

They ate that night in the dining room, on a table crafted from tropical hardwood and under the painted eyes of generations of large men. As they waited for Marjorie to serve them, Henry and Zoltán talked business.

"How much do you think you can make in two months?" asked Henry.

"In two month?" Zoltán replied. "I don't know. It depend on what time I having, what supply."

"Say I give you half a day, every day. So twenty-five hours a week and all the supplies you need. How much could you make? The local agricultural show's in August and I reckon this stuff'll go down a treat."

Zoltán Papp reached into his back pocket and pulled out a wad of paper and a pencil. He licked the nib and started scrawling down numbers just as Mrs Gritton came into the room with the tablecloth.

As he watched her pick the ashtrays and beer bottles from the table, Henry asked his wife. "There's a drinks category at Burwarton, isn't there?"

"Yes," she responded without looking up from her chores."My Aunt Agnes won it a couple of years back for her pear juice. Don't you remember?"

"How could I forget?" Henry chuckled. "By the time they opened the last of the batch, the sugars had fermented and they all got drunk. That's why she won."

"Don't be daft," said Marjorie. "That was just the bottle you left for a year before drinking. She's a marvel in the kitchen, my aunt. But she's just as good with flowers as with food and drinks. Did I tell you she'll be showing her roses at Shrewsbury again this year, she's on first- name terms with Percy Thrower and everything."

Zoltán looked up. "Okay," he said. "If I have all the ingredient and equ-ip-ments, I think can make maybe twenty litre every day. In two month that will about one thousand liter." He paused a moment in thought. "We have no space for to storage."

"You leave all that to me, Zollers," Henry boomed. "I'll sort you out. How much is a thousand litres?"

"Nearly two thousand pints," said his wife.

"Okay, that's good. Tell me Zoltán, does it keep?"

"Excuse me, sir? Does it keep what?"

Henry laughed from the bottom of his belly. "Does it keep, you know. Can it last for a long time?"

"Oh yes, in bottle with the good tops it last for many year. The sugar make it fresh, and there no air so it no go alcohol."

"So we can't lose. Let's make a deal."

The two men were shaking hands when Mrs Gritton returned, carrying a china gravy boat in one hand and a bunch of cutlery in the other. "So you've made a deal then?" she asked absently, laying the table. "I must say, Zoltán, your English has really come on since Christmas."

"Thank you, Mrs Gritton," Papp replied. "Your husband help us very much. We go many English lesson and we talk the English on the farm."

"I can imagine what kind of things you're picking up from the boys in the orchard." Marjorie chuckled to herself. "I haven't got to see you since, but I just loved having you all here for Christmas. You know, it was a very fashionable thing to invite a Hungarian for Christmas dinner, I heard all the great families did it. Do you remember the Queen even mentioned you in her speech? That was a special day. So how are your friends? Are they all okay? I heard the girl has left. What was her name? Noreen?"

"Nóra, yes. Is correct. She go in Leeds for to find her fortune. For her, very small the Clun."

"That's a shame," Marjorie mused. "Her and your friend seemed very much in love."

"They was. Gábor very not happy. How you say it? He's heart is break-ed."

"Oh, poor him," said Mrs Gritton. She stood staring at the table a moment before vanishing back out of the door.

"Say, Zoltán," said Henry. "Does this drink of yours have a name?"

"Yes. The name is 'A nagymamám citrusos-almás limonádéja'."

"What?"

"Is the name."

"Yeah, right. What is it in English?"

Zoltán pondered the translation. "My grandmother's citrus apple lemonade," he said.

"Oh no," said Henry, "that'll never do. It sounds old-fashioned. You need something snappier, something more modern, more like those American soda-pops."

"Szóda-pop?" said Zoltán. "How about 'my grandmother's citrus apple soda-pop'."

"Listen son, is your grandmother still alive?"

"No. She dead many year, in the war."

"Well then, why not take credit for this drink yourself?"

"How you mean? Like 'Zoltán Papp's citrus apple soda-pop'?"

"No, shorter. How about 'Papp's soda-pop'?"

Mrs Gritton returned to the dining room with a steaming plate in either hand. "What are you talking about?" she asked, serving the men.

"We're trying to come up with a name for the drink," her husband replied. "What do you think of Papp's soda-pop?"

"Papp's soda-pop," she said. "Papp's soda-pop. It's good, dear, I like the way the two s-sounds become one." She disappeared back into the kitchen and re-emerged with her own plate of meat and veg. When all were seated, Mr Gritton put his hands together in prayer. But before he could say a word his wife interrupted. "What about Papp Pop?" she said.

"Marjorie, dear, I'm about to say grace..." Henry Gritton's words trailed off at the sight of his young employee pinging the plosives from his lips. "Do you like it, Zoltán?" he asked.

"Papp Pop?" Zoltán said aloud.

"Yes, Papp Pop."

"I think very good the name," Zoltán replied, smiling. "Perfect in fact. Papp Pop," he said again, "Papp-Pop, PappPop, PapPop."

6. Rascals

22nd September 2032
Whitby

Helen Whitman had been peeking around the net curtain for an hour. But every time she'd done so, all she'd seen was the row of terraces opposite, with their mirror-image lintels three-stepping up Raith Street in time with the downstairs bay windows and arched doorways.

At what might've been her hundredth twitch of the netting, Helen's heart jumped at the sight of a white Delante van pulling up beyond the patterned-brick wall of their front yard. She grabbed an anorak, slung a canvas bag around her shoulder and darted outside.

Winston Humbolt beeped his van locked with a swipe of his Xi-fan sheet just as Helen flung her arms around him. "I've been waiting for you all day," she said, kissing his neck. "Tell me everything. How was it? Why don't we go inside and lie down for a while?"

Winston pecked her lips. "It was great, my Sugarplum fairy," he said. "Absolutely amazing, actually. But we can't be late for the Forum."

"Couldn't we? Just for once?"

Winston smiled down at his fiancée. "Maybe another day. But not today. I've got a lot to report."

"Then let's take the van down, that'd give us more time."

"I've been driving for hours, Sugarplum. And you know I prefer to walk. That way we get to see what's going on."

"I know," said Helen, "but you weren't the only one at the conference, were you? Why can't someone else report what happened? Paul Broddle was there, why don't you leave it to him?"

"No," Winston replied, turning on his toes. "Are you ready? We should get going."

A stiff breeze carried salt to their noses, the cackles of seagulls to their ears. They marched past ivy-clad ends of terraces which stepped down the hill with them.

"I had the radio on the whole way back," Winston was saying. "And there wasn't a peep about the conference. You'd think the founding of a new political party, at a meeting of tens of thousands of people from all over the country, well, you'd have thought we might've got a mention. But there was nothing. The only thing they could talk about was this attack on an air force base in Norfolk."

"What did you expect?" asked Helen. "You're always going on about how the State Broadcaster's nothing more than a mouthpiece of the establishment."

"That's true, Sugar. Very true. But I was hoping to hear something, even if it was rubbishing us. You know, there were journalists there from all the networks, and a good few foreign ones too. The organisers gave out more than five hundred press passes, so if they weren't there to report the news, what were they there for?"

"I don't know. What?"

"Some of them were certainly there to spy on us," said Winston. "This organisation's riddled with infiltrators. They're everywhere."

"Even here in Whitby?" asked Helen.

"Probably," said Winston.

"Who?"

"Oh, I have my suspicions..."

They skirted a row of cottages, wrapped in wine-coloured ivy, and the old town rose up before them as a stack of red-tiled roofs topped off with a church steeple. The sky above was a seething black. Thunder rumbled. A flash hit the spire. When the clouds broke they released a shower of hailstones, some as big as cricket balls. Winston and Helen dashed for the stone arches of the railway station, taking cover below the sign declaring 'Whistle Non-stop Whitby' in great yellow letters.

The downpour passed over as quickly as it had come on, and soon people were flooding the streets once more. But the wind still gusted up Baxtergate and Helen gathered her hair into a ponytail to stop it blowing over her face.

Along the pedestrian roadway, past tumbledown townhouses of whitewash or brick, one person after another greeted the couple. At the sight of an old lady hobbling along with a stick in both hands, Winston paused. He stooped to talk to her. "You all right there, Mrs Earnshaw?" he asked. "Do you need a hand with anything?"

"Oh, you are lovely, Winston," she said, her face wrinkling into a smile. She glanced up at Helen. "You're lucky to have someone like this to look after you, you know. Such a kind young man."

"I know," Helen agreed, clutching his hand.

Mrs Earnshaw turned back to Winston. "Don't you think it's dreadful what those terrorists did at RAF Snetterton?" she said. "Fifteen soldiers dead, they say, a group of radicalised leftists apparently. You don't know them do you? They're not part of your organisation, are they?"

"Ha!" Winston chuckled. "They attacked on the very day that their supposed allies were forming an alliance. They're not a group I or anyone else has ever heard of. So no."

"Good," said the old lady. "Because I don't like that sort of thing. Violence. You just make sure you stay well away from it, do you hear me?"

"Loud and clear, Mrs Earnshaw. No violence."

"Good boy. Now you two get on. Don't wait around for me, I'm not as quick on my pegs as I used to be. I'll be in the Pavilion to hear everything though, so don't start without me!"

They strolled on with Winston's paw smothering Helen's hand in his grasp. "So, who do you reckon did it?" she asked. "If it wasn't the radical left, as you say, then who was it? Islamists? The Black Block?"

"It could've been anyone, my Sugar. Despite the name, RAF Snetterton's actually a Greyskies base, part of Spokane Incorporated. All sorts of groups are at war with them, and most are neither Anarchists nor Muslims. It wouldn't surprise me if it was a revenge attack for what they did in Albania. The thing that troubles me though, is that whoever did it must be pretty sophisticated, to have M.R.S."

"What's that?"

"Magnetic Resonance Shielding," Winston explained. "Powerful electro-magnets that knock bullets out of the sky. I'd heard rumours there were prototypes but I'd never heard of it being used before today."

"Well, where did they get that from?"

"Not a clue," said Winston. "Maybe someone leaked PapSec's secrets. I doubt they developed it themselves but I suppose it's possible."

"And you don't think PapSec did it?"

Winston shrugged. "They could've, I guess, although I don't really see why they would. Whatever happened, I'm sure we'll never really find out."

Outside a whitewashed shopfront, with 'Whitely's of Whitby Quality Butchers' painted above the crimson-gloss window frame, someone called Winston's name and brought the couple to a halt. Out trotted a rotund man in a straw boater, with a moustache covering his upper lip like a white slug. He wiped his palms on his red apron and shook them both by the hand.

"I've been waiting for you to come past," said the butcher. "I wanted to thank you, Winston. Last week was our best ever. In all the five generations of Whitely's butcher's, I'm pretty sure none has ever seen business as good as this. I honestly thought this shop was done for, that the line would end with me. But not anymore. I've even got my boy back working with me. And it's all thanks to you and your 'buy local' campaign. We've got through so much Yorkshire lamb and Large White pork that I've had to double our order. We sold out of Whitby eggs three times last week, and my suppliers have already been out buying new birds to meet the demand. It's simply incredible what you've done for this town and my business." He rummaged in his apron pouch and held out a paper package. "My wife made you this to say thank you," he said. "I could've sold it a dozen times over, everyone wants one of Mrs Whitely's pork pies. But I was keeping it behind for you, to say thank you in person."

Winston beamed, but it was Helen who spoke. "That's very kind of you," she said, taking the package and stuffing it into her bag. "And make sure you thank your wife too. We'll have this for dinner."

Helen had never felt prouder than she did that day, walking arm-in-arm with her fiancé. As they strolled the old lanes of Whitby, she kept staring up at him and smiling to herself. Eventually Winston caught her glance. "What's wrong?" he asked.

"Nothing's wrong," said Helen. "I'm just admiring your face. You've got beautiful skin you know," she reached up and ran her fingertips over his coffee-coloured cheek. "I'm so proud that you asked me to marry you."

"Why?" he asked. "What have I done?"

"Everything," Helen chuckled. "Look how people are with you. You've turned this town around. You're an amazing man, Winston Humbolt. And I still can't believe I'm going to be your wife."

"Helen Humbolt, saviour of the Universe!"

She slapped his upper arm. "Don't be silly," she said. "You know I'm not sure about that name. I think it sounds a bit daft."

"I think you'll sound like a superhero," Winston responded.

"I know," Helen beamed up at him. "That's just another of the reasons I love you. You always see the bright side in everything."

Nestled into the side of the cliffs, the Pavilion theatre stood proud against the elements. In its 150 years, famous men and women of their ages had approached those various-shaped windows in their cream-coloured frames cut out of Victorian brick. But now, every Wednesday night, the owner had agreed to let the people of Whitby have the hall for free, on the condition that participants be encouraged to stop for a drink in the café bar afterwards, and before.

So through the foyer, Helen and Winston headed straight upstairs. They found the old-chromed café dotted with people they knew, mostly congregating around the varnished-pine bar.

"What do you want to drink?" asked Winston.

"Coffee," Helen replied.

"Milk and three sugars?"

"You know me," she said, grinning.

Winston went off to order, and Helenfound herself drawn towards a wall of glass panes. She loved this view, no matter the weather, and was so taken with the churning brown sea and black swirling clouds that she didn't notice her school friend approach.

"So come on," said Rebecca. "Let's see it!"

Helen span around, grinning. She held out her left hand to show off a stone sparkling square from a silver ring.

"Oh my," said Rebecca. "That's gorgeous. And it looks proper expensive. Where did he get it?"

"I don't think it's valuable," said Helen. "And it certainly isn't new. Winston redid the roof of one of those big houses on St Hilda's Terrace some months back. When he'd finished, the owners claimed they were broke so paid him in jewellery. I guess it's from there."

"And?" asked Rebecca. "Are you happy?"

"I am, Becky, I really am. I don't think I've ever been this happy in my whole life. I keep pinching myself, it still all feels like a dream. I just can't believe I'm going to get married to Winston Humbolt. Every new thing I learn about that man makes me love him even more. It's like I'm in the middle of a whirlwind, what with the bakery and everything."

"How's that going?" asked Rebecca. "Any progress?"

"It's all go, Becs! Again thanks to Winston. You know he's offered to make all the furniture, don't you?"

"Yep, you told me how much of a disaster his workshop is."

"He may as well have been raised in a barn," said Helen.

"That's where I'm lucky with Tariq, you see. He was well brought up."

"I don't care really," said Helen. "Everyone has their faults, don't they? And if he's just a bit messy, well, I can live with that. Did I mention he's got us an appointment with the manager of the District Bank? We're going tomorrow morning."

"That's great, Helen. I'm so pleased for you."

"And what about Tariq? Has his manager got him working Wednesday evenings again?"

"Not tonight," said Rebecca. "As far as the hospital's concerned we're still away till tomorrow. So they can't stop him speaking tonight, even if they wanted to."

"And you and him?" asked Helen. "Have you given any more thought to converting? Have you told your mum yet?"

"I'm looking into it," said Rebecca, "but I've got so many other things on that I don't really have the time. I haven't spoken to mum since Tariq couldn't get her that free flu jab. I dare say she was against him from the start though, being a good Catholic mother and all that. You know how people are in Glaisdale."

"I certainly remember," said Helen. "Isn't it a relief to be out of there?"

"Relief isn't the word," said Rebecca. "It's like I'm only just becoming a real woman, and not that village girl I used to be. I've learnt so much already, and you wouldn't believe how much I'm writing. I did six articles for the *Whitby Star* last week, and now they've got me doing five whole pages on the Space on the Left Conference. It's virtually a full-time job."

"I read the one you wrote about chopping the king's head off," said Helen. "It was pretty strong stuff. I'm not sure how much Harry Lanker would like to be compared with Oliver Cromwell, though."

"It wasn't really a comparison," said Rebecca. "More of a call for action."

Winston and Tariq arrived with drinks in every hand. They'd been deep in conversation but broke at Rebecca's words.

"I wish you wouldn't write such provocative things," said Tariq. "We should be making a positive change, not inciting violence."

"I'm supposed to be provocative," said Rebecca. "As Marx put it, revolutionary terror is a necessary evil to ease the birth throes of a new society."

"I don't know," said Tariq. "Even revolutionary terror doesn't need to involve killing people. We could simply ship all the aristocracy off in chains to foreign countries, like they've been doing to us for centuries."

The men handed out the drinks and Helen turned to the slighter man with the neatly cropped beard. "Did you enjoy the conference, Tariq?" she asked, taking a sip of sweet stew.

"It was brilliant, Helen," said Tariq. "To be around so many like-minded people. I still feel like I'm on a cloud now. Did Rebecca mention I got nominated for RASCAL's health committee? We are seriously looking into community takeovers of privatised hospitals."

"I bet your employers love that," said Helen. "I'm amazed they don't just sack you."

"They'd love the chance," Tariq replied. "But then us surgeons are a tight group, especially in Whitby. Whatever our politics or backgrounds, we've pledged that if one of us goes, we all go. If there's one thing that unites us it's a hatred of Monogon Medical, and their managers in particular. They swan around like little dictators while pretending they know our jobs better than we do. But even they're not stupid enough to get rid of all the surgeons, they know how difficult it'd be to find replacements, especially for somewhere like here."

As Tariq talked, Paul Broddle approached from behind. He laid a hand on the surgeon's shoulder and made him jump. "If only the teachers were still as tight as that," said Paul. "We used to have the strongest unions of all, but now it's every teacher for themselves. If we stuck together we could be safe as houses, but as it is, I fear for my job every day."

"Divide and conquer," said Winston. "I'd have thought you, as a history teacher, might be able to see that. It's pretty blatant – the oldest tactic in the book. And it still works, apparently."

"I understand perfectly well what's happening," Broddle retorted. "And with my historical background, I know just how significant RASCAL could turn out to be. Finally we've managed to organise ourselves enough to make a real difference. If we can stay united, we could take the country."

"Let's hope so," Winston replied. "But it wouldn't surprise me if it all broke apart as quickly as it's appeared. There's a lot of responsibility still on Harry Lanker's shoulders, and RASCAL has enemies everywhere before it even gets off the ground."

The theatre lent Whitby's Forums quite a different vibe to picnics by the Abbey or down on the beach. There were just as many people there; the boxes behind their rounded balustrades were full, as was the far balcony and every seat in the stalls. The houselights stayed on throughout – this was a meeting not a show – which is how Winston could see Mrs Earnshaw grinning up at him from the front row. But while the format was meant to be inclusive, whereby anyone could talk when they wanted, there now was a clear distinction between speakers on stage and listeners in the green-felt seats.

The sound system made the repetitions of a human microphone redundant, and those characteristic short phrases had descended into monologues. It seemed consistently to be the same few people that spoke, and as usual tonight it fell on Winston to open the meeting.

"Friends and comrades," Winston Humbolt announced through the mic. "What a sight it is to see the Pavilion full once again. As you all know, I was part of the elected delegation from the Whitby branch of the Yorkshire anti-Globalisation League at the Space on the Left Conference in Bolsover. That meant I got to address the General Assembly, and had the privilege of telling them about the amazing things we've achieved in our two years together. In front of thousands of people from across the country and the world, I spoke about our barter markets in front of the Tollbooth, about the childcare centres, our own newspaper, as well as the clinics you've put on and our efforts to have Whitby General classified a community hospital, so we can run it as we know it should be."

Winston took a moment to observe the faces, hanging on his every word. "There were groups there from all over the country, all with with similar stories," he continued. "The town of Dumfries, for example, has invested so much on wind turbines and batteries that they're completely energy self-sufficient. They've also cleared all the farmed salmon out of the Nith estuary and wild fish have started coming back. From there to Land's End, there were stories about people like us taking charge of their communities, growing their own food, providing the kind of care a private company never could. This movement is really gathering pace. And now it has a name. We are, from today, ladies, gentlemen and everyone in-between, all members of the Radical Alliance of Socialist and anti-Capitalist Associations on the Left, or RASCAL, as it'll be known. By working together across the country, we'll bring real and lasting change to this nation." he held his fist in the air. "The people, united, will never be defeated!"

"The people, united, will never be defeated!" hundreds chanted back.

With the audience on their feet, the bespectacled Paul Broddle stepped forward. Winston held out the mic for him without a glance in Broddle's direction. By the time his compatriot spoke, the larger man was off the stage.

"Comrades!" announced Paul Broddle to curtail the ovation. "We have much to talk about and little time to do it in. As you all know, I was with Winston there at the foundation of RASCAL, and I witnessed the great presentation he'd put together. It was top quality stuff, we should all be very proud of him and of ourselves."

There was an inkling of applause before Paul Broddle continued. "The main message we were given to take away," he said, "was that we need to get organised. This government could fall any day and we have to be ready as soon as that happens. If we pull together, we have a chance to throw out those old parties and bring in representatives that actually represent us, the people, not just themselves and their mates. RASCAL will give us a Harry Lanker in every constituency, not just Bolsover. Which is why, out of respect for yourselves and for the movement, I am putting my name forward as a candidate to be the RASCAL representative for Whitby and Scarborough. I look forward to a fair contest and the support of as many of you as see fit."

When people filed out of the theatre, most headed for the bar. Winston and Helen joined them to the café, but Winston insisted on hanging around by the door.

Paul Broddle spotted them and marched over. "What a meeting!" he grinned. "I'm going to get a round in to celebrate, and to thank you both for your support. What would you like?"

"I hope you've brought ID with you," Winston sniped. "I'm not sure they'll serve you otherwise. We won't have anything, thanks. We're just leaving."

"Are we?" said his fiancée.

"Yes, come on, get your coat."

"Okay, well, thank you for the offer, Paul," said Helen, "next time maybe. But I did just want to say I think it's great news you'll be standing at the next election. I'll finally have someone I want to vote for."

Rusholme

Brian Brownlow was ten-years-old when the doorbell rang and changed his life. His mother had been expecting the two men in tracksuits, one in his sixties and the other half his age.

She had a pot of tea brewing on the living-room coffee table, and after seating them on the sofa facing the TV, the first thing Mrs Brownlow did was to serve them both. With his father confined to an upstairs sickbed he would never leave, Brian's mother did the negotiating.

The elder man had introduced himself as Nigel Whitehurst and explained he was United's Chief Scout. It was he that did all the talking, in his broad Irish accent. "Your son's a prestigious talent," he said. "Which is why he needs handling by the very best. We all know what United means to this city, not to mention our reputation across the world. Signing with us means giving him the best chance he'll ever have to be a top-rate footballer."

"Aye," said Mrs Brownlow, supping her brew. "So go on then, what's the deal? You know.What are you offering?"

"Well, obviously he's too young to sign professionally," said the scout. "But we normally make some kind of arrangement with the parents. We generally pay a stipend of about five thousand pounds."

"Five thousand pounds?" Mrs Brownlow scorned. "Is that all? He's worth a heck of lot more than that. You know you're not the first club to show interest, don't you?"

"I mean five thousand pounds a month, Mrs Brownlow."

"Oh, well then. That's different."

"Of course, there are expectations from your side too," said Nigel. "He'll be on a strict diet, and you'll be expected to get him to training four nights a week. We also want him to do well at school. How is he academically?"

"You mean in lessons?"

"Yes."

"Not great. He's near the bottom of the class in most subjects."

"Well then," said the Chief Scout, "it shouldn't take too much to bring him up a grade or two, should it? We'll make that part of the deal."

Whitby

The storm now over, the clouds blown away, Helen and Winston walked home under a sky dotted with diamonds. The wind blustered at their backs as the couple strolled in silence through the starlight. Halfway up Raith Street, at the only doorframe glossed black, Helen let the pair in. Even though the heating wasn't on, the house was cosy and smelt of baking.

Helen went straight to the kitchen, pulled the pie from her bag, put it on a plate and searched around for a knife. She cut slices in the pastry, jelly and pork mash, and took their dinner through to the living room.

Winston was already sitting on the sofa with the television on, showing scenes of a still-smoking barracks. Helen sat down beside him and put the plate between them.

Her fiancé picked up a slice and inspected it. "This looks brilliant," said Winston. "Isn't it kind of Mr Whitely to give us a whole pork pie like this?" He took a bite, dropping crumbs onto his lap which he wiped onto the carpet.

"They're still showing the same news," said Helen, nodding at the screen. "The whole day on this one thing. I can see why you were so annoyed before. It must've be amazing actually being there at the founding of RASCAL. Imagine if we can really make a political party that actually represents rather than dictates. And I absolutely love the name RASCAL, it seems to say everything it needs to. I think Paul Broddle would make a great MP, don't you?"

"Not especially," Winston replied, spitting globules of pastry.

"What is it you've got against him?" asked Helen. "He seems a nice guy to me."

"I haven't got anything against him," Winston swallowed. "He thinks we should have some special kind of bond, because we're both black. But I don't like that way of thinking, I don't define people by their skin colour. I think he's immature and I don't trust him, nothing more. Let's just say I wouldn't be surprised if something turns up about him, that's all."

Helen swallowed a slice of pie. "You think he's up to something?" she asked. "If you've got suspicions, you should report them to the party. We don't want him messing things up, do we? Especially if he's standing for office. Do you think he might be an infiltrator?"

"I don't know," said Winston. "Maybe. I mean, I've got no proof of anything. But if I had to guess someone from the group... Let's just say he'd be on the list."

"Then why did you allow him to stand unopposed?" asked Helen. "Why didn't you stand against him? I'm sure you'd do well. There are loads of people in town who'd support you."

"That's not really my thing," said Winston. "I prefer not to have to big myself up on the campaign trail, drink tea with grandmas and all that."

"I'd have thought you'd be perfect for that. The grandmas are the ones who'll most likely vote for you, seeing how old Mrs Earnshaw was with you today."

"I'm not standing, Sugarplum, and that's that. Let's just leave it shall we? How about we brush our teeth and go to bed?"

"I just don't get it," Helen continued. "What is it that's stopping you? There's something you're not telling me."

Winston stared into his fiancée's glare and could see her searching his thoughts. "Look," he said. "There are things in my past that I don't want the Press getting all over, that's all. There's a lot of scrutiny when you stand for Parliament."

"What kind of things in your past?"

"Nothing Sugar, it was just a manner of speaking."

"No it wasn't. Tell me what you've done."

"No."

"Then I'll have to guess," Helen smiled. "Does it involve a crime?"

"No. Well, not in so many words, no."

"A crime in fewer words? Did you kill someone?"

"Let's just leave it Hells," said Winston.

"You did, didn't you? Come on, tell your wife to be. I want to know. I won't think any the worse of you, you know. Well, probably not. I promise I won't tell a soul, that's for sure."

Winston shook his head. "It was a long time ago, Sugarplum. It's really not important now. You know I was in the army. Well things happened that I've pushed to the back of my mind. I really don't want to go stirring it all up again, if that's all the same with you. Can we just go upstairs and get comfy?"

"We can go upstairs and go to sleep," Helen replied. "I'm not really in the mood for anything else, Winston. And we've got to go to the bank in the morning."

7. Bio-dome 1

26th October 2045
Manchester

In years to come, Naomi would tell biographers and gossip columnists alike that her earliest memory was the opening of Manchester's first Bio-dome. She would describe her awe at the lights, the noise, the dryness and the warmth. From a childhood mostly forgotten or discarded, the impression PapCorp made that day would stay with her for life. Not that the recollections of her four-year-old self told much of what actually happened.

She wouldn't recall the walk to the Bio-dome, for instance. Strapped to her mother's back, they traipsed through the drizzle for an hour. The plastic sheet over their heads kept off some of the rain, but couldn't stop it dripping over the hemp satchel on Minnie's hip.

Naomi would also blank out the PapSec troops in their yellow uniforms and bowling-ball helmets, surveying the crowd from the tops of buildings and third-storey windows with machine guns in their hands. And she would forget the bright yellow PapTrans buses that splashed puddles at them, just as much as the blank faces of their occupants crowded against the windows.

Hyde Road, eastern Manchester

On the leather backseat of the Prime Ministerial limo, Harry Lanker tucked a lock of hair behind his ear. He took off his specs and rubbed his hand from forehead to stubbly chin. "I can hardly keep my eyes open," he said to the driver. "It was only a hop over to Washington, I can't understand why it's affected me so much. I'm sure this bloody PapDrive interface doesn't help."

"They say it's designed to reduce strain on the eyes," said his driver to the rear-view mirror.

"They say a lot of things," the Prime Minister retorted.

"I guess you can never tell how the jetlag'll get you," said the driver.

"Well that's true…" said Harry Lanker. "They're making a big thing of the UN centenary over there, you know."

"Well they've not much else to celebrate, have they?"

"I guess not. But still, as leader of one of the original Security Council members, I was expected to stay around for a bit longer than I did. The French president's taking three weeks off to drive Route 66. He asked if I'd like to join. I mean, I wouldn't do that of course, I've got far too much on as it is. But I have to be here, don't I? To cut the ribbon at Michael O'Dillon's biggest vanity project yet. Surely this is the sort of thing the King should be doing. He's the one in charge of opening supermarkets and the like."

"It was in the contract, wasn't it?" said the driver. "The Prime Minister of the day would be the first to speak. You should make the most of it. I'm sure Lord Michael's right peeved that you're going to be opening the bloody thing, especially after you've put a stop to his plans for any more."

"I just hope I'll find a moment to get my head down," said Harry Lanker, staring out at the puddles on the empty pavement, the same colour as the buildings and the sky.

"There are courtesy caravans," said his driver. "All the VIPs have one."

"VIP…" Harry chuckled. "I'm not sure I'm ever going to get used to being considered a VIP."

"And nor should you. That's what makes you such a great Prime Minister."

"Thank you, Samuel," said the PM. "It's always nice to hear those things, even if I am just a failed soul like all the rest. Is that it?" he asked, nodding at the alien cupola over the city ahead.

"Certainly is," his driver replied. "Not long now."

Harry Lanker shook his head. "What a monster," he said to himself.

Manchester City Centre

The buses spewed out their passengers to walk the last few hundred yards to the Bio-dome. Across all three lanes, from one pavement of Oxford Street to the other, pedestrians shuffled through the drizzle. Further up the road, a line of yellow troops in solid round helmets blocked the way. They directed the crowds down Portland Street with the tips of their automatic rifles.

Her girl on her back, Minnie turned right with the crowds and got her first close-up of the Bio-dome. Its edge zig-zagged yellow like a child's first mechanics set, above the roofs of stone and brick warehouses, before curving up and away in glass and steel. Across the width of the road stood a line of yellow columns that looked like prison bars holding up the structure. And a yard under the lip of the Bio-dome, at the closest point out of the rain, doorless gateways filled the gaps between the columns, numbers stuck to their fronts.

Minnie Brownlow knew which security gate she wanted, and she worked her way through the crowds to number 19. She walked through on the signal, her daughter on her back and the bag around her shoulder.

The frame beeped as they went through, and a PapSec Community Crime Prevention Officer stepped forward in his peaked yellow cap and standard-issue PapDrive spectacles. Minnie smiled at the man as she removed her poncho and handed him the satchel. "There are so many people here," she said.

"They reckon there might be two million come today," the officer responded. "Albert Square's already full, so you'll have to go to Piccadilly Gardens and watch it from the screens there." He opened the bag and looked inside. "What's all this, Minnie?" he asked. "Didn't I say not to bring anything from the market? I'm not allowed to let you in with any of this, you know that."

"Brian, that's your four-year-old's lunch. What would you have her do? Starve?"

"Don't be like that, Min. It's not my choice, these are my orders. No exceptions, they said."

"Look, there are thousands of people behind us," said Minnie. "The longer we take, the more they'll have to wait. That's the best produce I could barter, so they're not dangerous or anything. And at any rate, there are millions here today, you said. Who's going to notice a couple of uncertified apples?"

"I don't know," said Brian. "There are cameras everywhere."

"Think of our daughter. Do you want her to go hungry?"

Brian Brownlow relented at his wife's gaze and gave back the bag saying, "Just be careful. Don't let anyone see you or I'll be for the chop."

"I'm sure it won't come to that," said Minnie, patting her husband's arm.

Piccadilly Gardens were just 500 yards from the edge of the Bio-dome, yet it still took half an hour to get there. Everyone was gawping up at the latticed ceiling so high above their heads, the rainwater cascading down the other side. The sight was so daunting that it sat heavily in Minnie's stomach, but Naomi on her back wouldn't sit still from the excitement.

"I love it here, mummy!" said Naomi. "It's dry and it looks funny. But what's that noise?"

"That's the rain against the Bio-dome roof," her mother replied.

"A dio-dome..." Naomi repeated. "Will we ever live in a dio-dome?"

"No," Minnie replied. "This is the only one. The Prime Minister said there can't be any more."

"Oh," Naomi responded. "Why can't we have one?"

"It's very complicated Nao, I'm not sure I can really explain right now. But you'll learn soon enough."

The Bio-dome roof wasn't the only sign of things to come. When they got to Piccadilly Gardens, they found it paved in concrete. Cranes towered over every building as they pieced together cylindrical structures that would soon occupy the whole dome, identical edifices reaching up to the artificial sky.

Giant screens flashed out from every wall, showing an old lady in an armchair with a blanket over her knees and half-moon spectacles balanced on her nose. She was watching children running around the garden outside, squealing and squirting each other with water. A voice from nowhere said "here's your tea, mum," and after a couple of blinks the world appeared as if through that old lady's eyes, looking through half lenses at a middle-aged blonde woman blown up a thousand times on the screens. A white box flashed around the face and underneath spelt out the words.

'Mariana. Daughter
Date of Birth: 16th June 1996
Likes: Cats and knitting...'

"Do you have memory problems?" boomed the commentary. "Or do you just want to remember life's most important moments in true-to-life Augmented Vision? Then PapDrive VI is for you."

In the crowd, Minnie gazed up at the pictures. "I can't think of anything worse," she opined to no one. "If I ever get to the stage where I can't remember my own daughter's name, I'd rather be put out of my misery than be forced to wear those things."

"Don't knock it till you've tried it," said a man in PapDrive specs. "These things have revolutionised my life. Now I'm never late for work, I never forget a name or a birthday or if a mate's wife's pregnant."

"I can do all of that without having some device record my every movement," Minnie replied. "You never know who could be watching you, following everything you do, everywhere you go."

"As they say," said the man. "If you've got nothing to hide, you've nothing to worry about."

Minnie tutted and shook her head away.

St Peter's Square, Manchester City Centre

Yellow columns flashed past the windows of Harry Lanker's car and the rain stopped. His limo slowed as they passed the stone rotunda of the Central Library, over which a yellow cylinder now towered forty floors. The driver pulled up beside one of some twenty static caravans, all arranged at the same angle in the square.

"Are we here?" asked Harry.

"We certainly are," said his driver, turning off the engine. "Just a moment, I'll get the door."

"I am capable of letting myself out," the Prime Minister retorted.

"Of course, Harry," said his driver, "but it's protocol isn't it? Like I tell you every time, I am your number one bodyguard – the first in line to take a bullet for you. And besides, this car pretty much drives itself. So unless you let me open the door for you, I've got basically nothing to do."

"Nothing to do but advise me," said Lanker, leaning forward and slapping him on the shoulder, "and to give me moral support. You're more than my bodyguard and driver, Samuel, you're the closest thing I have to a Privy Counsellor."

"That's right," his driver chuckled. "I'm employed to wipe your arse."

The Prime Minster laughed back. "I'd never make you do that, Samuel," he said. "But I will allow you to open my door, on the condition that you remember I'm acquiescing under protest. I'm the first servant of the nation after all, and servants don't have servants for themselves, not even Prime Ministerial ones. Just you remember that. In my eyes we're here as equals, which is why I want you on stage with me today, standing shoulder to shoulder. You got that?"

"Of course, Harry," said his driver as he pulled open the door and stepped into the Bio-dome air. Samuel Dietrich straightened his driver's cap and white tie, then scooted around the car to far-off chants of, "Har-ry Lan-ker, Har-ry Lan-ker."

Piccadilly Gardens, Manchester

Over every wall, the Prime Minister's yellowed smile and raggedy beard flashed from the screens. Minnie clapped her hands above her head, chanted Harry Lanker's name like most in the crowd.

But the man beside Minnie didn't join in. "I don't know how he has the cheek to show his face here," he said. "And without even bothering to shave. If Harry Lanker had his way, we'd all be digging the earth with our bare hands."

"Don't be ridiculous," said Minnie. "Just because he's making a stand doesn't mean we'll return to the stone age."

"You can't stop progress, that's all I say."

"This isn't progress and he's already put a stop to it," said a woman in the crowd. "There'll be no more PapCorp Bio-domes after this one."

"You mean the moratorium?" said the man.

"Of course," the woman replied.

"They'll never get that through Parliament," the man explained. "Those RASCALS couldn't pass a parcel, let alone a law as controversial as that. Minority government's a stupid idea, it never works. There'll be new elections soon enough, you mark my words."

"And when we're asked to vote again," the woman retorted, "then we'll show them. RASCAL'll get their majority and then we'll find out whose country this is."

"That scruffy Socialist could never win a majority!"

"You wanna bet?"

As her neighbours discussed, Minnie reached into her bag and pulled out a jar of water. She unscrewed the lid and sipped from the rim before passing it back to Naomi, who took it in both hands and tipped it up to her mouth.

Minnie didn't notice, but all around were staring at the little girl.

"Is that PapAqua?" asked the man who'd been arguing.

"No," Minnie replied, "It's just good old-fashioned water. Have you got a problem with that?"

"You can't bring that in here!" said a woman, "let alone feed it to your daughter! They could have her taken away for that. You never know what untreated water might contain. How the hell did you even get it in here?"

"What else's she got in that bag?" shouted another man.

Minnie found they suddenly had space to breathe, that people around them were moving away.

Approaching Albert Square, central Manchester

With his security patrol walking four in front, four behind, the only person alongside Harry Lanker was his driver, Samuel Dietrich. Together they strode past mock-gothic windows, under the pair of covered bridges linking the town hall to the old council offices – now one of many PapSec bases in the city. They could hear the crowd shouting his name the whole way, but when Harry Lanker stepped around the corner into Albert Square, the screams grew hysterical. The noise rebounded off the roof like it was trying to blow it away.

As he waved and smiled, it was obvious to all that Harry Lanker was enjoying himself. His tiredness forgotten, he spent as long as he could in taking the plaudits of the crowd before turning to meet the local dignitaries. They were lined up outside the town hall, all the way to the stage in front of the main entrance.

Harry Lanker had shaken two dozen hands by the time he got to Bernie Douglas-FitzAllan, the first of the O'Dillons' entourages. He, like the rest, held his hand limp in Harry Lanker's, deliberately avoiding his gaze.

Samuel Dietrich followed on behind, greeting all and sundry as if rather more than just the PM's driver. Most of the O'Dillon associates did as they'd done with his boss, ignoring him the best they could. But as Harry Lanker was walking up to the stage, waving both hands above his head, Lord Michael O'Dillon met the driver square in the eyes. Their handshake was firm, and when Samuel pulled away he found a square of paper in his palm.

Piccadilly Gardens

By one o'clock, every screen was filled with the Gothic clock tower of Manchester town hall, whose pealing bells accompanied the songs and chanting for Harry Lanker. In Piccadilly Gardens, screens flickered to a drone's image of Albert Square, where a spire-topped statue stood out as a solitary island amidst a sea of people.

Into the space around Minnie Brownlow and Naomi, now stepped two men in yellow jackets, caps, and standard-issue specs.

"What's in that bag?" asked the larger of the two PapSec Community Crime Prevention Officers.

"What's it got to do with you?" Minnie replied.

"We have information that says you are carrying illegal organic matter," he said. "And we're here to dispose of it or to escort you out of the Bio-dome."

"Sir," Minnie replied calmly. "I know the law. The first act of the RASCAL government was to kick that dreadful Fruit and Vegetable Act into the long grass, meaning I still have the freedom to choose what I feed my daughter."

"I'm not engaging you in politics, Mrs Brownlow, I'm merely doing my job."

"How do you know my name?"

"The Bio-dome is a private space where everyone's identity is monitored and recorded," the officer replied. "This enables the authorities to control access to whoever and whatever they want. The Bio-dome has been declared a clean zone, and in order to regulate the levels of bacteria in the air, all food and drink brought into this area should be purchased from Pap-authorised retailers. Therefore, I must insist that either you immediately hand over all such items in your possession, or I will have to ask you to leave."

As Minnie gazed up at the man, the image of Harry Lanker appeared on the tower behind him. At the sight of him striding out onto a flag-draped stage, in front of a pleated-stone arch, the crowd cheered and screamed.

"All right!" Minnie shouted. "Take the lot. I'm not missing Harry Lanker for anything!"

Albert Square

The Prime Minister stepped towards the podium and gazed over the mass of heads. Except for the journalists on the front rows of seating, most of whom stared at their Xi-fan sheets or PapDrives throughout his performance, all eyes were on Harry Lanker. "People of Manchester!" he shouted into the microphones. But the cheers and whistles would not subside, so again he shouted, and again.

"As you all know," he said when finally the crowd quietened, "I've cut short my trip to Washington to be here today, and your welcome has made it all worthwhile!" He applauded the crowd and they clapped back.

"It's amazing to see so many of you here supporting me," Harry Lanker continued. "But our movement is not all about me, and our work is far from finished. I've seen crowds like you gathered in towns and cities all over this country, and it's this momentum that has finally brought a party of the people into government. But I'll say this to you all. Now is not the time to sit back and relax, now is the time to take advantage of our situation, to start righting the wrongs of the past. Now you need to be more active than ever, and more aware of your every action – we've never been under closer scrutiny. Only by working together will we reclaim this country from its financiers!"

Approaching Albert Square

Nearly all the turnstiles at every entrance closed at one-fifteen. A few PapSec Community Crime Prevention Officers stayed on to process any latecomers, but Brian Brownlow wasn't one of them. So, like all his colleagues on a break, he followed in the footsteps of the man whose face was still flashing from the sides of every building.

Brian got to the corner of Albert Square, where the crowds were hanging on the Prime Minister's every word. If he'd looked up, he would've seen Harry Lanker in the flesh not fifty metres away. But Brian Brownlow wasn't bothered, he turned away from the action and marched instead through revolving doorways into the PapSec base in the old council offices.

He found a foyer crowded with men like him, in their uniforms of various yellows. Brian noticed the Chief Constable basking in the glory of a successful PapSec outing, in his black suit and medals, yellow patches on his gorget. But Brian didn't pause. He followed his colleagues down to the basement refectory and queued up for his allowance.

Bearing a tray of three courses while balancing a bottle of PapAqua, Brian sat down at a table in the middle of the hall and tucked in. He was so taken with his food that he didn't see the Chief Superintendent walk in, wearing his black dress suit with its yellow arms. "Which one of you is Brian Brownlow?" he shouted.

The room fell silent and Brian looked up from his lunch. He raised his hand. "That's me, sir," he replied.

"Stand up so everyone can see you."

Brian did as he was told, his heart pounding.

"This man," announced the Chief Superintendent, "has today jeopardised the lives of two million people. He single-handedly compromised the complex control systems that run this Bio-dome, defying explicit orders to do exactly the opposite. This man was responsible for an entire bag of unauthorised merchandise finding its way into the middle of Piccadilly Gardens."

"But sir," Brian stammered. "It was my wife and daughter, they..."

"It doesn't matter if it's the God-damned King, Brownlow! You were not permitted to make exceptions for anybody or anything. You have exceeded your authority, putting countless lives and livelihoods at risk in the process. So I have no alternative but to ask for your badge, your uniform, your gun and your PapDrive."

Piccadilly Gardens

Minnie was so enthralled by Harry Lanker that she never wanted him to finish. But finish he did, and after the reception the Prime Minster received, Lord O'Dillon's entrance was a huge anti-climax. Despite the fanfare of lights and the rousing trumpets, the best the audience could offer was a polite round of applause. Many, like Minnie Brownlow, didn't clap at all.

Lord Michael would drawl on for an hour about the challenges he had overcome in building the Bio-dome, ensuring the credit went always to himself.

But Naomi had soon had enough. Still strapped to her mother's back, she pulled at Minnie's hair. "I'm bored, mummy," she whined. "I want to go and play. Can't I go and find some other kids?"

"Not here," said her mother. "It's not safe. There are lots of strangers and you might get lost. Do you want to come down?"

"Yes, please. Then can we go?"

Naomi descended into the forest of legs and overcoats, but they couldn't leave; there was barely space to stand, let alone walk.

"Mummy," said Naomi, "I'm hungry."

"I know sweetie, but there's nothing we can do. We can't afford to buy anything in here even if we could get to a shop."

"Why didn't you bring a picnic? You said we'd have a picnic."

"Yes, Naomi, I did. But that man came and took it off us. Don't you remember?"

"But I'm really hungry, mummy," was all Naomi could reply.

Mrs Brownlow picked up her daughter and cradled her in her arms. "I know you're hungry, my darling. When this has finished, we'll go straight home and I'll make dinner. How does carrot stew sound?"

"Yummy!" Naomi exclaimed, cuddling herself to her mother's breast.

Rusholme

Mrs Brownlow, Minnie's mother-in-law, gave the last of her life to her husband. Even if he'd been dead five years, the decade she'd spent nursing him had turned her into an old lady. She now spent most of her days in an armchair, snoozing in front of the television with a duvet pulled up to her neck and a woolly hat on her head. Which was how Brian found her that day.

When his mother opened her eyes, Brian was already wrapped up in a sleeping bag on the sofa. "You're home early, aren't you?" she said. "Is something the matter?"

"No mum, nothing's the matter. I just want to watch the telly."

"I'm your mother, Brian," she croaked. "I gave birth to you. I can see when there's summat wrong with you. You know what they say. A problem shared's a problem halved."

"Nothing's wrong, mum. Please, just leave me alone. Let's watch the show. Zoltan O'Dillon's coming on now and you know how much I like him. He's such good fun."

Albert Square

When Zoltan O'Dillon took the limelight, Harry Lanker started to sway. Samuel Dietrich caught his arm and pulled him upright, whispering, "Not long now, Harry. Stay with us just a few minutes more."

Indeed, the younger O'Dillon's speech was quick and to the point, and as soon as he was done, Harry Lanker was off stage with his driver beside him. "I've got to get some kip," said the Prime Minister. "I could hardly follow what was going on out there, it was all I could do to keep my eyes open. Did they say anything important?"

Samuel smiled. "Well, Lord Michael declared he's going to build the world's tallest tower, and then Zoltan tried to outdo him by announcing the largest advertisement ever conceived. He's planning to have PapPop written in massive letters on a desert somewhere. He called it an advert for the aliens."

"You mean that thing?" said Harry, pointing to the pictures flashing from the walls of every building. "It's horrendous. Will those O'Dillons never be satisfied?"

They turned the corner of the town hall and vanished down the alleyway. As soon as they were out of camera-shot, Harry stumbled and fell into his driver's arms. "Jeez," said the PM, "I'm more knackered than I imagined. Give us a hand getting back won't you, Samuel, man? I've pretty much had it."

Samuel Dietrich took the Prime Minister under his arm. "What about the reception?" he asked.

"I can't go there in this state," said Harry. "I might say something I'll regret. No, better I have a couple of hours' downtime and see how I feel after."

Despite all the other attendants around Harry Lanker, it was his driver's broad shoulder that carried the Prime Minister back to his van. Samuel fumbled in his pocket and found the key, unlocked the door and walked Harry Lanker to the wrap-around sofa at the front end.

Samuel pulled the curtains closed. "You just rest," he said. "I'll be right here if you need me."

"You needn't do that," said the Prime Minister, relaxing his head onto a cushion. "I've got my whole security team here to keep an eye on me. I don't need my driver to look after me too. You've got an invitation to the reception, why don't you use it? I might join you later. I'll see how I'm feeling in a bit."

"All right," said Samuel, edging for the door. "If you're sure. I'll see you in there. It'll probably go on a while so don't worry about being late."

Samuel Dietrich stepped out into the Bio-dome night, through the PM's security cordon. From one of the vans he heard shouting.

Rusholme

Little Naomi had been asleep on her mother's back most of the way home. But her eyes opened as soon as Minnie's key turned the lock and they stepped up into the chill of their living room. "I'm hungry, mummy," she declared.

"I know love," Minnie replied, untying her daughter from her back and lowering her to the floor. "Let's get the fire on and I'll cook you something. Then I'll play you a couple of songs before you go to sleep, there's one I can't stop thinking of today. Would you like that?"

"Yes," said Naomi.

Neither husband nor mother-in-law acknowledged their homecoming, and Minnie knelt by the fireplace to arrange the kindling. "It's blooming freezing in here," she said. "And I need to get some food in that girl's belly. They took it all off us in the end, you know. The whole blooming lot. Threatened to kick me out just as Harry Lanker was coming on to speak."

"Oh," said Brian. "Did they?"

Minnie glanced at the screen to see what they were watching. She saw the picture of a high-up Earth with the letters PapPop shining out from southern Europe. "It's an audacious move by O'Dillon Junior," the commentator was saying, "to try and steal the limelight from his father. But now the plan is announced, the markets are already moving. PapPop is seeing big gains on international stock exchanges this evening, so it's obvious investors like the plan. They'll be wanting to see it through as quickly as they can, and organisations across the world will surely be queuing up to supply the billions in liquidity. In the meantime, the PapPound is at a new record high against Pound Sterling. At the end of trading in London, one PapPound was worth £1.42."

Minnie lit a match and soon flames were lapping the scraps of wood. "What are they talking about this rubbish for?" she asked. "What about Harry Lanker? He was the guest of honour, after all. Did you see him? Wasn't he great? I could listen to him talking for hours, you know."

"His speech was long and rambling," Brian replied, without breaking his gaze at the screen. "You know he never mentioned the Bio-dome once?"

Minnie tutted. "I wish you'd think for yourself sometimes rather than just repeating the endless diatribe of pap you get from that screen. There's so much real news going on in this world, but instead they're fixated on some stupid advert in the desert. It's the most ridiculous idea I've ever heard – I wonder how long it took them to come up with it. I bet it never even gets built."

Minnie Brownlow's rant may have fallen on deaf ears, but she was right about one thing; there were many other happenings that day, some of them of interest, most of which would never reach the public domain.

Old Mrs Brownlow, meanwhile, would fall into a permanent sleep just a matter of weeks later, in that very chair. She never knew what had happened to her son, he kept it inside until she'd passed. Minnie only found out when he stopped pretending to go to work. But Brian would never get over the resentment he felt for his wife, and over the years it would eat him up from the inside.

8. Bio-dome 2

26th October 2045
Manchester City Centre

The night before the first Bio-dome opened, Zoltan O'Dillon didn't go to bed. High on whisky and cocaine, he'd had a sudden urge to overshadow his father. And with Bernie's help he was sure they were about to do it.

As his limo took the pair into Manchester that morning, Zoltan turned to the Earl of Angus on the back seat beside him. "I can't get over what a great idea this is," he said. "It'll really knock Lord Mike for six. I can't wait to see his face when he hears it. Do you think it's going to be possible?"

"I don't see why not," Bernie slurred in reply. "PapEng are capable of pretty much anything, aren't they? If they're going to build the world's tallest tower, the largest advert shouldn't be too much of a problem."

"All right, I'll take your word for it. Now tell me again, where did we decide to build it? Spain, wasn't it, Bernie? "

"Yeah, that's right," said Zoltan. "Close enough to Gibraltar so PapSec can keep an eye on it, and far enough from the goons for them to have a go at smashing it up."

"And it's Spain, isn't it?" Bernie opined. "So I'd be surprised if there are two goats left living there now."

"Exactly," Zoltan slurred back.

With a flash of yellow the rain stopped. The driver pulled up opposite the Central Library and when Zoltan got out he found a thin man waiting for him. "Pickering?" he asked. "What the devil are you doing waiting outside?"

"I don't have a key to the caravan, do I?" Larry Pickering replied. "Only you and Bernie have copies."

"Oh yeah," said Zoltan, looking upwards. "What's that noise?"

"It's the rain on the Bio-dome roof," said Sir Larry.

"Is it really?" said Zoltan, rubbing his palms together. "Then that's the first obvious problem with Lord Mike's magnificent

Bio-dome, isn't it? People won't like hearing the pitter-patter of rain all the time as they go about their business. I wouldn't be surprised if this whole thing becomes a great white elephant. The one and only of its kind. That'll teach the good lord to be so damned arrogant. Did you get the supplies?"

"Of course," said Pickering. "But for Papp's sake, Zoltan, you look like you haven't slept. You're going to have to speak you know. Is it all ready? Do you know what you're going to say?"

"Of course, Larry old boy. Have some faith for once, won't you? Now come on, crack one of those bottles open. We've only got an hour till the thing starts and I don't want to be stood there sober."

Sixty minutes later, Zoltan and Bernie had devoured the bottle of whisky and were standing swaying in front of a gothic-arched window. Beyond a security cordon, crowds were staring up at the screens on the walls of every building except the town hall, waving at their bird's-eye reflections.

Lord Michael marched past and took two looks at his son. "Are you drunk?" he asked.

"I might be," Zoltan slurred back. "What's it got to do with you?"

"It's got everything to do with me," said Lord Michael. "If you make a tit of yourself today, I'll never forgive you. Got that?"

"Ay, ay ,daddio!"

"I'm being serious, Zoltan. This is my day and I won't have you ruining it with your idiocies."

"I know just what today is," said Zoltan. "Don't you fear Mike, when I get up to speak, I'll get straight to the point. I'll be not more than five minutes and I'll be as clear as day. You just watch me."

Lord Michael was about to march away in disgust when images of Harry Lanker flashed across every screen and the crowd went wild. He paused, shaking his head. "Look at that scruffy git!" he said. "He's supposed to be this country's Prime

Minister, and he comes to my big day with his hair all over the place and looking like he hasn't shaved for weeks!"

"Is that a bloody donkey jacket he's wearing?" added Bernie the Earl. "He looks like a homeless hippy!"

"His election cost PapCorp a hundred-million pounds in stock value," commented one of the Lord's six advisors.

"But PapCorp did all right," said Bernie. "As always."

"Only because of the tactical genius they have at the helm," said Lord Michael of himself. "As you've seen time and again, I'm an expert at turning crises to PapCorp's advantage."

"I bet you regret signing that contract though," said Zoltan.

"We wouldn't have got all that state funding otherwise," said another of the Lord's advisors.

"We just never imagined the Prime Minister would be him," said a third.

The crowd whooped louder than ever when Harry Lanker took the stage. The O'Dillons with their entourages followed; they had no choice but to stay in his shadow as the Prime Minister addressed the square and the world.

Lord Michael held his arms crossed with a fist over his mouth that looked like he was concentrating. In fact it was to hide his commentary on the performance. "He still hasn't mentioned the Bio-dome once," he whispered, "nor PapCorp nor any of us here. What are we on now? Twenty-five past one? He was only meant to have twenty minutes. Have you ever heard such long and rambling speech? Can't he see the audience has had enough?"

When Lord Michael finally got his chance to step forward, he found his reception underwhelming, despite the light show and the trumpet calls. He filled an hour with self-platitudes before getting on to the meat of his speech in the questions. "We have a very special moment now," he announced. "A pupil from the PapNews-PapEd Journalism Academy is going to ask his first live question. This young man is only thirteen but I've been assured he's a real talent. Vincent Humbolt, where are you?"

On the front row of the press seats, a boy with wild black hair and skin like Spanish porcelain got to his feet. He smiled into the cameras. "Lord O'Dillon," he said with confidence. "Thank you for giving me the opportunity to congratulate you on this magnificent achievement. But will it be just another chapter in the book that Lord Michael O'Dillon is writing across the face of this country? Or will it be the climax? With all new Bio-dome construction currently on hold, where can PapCorp go now?"

Lord O'Dillon stood nodding at the question. "I tell you what, son," he said. "You're more articulate than most of the journalists in this country who are four times your age! And you put the conundrum perfectly. As you so wisely point out, this country's extreme-left government is making it very difficult for PapCorp to bring the many benefits of Bio-dome life to millions of people. And I for one find that a great shame. But while they might currently be preventing us expanding outwards, the sky's the limit as far as building up goes. Everyone knows that it's PapCorp's engine that drives this country. We're a company on the move, heading further than anything ever witnessed in all of history. We are the masters of nature, the top of the food chain. Unconstrained by the limits of before, we are growing higher, wider, further than any humans have ever gone. And when we say we're going to do something, no matter how impossible it may seem, by golly we do it. So, tomorrow morning, PapEng are poised to begin work on the tallest structure humans have ever devised. On the edge of this very dome, between what will one day be the Ancoats and New Cross Bio-domes, it'll be more than five thousand metres high and dwarf anything on this continent. And it will be named, of course, in honour of the man who started it all. The Zoltán Papp Tower."

Plenty of polished questions followed, and Lord Michael gave a scripted response to every one. When at last Zoltan O'Dillon's turn came, he shuffled into the limelight without any of his father's fanfare. His eyes were still red from drink and drugs but, if he'd slurred at his father and everyone else, when he spoke to the mics he was firm and assured. He acknowledged the Bio-dome as he had to, waited for the applause to die down and then said what he'd planned, reading an autocue that ran across the bottom of his glasses.

"After all this time listening to the monologues of the Prime Minister and the Mayor of Manchester," he said. "You can relax now, I'm going to be very brief. Many of you might think that I've had an easy life. You probably imagine this route to the top has been planned for me. But it wasn't like that at all. I've had to fight for everything I've earned, from my Victoria Cross to being made head of PapPop – still the biggest fruit in PapCorp's basket. There's little doubt that the future of this great corporation lies with me. So, while my father chooses to pay homage to the past, in our hometown, my sights are set on extending the bounds of Zoltán Papp's great invention. We all know PapPop is the world's favourite drink, and we're working to make sure every single person has access to a bottle whenever they want. So to expand, we need to think outside Manchester, this country, and even off this planet. People know me as the hero of Jebel Shams, the man who tamed the desert with PapSec, winning a VC on my first engagement. Now, I'm going to tame the desert with PapPop. By covering thousands of square miles of wasteland in PapSolar Laminate, we're going to write miles-wide letters in the sand that will shine out into the heavens. That way, when visitors from other worlds do turn up, they'll know just whose planet this is. The world's first ever advert for aliens will say just one word – PapPop."

With pictures playing the graphics that Bernie had cobbled together, Zoltan O'Dillon milked the audience for everything he could. After his third encore, music rang out from the speakers. He turned to see the stage empty and decided it was time to leave.

Lord Michael was waiting at the bottom of the steps. He grabbed his son by the elbow and pulled him through the curtains below stage. "How dare you try to upstage me like that?" he whispered in the darkness. "If it wasn't bad enough having Harry bloody Lanker here, my own son then tries to outdo his father's grand announcement. Now all the channels will be going on about some ridiculous advert when they should be talking about my Bio-dome and my Zoltán Papp Tower. How long did it take you to come up with that idea? Five minutes?"

"A night," said Zoltan. "And you're just jealous because it's a much better idea than any idea you've ever had."

"You think?" his father sneered. "You should remember whose company this is, Zoltan. I made her what she is and I control the purse strings around here. There's not a chance in hell that I'm going to let you jeopardise my tower. All of PapEng's energies will be tied up in her and you're going to have go whistle for your advert."

"You want to bet?" said Zoltan. "How's Harry Lanker ever going to allow a five-kilometre tower in the centre of Manchester? I'll have my advert shining out into the heavens before you've even laid the foundation stone." Zoltan cast the curtains aside and stormed off towards his caravan, leaving his father smirking in the darkness.

St Peter's Square

By the time Bernie Douglas-FitzAllan got to the van, Zoltan was dozing on the sofa, a bottle of whisky half-full beside him and five lines of cocaine on the table. "Well, that was a nice day, wasn't it?" said Bernie, closing the front door.

"Where the fuck have you been?" said Zoltan, rubbing his eyes.

"I went shopping."

"What for? We've got everything we need right here, and anything we don't have we can just order. I've been waiting for you."

"It looks to me like you've already made a start," said Bernie, nodding at the bottle. "I needed a new suit for tonight."

"Oh yeah? Where're we going?"

"I don't know where you're going, Zollers," Bernie chuckled. "Judging by the state you're in, not very far. I'm going to see Miss Saigon with that fancy piece from Longsight. I told you about her, the tango dancer. Mind if I use the shower?" Bernie didn't wait for Zoltan's reply before darting off down the corridor.

O'Dillon Junior sat chewing on the situation, then jumped up and chased after his advisor. "Hey," he yelled, grabbing Bernie's shoulder and spinning him around. "Hey, yes, I do mind actually. I do mind you using my bathroom. You're pissing off to see some broad and leaving me alone on our big day."

"Our big day? Your big day more like it. We came up with that advert together, remember? But I haven't heard you sharing any of the credit."

"Because no one even knows who you are, Bernie," said Zoltan. "Do you think Michelangelo gave anyone credit for his Sistine Chapel? Did Christopher Wren share the glory with any of the actual men that built St Paul's? Of course not, they were great men. You are in the company of a great man."

"What you're forgetting, Zollers," said Bernie, "is that I've known you since we were three-years-old. I know who you really are, I've seen what you're capable of."

"Are you threatening me?"

Bernie laughed. "Of course I'm not, Zoltan. I'm saying that I'm your oldest mate in the world. That we've been through a million scrapes together, and you know I love you like a brother. But tonight, my brother, I'm going to do my own thing." And with that he shut the bathroom door, leaving Zoltan O'Dillon steaming in the corridor.

The CEO of PapPop kicked a wall in frustration, tearing a hole in the plywood. He clutched both hands against the sink, rocking back and forward in thought. Then he barged his shoulder against the bathroom door to find the Earl of Angus standing as naked and as plump as the day he was born. "Do you mind?" said Bernie.

Zoltan O'Dillon's answer was to grab a handful of his friend's blond hair and drag Bernie from the bathroom.

"Come on Zollers, man!" Bernie screamed. "Stop it, please. You're hurting me. Zoltan, I'll tell Pickering!"

"Pickering's off hobnobbing," said Zoltan, barging his schoolfriend towards the door. "And I do the hiring and firing around here. I should've done this years ago, Major Stinkovitch!"

"No, no, Zoltan!" cried Bernie. "Not outside! Please! I've got no clothes on, Zoltan, please! Zoltan!"

But O'Dillon ignored his friend's pleas. He barged Bernie out of the door, slammed it in his face and locked it shut.

"Zoltan!" Bernie yelled, banging the aluminium with his fists. "Zoltan, come on man. Don't do this to me, please. At least give me my clothes."

The bathroom window opened and out dropped Bernie's underpants, socks, shirt, shoes and trousers. Everything but the key to the caravan and his wallet.

Manchester Town Hall

Beside a marble fireplace, Lord Michael O'Dillon undid his tie and tossed it onto the dark-wood coffee table. He opened the top few buttons of his shirt and the fat flumped from his chin. He sighed, picked up his glass of whisky and looked at the man on the cream-fabric sofa facing him.

"I hope this Klein guy won't keep us waiting long, Atkins," he said. "Are you sure he's 100 per cent?"

"I'm sure," said the man in a yellow-felt tunic, with shiny brass buttons down the middle and an array of medals on his left breast. "He'll be here. I know him, he's not always on time but he never misses a call. Did he definitely get the note?"

"I gave it to him myself," replied Lord Michael. He sipped his whisky. "Strange name, Zachery Klein," he mused. "German, is he?"

"Absolutely not," said the PapSec Officer. "You've seen him. Did he look German to you? No, sir, he was a foundling brought up at the Zoltán Papp Memorial Orphanage in Prestwich. A computer app selected his name. I guess it could've been worse."

"It's certainly distinctive," said Michael O'Dillon. "Surprisingly fitting for a man like that."

St Peter's Square

Alone in his caravan, Zoltan O'Dillon was banging through cupboards in the corridor kitchen, leaving the doors open as he went. He found a bottle of 2035 Merlot above the sink, and as he searched for a glass he scraped the shelves with an ungainly paw. Ceramics smashed to the floor but he didn't care; he found a large round-bottomed goblet and bounded over the crockery. He plonked himself down on the sofa, unscrewed the cap and poured a large glass of red wine which he downed in two gulps. He poured another, and placed the bottle beside the empty whisky container.

Still churning with anger, he knelt down beside the coffee table, picked a plastic pipe from a box and snorted a line of cocaine. Sniffing, he sat straight up and wiped his nose with the back of his finger, then he picked another tube and went down for seconds.

After that one, he jumped to his feet, gazed first at the broken glass on the floor and then at the open cupboard doors. As the dopamine and serotonin raced across his synapses, rage overtook him. He stormed towards the cupboards and yanked a door from its hinges, loosening the shelving from the wall. He ripped at another, and another, until the entire unit could hang on no more and it collapsed around him in an avalanche of plates and tea cups.

The cupboard hit Zoltan O'Dillon square on the shoulder, but he wasn't done yet. He rubbed his arm, clambered over the bits of dinner set and grabbed the nearest cushion to hand. He took a cigarette lighter from the table and clicked the flint a couple of times until a yellow flame lapped against the upholstery. But it was no good, the fire-retardant cloth wouldn't catch. So he grabbed his wine glass and gulped down its contents, then poured himself another to take outside.

Manchester Town Hall

After two flights of stairs, Samuel Dietrich stopped for a breather. He took off his chauffeur's cap and wiped the sweat from his forehead with a handkerchief, then glanced both ways down the corridor. Between stone carvings, he strode off over a white-tiled floor decorated with ceramic bees. He paused only at a pair of walnut doors, which opened before he could reach for the bronze handles. Then he stepped inside and his identity changed.

"Ah, Zachery," said a soldier, getting to his feet. "Please, come in."

"Hello Francis," replied the driver, glancing at the three PapSec pips and crown brooch on his lapels. "Still a Brigadier, I see. I'd have thought you'd have been promoted a few rungs up the ladder by now."

"I didn't become a soldier to sit behind a desk," Francis Atkins replied. "And Brigadier's the highest rank that still allows me to get my hands dirty, when the time is right. Now I believe you've met Lord Michael O'Dillon."

"Only very briefly," said Zachery.

Lord Michael too was now on his feet. "Pleasure to meet you at last, Mr Klein," he said, holding his hand out in greeting. "I'm glad to have the chance to thank you personally for all the work you've done for us over the years, Francis here has been filling me in. And well noted about his rank, I keep trying to make him a General, but he always refuses. Now come and sit down, we have a lot to discuss. Would you like a glass of whisky?"

Only when all three men were on the sofas, sipping from their tumblers, did Lord Michael continue. "I've asked you here as two of PapSec's best men of action," he said. "This is a top-secret operation that can never see the light of day, ever. I know you're both PapSec through and through. I trust I still command your loyalty."

"Of course, sir," the Brigadier responded.

"I'll go to the ends of the Earth for you, Lord O'Dillon," said Zachery Klein. "I owe PapCorp everything. And everything I have I'd gladly give up to ensure your future success."

"Excellent," said O'Dillon, sipping his whisky. "Now this is the plan…"

St Peter's Square

In the Bio-dome night, rain splattered against the high-up roof and distant rumbles of thunder shook the air. There was a party going on just a couple of blocks away, a celebration for Lord Michael, organised by Lord Michael, paid for by the city of Manchester. A bang in the sky took Zoltan's attention, then another, and another, before colourful sparks fell in geometric patterns from the steel-mesh-ceiling.

"I'll show them fireworks!" said Zoltan to himself. He flicked an icon on the interface of his PapDrive specs to open the car boot, and removed a plastic fuel can before closing the lid with two flicks of the same hand. He took a sip of wine and marched straight back inside, carrying the petrol can over the debris. He splashed gasoline all over the sofa, took out his lighter and clicked the flint.

This time the couch caught with the first spark and the wave of heat sent Zoltan staggering backwards into the tea table. He dislodged the bottle of wine, but despite his state, his hand shot down and caught it by the neck. The curtains went up in a puff of smoke and Zoltan noticed that the last of his drugs were now strewn across the table's marble top. With flames lapping at the walls just metres away, Zoltan knelt back down, placed the glass and bottle on either side of his knees and gathered the dust together with his fingers. He took a tube, snorted the line and got back up, taking the bottle with him but leaving the glass behind.

Zoltan was still rubbing his nose when he got back out into the Bio-dome night. By now, one whole end of the van had caught and flames were lapping at the rest. He took a swig of wine and whooped. "Fuck you, Bernie Douglas-FitzAllan!" he yelled into the fire. "I hope she's worth it, because you've just resigned all hope of your future." He tipped the bottle to his lips then shook it at the inferno. "And you, Mike O'Dillon. Lord Mike. Fuck you too. My time will come, just you see if it doesn't. This advert is only the start! One day you'll be remembered as the father of Zoltan O'Dillon, the pace-setter for what was to come. I'll be Frederick the Great to your Frederick William. You just see!"

He drained the dregs from the bottle and threw it into the fire. "Screw the lot of you!" he shouted. "You don't know Papp about the world, you just go along with what my daddy says. But he won't be the boss forever, one day I'll be up there. Just you see if I'm not!"

The flames hit the fuel tanks and shot up towards the shallow edge of the Bio-dome. Zoltan screamed in delighted. "Fuck you Michael O'Dillon!" he hollered once more.

9. Flowering

21st August 1958
Stretton Gap, Shropshire, England

A queue of vehicles stretched out behind Henry Gritton's lorry as his bottle-green AEC Mercury with rounded wheel-arches and a split windscreen chugged uphill towards Church Stretton. Hedgerows and trees enclosed their route like a tunnel, breaking only occasionally to reveal the ridge of Long Mynd to their left.

In the middle of the cab, between the driver and his passenger, the engine clattered around the metal housing and infused the air with diesel fumes. Henry glanced at the young man beside him and found him staring intently out the front window. Gritton flicked the Hungarian's knee with the back of his fingers. "What's up, Zoli?" he asked. "You look like you've got the weight of the world on your shoulders."

"I'm just worried about today," Zoltán replied.

"You should try to enjoy today," said Gritton. "You've been working hard enough for it these past months. Go and make the most of being out of Clun, that's what I'd do. Have a wander around the show, you can use one of our passes."

Zoltán shook his head. "I couldn't do that," he said. "I want to be there the whole time to make sure everything is okay. I think we've made too much. What do you think, Mr Gritton?"

"I think you need to stop worrying, Zoltán. Remember how popular it was at Burwarton the last two years? Try to see the bright side for once. Just think how great it'll be if we sell all those bottles."

"If," Zoltán sighed. "That's a big word. And in any case, it twice came second in the drinks prize in a village show. What chance do I have here?"

"This is different," said Henry. "Prize committees at Country Fairs are notoriously corrupt, so don't put too much weight on coming second. If we don't sell all the bottles, we'll come up with some other plan. But just try to be positive. If you think it'll be a disaster, it'll be a disaster. If you try to imagine a success, well, just maybe..."

Close behind Henry, Thomas Gritton followed in his farmyard Land Rover. He was pulling a horsebox just like Marjorie behind him. But while the younger brother's trailer was plain grey, Henry's wife's had been painted the closest yellow they could find to PapPop, and the name of the drink was printed in bold black along the top.

In the back, Attila and Gábor Bacsik sat facing each other with their legs squeezed around the spare tyre and the tarpaulin-wrapped blocks of ice. Marjorie was alone in the front of her jeep but she nattered on most of the way.

"I can't tell you how excited I am about today, boys," she said. "Percy Thrower's going to be there. Do you know who Percy Thrower is? Do they have him in Hungary?" She glanced over her shoulder, saw the two men staring blankly through the windscreen and tutted. "I guess you don't," she continued. "Well anyway, he's a big celebrity. He's got his own show on the television and everything. My aunt Agnes knows him, she's been exhibiting in Shrewsbury for thirty-odd years. One of her granddaughters even goes to school with his eldest. Do you remember my aunt? She won first prize for her flower arrangement at Burwarton a couple of weeks back. Anyway, it's all thanks to her that we've got such a good spot. So many people are going to walk past the stall that I'd be surprised if Zoltán doesn't sell out by lunchtime."

On the back seats, Gábor turned to his brother. "Miről beszél?" he asked. 'What's she talking about?'

"Nem tudom," Attila replied. 'I don't know.' "But whatever it is, she's very excited about it. I just wish she'd watch the road more and not keep turning around to talk to us. Surely it's clear we don't understand a word she's saying."

Gábor smiled. "I don't mind," he said. "She can't do much damage at this speed and I'm quite enjoying being chauffeured around by the lady of the manor. Do you remember how the Ruskies used to go on about the imperialist class system and how it needed to be destroyed? I can see why no one wants a revolution in England; if two foreign farmhands get treated like this, then that whole class thing was obviously just another of their lies."

Cheshire Plains

A record hundred-thousand people would converge on Shrewsbury during those two days in late August. To marvel at the work of the most famous gardener of his age as much as the many exhibitors, people came from miles around on trains, buses and private cars.

Among their number, cruising through Cheshire in a peach-and-white Vauxhall Velux, sat two men in the front, two women in the back, all dressed up for Sunday. Through a curved windscreen, beyond the white bonnet with its chrome-lined headlights, the passengers would get a glimpse of the hills sloping by every time they passed a gap in the hedgerows.

The radio was playing, and a young blonde woman in a flowery dress shouted from the back. "I like this one!" she said. "Turn it up won't you, Callum?"

His knees against the passenger-side dashboard, her boyfriend reached for a dial and turned up the volume.

Beside Callum, the driver wore a pencil moustache and hair greased flat against his head, a polka-dot cravat tucked into his waistcoat. He flicked his younger brother's arm with a tanned-leather driving glove a couple of shades darker than his suit. "That Elvis Presley knows what he's talking about," he said, breaking into song.

"... *ever since the world began, a hard-headed woman been a thorn in the side of man...*"

"Oi, you!" his wife shouted from the back. "I am in the car, you know."

"I'm not talking about you, my love," the driver replied, "I was just singing along with the music."

"Well, don't," she instructed. "And will you please take it a bit steadier? With the petrol smell and the swaying in the back, Linda here's turning as green as her dress."

"Callum," said his brother, "if your bird fouls my car, you've got to clean it up."

"Do I 'ecker's like!" said Callum. "If she redecorates your wheels, it's nowt to do with me. Maybe you should listen to your missus."

"Thank you, Callum," said the driver's wife. "I hope he'll pay you some attention. He never does to me."

"Here we go again," said the driver. "Harold Macmillan was wrong when he said we'd never had it so good. He doesn't have to live with Doreen O'Dillon."

"That's quite enough out of you, Éamon!" said Doreen, slapping her husband around the back of the head.

Éamon chuckled. "I'm only joking, my dear. If you'd let me open the window, the smell wouldn't be a problem."

"And have my hair blown all over the place?" said Doreen. "No, thank you. I had this done special for today, and there ain't a cat in hell's chance I'm turning up at the flower show with my new perm all over the place. What if I meet Percy Thrower or get on the telly?"

Éamon glanced at his younger brother in the passenger seat. They exchanged a grin and shook their heads in tandem.

Callum O'Dillon was fifteen years Éamon's junior, the result of an affair that was never discussed. Only just out of his teens, the younger brother fiddled with the ribbons of his bow-tie, ran his fingers over the solid waves in his hair that met at the point of his forehead. He used so much pomade that he found not a single strand out of place. "How's business?" he asked.

"Business?" Éamon chuckled. "What business? I went to see one of my old clients in Rochdale, beginning of the week. A fella I'd been selling to since the war. Well now he says he's cancelling his order, says no one wants Tanzaro fruit squashes anymore, not now they've seen the ads for those American colas. That's all his customers ask for these days. Don't get me wrong, Mr Jewsbury's a nice man, but it feels like J&B's are on their last legs."

"It's not been the same since the fire, has it?" Doreen added.

"So what you going to do?" asked the younger brother to the elder. "Go and work for the Yanks?"

"I'll do what I have to," said Éamon. "You know me, I could sell sand to the Arabs. I want to find the next big thing."

"The next hula-hoop?

"For example."

"Then we should be heading to Hawaii," said Callum, "not bloody Shrewsbury."

"Callum O'Dillon!" Doreen scolded. "Go away right this instant and wash your mouth out with soap and water. What kind of impression do you want to give young Linda here? It's a stain enough that you've done time without you speaking like a convict as well. Now apologise."

Callum crossed his arms and stared out of the side window. "Sorry," he muttered.

Shrewsbury

Even though the Gritton procession steamed into town long before the show opened, they still found a queue of people stretching past their spot. They pulled up opposite the domed tower of St Chad's, in front of a long white tent which housed the indoor exhibits. They were to spend the day in a rounded alcove of the low promenade wall, fifty yards at most from the gates. There were no other stalls like theirs.

Zoltán Papp was the first out. People tutted as he forged a gap in the queue, but no one voiced their complaints until they were well out of earshot. The Bacsik brothers clambered out of the second vehicle, unhooked the horsebox and wheeled it into the recess, leaving it parallel to the pavement. The three Hungarians heaved the blocks of ice from Marjorie's Land Rover and piled them up around the far side of the trailer. When all were out, Mrs Gritton drove off to make space for Gábor to leap onto the flatbed of Henry's lorry and start heaving at wooden cases, clinking them down to Zoltán and Attila.

With every box stacked behind the stall, Henry Gritton too drove away. Zoltán came around the front of the horsebox, unlatched the flap which Attila had cut out, and lowered it on its hinges, revealing the words, 'PapPop, the new drink sensation' painted in bold for all to see.

Zoltán then did the same with the ramp of the trailer, lowering it to the floor so he could clear out a couple of empty barrels and slide out more ice blocks by pulling their tarps to the pavement. There he grabbed a crate of bottles to bring inside, and arranged them on a back shelf so that the labels all faced forwards.

In the meantime, Attila and Gábor were breaking up the blocks with mini pickaxes, chipping off shards of ice that they dumped into the barrels by the handful. When the containers were half full, the brothers began unpacking crates by ramming bottles deep into the ice. It didn't take long to find the first problem.

Gábor poked his head inside the stall, to find Zoltán talking to two young women in pinafores who'd just turned up. "Nagyon szép itt," he said. 'It's very nice in here.' "But we've got a problem."

"Nem ár!" Zoltán replied. 'Oh no!' "Go on, tell me the worst."

"It's these labels. As soon as they come into contact with water, they come off. Look!" Gábor scraped his hands over a barrel and collected dozens of paper squares with the word PapPop hand-painted on one side.

"Baszd meg!" Zoltán cursed, running down the horse ramp and staring into a barrel, hands on his head. "Mrs Gritton spent months on those labels, and now look. They're absolutely useless. How on Earth are we going to advertise now? What am I going to do?"

The PapPop stand was one of the last stalls people saw before entering, among the first they passed as they left. So as the sun broke through the clouds, a steady stream of customers paused to try Zoltán Papp's new drink.

When Marjorie got back from parking her car she found the serving girls, in their white aprons with ribbons around their heads, busily handing out bottles and tinkling change into a box behind the counter. Up the line, dozens were enjoying their first taste of PapPop. But, leaning arms crossed against the side of the van, the inventor's face told another story.

"What's wrong, Zoltán?" asked Mrs Gritton. "Haven't you seen how much people like PapPop? I heard someone say it was just what they wanted, and that they'd be picking up more on the way out."

"That's good," said Zoltán without expression. "But they won't know what it is. Look!" He picked a bottle from a barrel and showed her the plain clear glass. "All the labels fell off."

"Oh, that is a shame," said Marjorie Gritton. "They looked really good, I thought. Still, as long as people hear the name PapPop, I'm sure they won't forget it. Can't you see how popular it is?"

Éamon O'Dillon parked his car in a field on the edge of town. When all were out and ready to go, he reached onto the parcel shelf for his beige fedora hat with 'Denton's of Stockport' printed silver in the lining. He left his gloves in its place, clunked the door locked and ran his fingers over his car's tailfins.

Doreen was wearing a felt Breton with a curled-up rim and a blue flower that matched her gloves and handbag, Linda had a brown cloche pulled down to her ears. That left the younger O'Dillon brother the only one with his head bare. And it hadn't gone unnoticed.

"You not wearing a hat?" asked Doreen.

"Na," Callum replied. "It'll ruin my hair. Besides, I don't need one in the pub, do I? Come on Éamon, I'm parched. There must be some decent boozers around here and we've not got long till opening time."

"Éamon," said his wife. "I'm not having you and your brother gallivanting off on us. We've come for a nice family day out, not for you two to disappear into a pub. Maybe when we're on the way back you might have time for an half, but not before."

"Come on Éamon," said Callum. "We've been driving for hours, and you promised me a pint as soon as we'd parked up. I thought you wore the trousers in your marriage."

"That I do my brother," said Éamon. "But I also know what'll happen if I don't do as her tells me. I'll be on dry crusts and dripping for a week. We're going to have to do what her says."

"Okay, Éamon," said the younger brother, "I see the situation. But it still don't do nothing about my thirst, does it? I just thought we could go for a nice quiet pint."

"You know what thought did, don't you?" sneered Doreen. "It followed a muck cart and thought it were a wedding. Now, I've had my say. I'm sure we'll find a water fountain or something on the way. Come along. I hear the queues get quite long."

Henry Gritton sat perched on the low balustrade wall, watching Zoltán Papp stand guard outside the front of his stall. The Hungarian's arms were still crossed, his eyes down, but now he was muttering "enjoy your PapPop" to every customer who bought a drink.

At a lull in business, Henry went over to Zoltán and put an arm around his shoulder. "What are you doing?" he asked.

"I'm telling everyone to enjoy their drinks," said Zoltán. "And trying to make sure they remember the name. It's all because of the labels."

"I get that," said Henry. "But couldn't you do it with a bit more feeling? It's just, if you say it like that, it's like you resent even being here. Maybe show a bit more life? Try to smile, maybe?"

Zoltán looked up at the farmer, nodded his head. "I guess you're right," he said. "I just thought I'd…"

Zoltán didn't get to finish his thought before Marjorie Gritton called for her husband. "It's almost half eleven," she said. "And your brother's showing at midday. You know how much he wants your support."

"He'll need all he can get with that mare of his," Henry chuckled from the depths of his gut. "If she makes it round half the jumps I'll be amazed. Are you going to be all right here for a while, Zoltán?"

"We can cope, Mr Gritton. I wish your brother very much luck."

"Good lad. Just don't forget, while I'm away, try to look like you're glad to be here. Okay?"

"Yes, Mr Gritton," Zoltán mumbled. "I understand."

By the time the O'Dillon party got to the back of the queue, it stretched all the way down to the ancient town walls. Policemen in black tunics and half-egg helmets blew whistles as they directed the crowds uphill. Amid a line of people in their best top hats and flowing dresses, they shuffled past Georgian mansions, a medieval tower, the faux-Tudor range of Shrewsbury High School.

They must've been queuing for a good hour before a kink in the road revealed the white sandstone chancel of a church. In the forecourt, people stood around a wooden tripod supporting a box that spouted tubes from its front. As the other three waved at the camera, Éamon O'Dillon crossed the road to have a word with the man holding a microphone.

By the time he returned, the others were at the foot of a pedestal to the statue of a soldier with his stone-carved rifle reversed. "ATV," Éamon announced. "They're doing a report for a show called 'Midland Montage'."

"We won't get to see it then," said Mrs O'Dillon. "That's a shame."

As they paused at the thought that regional television meant they might get on the box and never know about it, Linda looked over the hundreds of people still standing between them and the blue gates. She saw the tall white tents inside the quarry, and the horsebox painted yellow with a hatch fashioned out of one side. She nudged Callum's arm. "You still thirsty?" she asked.

"I'm spitting feathers," he replied.

"Well there's a drinks stand over there. Why don't you get yourself something?"

When they got to the stall, they found a pair of pretty girls handing out bottles. Éamon pulled a shilling from his pocket and bought two. The serving girl removed the tops and plonked the bottles on the narrow counter for Éamon to take one for his brother, one for his wife.

Callum turned the bottle up to his lips and downed it all in one. He slammed the empty bottle onto the counter and belched. "It's good, that," he said.

Éamon nodded and looked to his wife.

"He's right," she said with a satisfied sigh. "This stuff's fantastic. Tanzaro ain't a patch on it. Could be right up your street this, Éamon. Here, try some."

Éamon took the bottle and poured the liquid over his tongue. He felt the bubbles sparkle down his throat, the sour lemon and ginger aftertaste, the sweetness of the sugar. He gulped, nodded to himself and turned over the plain glass bottle in his hand.

Zoltán Papp had been watching the group, and now he interrupted. "Enjoy your PapPop," he said.

"PapPop?" asked Éamon. "So that's what it's called. And you are?"

"I'm Zoltán Papp," he said, staring straight into Éamon's eyes.

"Are you now?" Éamon pondered. "Well, it's a pleasure to meet you, Zoltán Papp. I take it this is your drink?"

"Yes sir. I adapt it from an old family recipe."

"And let me guess, your family isn't British? Where are you from, son? Poland?"

"No sir, Hungary."

"Oh really? You're not a freedom fighter, are you?"

Zoltán nodded.

"That's a great selling point for a start," Éamon continued. "And this is a pretty decent product you've got, I must say. Tell me, do you have a distributor?"

"A distributor?" Zoltán pondered the word. "I don't know sir. At the moment Mr Gritton looks after all that. He gets me the ingredient and he brings me in his lorry."

"So I should speak to Mr Gritton about business then? Is he here?"

"No sir. You should speak to me about business. This is my drink, Mr Gritton just helping me."

"Excellent. Then let's go and have a chat. This is just my line of work, Mr Papp, and I think I may be able to make you a handsome offer. Let me buy you a beer."

"Hang on a minute," said Doreen O'Dillon. "Aren't you forgetting something?"

"Sorry, my petal," said Éamon. "Me and Callum just have a bit of business to do. That all right?"

"And what do you expect us to do?" asked Linda. "Wait here like a couple of wet lettuces, talking to us handbags?"

"Of course not," said Éamon. "You go inside. We'll come find you when we're done."

"And how are you going to do that?" asked his wife. "It'll be like looking for a needle in a haystack. There'll be thousands in there, you'll never find us."

"We could set a meeting place and time," said Éamon. "How about four o'clock outside the beer stand?"

"What?" said Doreen. "So you can carry on getting tanked up?"

"Not at all, my petal," said her husband. "It's just business, that's all."

"And does this business involve drinking six pints of Best Bitter, by chance?"

"It's about this drink," Éamon turned the bottle in his hand, "this PapPop. PapPop..." He smiled to himself. "Even the name's got a ring to it. You tasted it, you yourself said it was great, that Tanzaro weren't a patch on it, was your words. This just might be the opportunity I've been waiting for, my chance to cash in on all my hard work. If I could do this deal, Dors, it could change all our lives forever."

Mrs O'Dillon shook her head slowly. "I don't know, Éamon," she said. "You always find a way to get around me, don't you? Why does this meeting have to be in a pub?"

"This is gentlemen's business, my petal, and we need to be among gentlemen to do such a thing. Come on, we can still all enjoy our day out, and if things go well, we might be in for a whole lot more nice days."

"All right Éamon," said his wife. "Go do your business. But please don't have a skin-full, your driving's all over the shop when you've had a few."

As the O'Dillons talked, Zoltán glanced at the Bacsik brothers perched on the wall, smoking cigarettes as they eyed up the young women queuing past.

"Figyetek!" Zoltán shouted. 'Oi,' "I'm going with this pair."

Attila looked up. "Hova?" he asked 'Where to?'

"To the pub."

"Do you want some back up?" asked Gábor. "There's nothing for us to do here."

Zoltán glanced between the brothers. "I don't know," he said. "I don't really want to leave the van unguarded. There's a lot of money in there now, and what if something happens to the drink? Won't one of you stay here and one come with me?"

Attila Bacsik threw his cigarette to the floor and stamped it out on the paving slab with a turn of his toe. "I'll come with you," he said, getting himself onto his feet. "I don't like the look of that pair, they've got enough grease in their hair to keep a train running for a week. You stay here Gábor, I'll bring you something back."

"Are you alright guarding the van then, Gábor?" asked Zoltán.

Gábor shrugged.

"I can trust you, can't I?" Zoltán continued.

"Of course," Gábor replied. "What do you expect me to do? Just make sure you bring me back more than just a half pint of ale."

The crowds, it seemed, were either queuing for the show or actually inside, because the side lanes of Shrewsbury were virtually empty. Past rows of brick townhouses, the two Hungarians followed the O'Dillon brothers to the bottle-green door of a pub, where flowers hung from baskets between the upstairs windows. Inside, the room stank of pipe smoke and stale beer. The walls were bare brick, the ceiling pieced together from the boughs of old ships. Men sat, crowded around copper-topped tables, chatting, laughing, occasionally bursting into song as they enjoyed the exceptional licensing hours of show day, and the chance to drink all afternoon.

Éamon barged to the bar and ordered three pints of Best Bitter.

"Order for yourselves," said Zoltán. "I will buy my own and one for my friend."

"Oh," said Éamon, surveying Attila for the first time. "I didn't realise we had company, especially not someone of this fella's stature." He turned back to the bar. "Better make that four pints please, barman."

Éamon pointed towards a table in the far corner, and the Hungarians sat on wooden stools as they waited for the drinks. Éamon and Callum set down a glass of brown brew before every man, then pulled up stools for themselves. "So," said Éamon. "Is this your business partner?"

"No," Zoltán replied.

"He looks like security to me," said Callum. "He looks like he could crack your neck soon as look at you."

"He is my friend," said Zoltán. "We are together since Hungary and him and his brother are the only family I have. And he barely speak English. So whatever you say will go no further than this table. Now, I thought you wanted to discuss business."

"Straight to the point," said Éamon. "I like that in a man. Listen Mr Papp, I'm not one to mess around either. I'm going to make you an offer for your drink. How does a hundred pounds sound to you?"

"What for?"

"For the recipe and the name. You can keep the horsebox."

"A hundred pounds!?" cried Zoltán. "I might be an immigrant, Mr O'Dillon, but that doesn't make me an idiot. We'll make more than that today alone!"

"All right," said Éamon. "What if we increase the offer? How about two thousand?"

"I thought you invited me here to talk business, not for insult me." Zoltán stood up and so did Attila, pint glass in his hand.

"Hold your horses, son," said Éamon, "you haven't even finished your pints and there's still so much to talk about. Come on, sit back down."

Zoltán did so and Attila followed.

"Look," Éamon continued, "let me explain. I'm in the fruit-drinks business, have been for years. Ask anyone at the Manchester Bottlers' Association. I've got contacts with all the main wholesalers and friends in important places. I know what it takes to make it in this industry. I can get your PapPop into every shop in the land. Can you imagine that? There'll be adverts on Independent Television and everything."

"You want to put PapPop on television?" asked Zoltán.

"Of course," said Éamon. "It's the only way to go these days. The company I currently work for is dying on its feet because their advertising looks like a six-year-old drew it. But I've seen what it takes – a bit of sparkle, like PapPop for the eyes. You need to give this drink the success it deserves. Isn't that what you want?"

"Of course that's what I want. But I'm not going to sell it to you."

Éamon nodded. "I understand you, Zoltán," he said, "I really do. But we're grown men, I'm sure we can find a solution that benefits us all. We need something that's fair on all sides, an equal split."

"You mean fifty-fifty?"

"I was thinking more a three-way partnership," said Éamon, supping at the foam. "You, me, and my brother. You wouldn't have to put in a penny you understand, we'll arrange all the funding and the distribution."

"But then you have all the control," said Zoltán. "I know how good is this drink, Mr O'Dillon, and I know how much people like it. I already grow the business on my own and if I need any help I'm sure I can find someone. Mr Percy Thrower is a family friend, for instance. And it's already in the local shop."

"What? In Shrewsbury?"

"Clun."

"Where?"

"Clun. It's an hour from here, in the countryside near to Wales."

"Have you ever heard of that place, Callum?"

Callum shook his head.

Éamon O'Dillon put down his pint and leaned in. "You're in a place no one's ever heard of, Zoltán," he said. "Who are you planning to sell this to? The sheep? Manchester's a city of a million people, twice that if you count everyone around, in the mill-towns where I have all my clients. It's simple stuff, you need to be near your customers, and well enough connected to be able to get your drink to market. Even London."

"London?" Zoltán asked. "You think we could sell PapPop in London?"

"One step at a time, son. Remember, this is my profession. First we go for the local market in the north west. We build up a following there. And then, when we're strong enough and making enough out of it, we'll take it nationwide. These are things that a farmer and you and your refugee mates simply can't make happen. But this is what I can offer you."

"I'm glad for your offer, Mr O'Dillon," said Zoltán. "And I can see that it would be good for us all to work together. But there is not a chance I'm going to give up this drink to a couple of strangers I meet on the street."

Éamon nodded. "I completely understand," he said. "You want to keep control of your product, that's fair enough. If I'd come up with something that good, I wouldn't want to give it away either. But think a little about what we'll put in. We'll get you a factory in Manchester to work from, fitted with all the equipment you tell us you need. We'll get it into shops and cafes all over, you'll see. Why don't we say fifty-one-forty-nine? With you the majority shareholder. How does that sound?"

Zoltán pondered a moment, ran both sets of fingers over his cropped head and looked Éamon O'Dillon square in the eyes. "Where will we live?" he asked.

"I'll get you a place," said Éamon. "Somewhere close to the factory. You set out your terms and we'll do everything we can to meet them. We'll even wait until you're satisfied before signing the registration papers, if that's what you want."

Zoltán shook his head. "I still don't know that I can trust you," he said. "You speak like fine man. You use fancy words and make great promises, but I don't know who are you. How you expect me to trust you?"

"We'll prove it to you," said Éamon.

"Will we?" asked Callum.

"Yes," said Éamon. "Here's what I'm going to do. I'm going to get your drink on television, tonight." He turned to his brother. "They have ATV in Clun, don't you reckon?"

"If they can get any signal at all out there," said Callum, "they should do."

"Right," said Éamon, returning his attention to Zoltán Papp. "When you go home tonight, make sure you find a television and tune into channel three for a programme called Midland Montage. I'll expect a call from you in the morning."

He pushed a business card across the table and downed his pint. "Now, if you don't mind, my brother and I have some work to do. I look forward to hearing from you."

And with that, the O'Dillons got up and left.

Clun

It was still light by the time the Grittons and Hungarians got back to the farm that evening, with every bottle clinking empty in the crates. While the Bacsiks headed to the Stag for more drinking, Zoltán accepted Marjorie's invitation for tea.

Mrs Gritton served up a dinner of fried eggs, chips and beans, which she, Henry and Zoltán ate in the dining room before making their way to the lounge at the back of the farmhouse. Behind glass-panelled doors sat a neat garden and vegetable patch, but no one was bothered about outside.

In the corner was a wooden box with a little curved screen. Henry went straight over, turned one of the two dials and a black and white image faded into view, showing a cartoon advert for breakfast cereal.

Henry joined his wife on the sofa and Marjorie asked, "Is your brother not joining us?"

"No," said her husband, "He's still in a huff from the horse leaping. I've never seen him so angry at an animal."

"Me neither," said Marjorie. "Still, the show wasn't a total write off. Wasn't Aunt Agnes' flower display magnificent?"

"It certainly was," said Henry. "She thoroughly deserved that award."

"The Boyne Trophy's a really big thing," said Marjorie.

"I know," said her husband.

The adverts morphed into the two-eyed logo of ATV, flashing blue in the twilight, and they stopped to listen. The first report was from Shrewsbury.

"Look, Zoltán!" said Marjorie Gritton, "there's the van. There's Gábor!"

"Give it a rest a mo, won't you Marjorie?" said her husband. "Let's listen to what they're saying."

"Good idea," said his wife, leaping forward to turn up the volume knob.

"… Hungarian freedom fighters," the news reporter was saying, "showing once again the extra flavour our new foreign friends are bringing to the British Isles. His carbonated fruit drink went down a storm. Let's hope it doesn't take long to get PapPop on the shelves of every corner shop in the country. Meanwhile, in the horse leaping, Mr Charlesworth of Crewe won both grades A and B..."

Henry Gritton slapped Zoltán's knee. "Did you hear that, son?" he said. "On the shelves of every corner shop in Britain. You must be over the moon."

"Of course," said Zoltán. "That's what I want. I'm just not sure I want to be in business with the O'Dillon brothers. I don't know those guys, maybe they want steal PapPop or something."

"Ah, Zoltán!" said Henry. "Will you never see the bright side of anything? Come on, let's have a drink. I'm not normally meant to on a week night, but tonight we should celebrate. I'll go and get the whisky." He turned to his wife. "That all right with you, love?" he asked.

"I guess so," said Marjorie. "Just go easy on it, you know how you get after a couple."

10. Action

15th May 2035
In an aeroplane, destination classified

At just twenty-four years old, eighteen months after signing up and with no combat experience outside of simulations, Zoltan O'Dillon would never have been made Lieutenant-Colonel of any normal army, especially not with his reputation. But PapSec was no ordinary outfit, and Zoltan O'Dillon was not a regular man.

Despite the awards and the legend, Zoltan O'Dillon never visited Jebel Shams. His first and only act as Lieutenant-Colonel would be to lead a battalion into action thousands of miles from the Arabian peninsula. Not that anyone had been informed of that beforehand; the pilot himself only found out when they were over the Mediterranean, the passengers asleep.

There were a hundred seats on their Nordenfelt N630 jumpjet, but only three were occupied. Of Zoltan O'Dillon, Larry Pickering and Bernie Douglas-FitzAllan, it was the latter who awoke first that morning, was the first to peer through an oval window. But what he found below was not the blinding sand he'd been expecting. Rather, it was a landscape crumpled with mountains, where emerald capillaries disappeared into beige prairies.

Bernie reached for the panel above his head, clicked a button and his bed folded up into an armchair. He shuffled his buttocks to allow the night's sheets to be sucked into the armrests, glanced over at Zoltan O'Dillon to find the Lieutenant-Colonel lying face-up horizontal, snoring. "Zollers!" Bernie whispered.

More snoring.

"Zoltan!" he said louder, stretching out a black patent shoe and kicking his friend's dangling hand. "Zoltan!" he said a third time.

"What is it, Bernie?" O'Dillon replied without opening his eyes.

"Have a look outside."

"Why? What time is it?"

"It's eight o'clock. Look outside."

"What's so urgent about outside? It'll just be sand for as far as you can see. I've flown over deserts before you know."

"But that's just it. We're not over any desert. Have a look."

The Lieutenant-Colonel tutted, stretched up to the control panel and his bed folded away. But rather than glance through the window, he reached into a jacket pocket for his Xi-fan sheet, pulled out the corners to the size of a paperback and swiped the surface with his fingertips. A couple more flicks brought up a satellite view of the Earth. Then, by pulling thumb and forefinger apart over his device, he zoomed into a red dot flashing out their position. Only now did he glance outside. "You're right, Bernie," he said. "We're not over the Middle East. That's Africa down there.."

"What the bloody hell are we doing over Africa?" Bernie shrieked. "I thought we were supposed to be joining the Arabian Campaign! Have we been hi-jacked? Are we heading for the Angolan front? The fighting in those jungles is meant to be pretty hairy. Much better to be in the desert where we can see the enemy, don't you agree Zoltan?"

"Relax, Bernie," O'Dillon replied, scrolling over his Xi-fan sheet. "Don't get your knickers in a twist. There's an update on the mission notes. We're heading for South Africa, somewhere called Gariepdam."

"And what for crying out loud will we be doing there?" Bernie continued. "I told you I want to be kept well behind the lines, Zoltan. I really don't want to be involved in any fighting. You know I can't stand the sight of blood."

"Stop stressing, Bernie, for Papp's sake! We'll get the rest of the orders when we land. Just remember you're with me. What could possibly go wrong?"

"With you, Zoltan, anything could happen…"

They followed a stretch of jade as it meandered through copper-coloured hills. When the river widened into a lake, the peaks became bush-dotted islands.

Engines howled as they slowed over a concrete dam. Atop the closest promontory, the pilot lowered the plane onto a square of tarmac painted with lines and curves like the floor of a sports hall, its sides barely wide enough for the wings. The wheels kissed the ground and three hundred tons of aluminium landed like a feather, despite the gale blowing outside.

Gariepdam, South Africa

From the belt around his waist and shoulder, to the dark glasses and twilled regimentals, when Zoltan O'Dillon appeared at the door of the plane he looked every inch the military dictator. On his shoulders, black epaulettes stood out against his garish yellow uniform, sporting a golden pip below a single crown and the initials PS, for PapSec, scrawled above them in lightning-like lettering. He stepped onto the escalator and let it glide him towards the floor.

After him came Bernie the Earl. In a black suit with a yellow tie tucked into his waistcoat, he looked like he'd have been more comfortable on the benches of the House of Lords than on active combat. Which was the opposite of Larry Pickering, who was the last to descend the moving stairway, and did so in British Army khaki.

One after another they sat themselves into the back of a Pap-yellow Land Rover. Bernie clunked the door to and the driver was away, racing towards a cut-out in the rust-coloured rocks. They barely glanced at the lake below, hardly noticed the conical islands or the dam curving white like the frame of a picture. They certainly didn't see the people occupying the bridge with their flags and their drums and their games.

Zoltan pulled his Xi-fan sheet to the width of his shoulders and laid it on his knees. He swiped his fingers over the screen, tapping the surface like he was playing piano. He stopped and looked to his advisors. "I can't connect," he said. "I thought Xi-fan sheets covered the whole globe, so what's wrong with this one now? It worked before."

"That'll be the M.R.S," said Pickering. "The magnetic fields must scramble data connections as much as they do bullets."

"Then turn it off!" said Zoltan. "I need to get my orders. How can we speak to the driver?"

Zoltan flicked across his Xi-fan sheet for the driver-call icon. Bernie searched the cab for a button. But Pickering leaned forward and knocked on the window separating the front and back compartments. It rolled down. "Turn off the shields, driver," said the elder man. "Your Lieutenant-Colonel needs to make a call."

"Shta?" the driver responded. "Ne razumem engleski!"

"What did he say?" asked Bernie.

"No idea," said Larry, sitting back. "I guess he doesn't speak English."

"He doesn't speak English?" screeched O'Dillon. "What use is that? We're thousands of miles from our supposed destination and I need to speak to my commanding officer. Who is the commanding officer for this mission anyway, Pickering?"

"Brigadier Francis Atkins."

"Bomber Atkins?" said Zoltan. "What's he doing commanding an operation like this?"

"That I couldn't tell you," said Pickering. "All I know is that your father regards him very highly, and therefore gives him command of PapSec's more delicate operations."

"Oh, God!" Zoltan sneered. "I hope he's not another of Lord Mike's band of brownnoses. I've got enough of that with you, Pickering."

PapSec's base for the mission was a scaled-down version of what would one day cover Manchester and so much else – five miniature Bio-domes lined up along the tallest ridge. They pulled to a halt under the first dome, and when Zoltan got out the wind almost blow off his cap. Glass rattled in the zig-zag steel above. And below the roof's cover, men in tight black uniforms stood in ranks, berets slanted over their heads, rifles balanced against their boots.

A stocky man in baggier black marched forward with a pace stick under his arm. Following on his heels came two taller men, their heads shaven under black berets, chins stubbled, eyes deep set. "Lieutenant-Colonel O'Dillon, sir!" shouted the first man, saluting. "Sir, please allow me to introduce Major Branimir Stankovitch and Major Budimir Stankovitch, sir!"

Five hundred troops clicked their heels together as one. The men saluted and Zoltan touched a finger to his forehead. "Are they related?" he asked.

"Sir, yes sir," the man shouted. "They're identical twins, sir. And they've asked me to relay a message to you, sir. Major Stankovitch and Major Stankovitch would like to express their pleasure at being posted under a man so obviously destined for higher things. They are looking forward to working with you and to the swift and successful completion of this mission, sir."

"Right," said Zoltan. "Why can't they tell me this themselves? And who are you anyway?"

"Sir, I'm Regimental Sergeant Major Terzitch, sir," he shouted. "Reporting for duty. They can't tell you themselves, sir, because they don't speak English, sir."

"Oh, good God!" said Zoltan. "Does no-one here speak English? Go on then, what do they speak?"

"Serbian, sir. They can also communicate in Russian, German and a bit of Hungarian. But I'm afraid no English, sir."

"And does that go for the troops as well?"

"Sir, the vast majority, sir, yes."

Zoltan O'Dillon shook his head. "What use is an army if they can't even understand basic instructions?"

"Sir, if I may, sir?" the Sergeant Major continued. "Here you have some of the sharpest combat troops on the planet. We're Greyskies' 88 battalion. This is our first deployment as a PapSec unit, sir."

"Well, that's obvious," said Zoltan, "they look like they need a good kicking into shape. But Greyskies doesn't exist anymore, Sergeant Major, you should be in PapSec uniforms."

"Sir, yes, sir. It's just they haven't arrived yet, sir."

"They haven't arrived?" O'Dillon sneered. "How long have you been here?"

"Almost seven weeks, sir. We've not been allowed to leave the base in all that time, and we're running low on most supplies, sir."

"Well, that's no good at all. We need to speak to my commanding officer this instant. Come on."

Zoltan charged off around his yellow SUV and the others followed on, none closer than Larry Pickering. "I see you're not in correct attire either," said Zoltan. "Why didn't you order a PapSec uniform?"

"I did," Pickering replied, "eighteen months ago. And I'm still waiting for it. These fatigues are from one of my tours of Afghanistan. I might've been a kid then, but they still fit. Even though I only made colour sergeant, I'm still a damned sight more experienced in combat than you or Bernie."

"So the only person in this entire operation wearing a PapSec uniform, is me?" asked Zoltan.

"It would appear so, yes," Pickering replied. "And yours seems to be the only PapSec regulation vehicle."

O'Dillon shook his head, took his Xi-fan sheet from his pocket and pulled it out as wide as his arms would go. He balanced it on the car door and the ground, then tapped a few icons and the screen went blank. A tone rang out. He took three steps backwards to stand between his advisors on one arm, his senior officers and their translator on the other.

The screen filled with the face of Brigadier Atkins, all pink cheeks and blue eyes below a PapSec beret. The men stamped their heels, saluted as one, and the Brigadier tapped a finger to his forehead. "At ease, gentlemen," he said. "That's quite a view you have behind you."

"Is it?" Zoltan replied. "We haven't noticed. We haven't had time to notice. There are too many things to do to notice. Where on Earth are we, for a start?"

"If you've noticed anything," said the Brigadier. "It's probably that you're not in the Middle East. That expanse of water down below you is PapAqua's largest reservoir in southern Africa. Without exclusive access to that water, there'd be shortages of PapPop throughout the continent. A gang of natives have been stealing from the lake for some time, depleting the water levels. Now they've broken through the fences to occupy the dam wall. Your mission objective will be to secure the perimeter for PapCorp. But only when the time is right."

"And when will that be?" asked Zoltan.

"When I tell you it is, Lieutenant-Colonel."

"When my men have uniforms, you mean?"

"That'll be a start, yes," Atkins nodded. "It's been no small task assimilating Spokane's army of 80,000 into PapSec, let me tell you. And right now, uniforms are pretty low on our list of priorities. Do you have all the armaments at least?"

Zoltan glanced to the Sergeant Major, who shouted, "Sir, yes sir! We're well-stocked for ammo, sir, but fuel and food supplies are low, sir!"

"Yes," said the image of Francis Atkins. "I imagined they might be. You can expect a drop in a day or two. You'll be given good notice so as to prepare the men. Until then, your order is to stay put and wait."

"So we've flown all the way here just to sit around and do nothing?" asked Zoltan.

"For now, Lieutenant-Colonel, yes."

"Then why are we even here?" O'Dillon snapped at the screen. But it had gone blank. Zoltan huffed and looked to his advisors. "So what now?" he asked.

"Looks like we're going to have to lay low for a while," said Bernie. "Let's get the whisky out of the car, crack open a bottle and celebrate our safe arrival."

"Sir, if I may, sir," shouted the Sergeant Major. "Sir, we've been up here for seven weeks already, sir. Major Stankovitch and Major Stankovitch would like to request permission to take a closer look at our opponents, sir."

"You mean just the two of them?" asked Zoltan.

"Sir, no, sir. They mean everyone, sir."

"Yes," Zoltan pondered. "I was thinking something similar myself. I see we're going to get along just fine, you, me and the Stankovitches." Bernie sniggered but Zoltan ignored him. "Go and ready the vehicles!" he ordered. "Get the troops all loaded up, then wait for my instruction. Got that?"

"Sir, yes sir!" the Sergeant Major yelled, turned on his toes and marched away.

Zoltan was about to follow when Larry Pickering grabbed his arm. "What are you doing?" he said. "You heard what the Brigadier said as clearly as any of us. His strict instructions were not to leave the base and your first action is to disobey them?"

"Listen, Larry," said Zoltan. "You're here in a private advisory role, so don't push it. My officers and I have made a military decision on which you are not authorised to comment. I'll not hear another word. Now come on Bernie, get your shit together. I want you in the jeep with me."

"I think Pickering has a point, Zollers," said Bernie. "I mean, orders are orders and you can't just choose to disobey them when you feel like it. Besides, fuel's low, the Sergeant Major just said so."

"Bernie, stop being a pussy. We'll get a fuel drop soon, so in the meantime let's use what we have. Come on. You too Pickering. Let's go."

"Zoltan," said Pickering. "You're defying a direct order. Call this off before it's too late."

"You'd love that, wouldn't you?" O'Dillon sneered. "If I withdraw the first order I've given to my new battalion, I'll make myself look a complete imbecile. I've often thought you try to undermine me, Larry Pickering, but this just about takes the biscuit. Now come on, the pair of you. Let's go or I'll set the firing squad on you."

Their convoy consisted of dozens of vans and trucks, all matt black with the outlines of the Greyskies and Spokane logos still visible on the bodywork. At the head of the line was the only PapSec vehicle, on whose back seat Zoltan and Bernie were joking around.

"Major Stankovitch!" Zoltan sniggered. "Sounds like Bernie after a night on the vodka, although you'd be Major Stinkovitch, wouldn't you, Bern?"

"And you'd be Major Snoravitch!" Bernie retorted.

"You can talk..."

"Will the pair of you cut this out!" Pickering snapped from in between the men. "You're acting like a pair of kids. This is a very serious situation."

"You're right there," said Zoltan. "A mission in which no one can talk to each other because the M.R.S. fucks their Comms devices."

"Only this car has M.R.S." said Pickering. "The others are just old Greyskies stock. Remember RAF Snetterton? Well those are the same grade vehicles."

Zoltan tutted. "How are we going to turn it off?" he asked. "That's what I want to know. How can I confer with my officers?"

"We're not turning it off," said Pickering. "If you manage to get yourself sent home in a body bag, Zoltan, your father will make sure I'm not far behind you. You know I'm going to have to have words with him as it is, so let's just make sure all this goes off without incident."

"If they didn't want incidents," said Zoltan, "then why have I been given such a notorious bunch of thugs as 88 Battalion? Everyone knows what they did in Tirana. And now I've got them here under my command, even if they are still in their old uniforms. We all heard Brigadier Atkins' instructions, but only I was privy to his real intentions. What he was telling me was we can't have these natives blowing up the dam before we even get the chance to suss them out."

If Zoltan O'Dillon, or anyone else, had bothered to do any research, they'd have known that their opponents had no intention of harming the dam. Neither were they looking to fight; this was a show of solidarity, not of force. Old and young, women, men, and children, all had gathered from nearby homesteads to demand water for their parched lands and families, water they were denied by a foreign corporation with the law on its side; PapAqua owned the rights to every drop of the Orange River from the Drakensburg to the Atlantic.

Their cause had cut through racial barriers like nothing before in South Africa, uniting white Afrikaners with their black Xhosa and Sotho country-folk. The movement had built such momentum over the past few months that this could have been a defining moment in post-apartheid history, one in which people of all colours came to see each other as human beings, not as master and servant, ally not foe. But fate had other ideas.

Although they'd seen it from above, it was only when they got to shore level that Zoltan and his advisors saw how low the reservoir had got. At the base of every shrub-strewn peak, the water had receded and the mud dried until it cracked into geometric tears.

All were so taken with the parched lakesides that they only noticed the convoy slowing down when the view vanished behind slanted ventilation fins in concrete housings. At that moment, they turned as one to gaze through the windscreen.

Just yards away, children had been playing cricket. They stopped where they were to gawp at the great convoy of trucks and cars descending. Behind them stood their parents and hundreds of other adults, all dressed up for the occasion: tall white men in slouch hats and khaki shorts that finished well up their thighs, black women in intricately striped dresses and vibrant headscarfs, men holding pointed-oval shields cut from cow's hides, wearing feather headdresses but very little else, waving their knobkieries.

On the back seat, Zoltan O'Dillon tapped in anger at the surface of his Xi-fan sheet. "I need to confer with my officers," he said.

"Why?" Larry replied. "You know your orders. You've seen what you wanted. I suggest you turn around and go back."

"And how do you expect me to do…"

There was a bang on the roof, then another. Something smashed the windscreen and Zoltan ducked behind the driver's seat. "What the bloody hell was that?" he yelled.

"It was a stone," said Pickering, watching through the shattered front window. "That little girl just threw it."

"A little girl threw a stone and it got through the M.R.S?" said Zoltan. "What's wrong with the shielding?"

"Nothing," said Pickering. "It only works on metal, not stones."

"Right, that's it," said Zoltan, letting himself out of the cab. He crouched behind the open door, out of range of the shielding. Another pebble rang against the metal surface. He stretched out his Xi-fan sheet and tapped a couple of times until his Sergeant Major appeared before him. "It's pretty hairy out here, Terzitch."

"Sir, we can see that, sir," the NCO replied. "Major Stankovitch and Major Stankovitch think this clearly constitutes engagement on behalf of the enemy. They feel that we should reply with force, sir."

"My thoughts exactly," O'Dillon replied. "Muster the troops Sergeant Major, on my order I want them to fire at will."

O'Dillon stuck his head back into the car, "we're going in," he said to his advisors.

"You're doing what!?" Larry Pickering screamed. "Those are not your orders, Zoltan! You are exceeding your authority and I'm obliged to stop you."

"Stop me? Try stopping five hundred MX75 machine guns. I've given the order to muster. They're just waiting for me to give the signal. And knowing this lot, I probably won't be able to hold them for long."

"Zoltan, there are women and children in there."

"Look, if you bring your wife with you into battle, or arm your kids with stones and cricket bats and put them on the front line, then they become targets just like everyone else. Those people out there are occupying private land, they've been stealing PapCorp's property and preventing our employees from doing their jobs. They have now engaged us and they have to be cleared."

"I hardly think stone throwing constitutes engagement," said Pickering.

"Well there, I'm afraid, your opinion differs from that of my officers and myself. We're going in."

"But they weren't your orders!" Pickering persisted.

"Bollocks to orders, Larry. We're here on the ground for a reason, and that reason is not to sit up at the base and work on our suntans. We're soldiers, and our job is to take action. Why else send me 88 battalion?"

"A soldier's job is to follow orders, Zoltan."

"That's enough, Pickering. I don't want to hear another word from you until we're back at the barracks. Now are you coming, Bernie, or are you just going to sit there with your fat belly hanging out?"

"I told you I don't want to see blood, Zollers," said Bernie the Earl.

"You two are a whole lot of use, aren't you?" said Zoltan. "All I can say is it's a good job I've got five hundred troops to back me up, because if it was only you two I'd be screwed."

Zoltan O'Dillon ducked back out behind his car door. Beyond the shielding, he tapped furiously at the screen until the image of the Sergeant Major reappeared. "Are the men ready?" he asked.

"Sir, yes, sir!" the Sergeant Major replied. "Ready and waiting your order."

"Very good," said Zoltan. "Fire at will."

The clattering of guns went on for minutes, long after there was anyone left moving on the bridge. Shouting at his Xi-fan sheet, Zoltan O'Dillon called "ceasefire!" four times before silence fell. "Sergeant Major," he said, when finally they could talk. "I want the troops to advance, to check every body and make sure no one escapes. I don't want to leave a single witness. Do you understand?"

"Sir, yes sir," the Sergeant Major responded. "Consider it done, sir."

A thousand feet marched between the cars, spread out to survey every bloodied form. Young and old alike, if they looked like they were still breathing the assassins administered a few rounds to the head and they struggled no more.

Only when all the troops had trampled past did Larry Pickering come out to contemplate the scene. "This is a fine mess," he said. "Look at those bodies in the water. People were jumping over the sides to try and save themselves. You'll have to fish them out. The entire point of this exercise was to secure PapAqua's reservoir. The last thing anyone wants is for you to go and poison the supply by creating a cholera epidemic or something."

"You're right, Larry," said O'Dillon.

"I normally am," Pickering replied. "You should've listened to me before all this got so out of hand."

"Don't take that tone with me, Larry. We're all in this together now, we have to deal with it as a team like we always do. It's not like you and Bernie did much to stop us."

"You threatened to have me gunned down, Zoltan."

"That's what you say. The only other witnesses were a driver who speaks no English and Bernie Douglas-FitzAllan, and we both know whose side he'll take. Where is that old dog the Earl anyway?"

"See for yourself," Pickering pointed towards their jeep. "He's in there."

Zoltan O'Dillon peered inside the staff car. "Good God Bernie," said Zoltan, wafting a hand in front of his nose. "Talk about Major Stinkovitch! Have you shit yourself?"

The Earl of Angus was leaning his forehead into his palms. "I told you, Zoltan," Bernie said between sobs. "I told you I didn't want to see any blood. Then you went and did that. I'll never be able to forget this. I'll be having nightmares for the rest of my life."

"Oh, grow up Bernie, we're not in kindergarten now. And get yourself changed. You've got your luggage in the boot, see if you can squeeze your stinking fat arse into something else. It looks like we're going to have a bit of a bonfire. I'd advise you throw that old suit on it too." He slammed the door shut, then looked up to see his soldiers piling body on limp and bloodied body in the middle of the road. But Larry Pickering was nowhere to be seen.

That's because Pickering had climbed over the railings and was sitting on a maintenance platform, his feet dangling over the edge. He didn't look down, he didn't look anywhere in fact but at the Xi-fan sheet he'd pulled to the size of a postcard. Larry Pickering was so enthralled in his conversation with Lord Michael O'Dillon that he didn't clock the fingertips beside him.

"I had a feeling something like this would happen," PapCorp's CEO was saying. "I guess it was a bit daft sending him down there in the first place, worse still that he was there with that gang of incorrigible hooligans from 88 Battalion. Still, at least they weren't in PapSec uniforms, so if word ever gets out it'll look like a rogue unit of ex-Greyskies soldiers who went mad. And he did get the dam cleared, which was the objective after all. You leave the rest with me, Larry. I'll manage it from here. I'll make sure this never happened, that you were all obviously in some other place."

"Sir, with all due respect," said Pickering. "Don't you think your son should face disciplinary charges for this? I mean, what just happened was basically a war crime."

"There's no basically about it, Larry," said Lord Michael. "From what you've told me, you've just witnessed a massacre. I'll deal with my boy, you don't worry about that. What I need from you is silence. But then again, your discretion is precisely why I employ you to look after him. And you know how highly I value your loyalty. I'll make sure you're properly rewarded, Larry Pickering, have no fear there. How does a knighthood sound?"

"Very good, sir," Pickering replied.

"Excellent," said Lord Michael. "Now go back up there and do the best you can. They're going to need you." And with that, O'Dillon Senior vanished.

Larry Pickering shrank his Xi-fan sheet to the size of a stamp, plopped it into his shirt pocket and picked his feet out of the gorge. As he stood to gaze over the sandy valley, he heard a whimper from below. He peered over the platform edge and saw the blond head of a boy hanging on with his fingers. Larry knelt down to lift the kid up onto the concrete platform, then ushered him into the shadows against the dam wall.

"You sit here," said Pickering. "I'll stand guard above and make sure no one looks down. Just stay close to the wall and keep quiet. When night comes and everyone's gone, then you should go home." Larry put a foot on the stepladder. "Oh," he said, turning to the boy, "and I really am very very sorry."

11. Revolution

5th May 2045
Rusholme

Brian Brownlow came downstairs in his brilliant-yellow jacket and matching peaked cap. He found his wife curled up on the sofa and the TV blaring. He reached for the remote control, zapped the screen off and Minnie opened her eyes. "Hey," she said. "I was watching that."

"You were asleep."

"I just closed my eyelids for five minutes," she said, rubbing her face and sitting up. "Did you see the result?"

"I saw," said Brian. "A hung Parliament's what they're calling it."

"A hung Parliament?" Minnie replied. "RASCAL blooming won!"

"Well, I don't know, that's just what I heard. I've got to go to work."

"Why? What time is it?"

"Gone eight."

Minnie jumped to her feet. "Then why didn't you get me up earlier?" she said, "I still need to get Naomi ready."

"She's awake," said Brian. "I told her to get up, but you know what she's like." He pecked his wife's cheek and disappeared out the front door.

After washing and dressing her three-year-old, taking her to the toilet at least four times, Minnie Brownlow allowed herself a moment of television while Naomi put on her shoes. The pictures showed a mass of people surrounding cars that were inching their way through the crowds.

"There's Harry Lanker," a woman commentated. "In the middle of the five-car motorcade. He's just leaving the third-floor council flat in Bethnal Green where he grew up, where his mother still lives and which has been, up to today, Mr Lanker's official London residence. Their route will take them through the City, along Fleet Street and the Strand to Trafalgar Square.

Then down the Mall they'll go, into the Palace where we're hearing the King has spoken to the outgoing Prime Minister and accepted her resignation."

London

On the back seat of the new Prime Minister's Rover P9, Harry Lanker hadn't a moment to himself. Every time he finished a call on his PapDrive specs, there'd be another waiting. When finally he got a free moment, he lifted his glasses to his forehead and rubbed his eyes. He glanced outside, to find his escort crawling towards the end of a narrow lane, motorbikes speeding past on both sides to clear a path onto the main road.

Prime Minister Lanker leaned forward and tapped his driver on the shoulder. "What a night eh, Samuel?" he said. "You doing all right there?"

"Yes, thank you, sir," said Samuel Dietrich.

"Don't call me sir, Sam. You know I don't like it."

"Yes, Harry, of course. It was just, I thought, as you're going to be Prime Minister and everything, that maybe you'd changed your mind."

"Don't be daft," said Harry Lanker. "Now more than ever it's vital that people don't put me on a pedestal. Prime Minister means the first servant of the people, Samuel, you know that. Now, are you going to have a snooze when we get to Downing Street? You deserve it."

"Sure I will, Harry," said his driver. "How about you?"

"I'm running on adrenaline," said the PM. "That should see me through the days ahead." He tucked a strand of hair between his ear and the frame of his PapDrive specs.

The motorcade crossed onto Ludgate Hill and Harry Lanker glanced to his left, where the three domed towers of St Paul's loomed above red or yellow buses. "I camped there once," he said. "I was nineteen. I guess you could call that my first real political act. I was so excited to be part of it that I stayed every night, even though most people went home and just left their tents. That was thirty-five years ago, Samuel. And now I'm being escorted to Buckingham Palace to ask for the King's approval to run the country. What a ride its been!"

"A real rollercoaster," said his driver. "I was thinking about that day in Stoke, when we thought the police were going to smash our heads in. You spoke for about five minutes, and by the end the police officers were chanting your name as loud as anyone. No one'd ever seen anything like it."

"That was quite something," the Prime Minister mused. "Were you there the day we dressed as cows and occupied the offices of Moon Burger?"

"No, but I remember the story. Didn't the police refuse to charge you because there were no laws about arresting livestock?"

"Yep," Harry smiled. "They were good days, but there'll be none of that larking around anymore. I honestly thought we'd had it so many times. Remember when Swindon Council declared bankruptcy after it turned out every single RASCAL councillor had been transferring public money to bank accounts in the Virgin Islands? And there was all that hullaballoo in North Yorkshire. What was that guy's name again? Paul Brodie?

"Broddle," said his driver.

"That was him. You knew him, didn't you?"

"I met him a couple of times, that's all."

"Oh, okay. I lose track these days, there's so much to remember all the time. I thought you were in the same constituency party."

"We were for a bit," said Samuel, "but didn't really have much to do with each other. Isn't it amazing how many people have turned out?"

"It certainly is that," said Harry, glancing at the crowds down every inch of either pavement, cheering and applauding as if for a race.

Rusholme

As they did every weekday, Minnie and Naomi walked hand-in-hand to the food exchange. And as usual when they arrived, the little one ran off to join the other kids in the creche that'd been put up in a far corner.

Banners hung from the steel rafters of the former supermarket. Minnie had been one those who'd ripped up bedsheets while others splashed, 'Vote RASCAL' or 'Harry Lanker Loves You' in splodges and lines of black paint. But today, one of those sheets was turned around to face the far wall, acting as a screen for projections that tracked the Prime Minister's progress down the Strand like a hunting eagle.

Minnie's stall these days hosted a variety of vegetables grown close by. Alongside the onions and potatoes, Neville Jennings was one of a couple of delivery boys unloading hearts of artichokes and heads of asparagus, pods of peas and bunches of radishes bound up in hemp string.

But if the produce had changed, the workers had not. The moment she saw Minnie, Dahlia threw her arms around her. "Isn't it amazing?" she said.

"I just can't believe it's actually happened," Minnie replied.

"Me neither," said Dahlia. "I keep pinching myself thinking I'm going to wake up and find all this is a dream. Did you watch it all?"

"Every minute," said Minnie. "I thought I was going to fall asleep loads of times, and then a seat'd go from red or blue to RASCAL white, and I couldn't stop myself letting out a yelp of excitement. A few times I was so happy that I did a little jig around the coffee table. Silently of course, I didn't want to wake Brian or Naomi."

"We didn't have those worries in my house," said Dahlia. "I dare say the whole street was up all night. It was like watching a football match, every time RASCAL won a seat there were cheers all down the row. I've never known anything like it."

"Me neither," said Minnie. "Do you know why they're calling it a hung Parliament?"

"It means no single party's got a majority."
"So no one won?"
"RASCAL won," said Dahlia. "They're the biggest party by miles. But they'll find it hard to pass any laws, that's the thing."
"So what'll they do?"
"The theory I like the most is that RASCAL have to prove themselves. The idea is to show what Harry Lanker can do, and when the next election comes around we'll be even more ready. All we need is a couple of years of being taken seriously, and we'll get our majority next time around."
"I hope you're right," Minnie replied.

As they went about their daily business, workers and customers alike kept an eye on the projections. They watched the motorcade slowing through a gold-tipped fence, outriders peeling off until it was just the Rover P9 that carried on through the arch under the balcony of Buckingham Palace. It looped around the empty courtyard and parked up by the Romanesque columns of the north wing. The shot descended to the driver, showed him dart of out the vehicle and scoot around to the Prime Minister's door. But by the time he got there, Harry Lanker was already out, doing up the single button of his jacket and inhaling the air of power.

Buckingham Palace, London

"Harry," said the driver, hiding his mouth with his hand. "Remember the security protocol we discussed? You're supposed to stay in the car until I open the door."

Harry smiled and patted his driver's arm. "Don't worry, Samuel," he said. "I'm quite safe here. Now, wish me luck."

Samuel Dietrich smiled back and shook the Prime Minister's hand. "Of course, Harry," he said. "Best of luck in there. Do us proud."

While the Prime Minister met the King, screens up and down the country flicked to news of stock market crashes that few wanted to hear. In the food exchange, as around the country, they turned down the volume until Harry Lanker re-emerged into a lemon-stone courtyard. Only then was the sound pumped up across the nation for Carolyn Hargreaves' voice to ring out. "And that's him," she said, "our first shot of Harry Lanker, the King's fifth Prime Minister in thirteen years. Now for the journey that takes him out of Buckingham Palace, down the Mall to Downing Street where, as we already know, he's going to be given a rapturous welcome."

In view of the cameras, Harry Lanker undid his jacket and folded himself inside. Samuel Dietrich shut the door behind him, then dashed around to take up his position in the driver's seat.

The men didn't speak until they were out of the Palace gates, past the crowds surging down the steps of a golden fountain that glinted in the sunlight. As they drove between the rows of plane trees, Union flags fluttered in the breeze. Both pavements were taken up with people straining to get a view of the new Prime Minister, singing and chanting his name.

"Doesn't the Mall look spectacular?" said the driver. "We couldn't have asked for a better day for it."

"Yep," said Harry Lanker.

Samuel glanced in the rear view, but missed the grin he'd expected. "You all right, Harry?" he asked. "You seem kind of down. What did the King say to you?"

"That's exactly it," said the new PM. "It was a really strange meeting. We hardly talked about government at all. He said I need to watch my back. He reckons there are people out to get me. And he should know, shouldn't he?"

"I guess so," said Samuel Dietrich. "And he's right for sure, you can never be too careful."

Harry glanced at the fluorescent yellow motorcycles surrounding him. "I mean, look," he said. "Why are PapSec providing the security for the Prime Minister?"

"They won the tender, didn't they?"

"Tender my arse," said Lanker. "We all know how those tenders came about. It's a conflict of interest, that's what it is.

The only interest that my bodyguard should have is in preserving the life of the Prime Minister, not simultaneously to be working for my political rivals. I'm going to have to find a way out of this. I'm not sure I feel safe having PapSec looking after me."

"Sounds like a plan, Harry," said the driver, "although those contracts are aren't exactly easy to get out of. Remember how impossible it was to get all those houses back under public ownership after PapHomes took them over from Bridgeford Asset Management?"

"I'll never forget," said Harry. "But if they can use 'national security' to close down any kind of scrutiny, surely I can now use it to push through the real changes that need to be made. Can't I?"

"I guess so, Harry," said his driver.

Halfway down Whitehall, the convoy slowed to a crawl for the turn into Downing Street. People rushed through the security cordon to catch a peek of the first Prime Minister from a new party for 122 years. They banged the roof of his car, hammered on the windows and screamed Harry Lanker's name. But he could hear none of it beyond the inch-thick glass and armoured bodywork.

"Will you stop the car, Samuel?" said Harry. "I want to get out and walk among the people. If they can make the effort to come and see me, the least I can do is give them a little of what they want. It's like watching on TV with the sound off in here."

"I don't think that's a good idea, Harry," said the driver. "Remember what the King said? You need to watch your back from now on."

"Even here, among my people?" asked Harry Lanker, relaxing his grip on the door handle. "Do you think I'm in danger, Samuel?"

"All I know," said the driver, "is that as long as you're secure in this vehicle, with windows and doors closed, no one can get you. This car could withstand a nuclear bomb going off, provided you maintain the integrity of vehicle."

"Well, never have it be said that I'm not one for integrity, hey Sam?" The Prime Minister responded, waving at the faces against his window as he sat back into the seat.

Rusholme

In the food exchange, customers and workers alike wore looks of sleepless jubilation. There had been only one topic of conversation all morning, and when each spoke it was with the unfamiliar look of hope in their eyes.

Neville hovered by Minnie's side as she served a man in a string vest. Only when the customer had gone did he tap her arm. "Hey," he said.

"Hi," Minnie replied, straining for eye contact with the next customer.

"There's a party later, after work. We're going to Platt Fields for a bit of a knees up. Don't you want to join?"

"I can't," said Minnie, "I've got to look after Naomi."

Dahlia had been listening in. "I thought Brian was coming to pick her up when he clocks off," she said.

"Sure he is," said Minnie. "But then I've got to get her to bed and make his tea for him."

"And he can't handle that himself?" asked Dahlia.

"You'd think so, wouldn't you?" said Minnie.

"So you'll come to the party then?" Neville interjected.

Minnie thought a moment, glanced at the screen showing the black limo inching through the crowds around Downing Street. "All right," she said. "I haven't been out since forever. Like not since I was a kid. It'll be nice to let my hair down for a change. And when am I going to have an excuse like this again?"

Downing Street, London

Beyond the gates of Downing Street, selected RASCAL party members stood behind a crush barrier waving little white flags and Union Jacks. Samuel Dietrich held open the door for the Prime Minister, who got out waving and smiling to greet a few of his supporters in person before making his way to the podium.

When he turned from the crowds to the cameras, Harry Lanker had a smile as wide as the Dartford gap. He strode towards the blue-brick townhouse of number 10 with shoulders back and chest out, looking surprisingly fitting in his new role, despite the long hair, scruffy stubble and the open neck of his shirt.

Harry Lanker came to a stop outside a white doorframe surrounding a fan window and that famous black door. He grabbed both sides of a thin-steel lectern, with the royal coat of arms embossed on the far side, and grinned at the gaggle of cameras and reporters.

"Thank you," he said. "Thank you all very much. I have to tell you that I have just been to see His Majesty the King, and have accepted his offer to form a new administration of government in this country." He jutted his chin in pride, took a moment to compose himself.

"As I stand here before 10 Downing Street," Lanker continued. "I do so in awe at the people of this nation. You've been able to see through the propaganda and the smears to elect a truly radical government to act on your behalf. Corruption and cronyism have long had us by the neck, and yesterday you gave me a mandate for the wholesale restructuring of our society. As I've said so many times, if an economy doesn't work for everyone, it doesn't work for anyone. Big business has forced this country down paths we never should have trodden. Yesterday, you told them enough is enough."

Harry Lanker picked up the bottle on the lectern and took a sip, held it to his eyes and saw the PapAqua logo running all over it. He screwed the top back on and placed it by his feet, out of sight of the cameras. He tucked his hair behind both ears and turned back to the lenses. "When we founded the Radical Alliance of Socialist and anti-Capitalist Activists on the Left," he continued, "no one would have dared to dream that just twelve-and-a-half years later there'd be a RASCAL Prime Minister standing here on the steps of Downing Street. Its not been an easy few years by any means, but I assure you all that I keep in my heart the ideals and the objectives we set out with. I pledge to you today, that we will restore politics in this country to what it should always have been, about service to the public. This country of ours is about to stand on the feet of all, not on the heads of the many."

"As promised in our manifesto, my first act will be to put a moratorium on any further theft of public areas under the Biodome project. We will ensure that the right to food is protected, and will therefore kick the notorious Fruit and Vegetable Act into the long grass. And we will work to ensure every person on these islands has a roof over their head, food on the table and water from the taps. We have a long and proud history of reform governments in this country, and during my time in power, we at RASCAL will never lose sight of those who have gone before us. As we all know, this year is the centenary of Clement Atlee's post-war government, and I can't help but think of old Clem up there in heaven right now, watching down on his country with Nye Bevan at his side, smiling to each other. I thank every person in the country for giving me the chance to follow in such great footsteps, and I promise to carry out your wishes to the best of my abilities. So now, if you'll all excuse me, I must get on with the work of government."

Rusholme

The food exchange had stopped to watch Harry Lanker, no one wanted him to end. But as soon as he turned and vanished behind the black door, the shot went straight to the studio.

"High words indeed there from Mr Lanker," said Carolyn Hargreaves. "Charles Hawtry Montague, what do you make of all that?"

"To me," sneered a man with a public-school accent and blond chest hair spewing from the open neck of his shirt. "They sound like the words of a man about to discover that the job of government is significantly more difficult than opposition, especially when he can't even command a majority in the House of Commons. He mentioned 1945, but I'd draw more parallels with the 1923 Labour government. That particular minority administration lasted just ten months, and I'd be surprised if this one gets through a whole year either."

Dahlia tutted. "They always find someone to take down Harry Lanker," she said. "Whatever happened to talking up the government? Or does that only apply if it's your friends' party in power?"

"He's just bitter," said Minnie. "They're such bad losers, the lot of them."

Moskito Island, British Virgin Islands

Lord Michael O'Dillon had watched every British General Election since he was nine. But not this one. Even while the news commentators had been rubbishing the idea for months, the CEO of PapCorp could long see what was going to happen. Which is why he'd flown his closest associates to the O'Dillons' private island in the Caribbean, to be out of range of cameras or journalists, and outnumbered two-to-one by the most beautiful prostitutes money could buy.

When Zoltan O'Dillon arose that morning, wind was whistling through the gaps in the wooden walls and three women were dozing naked in his four-poster bed. He put on his PapDrive spectacles, wrapped himself up in a white-towel dressing gown and worked his feet into matching slippers. He creaked open the bedroom door and found every bare floorboard groaned as he stepped on it. The landing and stairwell were decorated with wood-mounted animal skulls, but Zoltan was too busy trying to get the news on his PapDrive specs to notice.

A veranda ran around both floors of the mansion house, supported by arches and cast-iron columns with rust bubbling through the white paint. Zoltan burst through the front doors and took off his glasses. He met a view that would once have extended over gardens and the ocean, that was now lost behind overgrown bushes and palms.

He found his father and Bernie Douglas-FitzAllan gazing into the overgrowth, whisky glasses in their hands. Zoltan went over to a Formica cabinet and helped himself to a tumbler which he filled to the brim. Then he sat in a wicker chair which creaked like the rest of the mansion. Whisky spilled over his fingers. "My PapDrive can barely connect," he said, brown liquid dripping onto his dressing gown.

"That's why we're here," said Bernie. "But I take it you know what happened?"

Zoltan nodded. "The end of civilisation," he said.

"Tell me about it," said Bernie. "Churchill would be spinning in his grave if he could see that hairy wanker representing this country at next week's VE day commemorations. It's just not right."

Zoltan nodded, then turned to his father. "So I guess this means…"

"Yes," said Lord Michael, staring out towards the sea. "There's no need to say it, Zoltan, I'm thinking precisely that. I wish we'd never signed that bloody contract now. Giving the Prime Minister the first slot at the opening of my Bio-dome means the first speaker will now be the very man who wants to tear the thing down. That man will be the ruin of us."

"Well," said Zoltan. "If you'd listened to me…"

"Not now, Zoltan!" barked his father. "This isn't the time nor the place."

The three men sat a moment, none daring to say another word until Bernie the Earl broke the silence. "Still," he said. "I see the PapPound's having a good day. Isn't it amazing how PapDrives can get you the financial news even when there's no other signal?"

Rusholme

It was dark by the time Minnie Brownlow staggered back down Welwyn Street. She fumbled in her pockets for the keys and scrambled around for the lock. When it clicked open, she tumbled inside and just about stayed on her feet. She found her husband awake, in his place on the sofa, watching a television screen of numbers and red downwards arrows.

But Minnie wasn't bothered about that, she threw her arms around Brian and planted a kiss on his cheek. "I've had such a good night," she said. "It was amazing. There were fire dancers. Have you ever seen them? And people playing drums and everyone sharing their drinks with everyone else, and dancing like crazy people. I danced for ages with one of the delivery boys. It was such a good night!" She sat down. "I'm as drunk as a skunk," she giggled.

Minnie glimpsed the screen. Beside the reams of negative numbers and the State Broadcaster's logo, a tired-looking blonde woman was reading into the camera.

"Trading on London stock markets was halted for two hours today," said Carolyn Hargreaves. "But it wasn't enough to prevent the worst slide for decades. The only thing keeping all UK-floated shares from complete oblivion was the reliable performance of PapCorp, and their internal stock index, the PapSie25. The company's currency, the PapPound, which decoupled from sterling just last year, saw the biggest gains against the national currency. At the end of the day's trading, one PapPound was worth £1.2583."

"What are they talking about this rubbish for?" asked Minnie. "Have they forgotten about Harry Lanker?"

"This is all his fault," Brian replied. "It's the worst day the pound has suffered for almost thirty years. The only thing saving the country from complete disaster is PapCorp. At work, people were saying Harry Lanker's sabotaged the stock market."

"Sabotaged the stock market? What bullshit! It was all the world's rich people that did that."

"Whatever," said Brian. "Are you going make me tea now? I'm starving."

"Are you saying you haven't eaten?" asked Minnie. "What about Naomi?"

"She said she wasn't hungry," he asserted. "But I am."

"Well there's plenty of food in the pantry."

"Yeah, but I don't know what to do with it, do I?."

"Brian, you're a twenty-three-year-old man. Surely you can fry an egg or something. Or at least get your mother to do it."

"You know she's not well. And in any case, cooking's your area of expertise."

"I wonder what your area of expertise is, exactly."

"I'm the breadwinner, aren't I?" said Brian. "The man of the house. I go out and graft so as we can afford the gas for the heating and this new TV we're watching. Remember what it used to be like?"

"Sure I do," said Minnie. "But I also work, you know. I've never had one night out since I've been with you. And the first time I do, to go and celebrate this new country of ours, all you're interested in is your stomach. I had a really good night, and now you've ruined it." She got up and stormed towards the stairs.

"So no chance of a bite to eat then?" Brian shouted after her.

Minnie didn't reply. As she bounded upstairs, she was lost in thoughts of laughing and dancing and the finely crafted shoulders of Neville Jennings.

12. Consequences

13th October 2035
Approaching Whitby

Winston Humbolt's Delante van breached the brow of Skelder Hill and the town of Whitby opened up below, nestled between the deep brown sea and clouds that unfurled like grey blankets. He reached for the radio dial and clicked it on.

"You're listening to State Broadcaster News," a man's droll voice filled the van, "where we're bringing you live and uninterrupted coverage of Lieutenant-Colonel Zoltan O'Dillon's visit to Buckingham Palace. Later today, the King will be presenting him with this country's highest military honour, the Victoria Cross. But before then…"

Helen saw the tension in her husband's face, his tightening grip on the steering wheel. She reached forward and pushed the dial off.

"Hey!" said Winston. "I was listening to that!"

"I know," Helen replied, "I could see what it was doing to you. The news gets you all wound up and we don't need any more of that."

"What's got into you, Helen?" asked Winston.

"What's got into me?" his wife scorned. "What's got into you, more like. I've given up an entire day to be with you, for you to go off and play your silly games with your mates. With Vincent at my parents', I could've been working on the bakery."

"I'm not asking you to play the games, Helen. And you could've stayed home if you'd wanted to. I thought you were excited about seeing Rebecca."

"I'm looking forward to playing paintball with her. We're quite a team, you know."

"I know, that's why I want you on my side. But would you please stop calling it paintball? It's Battle Tag."

"Same difference."

Winston sighed. "Just please do me a favour and follow my orders."

"You're not going to go all military, are you?"

"I want to win, Helen."

"And everyone else wants to have a nice time, so just try to relax, okay?"

"How can I relax when Paul Broddle's going to be there?" said Winston. "You don't know what it's like anymore, things have changed since you last came to a meeting. He finished a distant third in the elections but still struts around like he's some kind of political hotshot. Its made him more intolerable than ever. I know you've got a soft spot for him, Sugar, but Paul Broddle's not the man he makes out to be. So please, try not to contradict me when he's around, okay?"

"I told you I wouldn't," said Helen. "You never listen to anything I say these days, do you?"

"Sugarplum, please, don't be like that. You know I listen to you. All I'm doing is reminding you. Today's a very important day for me and I need you behind me."

Helen crossed her arms and sat back in the passenger seat.

Even as half a dozen others piled into the back of the van, the couple didn't speak for the rest of the trip. Their passengers, meanwhile, jeered around every corner, and sang all the protest songs they could think of, from Dylan to the Internationale. And while they considered the next tune, they filled each pause with chants of "Har-ry Lan-ker..."

Troutsdale, North Yorkshire

When the wheels of Winston's van slid to a halt on car-park pebbles, Helen was the first to get out. She stretched her arms and took a lungful of air. The dampness she inhaled was unlike that of Whitby town, where the sea salt and asphalt took away the edge. This was the fresh dew damp of autumn leaves on the turn, of cow manure with a tinge of wood smoke.

The others were still chanting Harry Lanker's name as they jumped from the back of the van. The last out was Fiona, cheeks rosy under her freckles, a gummy grin plastered over her face and an almost empty whisky bottle in her hand. "All right Helen?" she said. "Do you want a drink?"

"I was wondering why you lot were so boisterous," Helen replied. "No, thanks, I don't drink in the mornings."

"Suit yourself," said Fiona. "I for one need all the courage I can get before swinging around in the trees." She took a swig and crossed the trackway towards the activity centre. Winston beeped the van locked with a flick of his Xi-fan sheet and followed on without waiting for his wife.

The activity centre was a flat-out rectangle of wooden planks with slots cut out for windows. On the dirt forecourt stood some twenty people, most in cagoules and camouflage. But on the far side of the group, standing beside a man with an orange turban and a thick beard, was a woman in a black headscarf pulled to a circle around her face.

Helen would've known that figure anywhere, and she went straight over. "What's all this then?" she asked. "I never thought I'd see actually Rebecca Kingston in a burkha! So have you converted, have you? Are you really Muslim now?"

"It's not a burkha," said Rebecca, embracing her oldest friend. "It's just a hijab. And no, converting to Islam's a risky business these days, what with the security services looking out for it and all."

"So you're not even Muslim, what are you wearing that for?"

"In solidarity with my sisters and brothers," said Rebecca.

"I wish she wouldn't," said her partner in the turban. "I've specifically asked her not to. Islam should be a force for good in the world, it's only their enemies that use it as a political symbol. But you know what Rebecca Kingston's like, headstrong isn't the word."

Helen smiled. "Tell me about it," she said. "When she gets a bee in her bonnet, there's no stopping her. So how are you Tariq, or, er?"

"Parjit," he replied, "that's the name I go by these days, Parjit Agarwhal. Like every Muslim doctor still working, I've had to change religion and my identity. That way we're kept off the registers and not forced to wear those abominable green crescents, which make consultations all but impossible. So I'm now a Sikh, or at least officially. It'd be different if we'd managed to get Whitby General reclassified as a community hospital, of course. But then what hope did we ever have against PapMed?"

Helen shook her head. "It's dreadful what's happening in this country," she said before turning to Rebecca. "So your Muslim boyfriend's pretending to be Sikh. While you, a good Catholic girl, are dressed like a Muslim?"

"I know," Rebecca grinned. "It's interesting, isn't it?"

Neither Helen nor Rebecca much fancied the idea of swinging from the tree-tops, so they sat out the morning in the warmth of the activity centre café.

The others headed for an evergreen plantation down the hill. The division in the group was obvious from the way they walked; two men led from the front, with Winston's supporters on his side and Paul Broddle's gang on the other.

"I saw you in the *Star* again, Paul," Winston commented. "More mindless attention grabbing. A right petty little politician you're turning out to be."

Paul Broddle huffed. "If you'd bothered to read my article, bruv, you'd know I wrote about the role of the Whitby RASCALS in bringing down Spokane."

"I've told you before," said Winston. "We might both be black but that doesn't make us brothers. So quit calling me 'bruv', ok? I read your article, I thought it was typical Broddle babble. All you did was reword the same old stories and take the credit for everyone else's work."

"Aye," said Fiona, "We never saw you lining up to put your neck in a noose outside Moon Burger. If you're serious about this movement and retaining our support, we expect you to be with us. I mean properly with us. Not just for a couple of photos and an article in the *Star*, then home in time for the News at Ten."

"I can't be at every single protest, you know," said Paul. "I do have other things to do."

"He's got an election to win!" said a man on Broddle's wing. "And next time around it'll be a serious race."

"You want a serious race?" Winston retorted. "How about we race you lot to the start of the Monkey Trail."

"What are you?" Paul Broddle sneered. "Six-years-old? We're supposed to be serious members of a political party, for whose aims we all claim to agree. So let's have a nice day out without making everything into a competition."

"I thought that was the whole idea," said Winston. "My faction against yours. I mean, we're evenly matched numbers-wise, although of course the intelligence and physical dexterity are significantly in my favour."

"You what?" shouted the man at Paul Broddle's side. "You reckon your gaggle of losers are more intelligent than us? I say bring it on. We'll show you where the real brains are amongst the Scarborough and Whitby RASCALs."

So Paul Broddle found himself overruled even by his own side. It meant they raced over beds of pine needles and rushed through the Monkey Trail. They swung along zip wires and leapt from branches with abnormal relish, especially given they were forty feet above the forest floor.

In the meantime, Helen and Rebecca sat at a lacquered-wood table, mugs warming their fingers. Beyond a plate-glass window, the wind was whipping clouds across the sky and swaying the tree-tops in the valley below. But the women were too caught up in catching up to pay that any attention.

"I thought I'd be able to handle being a mum and a business owner," Helen was saying. "I even thought I might enjoy it. But it turned out to be way too much. The bank was so helpful though. When I realised I wasn't going to be ready on time, they agreed to extend the loan on the same terms with no costs. Which means hopefully next year I'll have my own bakery at last!"

"That was very good of them," said Rebecca, taking a sip of milky tea. "And how is your little Vincent? I bet he's grown!"

"He has. You'd hardly recognise him. He's got thick black curls and his father's eyes, not to mention the most gorgeous smile you've ever seen. He's talking too, hardly shuts up half the time. He'll be two next month, I'm going to make him a cake in the shape of a microphone. You should come to the party."

"I'd love that," said Rebecca. "I hardly get out these days. If Parjit and I weren't married to the same cause, we'd hardly see each other especially not now I'm editing the *Whitby Star*. You know our readership's gone past the *Gazette's*?"

"I know," said Helen. "I read it every day. I like how you're getting in different writers. I loved Paul Broddle's article last week."

"Hmm," Rebecca replied. "Well let me know about the birthday party. It'll make a change to see your Winston being a father as well as an activist."

Helen's face dropped at her husband's name.

Rebecca noticed. "What's up Hells?" she asked. "Everything okay?"

"I don't know," Helen responded, staring outside. "I've had this feeling for a while now, like something isn't right. Winston's a good father, don't get me wrong, but only when he's around. Many nights he only comes home to sleep. A few times lately he hasn't come back at all. I thought it was all party stuff, you know, organising protests and things. I told myself that for years. But now I'm starting to doubt myself, I wonder if there isn't another woman involved or something."

"I very much doubt that, Helen, I really do," said Rebecca, wrapping her warmed fingers around her friend's and gazing into her eyes. "He's a good man, your Winston. We've pulled some all-nighters, that's certainly true, at the hospital or outside the Moon Burger or wherever. Winston's very dedicated to us and he's great at what he does; he takes each of us out for a pint or two when we've been out on a job. And if there's ever a problem he comes and sorts it out. He bailed Fiona out a couple of months back. Took her for a fish supper to celebrate and everything."

"Fiona? Is that the ginger Scottish one?"

"That's her."

"He didn't mention that. Do you think there's something between them?"

"Between who?" Rebecca grinned. "Fiona and Winston? You must be kidding! Winston's as loyal to you as he is to the cause. And we think Fiona might be a lesbian. Kyle's been in love with her since they were at school but she doesn't even notice. So no, I don't think there's anything to worry about, Hells, I really don't." She paused at the concern in her friend's eyes. "I'd tell you if I suspected anything. You know that, don't you?"

"I guess so," Helen replied, staring down the valley.

Even as their limbs ached from swinging through trees, the group's spirits were soaring on a primordial rush as they strolled up for lunch. Despite all the exertion, there was little to choose between Paul's and Winston's groups when they got to the pinewood refectory with the big windows.

The two sides kept themselves separate as they ate, with Helen and Rebecca in between, lost in recollections of times gone by.

Winston and Paul had both understood the problem they were about to encounter, and had studied each other throughout dinner for who would be the first to move. With his meal done, Winston Humbolt wiped his lips and got up from his seat. He headed towards the women, knowing Paul Broddle would be mirroring him.

"Hello, Sugarplum," said Winston, kissing the top of his wife's golden hair. "Hello, Rebecca. Are you both ready for the Battle Tag?"

"Absolutely!" said Helen. "We were talking about the times we went paintballing as kids. We're a great team, me and Rebecca."

"You can't be on the same side today," said Paul Broddle. "You'll have to split up."

"Hang on," said Winston. "Why don't we ask them what they want? I think they should be allowed to stay together if they choose."

"And on whose side?" asked Paul. "Yours, I suppose."

"I say we let them choose," Winston insisted.

"Let them choose you," Paul sneered. "That'd give you an advantage of two people. No, we have to split them, one on my side and one on yours, that's only fair. You can choose who, if you want."

Winston glanced between the two women then shrugged at his rival. "It's not really a choice, is it? If I don't pick my wife, I'll be watching my back the entire game."

"Your back and your front," said Helen.

"Exactly," said Winston. "So, I guess Rebecca's with you."

"It certainly looks that way," said Paul, grinning.

The two men returned to their respective sides and Helen and Rebecca shook their heads at each other. "They're like a pair of toddlers, those two," said Helen.

"Tell me about it," Rebecca replied. "It's like that all the time these days. That Paul Broddle's a proper little scrote, he undermines Winston constantly. There's no way I'm going to help him win."

"Well if Winston wins I'll just have to endure him gloating, so I'm not sure which is worse. I was looking forward to being on your team though."

"We'll still be on the same side," said Rebecca. "Just in different uniforms."

The Battle Tag took place above the activity centre, where the forest was thinner and dotted with sheds, walls, and watchtowers. Everyone picked up masks as they walked into the game. They wrapped the goggles over their faces, turned on the Augmented Vision and their view became a battle zone of smouldering craters and branchless trees, the sticks they collected into MX75 machine guns.

Well into the game, Helen and Winston found themselves trapped in a shed with three others. Every time they popped a head up to see what was happening, shots crashed against the wood and made loud splintering sounds in their ears.

"Helen!" Winston shouted. "I need you to run to that tree and draw their fire."

"But that's a suicide mission," his wife protested. "If you want to do it, why don't you go yourself?"

"Because I'm the commander and I just gave you an order. Besides, you know I can't run so well."

"What kind of commander would sacrifice their best shot?" Helen continued. "I've hit more of them than all of you combined, and now you want to end my game so you can win? I tell you what, you'd make a rubbish officer in real life."

"Good God, Helen!" Winston shouted. "Will you never show me any respect? I'm ordering you over there to start the attack. That's Rebecca on the gate, can't you see? She'll let you through and we'll follow on behind."

"How far behind?"

"Right behind. Now, are you going? We'll lose our opportunity otherwise."

"All right," said Helen. "I hope you're right."

Helen Humbolt darted out from the back of the shed, sprinting from tree to tree until she stood facing Rebecca Kingston. The two women stopped a moment to look each other up and down and saw each other as masked warriors in augmented camouflage and helmets. Rebecca placed her stick to her shoulder and shot Helen again and again.

'Game Over' flashed over the lenses of Helen's goggles, a woman's voice spoke into her ear. "You are now dead," she said. "Please return to the activity centre where you can enjoy a relaxing cup of coffee or browse the many gift items in the…"

Helen tore the goggles from her head. "Rebecca!" she screamed. "What did you do that for? I thought you were supposed to be on our side!"

But Rebecca Kingston, her ears full of battle noises, saw only the image of a masked warrior lying blood-soaked and lifeless under the tree. She didn't hear a thing Helen yelled.

Helen Humbolt didn't know how long she'd been sitting on a log at the edge of the forest. She'd been staring at the fields enclosed in hedgerows, up inclines so steep that only sheep could graze. She listened to the dried leaves doing their best to hold on in the wind, the squawking of gulls, the occasional shout from the forest above.

Helen knew they'd finished the game from the chants of "championes, championes!" She got up and walked towards the noise to find the two groups of warriors coming through the woods.

Winston tore off his goggles, wiped his brow and was on to his rival. "Hey Broddle, you loser!" he yelled. "Are you going to be a good sport and come and congratulate the winners?"

"You only won by cheating," Paul Broddle replied. "It's all you ever do."

"We won fair and square!" shouted Kyle.

"Don't pull that one!" said Paul. "Your hijab heroine could've got you a dozen times, but for some reason she refused to shoot."

"She got Helen," said Winston, "our best player. So I'd hardly say she was on our side, was she? Now stop this prattling and be a good sport." He put out his hand to receive Paul Broddle's.

Broddle glanced at it, tutted and turned away.

But Winston wasn't done. "Wait a moment, Paul," he said. "I've got something I want to say to you and a few others." He shouted for Rebecca and Parjit, Kyle Clarke and Fiona McIntyre. Although he hadn't called for her, Helen strode towards the group and stood at Rebecca's arm, to bring their number to seven.

Winston stared a moment at his wife, wondering whether to ask her to leave. He decided not to and cleared his throat. "Friends," he said. "my closest and most faithful allies, my wife, we have a lot to be proud of. We've fought a campaign of passive resistance which even Gandhi would've admired, with an impact he'd only have dreamt of. We were part of a movement that brought down Spokane, one of the biggest corporations in the world."

"And handed all their brands to PapCorp," said Kyle. "What a success that was. We might as well have been working for them the whole time."

"I'm afraid that's the law of unintended consequences," Winston continued. "But it means we're now at a point where we must decide in which direction to go. We can keep chaining ourselves to railings or driving cattle down Whitby High Street until we get picked off one at a time, to pass away our days in some PapSec prison cell. Or we could step up to meet them head on. What I am therefore presenting to you all is a choice, Gandhi or Mandela. Passive resistance, public spectacles, beatings and meaningless torture, or the opportunity to catch them on the backfoot, to take the fight to the enemy and in doing so, defeat PapCorp. The reason you're all here is that I've been asked to gather together a small group of fighters who are dedicated to the cause."

"Good God, Winston!" screamed his wife. "What the hell do you have planned? Why are you looking for fighters?"

"I didn't mean fighters in the literal sense," said Winston. "It was a slip of the tongue. I guess I'm still playing Battle Tag. No, I'm not talking about combat, I'm talking about sabotage. And please, Helen, remember what we talked about."

"What I want to know," said Paul Broddle, "is who gave you these orders. Are you seriously saying RASCAL's developing an armed faction? I've not heard anything about it. The General Assembly certainly didn't vote on it."

"Look, Paul," said Winston. "You know Parjit and I sit on RASCAL's Security and Safety Committee. Let's just leave it at that."

"Let's not just leave it at that!" Broddle shouted. "I want to know the name of the person who gave you this order. I intend to take up this matter with Harry Lanker personally."

"Do what you want," Winston replied. "But you should remember, Paul, that you're just one of six hundred failed Parliamentary candidates. And I'm sure Harry Lanker has plenty on his plate without you bothering him. I've included you in this discussion for means of transparency, which is precisely what I was instructed to do. But if you're not interested, may I suggest you leave?"

"No," Paul replied. "I am interested and I'm going to have my say."

"Fine," said Winston. "Stay then. But I'm not talking any more about who gave me these instructions." He turned to the others. "Listen folks," he said. "I would hope that in the five years or so that we've known each other, that we've developed a kind of mutual trust. You know I'll look after you whatever happens, I'll be there to pick you out of any hole or any cell. I firmly believe that the moment is coming when we'll get to make a real change to bring down the entire system, not just one multinational. I'm asking you now to help bring that about."

"So does that mean we're finally going after PapCorp?" asked Kyle.

"That would be the logical move," Winston responded. "And PapCorp have an army, a force to be reckoned with. Just look at what Zoltan O'Dillon did in the desert with a few crack PapSec troops."

"I thought you said that story was bollocks," said his wife.

"I did," Winston replied. "It is, I mean. But whatever it was he got up to, PapCorp and his father were powerful enough to spin it into the story we all know. Violence begets violence, Hells. We are violently repressed, legal channels of protest have been closed down and we're left with no alternative but to retaliate in kind. Does anyone seriously think we'd have got rid of Spokane without those attacks on Greyskies? I mean, it's all very well hanging ourselves outside Moon Burger dressed as a cow..."

"I almost died that day," said Fiona.

"I know," Winston responded. "That's kind of my point. If we're prepared to put our necks on the line, literally in some cases, then we should risk our lives doing something that'll have a real, long-lasting effect. Now, who's with me?"

Rebecca's hand shot up. "Count me in," she said.

"Excellent," said Winston. "Now who else? Parjit? What about you?"

"Of course," said Parjit.

"I thought you were against violence," said Kyle. "I remember you telling me about how doctors were there to save lives, not take them."

"I never said that," said Parjit. "It must have been someone else. As the guru teaches, peace will never be possible when there is pain and suffering in society. We did everything we could to make Whitby General into a community hospital, but in the end it went to PapMed like everything else. All because their bid was 0.0001 per cent cheaper than ours. Unless we do something drastic now, there'll be nothing left of this country in ten years."

Shaftesbury Avenue, London

Like all their other restaurants, a blue moon still shone above the door of the PapBurger at Piccadilly Circus, indicating the chain's past identity. At a table on the upper floor, Bernie Douglas-FitzAllan finished his second Maxi meal and wiped his mouth on a jacket sleeve. "It's true what they say," he said. "You can't tell the difference between this bio-beef and the real thing. It's a good job too – I can't bear the smell of burning meat anymore."

"Hmm," replied Zoltan O'Dillon, masticating on his own meat sandwich. "You know what I've realised about all this?"

"What's that?" asked Bernie.

"Just how important I am," Zoltan said, in his PapSec ceremonial uniform with a solitary medal on his left breast. "I basically went down there and ruffled a few feathers, went a bit rogue on the orders and all that. But I got the job done and they've recognised it. You don't get a Victoria Cross for nothing, do you?"

"You earned it, old chap. You really did. I couldn't have done what you did that day. Getting out of the truck and all that. Going face-to-face with the enemy."

"I can still remember the stench from your trousers, Major Stinkovitch! I'll never forget that for as long as I live. But what I mean is…" Zoltan's attention drifted to the thin man in a grey suit who'd just got out of the lift. O'Dillon put down his bio-meat sandwich. "How the bloody hell did he find us here?" he asked.

Bernie the Earl didn't have the chance to reply before Larry Pickering was upon them. "It's nine-thirty," he said.

"Yeah? So?" Zoltan sneered, taking a handful of chips and stuffing them into his mouth. "How did you find me?"

"It's never hard to find you, Zoltan," said Larry. "You generally leave behind a trail of unpaid bar tabs and disgruntled young ladies, all of whom are happy to reveal your whereabouts. The barman at Ronnie Scott's was fuming. He told me you had two bottles of 2003 Margaux, then downed a couple of quadruple whiskies and left without paying."

"Did you pick up the tab?"

"Of course."

"Good boy, Pickering," said Zoltan. "Let the accounts department have the receipt and they'll reimburse you. Now, do you think you could kindly fuck off and leave us to have our dinner in peace?"

"That's not why I'm here," said Pickering. "You're out past your curfew. You know you're supposed to be in the hotel by nine, that was the agreement."

"Yeah?" Zoltan sneered. "Says who?"

"Says your father."

"Screw my father." Zoltan took a bite of burger and spoke as he chewed. "I'm a grown adult, free to enjoy our capital city as I chose. You should remember who you're talking to, I'm the hero of Jebel Shams. And I have this to prove it." He waved the bronze cross on his breast.

Sir Larry Pickering placed both fists on the table and leaned in on his knuckles. "Never forget, Zoltan," he whispered, "that I was there that day. I saw what you did. The only reason I don't denounce you in public is the respect I have for your father. I know that a stain like this would rub off on him as well, and that's the last thing any of us need. I'm sure you remember my advice to you that day, whatever you may claim. I suggest in future you heed my words and avoid any repeat of this unpleasant circumstance."

"This unpleasant circumstance you talk about," said Zoltan, "has landed me the highest military honour in the country. Not to mention the kind of publicity that can't be bought. Now, Bernie and I have had a heck of a day, so we're going to finish our PapBurgers, go for one gin and tonic over the road and toddle off to bed. We'll be home before the bells strike midnight, before the Earl of Angus turns into a pumpkin." He glanced at Bernie, saw his schoolfriend polishing off a third hamburger. "Then again," he said, "maybe it's already too late."

Glaisdale

Winston and Helen didn't speak until they'd dropped everyone off from the van. They'd driven half an hour over dark moors and were passing a solitary lamppost shining orange over a patch of grass when Helen broke the silence.

"I feel I don't know you, sometimes," she said, staring at the stone cottages making their semi-detached steps up the village High Street. "I just don't know where this anger comes from. You've helped turn Whitby around, you've brought down one of the world's largest companies, and your political party are on the verge of the big time. For the first time in your life you've got a real family, and now you want to go and throw it all away?"

"I'm not throwing anything away, Sugar. I'm trying to do what's right."

"Right for whom? Certainly not right for your wife and son."

"You and Vincent are always at the front of my mind," Winston responded. "No matter what happens, I'll always make sure you're looked after, please believe that. I'm trying to make the world a better place for you and for him. I want my son to be proud of his dad one day, which means I can't just sit by and let them beat us anymore."

"But violence? Really? What would Mrs Earnshaw say? Why can't you just keep playing practical jokes?"

"Mrs Earnshaw's dead," said Winston. "And our opponents aren't joking. They're deadly serious. Our next battle isn't with some bit-part, yankie hospital chain, our next target will be PapCorp. And PapCorp's army, PapSec, are much more than a bunch of gringo teenagers and mercenaries. They have the right of arrest in more than twenty countries, including this one. And they only understand one language. The system's violent to us so we have to react in kind. The only way to fight fire is with fire."

"Fire and Kyle Clarke?" said Helen. "He couldn't even play Battle Tag properly – he was too concerned about getting his shoes dirty. What good's he going to be to you?"

"He's all right is Kyle. He's methodical at least. And like the others, he has no family to leave behind."

Helen stared at the bald profile of her husband's head. "I guess you're happy Tariq and Rebecca's parents disowned them, aren't you? That means they're free to be your number one supporters."

"She's a strong character is Rebecca Kingston," said Winston. "I like that in a woman."

"So is that it?" asked Helen. "Are you doing all this to impress Rebecca Kingston? I suppose that's why she shot me, she got all defensive when I asked her about it. She used to be my best mate. Are you shagging her? Is that where you disappear off to at night times? To give her one around the back of the Pavilion?"

"Don't be ridiculous!" said Winston, stopping his van outside a bungalow where the projections onto the front curtain told them Helen's parents were watching television.

"Maybe you should just leave me here," she said, going for the door handle.

But Winston pulled her back. "I am not having sex with Rebecca Kingston," he said. "And I resent that you even think I would. There's only one woman in my life, Hells, one person I have sex with. Occasionally. And I'm not leaving you here. Your home is with me in Whitby, with Vincent."

Mayfair, London

It was gone two when Zoltan O'Dillon walked into the Consignia Bar on the corner of Grosvenor Square, forage cap under his arm, the top buttons of his tunic hanging open.

Bernie the Earl stumbled behind. His tie long lost, he was rubbing a pink hand mark that stung his cheek. He'd already forgotten who'd given it to him and what he'd done to deserve it.

Zoltan may have drunk just as much as his old schoolmate, but his memory was rather better. "It wasn't right what that girl did to you," he said. "That sort of thing shouldn't be allowed. Assault, that's what it was. And all because you wanted a feel of her little titties. I tell you, a girl at home wouldn't have reacted like that. Manchester bouncers would've thrown her out before either of us. They treat us with respect there."

"You're right," Bernie slurred, even though nothing of Zoltan's speech had gone in.

"We need to show these stuck up southern birds," said Zoltan. "They need to know that Zoltan O'Dillon, VC and Bernie the Earl of Angus are not people to be taken lightly. Look," he pointed to the end of the darkwood bar. "There's one sat on her own. That can only mean one thing. Let's go and talk to her."

With Bernie tottering after him, Zoltan O'Dillon went up to a blonde woman in her early twenties. She was perched on a stool upholstered in the same brown leather as the sides of the bar. Her eyes were lost in a Xi-fan sheet which she held in one hand, while the other pulled at the hem of her black dress to try and stop it riding up her thighs.

"What's a young lady doing in a place like this on her own at this time of night?" Zoltan leered.

"I'm looking for my friends," she replied. "I can't find them anywhere."

"They've probably all hooked up and gone," said Zoltan. "So it's lucky that you've bumped into a couple of gentlemen like us. What are you drinking?"

"Oh no" said the woman, yanking at her skirt. "I couldn't possibly. I was here with my friends..."

"Who've all left you," said Zoltan. He clicked his fingers. "Barman!" he hollered. "Three So-bod Mod-jars and make it snappy. This young lady looks like she's dying of thirst."

The two men took up stools either side of the woman, boxing her in. Zoltan dragged his seat towards her. "So how about introductions?" he said. "You know who I am of course."

"Yes, Mr O'Dillon."

"Good, well this is my old friend and top advisor Bernie Douglas-FitzAllan, the Earl of Angus. We've been to see the King today, you know."

"Yes," she replied. "I know."

"It's lucky you met us," said Zoltan. "We're still celebrating. We'll show you what a good time really is." He reached down and stroked his fingers against the inside of her knee.

The woman froze. "Mi-Mister O'Dillon," she stammered. "I'm sorry, but I'm a married woman."

"That's quite okay," O'Dillon replied, inching his hand still higher. "I don't mind if you're with another man, woman, horse, whatever. Tonight you've got me and Bernie the Earl to keep you company, and we're very open minded."

When Zoltan's touch reached the hem of her panties, the woman flinched and pushed him away. "I have to go," she said.

"Go? But our drinks haven't arrived yet."

"No, I, er, I'm. I'm going to the toilet."

She stood, balancing herself on her heels. When she turned, O'Dillon lifted her skirt and groped her buttocks. The woman jumped out of reach and trotted towards the toilets as fast as she could, pulling down the back of her dress while clutching at her handbag.

"Come on," said Zoltan. "She's giving us the sign."

"I don't think she is," slurred Bernie. "I think she wants to get away."

"To get away? What nonsense. You're too drunk to see it, but she's absolutely gagging for it. Quick, come on. Let's get her before she can lock the door." He pulled Bernie up by the shoulder and dragged him towards the women's toilets.

The woman's name was Sandra Shaw. Her disappearance that night led to a manhunt which occupied the front pages for months. Yet her body would only turn up twenty-six years later. By which time, England and the world would be a very different place.

13. Enclosure

26th November 2050

Carolyn Hargreaves spoke to the camera, "You're watching PapNews," she said. "On stock markets in Shanghai, New Delhi and London this weekend, PapCorp's the only word on everyone's lips. The PapPound continues its surge, thanks in no small part to First Lord O'Dillon's dual-currency policy. At close of trading yesterday, one PapPound was worth £2.7176. Meanwhile, the corporation's internal index, the PapSie30, soared a record 762 points to finish the day on 8,752. PapEng was Friday's biggest single climber, after the First Lord's announcement in Parliament that his Bio-dome project will be extended to other cities including Leeds and Liverpool, while twelve extra domes will go up over Manchester. When they're joined to the existing Manchester Bio-domes, they'll form the largest covered area in the world at over 8,500 acres. But the news doesn't stop there for PapCorp's engineering and construction division. PapEng is expecting another shot in the arm today when the Corporation's CEO Zoltan O'Dillon announces that construction has finally begun on his famous advert for the aliens."

Rusholme

Minnie Brownlow turned to her husband on the sofa beside her. "More Pap-nonsense," she commented. "Every day they have a new announcement. What was yesterday's? That every shop in the country is now legally obliged to accept PapPounds. And now this. The Whitworth Park Bio-dome'll come within half a mile of this house, and if the Longsight dome goes through as well, I mean, we'll end up getting cut off. Especially if they ever get their way with that new PapWay down Wilmslow Road."

"Good, I say," her husband responded. "You can't stop progress, Min. The pound was a dead currency, everyone said so. Having PapPounds in our virtual wallets will make us all richer."

"Do you even own a virtual wallet, Brian?"

"Me? Personally? Well, no I don't. Not anymore. But plenty of other people do."

"Not us though," said Minnie. "If we didn't have the food exchange, we'd starve."

"If you hadn't lost me my job, I'd still be out there now, putting PapPounds in my virtual wallet."

"Will you ever stop blaming me for that?" Minnie sighed. "That was five years ago, and what have you done since then? Sweet F.A., that's what. You could find another job, you know, if you ever got off that fat arse of yours. But you don't, do you? You just sit there saying it's all someone else's fault."

"That's rich coming from you!" said Brian. "You who blames Lord O'Dillon and PapCorp for all the wrongs under the sun. I tell you what, things would've been much worse under Harry Lanker. He was a scruffy, bumbling, good-for-nothing socialist, and this country is all the better for seeing the back of him, the hairy wanker."

Minnie Brownlow sat gawping at her husband. But she didn't get the chance to answer before a rat-tat-tat at the door took her away. She jumped up from the sofa, clicked open the latch and found Dahlia standing outside in a woollen hat and scarf. She was breathing heavily, panic in her eyes. "Minnie," she wheezed. "Minnie, it's the exchange."

"What about it?" asked Minnie. "It's closed now till Monday."

Dahlia wiped her eyes on her sleeve. "It's closed forever, Minnie. It's on fire. Can't you smell it?"

Minnie sniffed the ash in the air. She glanced over the red-brick school at the end of the road, saw a black cloud rising up behind it and her heart skipped. She hung to the door frame to stop herself falling. "But, but…"

"A bunch of scallies are throwing petrol bombs at the building," said Dahlia, having caught her breath. "They're still down there now."

"Right," said Minnie, "then I'm going to give them a piece of my mind."

Without a word to her husband or her girls playing upstairs, Minnie shut the door behind her and scarpered down the road wearing just a sweater against the northern winter.

CEO's apartment, PapPop Tower, Manchester

Before the Zoltán Papp Tower was finished, the headquarters of almost all PapCorp's divisions were split between two 'campuses', one over the river in Salford and one just east of the city centre in Ancoats. Both were clusters of cylindrical towers shaped like long thin cans of PapPop. At almost three hundred metres tall, seventy-odd floors high, the PapPop tower was the highest structure in Manchester at the time, one of few that broke through the Bio-dome roof. And the rooms of PapCorp's CEO took up the top six storeys.

Which is why Zoltan O'Dillon was, at that moment, lying naked in the penthouse suite. He rolled his body over crisp white sheets. "Are you coming back to bed, Jemima?" he asked his advisor.

"No," Jemima Kemal responded, slipping her legs into white lace panties and doing up her matching bra. "And you should get up too, we've got a busy day coming up, remember you're on the news later."

"I'm always on the news," Zoltan complained. "Don't they know it's Saturday?"

"The markets never stop, do they? Now come on, I'm finished in the shower. It's your turn."

"So you're nice and clean? Why don't you come and let me dirty you again?"

"Because we don't have time for that, Zoltan," said Jemima. "Now, I'm serious, get up."

"We never have time," Zoltan whined. "We should go away. Just the two of us. We could go anywhere, you know."

"And wherever we go," said Jemima, "there'd be someone that knows who you are. I'd love to show you around Istanbul, but it could never happen, could it?"

"Why not? I could dress up as a pleb. No one'd notice."

Jemima grinned with all her teeth. "They'd notice," she said. "A big blond man like you walking in the Grand Bazaar, I mean, you'd stand out a mile no matter who you are. And as your face's on screens every day, someone's bound to recognise you."

Zoltan sat himself up against the headboard. "All right," he said. "But promise me one thing. When I get confirmation from my man in Spain, I want you to drink a glass of champagne with me."

"I could probably stretch to that," said Jemima.

"And give me an hour with your body."

Jemima tutted. "You can have what I give you, Zoltan, and nothing else," she said. "Now get a move on. You're on air in two hours."

Rusholme

Minnie and Dahlia charged down alleyways, around the backs of houses and the extension to Naomi's school, past the wasteland that was now a garden and a car park piled with rubbish. With every step, the flames lapped higher.

A crowd had gathered in the old supermarket car park, watching the building going up in smoke and the young men dancing in front of it. The arsonists wore tight jeans tucked into black boots, their scalps all cropped. And each was carrying a clear plastic bag. One of the boys inhaled from his and the gas sent him into a frenzy of kicking and arm wailing and screeching like a bird in pain.

Minnie noticed Neville Jennings standing watching and went straight to him. She hugged his waist and looked at the gang of yobs and the craziness in their eyes.

"What are they taking?" asked Minnie.

"Drugs," replied Neville, wrapping his arm around her and kissing the top of her head. "It's a type of solvent called MX75."

"Like the guns?"

"The very same."

"Has anyone called the fire brigade?" asked Minnie.

"Who'd do that?" said Dahlia. "This building had no insurance and no one here has the money to pay, do they?"

A few people around mumbled in agreement.

Off to their left, someone threw a rock at the hooligans. Another followed, and another. "Get lost!" shouted a man.

"Fuck off or we'll make you!" yelled someone else.

"Yeah?" replied one of the thugs. "We'll see about that." He picked up a glass bottle, lit the rag that poked from the top and hurled it into the crowd. He watched it explode and took a drag from his bag, dancing and holding his crotch in celebration.

White-hot shards of glass fell on the heads of the melee. People screamed. A woman's leg caught fire and she dropped to the ground. She was still wriggling in agony as Minnie and Dahlia scarpered away down Claremont Road. They heard more bangs but didn't look back, didn't pause for a moment; all they could think of was to flee.

They didn't see Neville stop to put out the flames, the people helping the girl to her feet, the yobs chasing them away.

In the heat of the stampede, Minnie's toe caught in a pothole and she went flying on her hands.

Dahlia heard her friend go down and stopped. "Are you okay?" she asked.

Minnie scrambled to her feet. "I'm fine," she said. "Where's Neville?"

"There he is, look." Dahlia pointed.

Sure enough, Neville Jennings was bounding up the street as fast as his long legs could carry him. "Are you okay, Minnie?" he asked when he got to her, glancing back at the line of scallies sauntering across the road. "We should get going, come on, we'll hide in the alleys. I've never seen them fellas before. I'm sure they're not from round here. My bet is they'll be too scared of getting lost to follow us in there. Come on."

PapNews Studios, Manchester

From the moment Lord Michael O'Dillon announced it, work would continue on the Zoltán Papp tower every day and every night for almost a decade and a half. The city's Bio-domes rang constantly with crashing and hammering of metal. But just metres from the construction site, within an ornate factory shell and the soundproofed green room of the PapNews studios, neither Zoltan O'Dillon nor his two advisors heard anything at all.

O'Dillon Junior was staring at Jemima Kemal's thighs as they vanished plump between her tight black skirt and the sofa beside him. But she didn't notice his attention, because like Francis Atkins opposite she was scrolling through the gossip of the day as it shone through their PapDrive contact lenses.

It was all Zoltan could do to stop himself grabbing Jemima's knee, but she'd already told him not to three times, and he didn't dare try a fourth. He got up and marched to the fridge, pulled out a bottle of champagne. "You having one, Jemima?" he asked.

But Jemima was listening to reviews of diet pills, so was unaware of her boss/lover. Zoltan lobbed a peanut and it rebounded off her head. Jemima flicked her hands and removed an earphone. "Did you just throw something at me?" she asked.

"Sure," said Zoltan, "it was the only way to get your attention."

"You could've called me on my PapDrive, you know. What do you want?"

"Would you like some champagne?"

"Have you heard from Spain then?" asked Jemima.

"Not yet, no."

"Well you're on in like twenty minutes. What're you going to say?"

"I'll tell them the truth," said Zoltan. "Like always."

"Ha!" Jemima exclaimed. "That'll be the day! I'm sure all and sundry would love to hear about how you came up with your 'advert for the aliens', and announced it without any consultation with anyone but your drinking buddy, despite everything you've since claimed. Now, I'm serious, what are you going to say when they ask what's taking so long?"

"I'm going to say we've started," said Zoltan, pouring bubbles into a second glass flute. "Whatever happens, the markets are expecting it. And it's almost true, we've been clearing the locals out of the towns and villages for months now. There's basically no one left but a few hardcore fanatics. And not a single detail has made the news, anywhere. How good's that?" He held out a tall glass of sparkling wine. "Here," he said.

Jemima took a sip from the rim. "I just hope it doesn't backfire on you," she said. "I wish you'd let us script the interview."

"I'm best when I'm freestyling," said Zoltan, downing his drink and pouring himself another. "A couple of glasses of bubbly should do the trick, get me nice and relaxed. A line or two would be even better, of course. But you don't approve, do you?"

"Cocaine makes you into a complete arse," said Jemima. "And go steady on the bubbles. You should celebrate after something happens, not before. It's bad luck."

Zoltan put down his glass. "You've got a point there," he said. "The last thing this project needs is a curse on it. Maybe I should hold out till later."

But despite his promises, when Jemima returned her attention to her PapDrive advert-feed, Zoltan O'Dillon stole himself three more glasses. By the time he went on air he still had not heard from Spain. But that didn't matter by then.

In the studio, behind one side of the PapNews desk, Zoltan slouched in his seat as he watched Carolyn Hargreaves opposite him, talking to the cameras. "We have some exclusive breaking news for you now," she announced. "I'm joined here in the studio by PapCorp CEO Zoltan O'Dillon, VC. Mr O'Dillon, welcome to PapNews, it's a pleasure to see you as always. Now what would you like to tell us?"

Zoltan cleared his throat and shifted himself up the chair. "Yes, thank you Miss Hargreaves," he said. "I'm here with great news. At last, the promise I made to the world five years ago is bearing fruit. I just got off the line with my man in southern Spain, and he's confirmed that the ground's clear for work to begin on my famous advert for the aliens."

"That's great news," said the presenter. "I can only imagine how pleased you must be. This will cement PapPop's place in history, for sure. But something all our viewers want to know is what's taken you so long to get going?"

"Legal wranglings, Carolyn. Complicated law stuff. It's never easy moving five million people, even if you're PapCorp."

The presenter giggled nervously. "You mean a few dozen people, of course," she said.

Zoltan stared at the presenter. He blinked once, twice. "Yes," he said. "Yes of course, I was just exaggerating for effect. The goats have given us more problems than any people that might've lived there."

"Of course," said the presenter. "So can you confirm it'll be ready for PapCorp's centenary in nine years' time? You know better than anyone how much speculation there's been."

"You can bet your house on it, Carol," said Zoltan. "PapEng are the best engineers money can buy. And now my father's tower's well underway, the Bio-domes virtually build themselves so we'll get to spare some of that expertise in the sunshine. Happy days all round!"

Murcia, Spain

Aliyá Talavera had lived a good childhood. Safe in her family's flat in the city of her birth, she'd barely travelled ten kilometres in all her twelve years of life. With both parents to look after her and a little group of schoolfriends, she'd been secure, oblivious to the outside world. Until, that is, a knock at the door brought the outside to her, and robbed her from the only life she'd known.

They'd been expecting that knock. Aliyá's parents had been talking about this moment for weeks and it'd taken that long to get prepared; there was a pile of suitcases packed in the hallway, the car in the garage with a fully charged tank and a house in the mountains to go to.

It was Aliyá's father who opened the door, was the first to set eyes on the trio of men in yellow jackets and matching peaked caps. "Is everyone else out?" Oscar asked in English, fingering his black moustache.

"As agreed, Señor Talavera," an officer replied. "PapSec have checked and closed every building in the city. You're the last ones left. Are you ready?"

Oscar nodded, turned to his wife and daughter. They collected their luggage without a word and filed into the corridor. Dolores pulled the door to and bolted all three locks with a single key. She clasped the piece of metal in her hand, laid her other palm on the front door and closed her eyes in prayer.

"Dónde vas?" an officer interrupted in bad Spanish. 'Where are you going?'

Dolores glared at him. "Our destination is our own business," she scorched in her native tongue. "We're not prisoners, you know. Despite all of this, we're still free people, we can still go where we choose without first seeking your company's approval. Do you understand?"

The officer nodded. "I was only trying to be friendly," he muttered to himself in English.

Dolores tutted, glancing a moment at her neighbours' door. It was locked up, had been since the Ortegas left a month back. She pulled a length of string from her handbag and fed it through the hole in the top of the key. She tied the two ends and hung the necklace around her head. "I'll never take this off," she said, tucking the key into her lemon blouse. "I'm going to wear it till the day we return."

"Right," said Oscar, pacing downstairs with a suitcase in either hand and a guitar strapped to his back. "Even those locks won't keep out a bulldozer and a knocking ball."

"You never know," said Dolores, hauling a khaki rucksack and a suitcase in either hand, her jet-black hair piled into a bouffant. She followed her husband and their daughter down the stairwell.

"Just as long as you've also got the ones for Torre Guil," said her husband.

"Of course," said Dolores. "They've been in my handbag since my sister left."

"It's a good job she gave us her house," said Oscar.

"I guess so," said Dolores. "I just wish she'd stayed with us instead of chasing some romantic dream in Paris."

"She'll be okay whatever happens," said Oscar. "She's a wily old goat is your sister."

"Exactly," said Dolores. "And we've got our own worries now."

The sound of the front door shutting sent tremors through Aliyá, like the ground was opening, swallowing her whole. With her mouth sagging in tragedy, she looked like she might break down at any minute. But despite the tears gushing down her cheekbones, she held back her wails until they'd descended four flights of stairs into the basement parking lot. She placed her pink backpack in the boot, on top of the pile of cases and bags, then got into the back seat beside her father's guitar. It was the sound of her mother shutting the door that burst Aliyá, that unleashed a storm of howling and crying and thrashing of arms and legs.

With his wife doing her best to console their daughter, Oscar Talavera scooted the car up the ramp. He found the garage door being held open by a soldier in all yellow, and checked the road before pulling out even though he knew there'd be no traffic. They passed the other two officers fixing a solid panel to the main door of their building. And as they drove through Murcia for the last time, the only car on the road, they found similar yellow boards over every door and ground-floor window in the city.

Young Aliyá took it all in through her tears. She knew in her gut that this would be the last time she'd ever see her home, and she desperately wanted to remember every detail of how it looked. She watched the orange trees fly by as they accelerated up onto the motorway, past palms and ferns, all still green despite the season. The city vanished behind fences and walls on their right, while over the roofs to their left the setting sun was throwing fiery purples over long wisps of cloud.

Rusholme

Dahlia, Minnie and Neville stopped running only when they got to a chink in the fences. Hidden behind slimy-wood panels, they hung around with hands on their haunches, listening for the screams to subside, the sound of explosions to fade away. When they thought it safe to go home, Dahlia left Neville to walk Minnie back past the rows of two-storey council houses.

"What will I do now?" asked Minnie. "That building was my life."

"That building was just a building," said Neville. "It's them people what got burnt I feel sorry for."

"You said she was okay, which is more than can be said for our food exchange."

"There's loads of places in Rusholme for a market, Min, and if you can't find nowhere you can always just go help out in the gardens. There's never enough people for all what needs doing."

Minnie stopped, fed her hand into Neville's jacket pocket and worked her fingers around his. "You always find the positives," she said. "What would I do without you?"

"I wish you'd have me full-time," he replied. "Won't you come and live with me?"

"I can't Neville, you know that. I've got Brian and the girls at home."

"Then leave them. Come on, think of yourself for once."

"Neville, I'll never leave my girls, ever. You need to have that clear, okay? And Brian? Well, he's their father. He'd be dead in weeks if I left him, he can't do a single thing for himself. You know I love you, Neville, but this is how our life is. Won't you accept that?"

"I accept that every day, Min. I just wish you'd want to be with me more often."

"I always want to be with you, Neville." Minnie smiled. "If all this means we'll end up spending more time together, then maybe there's a light at the end of this long dark tunnel."

The television was on when Minnie got back to number 56, where the inside was colder than out, as usual. She shut the door, leaned her back against it and heard the commentator saying, "the strength of the PapPound is already having an effect on the High Street, where anyone left with old pound sterling in their virtual wallets will have noticed a spike in prices." Her husband was wrapped up in a sleeping bag, their eight-year-old Naomi likewise done up in her own sack beside him. On the floor between them and the TV, their youngest daughter sat cross-legged on the carpet, pushing trains around a wooden track. It was only little Ruth that noticed her mother's arrival, and she toddled over to wrap her arms around Minnie's leg. She noticed the rips in the knees of her trousers and looked up to see tears in her mother's eyes.

"What's the matter, mummy?" she asked. "What happened to you? Where did you go?"

"Oh, Ruthie," said Minnie, picking up her daughter and balancing her on her hip. "It's so horrible I don't want to tell you."

Naomi swivelled around in her seat. "What happened, mum?" she asked. "Where've you been?"

Minnie carried Ruth over to the armchair and sat her down on her lap. She shook her head. "They've burned down the food exchange, Naomi," she said.

"What!" Naomi screamed. "Who did? When?"

"Just now," said Minnie. "It was a group of scallies throwing petrol bombs. It's gone Nao, there'll be nothing left after this."

Naomi screamed, fell to the floor and banged her fists against it. But her father just turned up the volume and shouted over the television commentary. "That's what happens," he said. "You'd never see this sort of thing under a Bio-dome because PapSec keep a tight rein on security."

"And because PapCorp own everything under there," said Minnie, "they do all they can to look after their own property, but to hell with anyone else's. I wouldn't be surprised if PapCorp planned this, you know."

"What the heck are you going on about now?" said Brian. "You reckon PapCorp employ gangs of arsonists? You said it was a bunch of scallies."

"It's PapCorp that wanted us out," said Minnie. "They've been trying to evict us from that building since, well, since before Harry Lanker. All to make way for the expansion of Wilmslow Road into one of those bloomin' PapWays. They knew this was the only way they'd get us out."

"Bah!" exclaimed Brian. "And who told you that?"

"No one needs to tell me, Brian, it's obvious, We've been protesting about it being knocked down for ages, and now this."

"I don't see why you didn't take the money," said Brian.

"Don't be daft," said Minnie. "They didn't offer anything because no one owns that building. It probably used to belong to a Muslim family, but no one really knows and it don't matter a jot now. My job's just gone up in smoke."

"Then go and work at the PapMart," said Brian. "It's bound to be better paid than the exchange. And you'd earn PapPounds directly, so everything's going to be right cheap."

"No," said Minnie. "I'm not selling myself to PapCorp, come what may. And I'm certainly not letting my girls near any of that Pap-crap. I guess I'll go and work in the gardens. I'll find a way somehow."

"I'm sure you will," said Brian. "Resourceful girl like you. Now did you hear the great news? Work has finally started on Zoltan O'Dillon's advert for the aliens. Remember when you said that'd never happen?"

Minnie cuddled her three-year-old tightly, buried her face in Ruth's little neck and bumped her up and down so no one would notice her crying.

Murcia

Ten minutes after leaving their home, with Aliyá still bawling her eyes out, the Talavera family drove off the motorway, past the cladded walls of an old shopping centre, graffitied in tags or professions of love for people long gone. Even if they were still alive, they weren't in Murcia anymore.

That's because everyone left in the city, who didn't work for PapCorp, was in a parking lot under the department store. Oscar's headlights came on automatically as they descended into the gloom, illuminating some half a dozen other cars and vans. When he switched off the engine, the only light was that which fell through the ramp. Oscar and Dolores got out and stared into the gloom. They could hear a fierce debate going on among the group of people gathered around their vehicles. All seemed to be talking at once.

"I'm just saying we should've stayed together more," said a woman in a hemp jacket with half her head shaven. "If you hadn't been so intent on charging the earth to live in your flats, we could've all congregated in the city centre and formed a protective ring. As it is, we've let them divide us and drive us out without a fight."

"We put up a fight, Mimi," said an elder man in a three-piece suit and black tie. "Have no doubt about that. Five years we worked to try and stop this happening, going through every legal case in the book. Allowing squatters into my properties wouldn't have made any difference. What chance did we ever have, really? Their pockets were always going to be deeper than ours."

"It was when they sacked all us judges," said his wife, Carmen, beside him in her pastel blue dress and matching heels. "That was when we lost. Until that point they couldn't just turn off the water supply. But as soon as they'd got their people in the right positions, that's just what they did."

As the two Talaveras approached the group, a short man in glasses and a long-sleeved shirt turned to greet them. "Señor alcalde!" he said. 'Mister mayor!' "It's nice of you to join us at last."

"The mayor of a city that no longer exists," Oscar replied.

"Well at least the council's still all together," said the man. "Is everyone out then?"

"It looks that way, Chucho," said Dolores. "Every single door we passed had been boarded up."

With his eyes growing accustomed to the light, Oscar glanced at the congregation of vans around them. "It's a good job the roof of this parking lot is high enough."

"It's why I chose this garage," Chucho replied. "Seems a lifetime since I was the manager of this store, but I still have all the keys and the codes never got changed, so here we are."

On Oscar's other side was a man in a sharp suit and tie, with a chiselled jaw-bone and hair perfectly lacquered into place. "Are you looking forward to us being neighbours?" he asked.

"Just as long as you keep the noise down, Juanjo," Oscar replied. "I'm sure we'll get along just fine."

"You know me," Juanjo Cavernas smirked. "Parties every night!"

Oscar grinned back. "Wouldn't say boo to a goose, more like. Isn't that your van?"

"It is."

"And what've you got in there? I thought you'd already moved everything."

"I have," said Juanjo. "I've been up at Torre Guil for most of last month. Five gardens are already planted up for the spring, and I've shipped enough tinned food to keep us going a year or more. We're going to thrive up there, just you watch. It'll be like a new model community. And that van's part of the plan. It's got my senior partner's library in it."

"We're only taking a small selection," said Carmen Hueso. "The rest we've had to leave behind. And most of those books are mine, not my husband's. They're for the academy. Why should kids like your daughter be denied an education just because there are no schools where we're going?"

"That's a lovely idea," said Dolores Talavera. "I'm sure other adults would be happy to help. Oscar here could teach them English, for example. It almost makes me want to get started on this new life."

"You're telling me," said Mimi Rufián, standing beside her husband Paco in his pressed shirt and bright red cap. "The sooner we get started with building a new world, the better. There'll be no property where we're going. The alcalde won't be handing out any more special privileges."

"There were never special favours with Oscar Talavera," said Juanjo, glancing at the golden face of his wrist watch. "He's the cleanest politician we've ever seen, as you know full well. Now, we should get going. Twilight's the best time to travel. We'll be able to see where we're heading and not have to use headlights, which might attract attention. As long as we keep off the main roads, we should be able to avoid any PapSec traffic and get up to Torre Guil before it's completely dark."

When her parents had got out to meet the others, Aliyá refused to leave the car. She didn't want to see anyone, and sure as hell didn't want them to see her. So when there was a knock at the window, and Aliyá found her schoolmate Paco Rufián Junior outside, all she could do was bury her face in her hands.

Little Paco could see Aliyá was upset and wished there was something he could do. So he clicked the door open and peered inside. "Are you okay?" he asked.

"No," Aliyá yelled into her hands. "Leave me alone."

"It will be okay, you know," Paco continued. "My mum says so, and she never lies."

"It won't be okay!" said Aliyá. "Your mum's a liar. Everything's finished. Nothing's ever going to be okay. Now leave me alone." She grabbed the door handle and slammed it closed.

It was a clear night over the Guadalatín depression and the Milky Way cut a diamond streak across the darkening sky. There were no street lamps, not even the cathedral was lit up anymore. Apart from the rumble of their engines, the only sound was the chirping of insects.

Aliyá stared out, tears streaming down her cheeks. She was crying so hard that she struggled to breathe. Her stomach turned like she was falling into an inferno from which there was no escape.

Dolores reached back to hold her daughter's knee. "I know it's hard, love," she said, "but we'll be okay. As long as the three of us are together, everything will be fine."

"I don't want to leave, Mamá!" cried Aliyá. "Why do we have to go?"

"Because we have no choice," said her mother.

"But why?" the twelve-year-old continued.

"We don't know why," said Dolores. "Nobody knows why. We just have to. They've turned off the water and they'll shoot us if they see us. But we'll be okay at your aunt's place, up on the side of the sierra. You'll see."

Aliyá watched the stars streaking over the lifeless shell of what had been the city of her birth. She rolled up into a ball and hid her face in her arms.

The hole this change ripped in Aliyá's life would leave her crying for weeks. But the scars these events left on her soul would fester inside her for many years, until still greater tragedies took their place. Because they were far from safe where they were going, wouldn't be until they fled Aliyá's aunt's house and escaped high into the Carrascoy mountains.

14. Carrascoy

24th May 2055
Sierra de Carrascoy, Murcia Province, Spain

Aliyá Talavera dug her fingertips into the rock face. She pushed the bare ball of her foot against a jut of sandstone and heaved herself upwards. The seventeen-year-old shrieked from the effort, muscles rippling through her legs as she stretched. She balanced herself before reaching up with her hand, to find a tickle of grass that told her she was at the top.

With both feet on the cliff, Aliyá untied the rag from her deep-brown hair and shook it loose until it flowed halfway down her back. She stepped towards the forest, doing her best to ignore the man watching her, not five metres away.

"Aren't you even going to say hola?" the young man called after her. His nostrils ballooned around the great bauble that was his nose, his hair was a tangle of frizz and his mouth hung constantly open.

"Hola Paco," said Aliyá, stopping and turning her big brown eyes to him. "Why are you still here? I told you to go."

"I wanted to make sure you were okay."

"I don't need you to check up on me, Paco."

"I know," said the teenage boy. "I was just worried about you, in case you fall. And I thought we could go to the assembly together."

"You don't need to worry, I've been climbing these rocks since I was a little girl." Aliyá glanced at the sun hanging crimson over the dusty peaks of the Sierra Espuña. "But you're right about the assembly," she said. "We shouldn't be late. Come on, let's go."

Off just a bit to the west, but still high above the plains, Oscar and Dolores Talavera were far from alone; the ancient woodland through which they were walking was alive with the shuffle of chitter-chatter. Shoes of leather and wood rustled over a carpet of pine needles as people criss-crossed the pathways, while others shouted out their wares from seats between wicker baskets on the ground.

Like most in the forest that afternoon, Aliyá's parents were wearing the best clothes they had. Oscar was in a blue-white-check shirt with just a couple of strings hanging loose from the collar, sleeves turned up to his elbows and the top buttons open to unleash a bush of hair which continued down to his forearms, all as black as his profuse moustache.

Dolores Talavera never removed the house key from around her neck, although today it was tucked under the high cut of a brown dress with stylised ferns printed white. She had a khaki rucksack on her back, battered walking boots on her feet, and hair in a badger-coloured bun curled up onto her head. She inhaled. "Can you smell that?" she asked. "That kind of musty smell in the air? That means the acacia trees must be coming into bloom."

"You know it all just smells like countryside to me, mi amor," said Oscar, stroking her arm. "But it's certainly a lovely evening for a stroll."

The Talaveras walked on barely three steps before there was a shout of "Oscar!" from the base of a tree trunk. They looked down to see a man in a faded-red baseball cap, his bush of beard protruding grey from a face the colour of almonds. His clothes were so ingrained with sand that it was impossible to tell what colour they once were. "Cabrón!" he said, rummaging around in a muddy sports bag. "I thought you weren't coming today."

"Paco, tío," said Oscar, "when have you ever known me to miss a general assembly? Trying to keep this rabble in order is the highlight of my week."

"And you do it so well, Señor alcalde!" the man slurred, looking up through his bloodshot and foggy eyes. "Listen, I've got something for you. I know how you're always up a new tipple, so I've kept this for you. Here." He held out a half-litre plastic bottle, filled with orange-brown liquid.

"What is it?" said Oscar.

"It's my orange aguardiente," said Paco Senior, struggling to his feet. "You remember how Junior and I went down to the orangery every night for two weeks last autumn, when I could still see a bit better? Everyone said we'd get caught but we never were. Well, this is the result. One of my better efforts, I think you'll find. And this bottle has your name on it."

"That's very kind of you," said Oscar. "What can I offer in return? I don't suppose you want some green beans do you? I've got a pile of them up to my balls."

"You can keep your beans," Paco said. "Señor Seda's got so many he's trying to ferment them into alcohol. Have you ever heard of anything like that? It'll taste horrendous, but if it works, well, who cares, eh? Chucho Molino exchanged a bottle for a handful of his goat's cheese. Have you tried it? It's almost like in the old days."

"Then what would you like from us?" asked Dolores.

Old man Paco leant an arm around Oscar's shoulder. "I don't want anything off you but a favour," he said.

"And what might that be?" asked Oscar, his face scrunched at the man's odour, safe in the knowledge that Paco Senior couldn't see him.

"I need you to have a word with your daughter," he replied. "My boy's crazy about her, but she acts like he doesn't exist. I hear him crying sometimes, I guess it's for his mother as much as for your daughter. But if you could just ask her to be a bit kinder to him, well…"

"He could be crying for lots of reasons," said Dolores. "Aliyá certainly does it enough and it's not over your Paco or your Mimi, rest her soul. I don't know what you want us to say to our daughter, she'll do whatever she feels like and to hell with the rest of the world."

"Just do what you can," said Paco, forcing the bottle into Oscar's chest. "Please."

"All right," said Oscar. "I can ask her to be kinder, at least. But I'm not promising anything, okay? She's more headstrong than the hostia, my daughter." He took the bottle and handed it to his wife.

Dolores tutted as she stored the drink among the beans in her rucksack. Then she worked both hands around her husband's elbow and dragged him away. "You shouldn't have accepted that," she said. "You'll never be able to give him what he wants. Aliyá doesn't listen to us at the best of times, let alone for something as personal as this."

"You saw how insistent he was, Lola," said Oscar. "And I think we were quite clear. Aliyá's her own boss, she'll do whatever pleases her. In the meantime, we're got a bottle of orange aguardiente to have with our beans at dinner."

"It's not exactly pata negra ham and red wine, is it?"

Oscar grinned. "Well, until the delivery arrives from La Rioja, this'll have to do."

Dolores smiled back. "All right," she said. "Let's just hope it doesn't make you blind like old Paco Rufián."

Aliyá bounded shoeless down the hillside, her hardened soles crunching over twigs and fir-cones as if they weren't there. Her suitor trotted a couple of paces behind, equally barefoot, his eyes transfixed on her t-shirt flapping in the draught and her buttocks bouncing around her short denim shorts.

Skipping over the green leaves of a ditch that ran along the contour of the hillside, Aliyá grabbed a tree trunk and wrapped her arms around it to stop herself. Paco did likewise at the next tree along. "What's wrong?" he asked.

"Over there," she pointed. "I saw something moving."

Paco peered into the shadows. He could make out bodies running through the forest, apparently naked. "Ha," he chortled, "you know who that is?" He stepped into the path and shouted "Juanjo!"

The movement stopped. "Who's there?" asked a man.

"It's okay, it's just me Paco Rufián and Aliyá Talavera. We didn't want to startle you. Are there many of you?"

"We're ten," shouted another voice. "We're on our way to the assembly. We're a bit late though. If you want to come with us, you'll have to get a move on."

Paco shrugged. "Okay," he said. "Why not?"

He paced forward but Aliyá pulled him back. "Be careful!" she said. "You nearly stood on a lettuce."

"I knew it was there, come on."

"Are you sure you really want to go with Juanjo?" she continued, stuck to the spot. "Remember what Señora Hueso told us about God taking revenge for his sinful ways? Maybe we'll get hit by a lightning bolt too. Or worse, maybe they'll make you join them."

"For such a smart girl, Aliyá, you really are daft sometimes," said Paco. "Old Carmen Hueso says a lot of shit. Juanjo lost his house because PapAqua said it was theirs, and they sent a drone to blow it up. That's the truth, you saw it with your own eyes. I mean, he wasn't even gay then so how could it have been in retribution? And besides, you of all people should know that guys don't interest me."

"Why me of all people? I've never seen you with a girl."

Paco's jaw dropped. He wanted to say so much, but all that came out was, "Come on, let's go."

The two teenagers darted towards a group of men with rippled stomachs and shoulders that could carry the world. Around their waists they wore the furs of small animals, but their bodies bore no other clothes.

"Why are you dressed like that?" asked Aliyá.

"For the assembly," answered one of the younger men.

"Why?" Aliyá continued. "What do you normally walk around in?"

"Walk, lie, sit," said another of the boys. "We find it much more sensual to be naked. But we know what some of the old ladies at the assembly think, and it's not worth antagonising them further, so we made these from rabbit skins."

"We like to think of it as getting closer to nature," said another lad, "to becoming one with the world and all that's in it. And as good Professor Cavernas points out, this way we don't leave a trail, no-one will find a bit of our clothing and be able to track us down."

"Are you still a wanted man?" Aliyá asked Juanjo. "Are they looking for you?"

"I can never be too careful," said Juanjo. He was some twenty years the elder of his group, with skin like leather and a fur-like fuzz over his chest, shoulders, neck and chin. "I was wrong about them sending the army up here, though. Maybe they assumed it was an accident, the guy's own fault. He might have worked for PapAqua, but that man I killed was local, he spoke pure Murciano. I suppose he wasn't as important to them as I thought. Anyway, we need to make a move. It'll be dusk soon."

The slopes of the Carrascoy would have been no-one's choice to site a closed community. The bedrock was hidden under a thin covering of bone-dry soil, and that was riddled with stones and clods of hardy grass. Life wasn't easy, certainly not at the beginning, and Mimi Rufián wasn't the only one to have fallen along the way.

But as the survivors stretched out the supplies they'd bought with them, they built themselves shelters, composted their waste, dug out ditches and planted every seed they had. They built a network of pipes from hollowed-out branches to catch the rain and bring the soil to life. As the first high ground inland from the sea, they were lucky to have enough water to store it in great cisterns they'd dug out of the rock.

With no clocks in the sierra, or at least not for most of the exiles of Murcia, meetings were dictated by the movements of the heavens. Every Tuesday afternoon, the scattered inhabitants made their way along paths scraped out by their own footprints. They first bartered their weekly produce, then as the sun descended over the mountain ranges off to their west, hundreds congregated in a glade.

Oscar and Dolores stopped to greet more of their friends on their way to the forest arena, to exchange their beans for orange medlar fruits or black haw-berries, long courgettes and miniature cucumbers, potatoes and carrots, all of which went straight into Señora Talavera's backpack on top of the bottle of spirits.

The pines thinned out into a sloped clearing and the couple made straight for the highest point. There they found an old woman sitting on a rock in the cream dress and shoes she used to wear to church. The frames of her glasses were square and blue, her hair bobbed grey atop her head.

"Hello Carmen," said Dolores, bending down. "No, don't get up. How are you? What would you like from us this week?"

"I don't suppose you want some green beans, do you?" said Oscar. "We've got a mogollón."

"No, thank you," Carmen replied in an aged croak. "I saw Señora Seda earlier and she's got the same problem, so I took five handfuls from her. They've got so many that her husband's trying to make alcohol from them."

"Let's hope he doesn't succeed," said Dolores. "There's quite enough liquor in this sierra as it is."

"Of which Señor Seda drinks about half," added Oscar. "I'm sure his good señora wouldn't mind if he drinks himself into the grave."

There was a silence as the same thought fell on all three, one that none would dare enunciate; the very same could have been said of Carmen's husband Eduardo, the former lawyer, who no longer accompanied her to these assemblies.

Dolores broke the impasse. "Aliyá's really taking these exams seriously," she said. "It doesn't seem to matter that they count for nothing, that there are no exam boards or universities for her to go to. Even without any paper, she studies the pages and she seems to memorise the ideas."

"She's certainly an exemplary student," said Carmen. "If it weren't for young Paco Rufián trying to distract her all the time, she'd do even better. Sometimes it takes everything I have not to throw him out of our classes, but then I think of his poor mother and how ashamed she'd be to see what's become of her Pacos. I just take a deep breath and carry on. But Aliyá seems to be able to clock it all out."

"She clocks most things out," said Oscar. "She lives in a world of her own half the time."

"She certainly is a strange bug," said Carmen, "I'll give you that, never comfortable unless she's got her head in a book or her feet on a rock. She's so intelligent, it's such a shame she was born when she was. She could've been a scientist or a doctor if she'd been born in our time."

"But she wasn't," said Dolores. "And that fact eats away at her every single moment of her life. She's better now she has these exams to focus on, but I really worry what'll become of her when your schooling finishes. Who knows how long she'll have to stay up here, climbing the rocks. Thank God for people like you, Carmen Hueso, that's all I can say. You've been a huge support to her. You know she prays every day because of you?"

"I'd hope she prays for the solace only the Lord can offer," said Carmen. "If anyone can help her through her woes, it's the Lord Jesus Christ. I just wish she'd dress a bit more modestly."

Oscar smiled, was about to crack a joke when a hand slapped his back. "Our Lord and Master!" proclaimed Chucho Molino, peering up through the single cracked lens of his spectacles and grinning with all the teeth he had left.

"In the sierra where everyone's equal," Oscar replied, "he with the most beans is king."

"You reckon you've got the biggest bean harvest in the Carrascoy?" asked Chucho. "Old Señor Seda has so many he's now trying to distil a bucketful into bean gin."

"I heard," said Oscar. "And rumour has it you've been working on your own product."

The man smirked. "That's right," he said, "and I've saved a piece for you." He rummaged in his pocket and brought out a large leaf folded up into a packet, which he unpicked to reveal a handful of white dice. "Have one of these," he said.

Oscar took one for himself and Dolores did likewise. She studied the bite-size piece of cheese before popping it into her mouth, then churned it around her cheeks for a good while before swallowing. "Oh my," she said. "I haven't had cheese for years. And this is really good."

"And there'll be more," said the man. "this was just the trial batch. I'll make sure you get your share when I've refined my technique."

Dolores glanced up into the sky and saw the reddened haze above. She tapped her husband's arm and pointed. "It's almost time," she said.

"And there's Juanjo and his boys," said Chucho, pointing at the nearly naked men climbing towards them. "Which means the Council of Murcia is all here. All those that can be that is. It's time to start."

"Is Aliyá here?" asked Oscar.

"I can't see her," said his wife, "Paco Junior neither. But there are no special privileges, we should make a start before the light goes."

"Quite right," said Oscar, kissing his wife's forehead. He turned to the others, perched on rocks or dry ground. "Mic check!" he shouted.

"Mic check!" dozens of others responded.

Aliyá and Paco were some trees behind Juanjo when the forest started to thin. Aliyá heard the repeated shouts of the assembly and she stopped to grab Paco Junior's bicep. "They've already started," she said.

"Yes," Paco replied. "I guess we should hurry."

"No," said Aliyá. "If we arrive late then people will talk. It's better not to go at all now, you should've run faster. Let's go and sit somewhere."

"Is that what you want?" asked Paco, trying not to smile.

"Yes."

"Great. I've a bottle of my dad's aguardiente in my bag. We can drink that."

"You know I don't like alcohol."

"Well maybe you could have a sip."

Aliyá stared at Paco so intensely he thought she was looking straight through him. She shrugged. "Maybe," she said, then brushed past her friend and led him back out the way they'd just come.

Perched on the highest rock in the clearing, Oscar Talavera directed the meeting like the conductor of an orchestra, one with no instruments but their own shouts. People sat cross-legged on cuts of wood or shards of rock. Only the speakers stood, and at this moment, Juanjo Cavernas was on his bare feet.

"We don't know when the next rains will come," he said

"We don't know when the next rains will come," dozens around him repeated so all could hear.

"But we have to be prepared when they do."

"But we have to be prepared when they do."

"The collection system is very complicated."

"The collection system…"

"You all have your patch to inspect."

"If you notice any problem, you need to tell us."

"Use the three-owl hoot."

"Or tell us now."

Oscar looked over the scene. "Does anyone know of a leak in the system?" he asked.

"Does anyone know of a leak in the system?" went the Chinese whisper.

A dozen or so hands went up. "This is a problem," Oscar said to his wife. "We're going to have to get this sorted before the next rains come. Okay, who's first? Señora Seda."

Beside him, Juanjo noticed Carmen with her hand raised. The almost-naked man leaned in and whispered. "Why didn't you say anything, Señora?" he asked. "You know you only have to call and I'll be right round. I won't have you and Eduardo wanting for anything, not after all you did for me over the years."

"I don't know," Carmen replied, refusing to return the man's gaze. "It's like I don't even recognise you anymore, Juanjo. You've allowed Sodom and Gomorrah into your life and I don't want you infecting my husband with any of your wickedness. Things are hard enough for him as it is without having to see what's happened to his protégé. So thanks for the offer, but I'd prefer someone else helped us."

Aliyá plonked herself down on the ledge of a rock and dangled her legs over the side. Paco sat down right beside her and Aliyá shuffled away. But Paco didn't follow, he reached instead into his bag and pulled out a battered plastic bottle filled with brown-orange liquid. When he looked back at Aliyá, he saw tears running down her face.

"What is it, Ale?" he asked. "Why are you crying?"

She shook her head. "It's just everything," she said. "I mean, look at that. That used to be our home. Now we have to live up here like cavemen while some foreign corporation tears apart our houses. What did we do to deserve this? It's so unfair." She bent her face into her palms and broke down in tears.

Paco shuffled over and put an arm around his friend, but she shrugged him away. Unsure of what to do next, Paco said, "at least you've got both your parents, and you're all healthy."

"What's that supposed to mean?" said Aliyá, lifting her head to look at him. "Just because my mum's not dead and my father isn't a blind alcoholic, I can't feel sad sometimes?"

"I didn't mean that, I just meant that we're all living through difficult times."

"I can't believe you'd attack me for having both my parents alive."

"I didn't attack you, Aliyá. I'm just trying to say I understand how you're feeling."

"You don't understand, Paco, that's the problem." She tucked her knees to her chin and gazed out at the red fog consuming the valley.

The sunsets over the Guadalentín depression made Aliyá think the universe was on fire, the burning dust clouds below, the pink and orange flames lapping the sky. As the sun's light faded, so too did the pencil-line peaks on the horizon. Aliyá and Paco sat dwelling on the plains, at the crashing of distant bulldozers under the kicked-up dirt or the tree-shaking tremors of the explosions. Paco Junior took another swig of homemade liquor. "My dad's got a new theory," he said.

Aliyá didn't respond.

Paco tapped her arm. "I said my dad's got a new theory," he repeated.

"I can hear you, Paco," said Aliyá, drying her cheeks on the hem of her t-shirt.

"He's now convinced himself that they're building an advert for extra-terrestrials. He reckons it's the only logical explanation."

"Qué dices?" Aliyá sneered. 'What are you saying?' "You think they're going to all that effort for some advert? One no one could even see unless they come from another planet? That's ridiculous!"

"I didn't say I believe it," said Paco. "I said that's what my dad now thinks. I'm still convinced it's a launch station for a mission to Mars."

"I know," said Aliyá. "And my mum reckons it's an enormous solar panel farm. That's the best explanation I've heard. You can see it sometimes, like great flat sheets that glint in the sun when it's windy enough to blow away a bit of the dust."

Paco held the bottle towards his friend.

"No," she said.

"Come on, Aliyá," said Paco. "It's fine. My dad said it's one of his best."

"Paco, your dad's almost blind from his own alcohol. Just because he's tried it doesn't make it okay to drink."

"I've already had some. Look!" He raised the bottle and took a swig, then held it out to Aliyá. "Go on," he said. "Just try it."

Aliyá glanced from Paco Junior to the bottle and back again. "Is it good?" she asked.

"It's the best there is," Paco replied.

Aliyá took the bottle by the neck. She watched the liquid as she swilled it around, then held the rim to her lips.

Aliyá swallowed and the moonshine burned down her throat. She scrunched up her face. "Urgh!" she exclaimed, spitting onto the rocks. "That's absolutely disgusting! I can't believe you like it."

"I didn't say I liked it," said Paco Junior. "I said it's the best there is." He grabbed the bottle back and tipped it vertically to his lips. With three large gulps, most of the liquid was gone. "That's what I mean," he said, swaying on his rocky seat. "That's the kind of thing that we need to get us through living in this shit hole."

"Did your father give you that bottle?"

"No. I earned it."

"What for?"

"For helping him make it, of course."

"But does he know you've taken it?"

"Not this one, no. Why? This is a sharing society, isn't it?"

"That's not how it works," said Aliyá. "We might have no property, not like they used to, but your dad made that so it was his to do with as he pleased. It's stealing no matter what you say."

Paco tipped a last mouthful down his throat. "He doesn't even know how many bottles we made," he said. "He was never any good at maths, even when he could see."

"I just don't like stealing, that's all," said Aliyá.

"What does it matter? If I don't take them, my old man will only drink them or hand them out for favours. There are too many old drunks among us, that's our problem. They're too happy to sit around up here and share out homemade liquor, while some foreign invader flattens our homes. We need to organise ourselves, to take them on."

Aliyá scoffed. "You've had a bottle of your father's aguardiente and now you're ready to fight that lot down there?" she said. "Well, good luck with that. Whatever PapAqua is, if it can clear a city by buying all the water and then make this much mess, well, it must be pretty powerful." Aliyá hugged her knees closer to her chest.

By now, the sun had set and the last of its flames had gone out. Overhead, the moon fuzzed pink in the dust and a few stars sparkled red. The only noise they could hear was the rustling of wind against leaves and the clunking of machinery from below.

It was agreed that the assemblies would last only as long as Oscar could still see hands waving among the participants. Even though the moon's reflection gave a reddish glow to the forest arena, it was soon time to bring the weekly meeting to a close, to break up into small groups of friends or committees, to leave the glade over footpaths or rocks.

Oscar and Dolores always waited to see everyone off before heading home themselves. When they were the only two left, Dolores turned to her husband. "Do you think Aliyá's all right?" she asked. "She wasn't at the assembly and she did say she was going to be there."

"I guess she changed her mind," said Oscar. "But old man Rufián was on his own as well, so I guess young Paco must be with her."

"I suppose," said Dolores. "I just wish she wouldn't go off like that without telling us."

Oscar shrugged. "It's how she is," he said. "Come on, let's go home."

Like most of their compatriots in the Carrascoy, the Talaveras lived in a single-room shack cut out of the hillside. Its roof was a softly pitched tangle of sticks and dried grass with turf piled over it. In the darkness of the forest it would've been impossible to spot had Dolores not painted ever-enlarging white 'T's on the bark. Which is how they found their way.

The moon and stars lit Aliyá's path in a hazy pink reflection. She led Paco Junior by the hand as he staggered along with an empty bottle in the other. All she could think of was making sure he didn't fall and hurt himself.

Aliyá came to a halt at the sight of a large 'T' painted white on a tree trunk.

"Why have we stopped?" Paco Junior slurred.

"This is my house, Paco, I'm going in now. Do you think you'll be all right getting home on your own?"

"I don't want to go home on my own," he slurred. "I want to come home with you." He took a step towards her.

"There's no space at my house for you to sleep, Paco. And after all that drink, you'll probably snore like a pig. What are you doing?"

Paco had his hands around Aliyá's waist and was rubbing himself against her. "Kiss me, Aliyá," he said.

"What!?" she yelled, pushing him away. "What are you doing, Paco?"

"I love you, Aliyá. I want to kiss you."

"Stop it, don't say things like that. You're only saying that because you're drunk!"

"I needed a drink to tell you," Paco slurred. "But this is how I always feel. Come on, kiss me. Just a little bit. I love you so much it hurts."

"What do you know about love?" asked Aliyá, shoving Paco in the chest with both hands. He staggered backwards, balancing himself on a tree and made sad eyes at her. She saw his expression, tutted, shook her head and vanished off into the forest.

Aliyá barged through the door of their hut, a hessian sack covering a gap in the pile of half-split tree trunks that made up the front wall. She went straight for her straw bed and collapsed face-down into her arms.

"Aliyá?" asked Dolores in the dark. "Is that you?"

Aliyá sniffed.

"Are you crying again?" said her mother. "What's happened now?"

"Leave me alone, mamá," she replied.

"Come on Aliyá, tell me. I'd like to help if I can."

"Just leave me alone! That's all I want."

Dolores listened to her daughter whimpering and sobbing for as long as she could before finally she asked, "Are you sure you don't want to talk?"

Aliyá sniffled. She got up from her bed and pulled aside the door-bag. "I just wanted a bit of peace and understanding," she muttered.

"Hey," Oscar shouted after her. "Are you going to see your friend, Paco?"

"No."

"Don't you think you might want to? He's a nice guy, don't you think?"

"No."

"Okay, well just be careful out there. In God's name, don't get spotted by a drone."

"Venga, papá!" Aliyá replied from the other side of the curtain. 'Come on, dad!' "They're not looking for us anymore." And with that she was gone.

15. The Referendum

1st June 2053

Carolyn Hargreaves, with her bobbed blonde hair, smiled plastic pink from every screen. "You're watching voting day coverage from PapNews," she said. "I and my colleagues will be with you throughout the day, bringing you uninterrupted coverage of what promises to be an historic event. Thanks to one of the many innovations in this referendum, we'll be able to bring you the result the moment polls close at ten this evening. Shortly, we'll be taking a look at the more revolutionary aspects of this vote, from the use of PapDrive voting technology to extending the voting age to fourteen-year-olds for the first time ever. But first, we're going over to the Houses of Parliament where our reporter Vincent Humbolt is waiting."

The shot flicked to a man standing on the lawn between the Abbey and the Palace of Westminster, before a backdrop of the four-columned Victoria Tower and the criss-crossed ceiling of a Bio-dome. His hair was as neatly combed as possible, but still curled up at his ears. His eyes sparkled, and when he spoke it was with a North Yorkshire twang. "When Lord Michael O'Dillon was asked to oversee the country," he said to the camera, "Britain was on the verge of a major crisis. Five years on, and his reforms have helped this nation to its longest period of sustained economic growth since the turn of the century. While many are seeing this referendum as a vote of confidence in the First Lord, the new constitution is thorough and varied. It'll reduce membership of the House of Commons to 427, the number of seats in the chamber. A percentage of those members will be appointed by the Prime Minister, so Britain will never again get stuck under the rug of minority government. But the referendum is about more than just politics, because if enough people say yes today, you can say goodbye to the pound in your pocket – all pound sterling still in accounts will be transferred to PapPounds at midnight, at the very generous exchange rate of four-to-one. There will also be some more technical elements such as the full use of PapDrive Augmented Vision throughout the country and the liberalisation of planning laws to fast-track vital infrastructure..."

Rusholme

At 56 Welwyn Street, six-year-old Ruth Brownlow was sitting cross-legged on the carpet, tapping away at her old laptop computer. In the girls' room upstairs, Naomi was singing into the mirror so loudly that her father had to turn up the volume on the telly to max. Minnie was beside him at his normal place on the sofa, glued to the screen like he was. "Are they serious?" she asked. "What about the most important bit? If Michael O'Dillon wins today, he'll be made Prime Minister for life! How can they not mention that we're voting for a dictatorship?"

"You can't vote for a dictatorship, Minnie," said her husband, "that doesn't make sense. What this country needs is firm and decisive leadership. As everyone knows, representative democracy brought this country to its knees. Which is why I'm voting yes."

"So you're going to leave the house?"

"I have to, Minnie. It's my patriotic duty. Even the King said so."

"And how, precisely, are you going to do that? You've hardly moved beyond this sofa and your bed for eight years. And now you're going to leave the house to help make Lord Michael O-bloody-Dillon Prime Minister for life? I was just wondering how you'll be able to do it, with your bad knee and everything."

"My knee's only bad sometimes."

"Sometimes, like every time I've ever asked you to take the girls outside. Little Ruthie's never once been to the park with you in her entire life."

"It's not like that, Min. I'm normally a bit unsure on my pegs these days, but today I feel fine. And I've made plans."

"Oh really?" asked Minnie. "And what might they be?"

But Brian didn't need to respond because a knock on the door did it for him. When Minnie Brownlow opened the latch she found three large men in tight yellow uniforms. "Yes?" she asked.

"We're here to provide an escort to the polling station," said an officer.

"Are you?" said Minnie. "It's only at the end of the road. I think we can manage, thank you very much."

"Ma'am," said the man. "PapSec Community Crime Prevention Officers are providing assistance to millions across the country today. We're helping anyone too infirm to walk themselves or too scared of going through a no-go zone like Rusholme. We have a request here from a Mr Brian Brownlow."

"Have you now?" she asked, glancing inside to find her husband standing with a coat around his shoulders. She couldn't help smiling. "You won't need that," she said, pinching his collar.

"I don't know, Min," he replied. "It's a bit chilly."

"And about ten degrees warmer outside, as always. Come on girls!" she shouted, "We're going out."

The red bricks of Welwyn Road shone warm in the afternoon sun, front yards buzzed with wildflowers. But Minnie barely noticed as she staggered under the weight of her husband's arm around her shoulders. The three PapSec men kept watch with guns at the ready as if guarding a VIP through a war zone.

"Isn't it great that PapSec make it safe to vote?" said Brian between breaths. "I wouldn't feel secure here otherwise, not these days."

"There's no one here," said Minnie, gazing around the street. She found Ruth was walking beside her, but eleven-year-old Naomi moping behind. "Come on Naomi, keep up!" Minnie shouted.

"I don't see why I have to come," Naomi replied, eyes to the ground. "It's not like I get to vote, is it? Why do I have to go to school on a Sunday? We could've stayed at home, I could've looked after Ruthie."

"Because you're eleven and I'm not leaving you at home alone for any reason, anything could happen. Besides, this is something very important you're witnessing today."

"A stupid vote?" said Naomi, "it doesn't really matter."

"How I wish you were right, Naomi," her mother replied.

"Yeah," said little Ruth. "If Michael O'Dillon wins today, we'll never be allowed to say anything ever again."

The polling station was at the bottom of their road, in the school which both Ruth and Naomi attended, the only non-PapEd place around. It may have been some two dozen houses from their front door, but in those few hundred feet, and despite Minnie's help, Brian had to stop for breath twice. When they got to the school gate, he was panting so heavily that he couldn't talk. Between the PapSec officers guarding the fence, an elderly lady with a bow in her grey hair and a cravat around her neck was waiting to welcome the voters. "Hello," she said, smiling. "Haven't we got a lovely day for it? Now I hope you've got your voting slips."

Minnie waved two pieces of paper.

"Very good," the lady continued. "I suppose your daughters still aren't old enough."

"No, they're only eleven and six," said Minnie.

"Well. they'll be voting soon enough," said the woman. "This place has been full of kids all day, you'd hardly believe it. I remember when you had to be an adult to vote, but not anymore. Fourteen is old enough these days." Her eyes flicked at Brian and saw he wasn't interested. She scanned their cards and irises, then pointed to the computer screens lined up like self-service check-in desks along the school wall. "So if you'd kindly head over to the polling terminals," she said. "You're ready to vote."

"Where are the booths?" asked Minnie. "Can't I just write an anonymous 'x' on a piece of paper like we usually do?"

"No, my dear, not anymore. They've finally updated the system to be fully digital. If you had a PapDrive you could've voted from the comfort of your own home. This new system means we won't have to spend hours counting little bits of paper. We'll get the final results as soon as the polls close, so we can all be in bed at a reasonable hour."

"But isn't that open to abuse?"

"Abuse?" the woman smiled. "Of course not, dear. PapTech have designed it in such a way that it's impossible to breach the security system."

"PapTech built it?" asked Minnie. "Lord O'Dillon's company? Isn't that a conflict of interest?"

"What's that now, dear?"

"I mean it's a vote on Michael O'Dillon, the former CEO of PapCorp, whose son now runs the company, about whether to allow him to stay in power forever. And the voting system was built by the tech division of that very same PapCorp. It might be impossible for anyone else to break in, but PapTech have all the codes, haven't they? They can alter the result any way they choose."

"Oh, they wouldn't do a thing like that," said the lady. "PapCorp's an honest company, and Michael O'Dillon's a good man. They wouldn't cheat the system, they don't have to."

PapPop Tower, Manchester

Zoltan O'Dillon was watching a 3D-projection of naked women through his PapDrive lenses when Jemima strolled into his office. He swiped the back of his hand before his face to see her standing in front of him, in a cream dress that hung to her hips and thighs. She flashed her teeth and sat down opposite. "We have to talk about this interview," she said.

Zoltan rearranged himself. "Have you read over the transcripts then?" he asked.

"Of course," she replied. "You sent it to me three hours ago."

"Did I? Well, doesn't time fly when you're enjoying yourself? So go on then, what do you think?"

"Are you really going to say all that?"

"Of course," said Zoltan, leaning his elbows on the desk. "Why? Should I change something?"

"Change something?" she said. "It's your father's big day and you're going to try and sabotage it. This bit here, let me read it to you. 'If Michael O'Dillon becomes the dictator of Britain, he'll destroy this country. Take my word for it, my father is the most evil, corrupt and dishonest person in the world, and there's no way he should be allowed all this power'."

"So should I moderate it a bit?" asked Zoltan. "Maybe not call him a dictator?"

"Nor evil nor corrupt nor dishonest. Zoltan, you really can't say all this stuff live on air."

"Can't I? Why not? I'm the CEO of PapCorp, for goodness sake. I can say what I want and people have a right to hear my views."

"Okay, just imagine this," said Jemima, "if your father were to lose this vote because of you, you've had it. You're only CEO because the establishment thought it too much for him to be head of both the country and PapCorp at the same time. If he's no longer Prime Minister, he'll want his old job back. Your job."

"Well he'll have to go whistle for it then, won't he?"

"Zoltan, try to be serious for a moment. If he goes to the shareholders, you're done for. Even without opening that enormous box labelled 'Zoltan O'Dillon Cover-ups', he's still got more support than you by a mile. You'll be out of a job and disinherited, and that's if they don't throw you in jail for the rest of your life. It's in your interests to support him. I mean, we don't want the possibility of another Harry Lanker now, do we?"

Zoltan closed his eyes, shook his head slowly. "How do you always do that?" he asked.

"Do what?"

"Always see the angle I've missed. I don't know what I'd do without you, Jemima Kemal. You truly are my Number One Lady. I could kiss you."

"Not now," she replied. "We've got work to do. Do you want me to redo the script?"

"Nah, don't worry. I'll just repeat the same old bullshit about Augmented Vision and the PapPound, I won't even have to think about it. So it looks like we'll be free for an hour or so..."

Rusholme

With Naomi and Ruth asleep upstairs, and a day of picking vegetables to look forward to, Minnie Brownlow wanted to go to bed. But Brian had begged her to stay up for the result, and in the end she'd relented. As ten p.m. approached, she was sitting with her arms crossed and sulking.

"Isn't it exciting?" said Brian. "I so hope he wins. He'll really shake this country up."

"What's he going to shake up?" said Minnie. "He's already been in charge for five years and has done quite enough shaking, as far as I'm concerned."

"That was different. Until now he's only been First Lord. From today he'll become Prime Minister for real."

"And for life..."

As every minute ticked by, the background music to the television commentary grew steadily faster. At thirty seconds to ten, the screen filled with a Grenadier Guard in his red coat and bearskin cap. He was strumming an angled drum on his left thigh, rolling it ever quicker as a clock ticked down in the corner of the screen. The timer reached zero to a crashing crescendo, the screen went blank then flashed with

'Yes: 87.7 per cent,

No: 12.3 per cent'.

Brian's fists shot into the air. "Yes!" he shouted, with a look he hadn't shown since he'd last scored a goal, twelve long years ago. He jumped up from the sofa, forgetting his bad knee, and danced a couple of steps.

"I don't believe it," said Minnie. "It's only five years since most people voted RASCAL, and now we're supposed to believe everyone's changed their minds about O'Dillon?"

Brian pointed at Minnie. "Sore loser!" he yelled.

Minnie shook her head. "If it weren't for our two girls," she said, getting up from the sofa, "I'd have left you long ago. I'm off to bed. Please don't make too much noise." She made for the stairs.

"Aren't you even going to stay for O'Dillon's acceptance speech?" Brian shouted after her. "Come on Min, don't be such a bad loser!"

But Minnie was upstairs in a flash, so Brian had to celebrate alone with only the television news for company.

10 Downing Street, London

At ten-thirty that night, on screens and lenses across the spectrum, Lord Michael O'Dillon addressed the nation. With a Union Jack and the yellow flag of PapCorp hung crossed behind his shoulders, he leaned his forearms on a mahogany desk and spoke straight to camera. "People of Britain," he said. "What you have done today will go down in history. Today will be remembered as the day Britain stopped obsessing about past glories and embarked on a new future. As you've proven, the great majority of people agree that universal suffrage led to the worst decline in this nation's history. Giving the vote to every Tom, Dick, Harry, and Harriet shattered our industry and sapped our spirit, lost us the empire and our place atop the world. Some say all history is a repetition of past events, but what we have witnessed today is something completely new. This is the first time ever that a democratic country has freely chosen to give up the privilege of voting in order to secure a safer, more prosperous future for all our children. Universal suffrage and human rights bred one entitled generation after another, who thought it their responsibility to break down the system and rebuild it in their own image. They failed. I have succeeded. Now we will see what true glories my PapState can bring to Britain. God Save the King!"

On every device in the country, Lord O'Dillon's fat grin faded into a fluttering Union Jack and the first notes of the national anthem.

In Rusholme, Brian Brownlow stood with a fist on his heart and belted out the same verse three times.

16. Business

17th September 1959
Ancoats, Manchester, England

Attila Bacsik rolled out from under a tangle of copper pipes, screwdriver in hand. "Probáld ki most," he said. 'Try it now.'
Standing over his brother, Gábor twisted a brass wheel until steam was panting through the system. He flicked switches and the conveyor belt passed bottles under a nozzle dribbling yellow liquid.
"Kurva életbe!" Zoltán Papp cursed. "Now it's far too weak! It's going to be impossible to get this right. Either it's so strong it almost smashes the bottles, or it's so weak that there's barely three drops in each. It's so frustrating. We've got everything ready to go except this, I can't believe this one thing is so difficult. How will we ever get this plant running?"
"Calm down, Zoli," said Attila. "We're doing really well. They gave us a month to finish. We've not even been at it three weeks and we're already making adjustments. A couple more days and we'll be ready to go."
They were in a long warehouse, under the last in a series of pitched roofs with windows along each side of the apices. H-section pillars held up the lower ledges of the zig-zag ceiling and separated the warehouse into bays, each with moving gantries that clattered over rivets as they picked up sacks of potatoes from one end and piled them up elsewhere.
Papp and the Bacsiks could hear the workers shouting, but they couldn't see them because the Hungarians had closed off their end with sheets of white linen. Hidden from the eyes of the warehouse workers, they'd assembled a jumble of pipes and glass globes, conveyor belts and machinery for mixing, bottling, capping and labelling.
Their own moving gantry sat stilled above the far wall, where wooden crates of empty bottles were piled up either side of the only door.

In through that opening walked Éamon O'Dillon, carrying a bowl covered in a tea-towel which dropped from the circular rim. "You're going to like this one, boys!" he said. "It's the missus's speciality cottage pie. I had it for me tea before I come here. Bloody lovely it is, let me tell you."

"Thanks," said Zoltán Papp, taking the bowl and laying it on a workbench.

His hands free, Éamon retrieved a pipe from one jacket pocket, stuffed it with tobacco from another, and lit it with a match from a third. "How you progressing, young Zoltán?" he asked. "We're getting there," said Papp, removing his cap and dabbing it over his forehead. "We're just making adjustments."

O'Dillon puffed a cloud of smoke through his nostrils. "Excellent," he said. "Have you been outside today?"

"We don't go outside since you drop us off here," said Zoltán. "We hardly have a breath of fresh air. Is like working in a sauna. Is Manchester always like this?"

Éamon chuckled. "Of course it is, Zoltán," he replied. "Manchester's as famous for its weather as it is for its air. Now, there's something you need to see. Come on. Bring your mates and all, I think they're going to like it."

Zoltán shrugged. "Fiúk!" he yelled. 'Guys!' "Éamon's got something to show us."

Attila pushed himself from under the bottling plant. "We're in the middle of this," he replied in Hungarian. "We can't stop now."

"Well, come as soon as you can," said Zoltán, and followed his business partner outside.

As they stepped out the door, a double-decker bus chugged past and left a cloud of black smoke in its wake. It was corporation red with a cream stripe above the lower windows, below an advert running along the upper floor that read 'ssschweppesss'.

Zoltán felt a hand on his shoulder. "That'll be PapPop on the side of buses pretty soon," said Éamon, turning his business partner to face the warehouse. "Now tell me, what do you make of that?" He pointed up towards the roof which undulated down Oldham Road, circular windows below the point of every sooted-brick triangle. All units were identical, except theirs, because between the rose window and the door of their end unit, bold yellow lettering now proclaimed

'Papp Beverages Ltd.

Makers of PapPop'.

Zoltán gawped up at the sign.

"Doesn't it make you proud?" asked O'Dillon.

"Is ok," said Zoltán. "But won't stay this bright for long with the air like this. Are you sure this is the best place for a drinks manufactory? Next to all these chimneys and the train station, I mean."

Éamon chuckled. "They've been bottling water and fruit juices in this city for two hundred years," he said. "And no one ever complains at the purity of J&B's Lemonade or Slack & Cox's Eau de Seltz now, do they? If it's good enough for Charlie Boddington, it's good enough for Zoltán Papp. Don't you agree?"

"Who's Charlie Boddington?"

"Never mind," Éamon chuckled. "Besides, this air? This is nothing. It was far worse before. We used to have some real peasoupers up here, until they changed the law. The new smokeless fuels have made a right difference." He edged towards the door. "But you haven't seen the half of it," he said. "You see them tubes around the letters? Well, they're not filled with PapPop, let me tell you that. Prepare to be amazed." He reached inside the door frame, clicked a switch and the letters flickered fluorescent. "Well?" Éamon said, standing back in admiration. "What do think? I bet they don't have signs like that in Clun or communist Hungary."

"Not in Clun," said Zoltán. "But there plenty lights like that in Budapest. Is big city…"

The men didn't dwell long on the fallacies of Western propaganda before the roar of an engine and skidding of tyres announced a bright blue Turner Sports car with the top down. Callum O'Dillon brought the frog-eyed headlamps to a halt just inches from the chrome bumper of the only other car around.

He honked his horn, clapped his hands above his head and jumped out onto the pavement. "Will you look at that?" he yelled. "Papp Beverages Limited, our very own company! All that's left to do is sign the papers and we'll be ready to take on the world. I've got a great feeling about this fellas! PapPop's going to be the next big thing!" He slapped both his partners on their backs.

In the rush of Callum's appearance, the Bacsik brothers had emerged from the warehouse, their faces and overalls smeared with grease. But they weren't admiring the sign.

"Mik a fasz azok?" shouted Gábor, pointing at the pair of cars. 'What the cock are those?' "Our labour's paying for them. Are we breaking our backs every day just so those two can drive around in flash automobiles? They've got new cars while we're sleeping on the wooden floor of a potato shed. And they still haven't paid us a penny. Zoli, you're supposed to be the boss. You need to stand up to them, for all our sakes. Go on, you speak good English, tell them we're not happy."

As Zoltán listened to the Hungarian, he didn't hear Callum address him in English. So he was surprised to find the younger O'Dillon shouting at him from just feet away. "I said, is it all set up yet?" asked Callum. "We have to get on with production."

"You give us four week for finish," Zoltán replied with all the calm he could muster. "We are only in the week three and we already on the fine tuning. We'll be ready on time."

Callum tutted, shook his head. "I knew we should've brought in Meadowcroft's own men," he said. "It's their kit, after all. What do these guys know about assembling a bottling plant?"

"You should go and see it," said Éamon. "They've done really well. The place looks great, proper professional."

"The workers of Csepel are the best mechanics in the world," said Zoltán.

"I'm not doubting their abilities with iron bashing or whatever they did," said Callum. "But we're not behind the Iron Curtain now, you know. You're in the crucible of the Industrial Revolution, just you remember that. The Mancs invented the machine, pretty much. There's nothing these guys can teach us."

"The English also invent a game called football," said Zoltán. "And we Hungarians teach you a lesson there, didn't we?"

Callum shook his head. "I'm not talking about football," he said. "If we hadn't had to wait for you lot to finish mucking around on Gritton's farm, we'd be up and running by now."

"Mr Gritton was very good to us," said Zoltán. "We couldn't just leave him, after everything he did. He needed us all the summer, and we still would be working there now if you didn't persuade him for let us go at end of August. He would pay us as well, and even the little caravan we slept in was better than a bed of sacks on the factory floor. You said we have a month. We only three week in so we on time, don't worry about that. And while we break our balls to try to get this finished, why are you two driving new cars?"

"These cars are necessary for our business," said Éamon, between puffs on his pipe. "And you'll get paid at the end of the month, like all of us. Now, we've got things to discuss. Let's go."

"Just a mo," said Callum, fumbling around in his car. "We should record this moment for posterity. We need to take a photo. Maybe one of the boys can do it?" He stood to face the others, brandishing a Bakelite box.

"Why we need to make photo?" asked Zoltán. "We very busy, you know."

"All in its own time," said Callum. "No need to rush, it's still ten minutes till opening time. We should savour the moment. It's not every day you start a new business empire, is it? Now come on, come over here and stand in front of the sign with us. Can you get one of your mates to take the photo?"

Zoltán shrugged. "Átosh!" he shouted to the older brother. "Do you know how to use one of these?"

"Persze," replied Attila, taking the camera. 'Of course.'

The three directors lined up with their backs to the factory.

"Okay," said Callum. "Now this ain't going to be one of them old Victorian-type photographs where everyone stands around looking unhappy. We should be a bit more 'with it'."

"What you mean?" asked Zoltán.

"I don't know," said Callum, "let's make it a bit funny."

"We might want to send this photo to the Press," said Éamon. "We need to be looking shipshape and Bristol fashion."

"Jeez, come on brother, loosen up. Things are changing, old man, you mark my words. The Sixties are just around the corner and it's my generation who'll be running the show from now on. It's us we have to appeal to."

Éamon shrugged. "All right," he said, "if you insist. We'll do one sensible one and one silly one, how's that?"

"Fine," said Callum, "but the daft one first. Now come on, pull faces like me."

As the three men posed, Attila peered through the square lens and clicked a circular button.

He took the camera from his eye and shifted the grooved-plastic dial with his thumb. "Take another now, Attila," said Zoltán in Hungarian. "This is the sensible one."

But Attila kept winding. "Nincs több film," he said.

"What did he say?" asked Callum. "He said there's no more film."

"Well, was the picture okay?"

"Jó volt a kép?" Zoltán translated.

"Nem, kurva szár volt," Attila replied. 'No, it was whoring shit.'

"What did he say?" asked Callum.

"He said it's fine."

"Should I get another film?" said Callum.

"Don't bother now," said Éamon. "We can do that tomorrow or some other day. Come on, we need to talk."

"Okay," said Zoltán. "Talk."

Callum glanced at the Bacsik boys. "We mean in private," he said. "Let's go to the Dans."

"They no even understand English," said Zoltán. "You can say what you want."

"What we want to say ain't for their ears," said Callum, "Whether they understand it or not. We're the bosses and they're our workers."

"Let's put it this way," said Éamon. "We've got some papers to sign and it'd be better if it was just the three of us, the three directors of the company and nobody else."

Zoltán looked the O'Dillon brothers up and down, at their new tailored suits and lacquered hair. He shrugged, shook his head and turned to the engineers. "I've got to go," he said in Hungarian.

"Where?" asked Gábor. "To the pub? Are you going to buy us a drink?"

"I can't," Zoltán replied. "I mean, I'm going to the pub, but you can't come."

"Why not?" Gábor continued. "We've been working as hard as you."

"I know that," said Zoltán. "But it's a directors' meeting, and they don't want you there." He reached into his jacket and produced a folded note printed red with the Queen's head on one side, Britannia on the other. "Take this," he said. "Go and have a few drinks. You're celebrating as much as I am. This company's as much yours as it is mine. I might see if I can find you later, so don't go too far, okay?"

Zoltán pulled a metal shutter over the door and fastened it with a padlock. When he turned back, his countrymen had gone.

"You coming with me?" asked Éamon. "There's plenty of space."

Papp shrugged. "Is not far, is it?"

"No," Éamon replied. "Ten minutes on foot, two in the car. Have you ever been in a Rover P5?" He pointed to the black vehicle in front of his brother's, with its chrome lines along the doorframes and down the middle of the grill.

Zoltán shook his head, opened the passenger door and released a waft of new leather and freshly polished cherrywood. He sat in a beige seat and it engulfed him.

Éamon turned the ignition and the engine coughed into a steady purr. "What do you think?" he asked, putting his hands on a steering wheel around an inner ring of chrome. "Isn't she a beauty? I've not had her two weeks, but I've already taken her up Preston to stretch her legs a couple of times. Got to almost a hundred in fact. Have you heard of the Preston bypass, Zoltán?" He pulled out into the road.

"No."

"They're calling it a motorway," Éamon explained. "First in the country. Soon they'll be everywhere. Great wide stretches of tarmac without any bikes or horsecarts to slow you down, and barely any cars either, certainly not ones that can go over ninety miles an hour!"

"That sounds good," said Zoltán blankly. "Did you buy this car?"

"You mean me, personally?"

Zoltán nodded.

"Well no, of course not. I can't afford a machine like this. Papp Beverages paid for it. It's for work, after all."

"How could the company buy it?" said Zoltán. "When the company no even exist? I mean, before we sign the registration papers."

Éamon grinned. "The same way I got you that giant chemistry set," he replied. "When I said I was well connected, son, I meant it. Between you, me and the gatepost, the manager of the local District Bank is in my lodge, so he's pulled a few strings for us, if you see what I mean. We need these cars to do our work just as much as you need them pipes and cylinders to do what you do. We're scouring the family stores and tea rooms of Lancashire trying to flog the bloody stuff, and just imagine if we show up on a bicycle or in a shitty old van. What'd they think of us then? That we were small-time wasters, that's what. There's too many drinks makers in Manchester as it is, and most of them have factories what look like palaces. So if we want this company to be a success, we have to think big. We have to make ourselves stand out and make it look like we've got a bit of brass

behind us. Hence the bright yellow sign and the smart automobiles. And our investment's already started paying off."
"Why's that?"
"Because we've got our first orders, Zoltán."
"Really? So soon?"
Éamon slapped Papp's leg. "Let me get the beers in and I'll tell you all about it," he said, turning his car into a side road. He parked beside a ground-floor wall of white-washed plaster, below two storeys of smoke-blackened brick.

Gábor and Attila had been walking the flagstone pavement when the two cars roared past.
Gábor spat. "Kurvák jampecak!" he cursed. 'Whoring spivs.'
"What the cock is your problem?" asked Attila. "Ever since we got to Manchester you've had a face on you like you're ready to take on the world. You need to calm down, my brother."
"Don't tell me to calm down!" said Gábor. "How dare those Irish conmen treat us like this? We're the ones building this company. It's Zoltán's drink, for goodness sake. But he's sleeping on the floor with us, eating leftovers from Mrs O'Dillon's family meals while those two are off driving around in those things. This is worse than working for the communists, at least they paid us. It's not right."
"Listen, Gábor," said Attila. "Things are moving quickly here, can't you see? We only left the farm a few weeks ago. You can't just expect everything in life to be rolled out for you. Sometimes you have to accept things aren't going your way for a while. It'll come right though, you'll see. Zoltán'll make everything okay. Otherwise they won't get any of his precious PapPop, will they?"

On the corner of Cornwall Street, in the place of an upstairs window, a claret sign declared 'The O'Connell's Arms, Chester's Ales' in gold capital letters. But to the locals this pub was the Dan's, and they knew that the doorway in the middle of a three-sided apse on Oldham Road was there just for show.

So Zoltán followed the O'Dillons around the end of the back-to-backs and in through the entrance on the far corner.

The air in the pub hung heavy with pipe smoke; it had left the walls a tarry yellow and drifted like mist above a bar of unvarnished oak. There stood a handful of regulars, men in flat caps and bare heads, all supping at pint pots and all in the workwear of their factory. "Ey up," said one of the men, "here come the gaffers."

"What you talking about?" scoffed the barman, "That's Éamon O'Dillon and his little brother Callum. What can I get you lads, same as usual?"

"Ay," said Éamon. "What you having, Zoltán?"

"I don't know," said the Hungarian. "White wine and soda water?"

Callum laughed. "White wine and soda water?" he mocked. "Do you have any idea where you are? This ain't the Midland Hotel you know. This is a man's pub. In the O'Connell Arms you have a choice of Chester's bitter, Chester's stout or Chester's mild. That's it."

"Well, I don't know," said Zoltán. "Where I come from, bars have selections of wine but only serve one type of beer. What you recommend?"

"Have a few pints of mild," quipped Callum.

Zoltán shrugged. "Okay," he said.

In his tie and waistcoat, the barman chortled as he pulled at the middle of the three brass handles.

The directors locked themselves away behind a frosted-glass door with the word 'Snug' written in crystal-clear swirls. Inside was a corner room of red-leather seating, big enough for six men to sit around a circular table. A hatch in the wall gave them access to the bar, and there was a brass bell to ring for attention.

Having instructed the barman to let no one else in, Éamon laid his briefcase on the table. "So I was about to tell young Zoltán, here," he said, "about our meeting with Colonel Woodhall."

"You should've seen the place," said Callum. "We were at the Café Royal on Peter Street, it's one of them new Berni Inns. Very lively indeed."

"That's right," said Éamon. "Colonel Woodhall's the owner of the Blue Moon of Kentucky Burger chain. A very important man in America, let me tell you. He could see the potential in PapPop with almost no persuading. He's already opened his first restaurant in London, says he's coming to Manchester next. They've plans to open hundreds of franchises all over the country, and he reckons they'll have overtaken Wimpy in no time at all. But what he wants more than anything is a local drinks provider – something new and fresh to go with their image. He signed us up on the spot, Zoltán. Said it was the finest drink he'd ever tasted."

"And he went ape at our advertising plans," said Callum. "Said it's just what he were looking for."

"No word of a lie," said Éamon. "From this day forward, as Blue Moon of Kentucky restaurants open all over the country, every single one will be selling PapPop by the gallon. It means we're going to be rich, Zoltán me old mucker."

"How much did he order?" asked Zoltán.

"Ten crates for the end of this month," said Callum. "Do you think you can do it?"

"Ten crates? Is not too much."

"It's a start," said Éamon, "a trial run. Can you do it?"

"Of course," Zoltán sneered. "An amount that small I do no problem from Henry Gritton's barn."

"Good man," said Éamon, "then you know what this means, don't you?" He clicked the latches of his briefcase with both thumbs and popped the top open. Then he picked out a pile of papers which he pushed toward Zoltán Papp. Éamon reached into his blazer pocket, pulled out a pen and laid it on top of the paperwork. "That's my lucky pen," he said. "I use it to sign all my contracts."

"So this is why you bring me here?" said Zoltán. "To finalise our agreement?"

"That's right," said Éamon. "What were you expecting?"

Zoltán took a sip of beer and licked the foam from his stubbly lip. "You still don't meet all my criteria," he said. "You two drive around in your fancy cars while me, Attila and Gábor sleep on the floor of a warehouse and eat the food you no want. Is not right, and is not what we agreed."

"I think you'll find you're wrong there," said Callum, grinning. "You set us a number of challenges before we could incorporate the company. As far as I'm concerned we've fulfilled them all."

"All but one," said Éamon, fumbling in his jacket for a set of keys which he jangled onto the table-top. "Flat 35," he said. "Third floor, just around on the right-hand side. It's all set up and ready to move into. We've even hired you a television."

"Where is it?"

"Victoria Square."

"Where's that?"

"Where's that?" Éamon chuckled. "We just blooming drove past it, that's where it is. Didn't you notice that big fancy building almost opposite the factory?"

"No. Like I tell you, we no go outside since you dropp-ed off us. We spend every night on the floor with only sacks to sleep on."

"Well, tonight you'll be sleeping on a spring mattress under real blankets," said Éamon. "In the mornings, you'll just have to cross the road and you'll be in the factory. How does that sound to you?"

"There is room for Attila and Gábor?" asked Zoltán.

"Sure there is," said Éamon. "There are two bedrooms and a living room. And if you want somewhere bigger, when the shillings start rolling in, you'll have your pick of places out of the city, where the air's much sweeter. Who knows, maybe you could even learn to drive a good British car." Éamon O'Dillon downed his pint in one go and slammed his glass onto the table. "I think it's your round, Zoltán," he said.

"But I still have most of my beer." Papp replied. "I no really like it, to be honest. Is too warm and flat and, well, mild. I prefer cider to this. You want mine?"

"Don't be daft," said Éamon. "It's not right to drink out another man's pint pot. Callum, get them in. We're celebrating, after all."

As Callum stood to ring the bell, Éamon pushed the contract towards Zoltán. "I believe you've already had the chance to read this over," he said.

"That's right. You don't added nothing or taken nothing out?"

"Not a sausage," said Éamon. "But please, take your time to read it, we've got all afternoon." He pulled his pipe from a jacket pocket, tobacco from another and stuffed it into the bowl to light with a match that he dropped to the floor between his feet.

It took Zoltán Papp twenty minutes to re-read the contract and sign all three copies. Then Éamon broke open a bottle of whiskey and served it out into highball glasses.

By the time the bottle was empty, all three men were lounging with their arms out along the humped-leather upholstery.

"So, gents," said Éamon. "Seeing as how we're now formerly business partners and everything, I have something I'd like to suggest. An extra piece of advertising to add to the factory door. What do you think?"

From the bottom of his briefcase, he produced a poster showing a greyscale photo of a husband, wife and daughter sitting for breakfast. On an orange background at the top ran the slogan 'Life's better with the Conservatives' in black letters, an orange rip at the bottom of the picture said 'don't let Labour ruin it'.

"So what?" asked Callum. "Get the door put through and have everything nicked? I don't think so. Ancoats is Labour to the core, and I'm with them."

"You're going to vote Labour?" said Éamon.

"Of course I am," Callum replied. "I'm Manchester born and bred. Up here, only class traitors vote Tory."

"Class traitors and factory owners," said his brother. "Just try to think who you are these days."

"Well, I'm against it," said Callum. "I'm not having the Conservative Party anywhere near PapPop."

"Then it looks like it's a decision for our majority shareholder. What do you think Zoltán?"

"I not political," Zoltán replied. "I see too many politics in my life to be concerned with any more. I think we should not take sides. We want everyone to drink our PapPop, and most of our customers are from Manchester, therefore we will lose business if we support one side against the other."

Éamon shrugged. "All right," he said, lifting his glass. "I can accept a democratic vote like anyone. Then here's to Papp Beverages Limited, and our continued political neutrality. The Switzerland of the drinks' world."

It was dark by the time Zoltán Papp staggered out of the O'Connell's Arms. He dug his hands into his jacket pockets, jingled the keys between his fingers and remembered the flat, picturing the Bacsik brothers about to spend another night on the warehouse floor.

Zoltán's route took him past his new home, a brick monument to social housing that towered over the corrugated roofs of the warehouses opposite. A train whistle blew through the smoky air and Zoltán noticed the glow of a pub sign on the next corner. It announced the 'Nelson Vaults', and music was drifting out of the open door. He poked his head inside, saw the crowds of late drinkers and listened a moment to a man strumming a guitar and singing

"Found my love by the gaswork croft,
Dreamed a dream by the old canal,
Kissed my girl by the factory wall,
Dirty old town, dirty old town."

Zoltán wasn't in the mood for crowds and music, tomorrow was just another working day. He crossed the road, making sure to look both ways as he did so, but he saw no cars or buses either driving or parked.

The air tingled against Zoltán's teeth and smoke particles swarmed like insects around the yellow incandescence of the factory sign. He reached into his pockets and pulled out two sets of keys, was fumbling with the bits of metal when a woman said "Szia Zoltán." 'Hi.'

He spun around to find a familiar figure before him, scarf around her head. "Nóra?" he asked. "What are you doing here? I thought you were in Leeds."

"I was," she replied. "And now I'm here. I heard you had a business going and I thought you might need a hand."

"Well, yes," said Zoltán. "Yes, I guess maybe we will. We haven't opened yet though, not really. How did you find us?"

"Gábor wrote and told me. I've been waiting here all day."

"Have you?"

"Yes," said Nóra. "The brothers still aren't here."

"Aren't they?" said Zoltán, putting the keys back in his pocket. "Well, where are they?"

"I don't know, but they've not been here since you all left at five."

"Oh," said Zoltán. "Well in that case, I've just got the keys to a new flat. It's in that building there. Shall we go and see what it's like?"

17. Going Back

17th September 2059
Sierra de Carrascoy, Spain

Aliyá Talavera cried most mornings, but at least she could normally get up. Not today though. Because as strips of sunlight streaked through the shack wall, Aliyá was inconsolable. She'd tried lifting herself a couple of times, as she knew she must, but never got further than sitting upright and looking around the hut, before her face cracked and she collapsed into another wave of sobbing.

As she got on with the many chores of that day, Dolores whistled along with the birdsong and ignored her daughter the best she could. Eventually, with the hut empty but for a couple of tree-trunk stools and Aliyá's bed, her mother could hold out no longer. "Vamos Ale!" she said. 'Let's go!' "Everything's outside except you and that blanket. So I need you off it, it's time to leave."

But Aliyá turned over and shut her eyes. "I don't want to go," she muttered to the earthen wall.

"Come on Aliyá," said Dolores, tugging at the blanket. "Just think, the next time you go to sleep will be on an actual real bed."

"I have a real bed," said Aliyá. "This is my real bed. It's been my bed most of my life and it's fine. I'm staying here."

"Listen," said Dolores, pulling up a slice of tree-trunk on which to perch herself. "We've been over this a thousand times. We're the last ones up here for goodness sake. You can hardly stay on your own now, can you?"

"Why not?" asked Aliyá, "I know this hillside better than anyone in the world. I've grown up here, I could survive. Besides, Juanjo was talking of staying. I could live with him."

"Don't be daft, Aliyá, you're coming with us and that's the end of it. Juanjo too, he's probably there waiting for us now. Do you really think he'd let his gang of boys leave without him? Now come on, we need to go."

"I'm not going and you can't make me."

Dolores grasped at her daughter's arm but Aliyá pulled away.

The cabin got suddenly lighter as Oscar pulled open the door. "So you're awake at last, mee-khá," he said. "Come on, we're already late."

"She's not coming," said Dolores. "She says she wants to stay here."

"I'm sure the wolves will be happy," Oscar grinned. "With no more chickens or goats to pick off, they'll be getting hungry. A young lady of Aliyá's stature will feed a family for a week or more. I mean, what use is a cloth door against a pack of hungry dogs?"

"It's not fair," said Aliyá, lifting her head and wiping her tears with the heels of her hands. "Why does no one ever think about what I want? You forced me to leave my home when I was twelve. And now you want me to leave again just like that, to give up my entire life and follow you, again. I am an adult you know, I should be able to make my own decisions."

"It wasn't just us that made this decision," said her mother. "The community's been working on this for months, as you well know. We wouldn't be leaving unless we had to, unless we knew that things would be better in the city. These last few months have been really tough, Ale, you know how it's been. After they blocked off all the springs and destroyed our water collection systems, what choice do we have? There's safety in numbers, that's all there is to it. That's why we have to go back. Almost everyone's already left as it is. We Talaveras are the last, as always. Now come on."

"There's nothing to climb down there," Aliyá whined.

"You could climb the cathedral," said Oscar.

"And have everyone watching me? No thank you. I remember what it used to be like. There'll always be people in the city, and nowhere I can go to be completely alone."

"You'll have your old bedroom back," said her father. "With a door and a bed and everything. You'll be able to stay in there as long as you want and be on your own whenever you need to be. And besides, Murcia won't be like any of us remember. From what I've heard, there's almost no one there, and those that are in in the city these days are mostly strangers from elsewhere. There'll be no cafés or cars or electricity or anything, but at least we'll be home."

"This is my home," said Aliyá. "I can tell five different types of honeysuckle just from their smell. Down there I know nothing."

"Venga Ale!" said her mother. 'Come on Aliyá!' "You'll learn soon enough. A smart girl like you can adapt to anything. And think of all the new possibilities you'll have down there, all those new people you'll meet. You'll even be able to practise your English."

"I don't want to meet new people," said Aliyá, "I don't want to practise English. I just want to stay here, to live like we used to. I don't want to change." She slumped back down and wormed her body to the wall.

"Fine," said Oscar, tapping his wife's shoulder. "Come on Dolores, let's go. If she wants to stay here, she can stay. But we need to leave. Bye then Aliyá!"

"Yes," said Dolores, following her husband out the door. "Adios!"

After not more than five minutes of churning her mind over, Aliyá appeared outside with her folded blanket under one arm. She took a look at the pile of bags and said, "That's a lot for us to carry."

"We brought it all up here," said her mother. "So we can surely carry it all down."

"We didn't carry it all though, did we?" said Aliyá. "We brought it in the car most of the way."

"Well, now we have to carry it," said Dolores, picking up a suitcase in one hand and a basket of fruit in the other.

"Are we going to get the car?" asked Aliyá.

Oscar swung his guitar case onto his back and chuckled. "After standing still for ten years," he said. "We can be pretty certain it won't start."

"But can we try at least?" asked Aliyá.

"Sure, I'll try," said Oscar. "But I wouldn't get my hopes up."

Their backs and hands fully loaded, the Talaveras followed an earthen track through a forest of Carrascoy pines. As they descended, the path turned from dirt grey through an iron-infused purple to the light-coloured clay of the valley. Evergreens gave way to cork oaks whose roots invaded the pathway and their leaves gave shade from the sun.

But while the flora and the bedrock were changing, Aliyá's mood stayed stubbornly down. She felt like every step along that trackway took her closer to an abyss which she could already sense in her gut. Tears dropped from her cheekbones, her face told of utter despair. But she let out not a whimper.

When a gateway appeared in a rock wall, Oscar and Dolores vanished inside. But Aliyá hung back. She looked up the hill, where her home was now lost among the trees. She took a deep breath, then another, and dried her cheeks with the short sleeve of her t-shirt.

Through the gateway, Aliyá trudged behind a shack the same orange stone as the wall. Into a miniature amphitheatre she went, where three rows of concrete curved around a well which was cemented shut and topped by a thick metal sheet with the words 'Property of PapAqua' stamped over its yellow surface.

Aliyá found a small but familiar group gathering up their rucksacks and baskets. Juanjo and a couple of his boys were there, all done out in animal-fur G-strings and carrying only baskets of produce. There was little Chucho Molino in the shadow of his wife Belén, their ten-year-old son hiding behind them. Old Carmen Hueso was among them, but Eduardo was not; her husband's was one of so many bodies they'd had to leave buried on the hillside with sticks and stones to mark their resting places.

Old Paco Senior was also alone. He wore a backpack over his filthy shirt and was, by now, completely blind.

"Is your Junior coming to collect us?" Oscar asked, tapping Paco's arm. "I thought he'd be leading us."

Paco nodded. "He left me here this morning to wait for you all," he said. "He's going to meet us down there, at a roundabout just outside Sanganera la Verde, where the sheet goes over the river."

"Then how are you going to get down the mountainside?" asked Dolores.

"Do you need a guide?" said Aliyá.

"That'd help a lot," said old man Rufián. "Is that you Aliyá?"

"Yes."

"And will you help this poor infirm old man out of the sierra?"

"Yes."

"Oh you are a treasure," said Paco Senior.

"Then if we're all here and ready," said Juanjo. "I guess it's time to leave."

So after the shortest of breathers, the most boyish of Juanjo's gang took hold of Aliyá's luggage and the Talaveras were off once again downhill. No one's footwear had survived ten years in the mountains, but most of the group wore wooden clogs which clunked against the rocky roadway. Only Juanjo and his boys were shoeless like Aliyá. She held Paco Senior's arm in hers, focussing on his every step. It meant, for a while, she could blank out the tragedy of the second exodus she'd experienced in her twenty-one years of life. One she sensed it would not be her last.

They clip-clopped over asphalt which had blanched under decades of sun. The surface had split a little more with every frost and what remained was dotted with tarry shards, too much even for soles as hardened as Aliyá's. Behind Juanjo and his boys, she was helping Paco Rufián along the grass embankment when they almost walked into the broken breeze blocks of a hut, hidden behind the overgrowth. From then on, the soft shoulder gave way to flat-stone pavements wide enough for two, with low walls down both sides of the road.

At a curve without trees or buildings to block the view, the group slowed to gawp at the valley. Aliyá had spent hour on hour pondering this scene, alone from the tops of rocks. But for the majority, this was their first proper sight of the vast beige sweeps and lines that covered the plains after the dust of construction had settled.

"Madre Mía," rasped Belén Molino, pointing to their left. "Look, Librilla's completely gone. It was there, under that long straight bit. I used to spend every summer there with my grandparents. We even talked about moving to that house when we left the city. Do you remember Chuchi? We thought it might've been better to live in an actual house on our own than with the community. It's a good job we made the right choice, isn't it?"

Her husband grunted in response.

"It doesn't look real," said the animal-skinned man wearing Aliyá's rucksack. "What do you think it is, Professor?"

"I still couldn't say," said Juanjo, "but it's real enough. As is the damage they've done. Look at the Sierra Espuña. It's like they've dug an enormous roadway right the way through the middle. I just don't see why anyone would want to walk back into that."

"I'm with you there," said Aliyá, as she stepped onwards.

Rusholme

Today was life-changing for more than just those few remaining occupants of the Carrascoy mountains. For Naomi Brownlow, it felt like almost every day for the past three months had been the biggest of her life, but today would trump them all. She'd been through three lots of auditions, nine weekends of knock-out rounds, quarter-finals, semis. And now, at last, she was in the final. Today she would be crowned PapStar59. Or at least that's what the Press were saying.

Brian Brownlow lowered himself onto the coping stone of a brick wall. He sighed. "I'm sorry for holding you all up," he said. "Its been a while since I've walked so far. I don't want to make you late though, Naomi. Maybe you should leave your old dad here."

"Don't be daft," said his seventeen-year-old daughter, in a sleeveless dress her mother had sewn from scraps. "We left half an hour early so as you'd have time to walk me to the Biodome. Look, this is already Platt Lane. It's only a couple more hundred metres. You can already see where we're going."

Sure enough, a great yellow wall blocked off the end of the road, dwarfing the church steeple and the trees that lined the street. But it still took twenty minutes and another few breathers before the Brownlow family were at the base of the security wall.

As the family approached the flawless barricade, two vertical slits slid open. Minnie flung her arms around Naomi. "Best of luck," she said, kissing her cheek. "You just show them what you're made of. This is the moment you've been waiting for your whole life. Go out there and grab it with both hands. When you come home, after you win, we'll open that bottle of wine I've had hidden away. Then we'll celebrate together. But you've got your sister there with you for support. Just don't forget her in the melee, will you?"

"Of course not, mum," said Naomi. "She'll be by my side the whole time. When I'm not in make-up or on stage that is. You've nothing to worry about." Naomi turned to her father. "Thanks for coming, dad," she said. "It's so good of you to come and see me off. I know how much effort it was."

"Well, I want to show my daughter how much she means to me," said Brian, between heaving breaths. "You've always been a class above people around here, Naomi, and I'm sure you'll be in a different class again this evening. Just like you are every week. Go and make us proud."

The girls disappeared inside the narrow doorways and each swallowed them whole when they slid closed behind. Minnie hugged her husband's belly. "I'm so proud of her," she said. "I feel I could burst! Isn't it a shame we couldn't go with them?"

Brian chuckled. "With tickets at five hundred PapPounds a piece and only one for free, there was never a cat in hell's chance we were going to be there."

"No," said Minnie, gazing over his shoulder. "I guess not... Will you look at that?" She pointed towards the park. Over the browning tree-tops, images flashed out of the Security Wall, showing a black and white photograph of three men pulling faces below a neon sign declaring 'Papp Beverages Ltd. Makers of PapPop'.

In the park, people sat on blankets as they stared up at the great collages of colours and monochrome that danced over the wall. "Don't you want to stay for a while?" asked Minnie. "We could watch some here on the big screen before we go home."

Brian thought before answering. "I mean," he said, "it was such an effort to get here. We might as well make the most of it while we can. Come on, I could do with a sit down."

So they strolled through a cast-iron gateway and parked themselves under an oak. As they looked up at the screen, Minnie noticed an elderly man staggering under the weight of a yellow crate hung around his neck. He wormed his way towards them. "Do you have your PapPop ready?" he asked in a broad Irish accent.

"We don't really drink that stuff," said Minnie. "And we don't have any PapPounds so we couldn't buy one anyway."

The man smiled. "You don't have to buy them, Minnie," he said. "Didn't you see it advertised? It's been on TV for weeks. You can have a bottle for free. PapCorp haven't only put up millions of screens like this on streets around the world, they're giving out nine billion bottles of PapPop to open at the moment Zoltan O'Dillon turns on his advert for the aliens. Now, how many would you like? Two?"

The man paused at her husband's face. "Is that you, Brian?" he asked.

"Yes."

"Well, look at you!" the man exclaimed. "I haven't seen you for, ooo, must be ten years at least. I can still picture you that day we knocked on your mum's front door. Do you remember me, Nigel Whitehurst? I was the fella who signed you up."

"I remember," said Brian. "But it's been more like twenty years. I left United in 2041."

"That's right, it was that bad tackle in training, wasn't it? Just before the takeover. I wasn't far after you, son, but I'd been lucky enough to have had my career by then. Not that I can retire, of course. Hence this PapPop gig. I don't suppose you still play?"

"Not at all. I can hardly move most of the time."

"No," said the man, glancing at the screen and back at the Brownlows. "But you're..." He glanced around again. "Then you're Naomi's parents, aren't you?"

Brian smiled and nodded.

"You must be so proud!" said Nigel. "Do you think she's going to win? Of course she's going to win. Anyway, Brian, I've got to get on. Let's have a pint some time. What do you think?"

Brian looked to his wife to ask what to do, but she wasn't paying attention. So he took the bottles of PapPop with a "thanks" and said "that'd be great," for want of anything else to say.

The whole time the men were talking, off in the distance Neville Jennings had been staring at Minnie. And as soon as she saw him, she found it impossible not to return his gaze.

Sierra de Carrascoy

Juanjo Cavernas grew twitchier with every step downhill. At a sign half-hidden in the bushes, declaring 'Torre Guil', he conferred with his boys. "We're going to run ahead," he said to the group. "I don't really want to dwell too long here, I'm sure you all know why. We'll wait for you at the junction with the main road."

"Of course," said Dolores. "You go Juanjo. We understand."

So Juanjo and his friends belted off down the roadway, arms flailing.

The rest of the group soon paused at a house that had never been plastered, behind a wall a couple of breeze blocks high. With old man Paco on her arm, Aliyá gazed at the concrete frame filled up with sun-pinkened tiles and the balcony that used to be hers.

Aliyá felt her mother's hand work its way into hers. "Do you remember?" asked Dolores.

"Of course," said Aliyá, watching her father yank open the garage door. "I might only have been twelve, and we hardly stayed any time, but I remember this place so clearly…" She glanced over the neighbour's wall and saw the heaps of bricks where Juanjo once lived, now just a hole in the ground.

In front of the crater stood a concrete cross the height that the house had been. Dolores hopped over the wall towards the yellow flowers arranged at its foot. She knelt down and rubbed them between her fingers. "They feel real," she said. "I wonder who's been leaving fresh flowers here."

"They're probably some type of GMO we've never seen before," said Belén Molino. "We've been ensconced in these hills, hidden away from the world for a decade. We're bound to find things we haven't seen before when we return to the real world."

"The real world?" chuckled her husband, Chucho. "We're going to be living inside a two-kilometre ring of plastic. We'll be more cut off in there than we were up on the side of Majal Blan…" He faded off as he noticed the others staring at the expanse that used to be farms and villages. The plastic sheeting was suddenly ablaze in yellow, shining brighter than the sun.

From inside the garage, Oscar could see only the daylight brighten and he rushed out to see what was happening. But by the time his gaze joined the others, the illumination had gone. All he saw was that dust-coloured carpet covering the valley. "What was that?" he asked.

"It was, um," Aliyá stumbled on the words.

"What was it?" asked blind Paco. "What happened?"

"The whole sheet just lit up," said Carmen Hueso. "The entire valley was glowing yellow. I've never seen anything like it."

"Me neither," said Aliyá. "How strange. How about the car, Papá?"

"Completely flat," said Oscar. "I can't even get it to open. Looks like we'll just have to keep going on foot."

With no access to PapDrives or other devices, to radio nor television, the word-of-mouth campaigns nor even the banners held between low-flying drones, those to whom this valley once belonged were some of the few people on Earth not to know that today marked PapCorp's centenary. They had no idea that this was the day Zoltan O'Dillon would turn on his advert for the aliens.

Aliyá had never heard of Zoltan O'Dillon. Like the others, she hadn't a clue that, at that very moment, southern Spain was playing host to one of the most important people imaginable. In a Nordenfelt N690v Jumpjet, where the 'v' stood for VIP, the CEO of all PapCorp was flying above his flagship project. Not a hundred miles from the returning Murcianos, he and his two advisors were speeding from the PapSec base on Gibraltar to the only peak above 2,000 metres in all of Murcia Province.

Over southern Spain

By now, Zoltan O'Dillon's brow was bald, his belly and jowls had expanded to match his role. It was for his benefit that the sign flashed on, and when he glanced at his aides opposite, his smile was so wide that he looked almost reptilian. He stared at his junior assistant, Lucy Hardcastle, the daughter of an old schoolfriend. "Isn't it magnificent?" he exalted. "A fitting tribute, don't you think? The greatest company that's ever graced the face of this Earth, and it does so with a thing of simplistic beauty. Kill it won't you, Lucy?"

"Kill what?" she asked. "Do you mean kill the sign? How am I supposed to do that? Is it even alive?"

"He means turn it off," said Francis Atkins, beside her. He noticed her blank stare and said, "On second thoughts, I'll do it." His hands weaved a PapDrive dance as he selected icons only he could see, and in seconds the valley was restored to the colour of sand.

Lucy stared outside. "I just can't believe it," she said. "I can't believe I'm actually here. Billions of people across the planet are going to be watching today, it'll be bigger than the death of the

King. And a whole lot happier. Just think of all those PapTech screens on every corner in the world, all the PapBurger street parties and the collective pish of nine billion bottles of PapPop being opened all at once..."

Francis Atkins stared at the woman. "Don't tell me," he said, "you've forgotten the bottles, haven't you?"

"I, um, I meant to get them," she said. "I left them on the side to take with me. But then you made us leave in such a hurry and we were looking for Zoltan's medal. Remember? I must have left them in the rush. What should we do Francis? Zoltan?"

But neither man responded. Zoltan flicked his fingers and the news appeared in his lenses. "...and don't forget to join me later this evening," Vincent Humbolt said into his ears, "when I'll be presenting the final of PapStar59."

Murcia Province, Spain

The lump in Aliyá's stomach weighed ever heavier, but as long as she was leading blind old Paco she could ignore it. With her eyes on his footsteps, she caught only glimpses of houses splitting in the heat, their shutters rusted closed and chunks of plaster missing from the sun-faded walls.

Between razor-wire fences guarding overgrown groves of oranges or lemons, the slope flattened out. In place of the Carrascoy pines and oaks, tall palms now dotted both sides of the road and lent no shade from the September sun.

The group found Juanjo and his boys at the junction, lazing under a couple of giant oaks that had once given shelter to roadside cafés. The buildings now stood roofless, their vibrant purple façades pinkened and flaking. The boys had seen the group coming and were waiting for them at the junction.

"Did you see it?" asked Chucho Molino.

"Of course," said Juanjo. "You could hardly miss it. I never thought a day could get brighter than Murcia in the middle of summer, but I was wrong."

"So what was it for?" asked the boy with Aliyá's rucksack.

Paco Senior coughed. "It's what I've been saying all along," he said. "Even without the use of my eyes, I told you it was a sign to extra-terrestrials. Do you believe me now?"

"No," said Carmen. "Sorry Paco, but it still makes no sense to me. I mean, we now know this thing lights up, but not for an advert. It could be the signalling for a Mars mission or something, like your son always said."

"Yes," whiled the old man. "Maybe."

One of the boys wearing a rat-skin around his genitals stepped towards old Paco. "I'll guide you for a while if you want," he said. "I know it's not far but it'll give you a break, Aliyá. Is that okay with you?"

Aliyá shrugged. "Okay," she said.

Without the old man's feet to watch, his arm to hold, Aliyá felt suddenly alone. The weight in her belly seemed to pull her further and further into the cracked roadway, and she was surprised her footprints didn't leave indents like the tyre-troughs which grooved its surface. She watched her toes and her tears as they splashed onto the dirt.

The group headed down one side of a dual-carriageway, with bushy palm trees down the middle between concrete stumps which once would've held streetlights. The air was alive with the chirping of cicadas and the swooping of birds.

With the plain beige sheet getting ever closer, they skirted a roundabout where roots had cracked through the kerbstones. They stepped off the road and picked their way through the thistles and pebbles. The sheeting curved towards them and they saw for the first time the aluminium scaffolding that held it dead level.

The earth gave way at a river channel. On its bed, a path had been carved out through prickly bushes and dead reeds. On the other side was a concrete wall graffitied in faded tags and squirls. This was the meeting point, just as old man Paco had described. The only thing missing was his son. The father shouted Paco Junior's name, as did everyone else. But they soon gave up their calling, it was obvious that young Paco wasn't there.

Manchester

On the far side of the security wall, Naomi and Ruth Brownlow found a yellow taxi pod waiting for them on the hard shoulder of the PapWay. It stood open down the middle like a clam shell, displaying a yellow-padded interior that left no room for a driver, no seats or windows either. The moment the girls had clambered in, the lid closed and they were away.

Two hatches opened in the ceiling, each containing a pair of glasses, and the car spoke to them in a woman's voice. "Naomi and Ruth," she said, "thank you for choosing PapAuto. We hope you enjoy your journey to the Atom Complex, door 28C. Please put on your PapDrive glasses so you can see the ride in true to life Augmented Vision."

They did as instructed, fitted the arms over their ears and the earphones inside. They held a button on the rim until the lenses flashed with the word PapDrive IV. When that pixelated away, they found the cab transformed into an old video reel showing a black-and-white metropolis of smoking chimneys.

Carolyn Hargreaves commentated directly into their ears. "Zoltán Papp was a remarkable man," she said. "After being exiled from his native Hungary by the communists, his new life in England would give birth to the most ground-shattering soft drink in history: PapPop. Not much is known of his early years, although we do know his father worked at the telephone exchange and his mother sang in numerous Budapest jazz bands. Little could they have guessed what impact their son would have on the world. Papp Beverages Limited was founded on this day a hundred years ago, in the O'Connell's Arms on Oldham Road in Manchester."

Their visions filled with a black and white photo showing a sign for Papp Beverages Ltd. Under it stood three men, the outer two looking awkward but the one in the middle was sticking out his tongue. "PapPop would be an overnight sensation," she continued. "But just three years after the founding of his company, Zoltán Papp would sell all of his interests so he could retire with his family to an island in the

Caribbean. The buyers, as everyone knows, were Éamon and Callum O'Dillon..."

"I read that whole story's a complete fabrication," Ruth commented. "There's a theory that they never paid him anything, but instead had him murdered."

"What are you talking about now, Ruthie?" said Naomi. "Where do you even get such stories?"

"From the internet, of course."

"You mean the dark web? You spend far too much time on there for your own good. I'm amazed that old laptop of yours can even connect."

"It's not always easy," said Ruth, "but I usually find a way through. You know what I'm like."

"I know," said Naomi, "a right little computer genius. Just do me a favour and don't go spouting any of your political crap today? Okay?"

"What do you mean? If a journalist asks me a question I'll answer it as truthfully as possible."

"Just don't say anything that'll make you sound like some crazy conspiracy theorist. It might lose me votes, and I'm going to need all I can get against Leon J."

"You'll beat him no problem, sis. I have complete faith in you. Everyone's saying it's your destiny to be PapStar59. It's what you've wanted since forever and you'll get there. I'm sure of it."

"Thanks Ruthie," said Naomi. "I know I'm better than him, but there are all those rumours about him buying votes so you just never know."

"I'm sure they won't be able to do that this time around, not in the final. PapStar certainly wouldn't want that to happen, and they've put in all those extra controls, haven't they? They're making everyone declare a whole year's bank statements before they can vote. You're not nervous are you?"

"Of course I'm not. I know I'm going to win, it's like I was born for today. I just can't quite believe it's here so soon."

Ruth took off her glasses.

"What is it?" Naomi asked.

"These things make me dizzy," said Ruth.

"You'll have to get used to Augmented Vision, Ruthie, especially when you come and live with me."

So Ruth put them back on to please her sister. But the movement of the taxi and the dislocated images gave her car sickness, so she passed most of the journey with her eyes closed.

In a week when the news left little time for anything but PapCorp's anniversary celebrations, the unanimous predictions of Naomi's victory had filled fewer columns than the scandals around her opponent. His family came from all over the globe, but if they were mixed in origin they shared one thing in particular; they were all incredibly rich. Which is how Leon J. Handlykken was able to afford the chip in his voicebox that automatically tuned the sounds as they were produced. A chip which had been deemed illegal and surgically removed just days before. But that was old news, now the allegations centred on his people buying votes.

Bio-dome 4, Manchester

Ruth Brownlow's head felt better when the taxi stopped, when their yellow egg-taxi cracked open and revealed a pile of great spheres spurting out of the concrete. In the air above, smaller balls levitated their way around the nucleus of the Atom Complex, all declaring allegiance to one PapCorp division or another. The ground was a storm of shouting and camera flashes.

"Naomi!" people were yelling.
"How do you feel?"
"Are you confident?"
"Do you think Leon J's performance will be better without voice enhancers?"

Naomi knew to answer no questions, at least not till PapStar had properly vetted them. So she grabbed Ruth in one hand, waved with the other, and made her way to an open slot in the nearest nucleon.

The door slid closed and dampened away the commotion. Through their PapDrive glasses the girls saw a dark passageway lit by millions of augmented candles that seemed to be floating. Before them stood a pair of women, one blonde, one brunette, resplendent in their layers of soft-curled hair and enhanced bodies. Both were the perfect height of 5 ft 8 ins, their smiles surgically similar, and both wore patchwork dresses not a million miles from Naomi's own.

"Oh Naomi," said the blonde. "You look stunning as always, I absolutely love that bow on your dress. Did your mum make that as well?"

"Sure," said Naomi, "My mum makes all my clothes. She always has."

The women smiled as unpatronisingly as they could manage. "Come on," said the brunette, "Let's get you made up." They each grabbed one of Naomi's arms and marched her off down the corridor.

"Good luck then, Naomi!" Ruth shouted after her. "See you when you're PapStar!" As she watched her sister being escorted away, Ruth felt this was the end of something.

Pico de los Obispos, Murcia Province, Spain

The wings of Zoltan O'Dillon's jumpjet fitted perfectly onto a square of concrete just below the highest point around. When they got to the bottom of the escalator, the three passengers didn't pause to take in the mountaintop views; the wind was so strong that they hurried the twenty paces up to the metal pod which had been hoisted in, hours earlier.

A couple of engineers were at work near the doorway, but Zoltan strode past as if they weren't there. He stopped at the window which curved around the far end of the studio, peered out at the peaks jutting from the flat sheeting below like islands in a lake or a reservoir.

"Here you are, Mr O'Dillon," said Lucy.

He peered around to see his young assistant holding out a bottle of PapPop. "Where did you get that?" he asked.

"Francis bought it off the engineers," she replied with flittering eyes. "You know nothing's too much for you."

Zoltan tutted, turned away. "It reminds me of somewhere, all this," he said. "From my PapSec days in Africa."

"You were in Africa with PapSec?" said Lucy. "That's not in any of your biographies, and I've seen them all."

"No," said Zoltan. "It was special operations. Still very hush-hush. Do me a favour and get me Bernie the Earl, won't you?"

"Who's that, sir? Bernie The-what?"

"Bernie the Earl. Get me Bernie the Earl!"

"I'm very sorry Mr O'Dillon, but I don't know who Bernie Theeul is."

Zoltan glared down at his assistant. His nostrils flared, he had the urge to lash out but he remembered what Jemima would say and he put his hands away in his pockets. His words came slowly. "I want you to find me Bernie Douglas-FitzAllan," he said, "the fifteenth Earl of Angus. And I want you to do it this instant. Do you understand?"

"Yes, sir, Mr O'Dillon, sir," Lucy stammered. "I'm very sorry, sir, I didn't realise you were saying Bernie the Earl, I thought it was Bernie Theeul or something. He was my predecessor, I know who he is, of course I do. So, where can I find him?"

"How in Papp's name am I meant to know where he is?" Zoltan yelled. "I pay you to be my assistant. Now assist me in finding Bernie the Earl."

He span his head back to gaze over his great monument. But no sooner had he returned his view to the valley than a woman's face appeared before him with her rosy-red cheeks and a smile that was all teeth.

Zoltan answered the call with a flick of his fingers. "Jemima," he said. "Tell me you want your old job back."

Jemima Kemal chuckled. "What would I want to do that for?" she asked.

"Because this imbecile child I got to replace you is a complete waste of space."

"That's what happens when you make appointments with your penis, Zoltan."

"It worked okay with you."

"That was different," said Jemima. "I'm different. You just got lucky with me."

"She forgot the bottles of PapPop," said Zoltan. "Can you imagine that? It was pretty much the only thing she had to do. Now I've asked her to find me Bernie the Earl, and she didn't even know who he is."

"You won't be able to find Bernie," said Jemima. "I tried to contact him for years. I needed his passwords, but we could never get hold of him. Apparently he's in Scotland, living off his land like a hermit. He doesn't even have a telephone, let alone a PapDrive or anything we could use to locate him. He's completely off the radar."

"Well, that is a shame," said Zoltan. "The view from here reminds me of a day we spent together many years ago. Still, never mind. I wanted to talk to you about that photo you keep showing, the one where my grandfather looks deranged."

"It's the only shot there is of all three of them, Zoltan. You know that. Now I don't have all night to chat, I'm producing this entire evening's output. I'm only calling to make sure you're ready."

"For you Jemima, I'm always ready." Zoltan winked but she'd already hung up.

Sangonera la Verde, suburbs of Murcia, Spain

Beneath the rim of that unfathomable sheeting, the group sat on the banks of the dried-up river. They waited together in silence, Aliyá with her arms around her knees, a blankness in her eyes and an emptiness in her soul.

Her father got up. "I'm going to the bathroom," he said, and scrambled up the bank.

As he urinated onto an aluminium strut, Oscar gazed over the great expanse of sheeting. He listened to the passing of his water, watching the fine weave that patterned the beige veneer and the wires that disappeared into circuit boxes on the ground. Oscar hummed to himself, pondering when Paco Junior would eventually turn up.

Brilliant yellow flashed across the surface. Oscar covered his eyes and turned away, leaving an arc of urine on the bare dirt ground. He did up his trousers with his eyes closed, felt his way down the bank with the fold of his arm across his face. He was still blinking when he found the others, huddled over with their faces to the floor.

"It's really bright," said Oscar, "like looking at the sun."

"We noticed," Belén Molino replied.

"There's no way we'll be able to get under that," said Juanjo. "If we have to crawl under there for two kilometres, we'll all end up blind, if not roasted to death."

"I wouldn't worry," said Chucho Molino, "it's like we saw in the afternoon. I'm sure it'll go off again in a minute."

18. Moving Forwards

17th September 2059
Pico de los Obispos, Spain

Zoltan O'Dillon turned from the light that now flooded the plains. He lowered his bottle of PapPop and grinned into the camera. "Let there be no doubt," he said. "When lifeforms from other worlds do finally pass by this corner of the Milky Way, they'll know it's PapPop that keeps this planet spinning. From the moment Zoltán Papp brewed his first bottle in a cowshed in Shropshire, all the way through to today, our story has been one continuous line of ever greater success. And we haven't finished yet." He sipped from his PapPop bottle. "So here's to the past," he said with another swig, "to the present." He downed what remained, "and the future. One in which every single division of PapCorp works to make the world a better place for all."

To soaring trumpets and triumphant strings, on a billion screens around the world, the shot broadcast ever higher views of the Iberian Peninsula and the word that now dominated its south-east corner; 'PapPop' shone out against the encroaching night.

"Now stay tuned for this evening's next course," Zoltan O'Dillon narrated. "What is already being called the afterparty to end all afterparties is coming up very shortly. In just a few moments, all PapTV channels will be crossing live to the Nucleus Hall of Manchester's Atom Complex for the much-anticipated final of PapStar59. I for one will be watching it on my PapDrive as I fly back. And all being well I'll be there to present the award to tonight's winner. I look forward to you joining me for what promises to be a great show."

Bio-dome 4, Manchester

Ruth Brownlow felt like an emperor when she stepped into the auditorium. Under an augmented ceiling of stars and galaxies and black holes, rows of tiered seating sloped down to the stage. The only people there at that time were the stage hands, but screens around the auditorium were already flashing with PapMode adverts for their latest patchwork dress.

As eight p.m. approached, the Nucleus Arena filled with people in suits or 'hand-stitched' dresses. They waved flags, cheered and clapped as Zoltan O'Dillon ignited the sign, and drank their complimentary bottles of PapPop on his instruction. And that was before the house lights dimmed and a panel of celebrities seated themselves behind a long-prop desk, each uttering their individual platitudes to PapCorp, Zoltan O'Dillon, and his advert for the aliens.

The host for the night was the new star of PapNews, if not all of PapTV. His nightly Humbolt Hour was the top-rated news programme ever, and he was now popping up on every channel, including the finals of talent contests such as this.

When he'd done interviewing the judges, the stage wall flickered into a screen showing crowds standing outside and waving their arms. "Look at all those people out there in Rusholme," said Vincent Humbolt. "It's like everyone in the township has braved the cold outside the Bio-domes to witness this moment. And they won't have to wait much longer. Because if it's warm here under Bio-dome Four, inside the Atom Complex it's about to get a whole lot hotter. This is the moment all those people in the rain and wind have been waiting for. Ladies and gentlemen, I give you Naomi!"

The audience stood to cheer as the pictures vanished from the stage wall to leave a pair of dancing spotlights the only illumination. They met in the middle, at the top of a staircase which had appeared in the darkness. In her homemade dress and a pair of borrowed heels, Naomi looked the pinnacle of a fashion she herself had set. Her out-turned hair bounced with every step she took down.

On the stage below, Vincent Humbolt watched the young woman descend. He hugged her bare shoulder when she got to him, bringing her face to the mic. "Oh Naomi," he said. "What a pleasure it is to meet you at last. I love this dress your mum's made, another one for PapMode to replicate." He focussed on the camera. "And you can order one now with just a flick of your fingers." He turned back to the contestant in his arm. "You know, Naomi. When I learned I'd be presenting PapStar tonight, the thing I was hoping for the most was that you would be here. And let me tell you all at home, if you think she looks good on screen, you should see her in the flesh!" The catcalls in the audience were short-lived. "So tell us what you've got for us tonight."

"Thank you, Vincent," Naomi replied, "it's a pleasure to meet you too. For tonight's show I'll be singing three songs that are all close to my heart."

"And all of them classics," said Vincent Humbolt. "All at least sixty years old I believe."

"Well 'Love don't cost a Thing' is from 2000," she smiled.

"Of course it is," he said, grinning back. "That'll be your second song tonight. But your first piece will be the oldest number ever performed on PapStar. It was written all the way back in 1970! Can you tell us what it is and why it's so special to you?"

"Yes, Vincent. Ever since I've been coming to PapStar, there's one song what's always been in my head. It's something my mum used to sing to me when I was a kid. She'd play the guitar to send me to sleep, you see. I remember this one because she played it over and over again the night we came back from the opening of the first Bio-dome, when I was just three. That was my first memory, so you could say I've known it my whole life. The song is called Big Yellow Taxi, by Joni Mitchell, because every week now for months, I've been coming here in a yellow taxi."

Music swirled, lights dazzled and Naomi burst into song.
"They paved paradise and put up a parking lot
With a pink hotel, a boutique and a swinging hot spot.
Don't it always seem to go, that you don't know what you've got
Till it's gone..."

In the air over Spain

By now, Zoltan O'Dillon and his advisors were hurtling northwards aboard their Nordenfelt N690v. All three passengers were watching the pictures through their PapDrive Corneal implants, hearing the same lyrics being belted out with such force. But if the irony of Naomi's song was lost on a singer and audience fed a constant diet of pap, it was picked up seven hundred miles due south.

"Whoever approved this song must be a complete imbecile," said Francis Atkins.

"Why's that?" asked Lucy, gazing at the pictures. "I think it's good. I've never heard it before. I was just looking at her dress."

"Listen to the words," said Francis.

"Yeah? So?"

"They paved paradise and put up a bloody parking lot!" said Zoltan. "She might as well be talking about PapCorp and Manchester."

"I don't see what you mean," Lucy responded. "Manchester was never exactly paradise, was it? And I liked the personal touch about her arriving in a yellow taxi. They have them you know, yellow taxis."

Zoltan glared at his young assistant through a box in his vision. "Did anyone ask for your opinion?" he sneered. "That Naomi might be as ignorant as you, but at least she has one talent. You have none at all. You're insolent, lazy, unable to concentrate on any single thing, forgetful, clumsy, thick as a brick and an all-round waste of space. If you were a man, I'd take my fists to you and show you what for. I was thinking of giving you one last chance, on the condition that you let me have you until you're begging for mercy. But now I've changed my mind. You repel me. You're so stupid you wouldn't even be able to turn me on. As soon as we land, you're on your own. From this moment, you are out of my team. And if you ever say anything to anyone about me, about anything, I'll have you and all your family locked up in a cage with a pride of hungry lions. Do you understand?"

Lucy couldn't breathe, the air caught in her throat. She closed her eyes to hold back the tears, and nodded her head to show that she'd heard.

Bio-dome 4

Voting closed just fifteen minutes after Leon J. had finished his final piece, a mix of techno and K-pop which he claimed to have written himself.

Zoltan O'Dillon's plane was so fast that he got there with minutes to spare. He entered the stage to a beating of drums, which rolled only faster as he flipped open an envelope and peeked at the note inside. He smiled to himself. "Ladies and gentlemen," he said. "I think there's no doubt who here is the winner. We've all been watching the same pictures, hearing the same tunes. And the people, it seems, agree wholeheartedly with me. Because with a walloping thirty nine million votes, which is incidentally more than my father's ever managed, the winner of PapStar59 is... Naomi Brownlow!"

Rusholme

In Platt Fields Park, Minnie and Brian had been standing, watching the screen with such intent that they didn't realise a crowd had gathered to see the couple's reaction, that they themselves were the centre of attention.

On Zoltan O'Dillon's word, the Brownlows' hands shot into the air. They lowered them onto each other's shoulders and danced a merry jig; Brian seemed completely to have forgotten his bad knee, he was just too elated. "Oh Minnie!" he shouted, smiling into his wife's eyes. "Oh Minnie, isn't it wonderful. This is the happiest day of my life!" He bowed his head and kissed his wife on the lips with a desire he hadn't shown since they were teenagers. "I've decided things are going to change," he continued. "I've decided I need to get out of the house, to join the real world. The Fifties have been really shitty, Minnie, on that I'm sure we can both agree. But the Sixties will soon be upon us, and if they're half as swinging as they were last time around, what with Naomi now being a superstar and everything, well, I want to be part of it." He gazed into his wife's eyes and they kissed again in jubilation.

Only when the Brownlows finally broke their embrace did they notice the crowds applauding. But rather than waving their arms at the screen, they were encircling the couple and chanting Naomi's name. Right at the front, there was only one person not joining in. Neville Jennings stood staring at the woman he loved, his arms crossed. And when Minnie caught his eye, she could barely look back at her husband.

Bio-dome 4

Vincent Humbolt had his arm clamped around Naomi's waist. "What can I say that hasn't already been said a thousand times?" he said into the mic. "You look absolutely stunning, Naomi. You always do. Over these few last months, we've watched you transform in front of our eyes, and you've changed us. Thirty-nine million of us! We've seen how tough its been adapting to life here sometimes, but you've really put your heart into this and grabbed your opportunity with both hands. You've shown what Manchester souls are made of, true northern grit. I'm sure everyone in the audience and watching at home will surely agree that you, Naomi, like your last song, are our Ghetto Superstar!"

Naomi gazed in wonder at the famous man who was stroking his thumb on her hip. She grinned. "Thank you, Vincent," she said into the microphone. "This is just all unbelievable. I don't know what to say." She looked out into the spotlights. "Ruth?" she said, "where's my sister Ruth? I want her here with me."

Ruth had barged her way to the front of the stage, but still had to persuade the security guards that it was indeed she who Naomi wanted.

In the meantime, Vincent lowered the mic and whispered into Naomi's ear. "I mean it," he said, "When I say you're gorgeous. You really should let me take you for dinner some time."

Naomi's eyelids fluttered like her heart. "That'd be lovely," she whispered back. "And Vincent, I want you tell you how much…"

But she was unable to finish the thought before Ruth's arms encircled her. "I always knew you could do it," Ruth said. "I always believed what you told me, about winning PapStar and living in a mansion under the Bio-dome. Oh Naomi, I'm so proud to be your sister."

Vincent relaxed his grasp and turned to the audience who were all still on their feet, howling and applauding the new superstar. He clapped his fingers against the mic and the ovation grew even louder.

Sangonera la Verde, outskirts of Murcia city

Although the sun had long since set, the scrubland above the old river channel was still as bright as daytime. Aliyá and the group had clambered out from under the canopy. They perched on concrete foundations, piles of bricks or tyres, looking out over the plains for any sign of their guide.

When Paco Junior appeared, the light of the sheeting lit his way as he staggered and wobbled. The group had seen him from afar, and as he got closer they could make out his dark glasses and the bottle in his hand. But only when he was upon them did they notice the stench of alcohol that hung around his head. The group watched on in silence as he plonked himself down by his father.

"Ay por fin," said the younger Paco, uncorking the bottle with his teeth. He took a hefty gulp and patted his dad on the back 'At last.' "Have some of this Papá, it's real alcohol." He placed the bottle in his father's lap.

"Joder, hijo!" said Paco Senior. 'Fucking hell, son!' "Where have you been? We've been waiting for you for hours. Are you sure you're going to be able to get us through with the light on?"

"What do you mean with the light on?" asked Paco Junior. He swivelled on his seat, looked over the rims of his sunglasses at the expanse of gleaming yellow. "Oh," he said. "It is bright, isn't it? I didn't realise they were doing that today. I thought it was next week some time."

By now the whole group had gathered around the two Pacos. "So you knew this was going to happen?" asked Carmen Hueso. "You knew they were talking about doing this, and you didn't mention it to anyone? You've stranded us outside the city, Paco. You've let us all down."

"Don't talk to me like that!" said the younger Paco, staggering to his feet. "You're not my school teacher anymore! You're just some old woman whose husband drank himself to death because he couldn't bear to spend another day with you. You lot know nothing at all, you don't even know what all this is for!" He pointed at the sheeting. "Most of you at any rate. Now, are you coming or what?"

"But you're drunk!" said Dolores.

"So?" he scoffed. "I'll have you know I can handle my drink, unlike some others. And this is quality vodka, look." He picked the bottle from his father's lap to show off the label declaring PapVodka in big yellow letters. He took another swig.

"But can you get us to the other side?" asked Oscar. "That's the question."

"Of course, Señor Talavera. I've done this route a hundred times, mostly in the middle of the night. I'll do it blindfolded if I have to, it's simply a case of following the river bed. I'll show you."

The young Paco Rufián barged towards Aliyá. Skulking behind her parents, she held her gaze firmly to the ground. She'd spent years cultivating her anger at Paco Junior, but even though she knew he would be their guide, she had told herself so often that they'd never meet, that she hadn't even considered how to react when they did.

Paco brushed past Aliyá's shoulder and mumbled, "You should've worn shoes," in the full knowledge that she'd outgrown her last pair a decade before. He took off his shirt to wrap around his head and cover his eyes, then disappeared down the old riverbank.

Bio-dome 4

The PapStar afterparty took place in one of the complex's electrons, in a sphere of metal that hung on electro-nuclear repulsion, much closer to the Bio-dome roof than the ground. There must've been a hundred people there at most, the great and the good of PapCorp. And all, it seemed, wanted to talk to Naomi. She felt herself in the middle of a whirlwind, was glad to find Ruth hanging on tight.

Vincent Humbolt barged his way through the crowd. "You haven't got a drink," he said.

"No," Naomi replied, "there hasn't really been time."

"Let me get you a Szabad Magyar."

"What's a 'Sow-bodge mod-year'?" asked Ruth.

Vincent smiled down at her. "So-bod mod-jar," he repeated. "It's an adult's drink. I'll bring you the alcohol-free version, a PapPop. You just stay with your sister." He stroked Naomi's forearm. "One for you?" he asked.

"Of course," replied Naomi. "What else?"

Vincent vanished off and Ruth pulled her sister's ear to her mouth. "What the hell's one of them then?" she whispered.

"It's like what they drink on TV," Naomi whispered back. "I wonder what it tastes like. I guess I'll find out soon enough, though. Isn't all this amazing?"

"Yeah, great," Ruth sneered, staring over at the man. "He's a smarmy git, that Vincent Humbolt. I can just imagine what mum'd say about him. He thinks he knows it all just because he reads PapCorp propaganda on the telly."

Naomi tutted, turned her attention to her audience and smiled.

When Vincent returned it was with a triangle of glasses, all filled with sparkling yellow; only Ruth's came with a straw. Vincent handed them out and raised his glass. "Well, cheers," he said. "To a great day for PapCorp and an even greater day for Naomi Brownlow." He sipped his drink, as did Naomi. But Ruth did not. "Don't you like your PapPop?" said Vincent.

"No," she replied.

"Well you haven't even had any, how do you know?"

"I hate PapPop," said Ruth, putting down the glass on the nearest table. "They commit genocide."

"Excuse me?" said Vincent. "What in Papp's name are you talking about? Genocide?"

"Please excuse my sister," said Naomi. "She promised she wouldn't go into any of this political stuff tonight."

"It's okay," Vincent responded. "I've got a little brother who's outspoken like her. It must be something to do with younger sibling inferiority syndrome. Still, we're all adults here. Well, almost all. Those are some pretty heavyweight allegations you're making, little girl."

"Yes," said Ruth, "and don't patronise me, Mr Humbolt, I might be young but I know how things are. We're ruled by a dictator who thinks him and his company are at the centre of the universe and who took power by killing the elected Prime Minister."

"Wow," said Vincent. "All that bile without even taking a breath. You want to hope no one's recording this conversation, Miss Brownlow, or you could end up being sued for slander. Or worse, you could damage your sister's reputation before she's even got going. I've never heard anything so preposterous. Michael O'Dillon won the election."

"Six years ago he won a vote, and who knows when we'll get that chance again."

"He'd win tomorrow if he had to," said Vincent. "It's hardly his fault there's no opposition to speak of, is it? Who would stand a chance against the proud record of Lord O'Dillon's PapState?"

"Can't you hear yourself?" said Ruth. "You're like a propaganda machine whether you're on screen or off it."

"Ruth!" Naomi barked. "Now stop it! Be quiet! Mr Humbolt here is a very important man and you're making him think bad of me. You promised me you wouldn't do this. What is wrong with you?"

"Don't worry, Naomi," Vincent said, stroking his thumb over her buttock. "I don't think any less of you because of your sister. We can't choose our family, right? This is your big day – you're PapStar59, for goodness sake. You're the Queen of PapCorp on the day of her centenary. Come on, let's dance."

"I'd love that," Naomi replied. She let him lead her away by the hand without a glance back at her sister.

Suddenly alone, Ruth sulked off towards a table stacked high with strange foods. She scanned the plates for something she recognised but found nothing at all. So she picked up a puff pastry that oozed with pink cream. She took a bite, munched twice on the vol-au-vent and her face soured at the artificial flavours. She spat it into her hand. "Ugh," she said, looking about her. She couldn't see Naomi, or anyone she knew. So she scarpered for the toilet.

Ruth locked herself inside a cubicle. She threw the mashed-up hors d'oeuvre into the bowl and wiped her hand clean with a piece of toilet paper. Then she flushed it all away and sat on the seat fully clothed, resting her elbows on her lap and her face in her palms. A tear appeared in the corner of her eye and she brushed it away immediately.

Naomi hung off Vincent's shoulder, dancing as if on a cloud. She, Naomi Brownlow, was PapStar59. And the queen of the night couldn't let go of the man in her arms. She pulled herself closer to Vincent, moved her body against his and nestled her nose into his neck. She took a deep breath, flying higher still on his muskiness of his flesh.

She could resist no longer. Her lips pecked his neck, one kiss, one more, three. Then two strong hands nudged her away by the waist. Vincent stared into her eyes. Even though they buzzed with a million coloured pixels, through her own PapDrive specs Naomi could see the desire in his gaze. When their lips met she felt like she might just fly away and never come back down to Earth.

In the safety of the cubicle, Ruth sat listening to women's conversations when they thought they were alone. She'd been there at least an hour when she heard a woman say, "I hate that Naomi Brown-nose. I mean, who the hell does she think she is? Some tart from the 'block'? I've been seeing Vincent for like four months now. I know he's a cheating bastard but he invited me here for goodness sake. And now look at him prancing around with her wrapped around him."

Below the sheeting, outside Murcia

Under the constant glow, every inch they gained was harder than the last. As Aliyá felt her way through the aluminium struts, it seemed they were making progress. But with the scarf around her eyes she couldn't tell how much.

Aliyá, like the rest, was crawling through a shallow channel, the sheeting close enough to make her hair stand on end. The group kept together by blowing owl sounds into their hands every so often, when they took breaks from the dragging of cases and baskets along the rocky floor.

She knew her father was beside her by his rasping.

"Aliyá," Oscar huffed. "Lola, mi amor. I've got a really bad feeling about this. Something dreadful's about to happen, I just know it is."

"Come on now, Papá," said his daughter. "Just keep going a bit more. We can't be far. How much further, Paco?" she shouted. "You said this was going to be easy, that we'd just walk down the river. Are we lost or something?"

"Lost?" Paco Junior shouted back. "Don't be ridiculous! I know just where we are."

"Then where are we?" asked Belén Molino.

"We're nearly there," said Paco Junior. "I think."

Aliyá heard a wheezing to her right and asked, "Is everything okay Papá?"

"I hope it's not much further," said Oscar as he struggled for air. "I'm not sure how much more of this I can take. My fingers are starting to tingle."

Manchester

It was only when the security guard came to clear the venue that Ruth was discovered, and promptly escorted down to the street without any idea of where her sister had gone. With no money for a taxi, she would have to walk home. A few swipes of her hand brought up the navigation function of her PapDrive specs, and she studied every turn of the route until she was sure she'd memorised it. She followed the navigation arrow until it imposed itself yellow over a footbridge, then took off the glasses and dropped them into the Bridgewater canal.

Ruth Brownlow walked home with hands in her pockets, her feelings decidedly mixed. She was elated for her sister, of course she was. But at the same time, she'd never felt more abandoned, more deeply let down or betrayed.

Still under the sheeting around Murcia

Either side of their man, the Talavera women were now dragging Oscar's luggage as well as their own.

As she crawled alongside her husband, Dolores whispered memories to him. "Remember those evening promenades along the riverbank?" she'd said. And, "You used to have a glass of brandy for breakfast almost every day, and pretended you didn't. I always knew, you know."

Oscar rasped louder. "Lola!" he heaved. "Aliyá, I can't breathe. I feel like my face is on fire. I need to take this off."

Aliyá grabbed her father's hands to stop him removing the scarf from his face. "Don't do that Papá!" she said. "You'll be blind the moment you look at it."

"I have to," Oscar gasped. "It's my heart, I…"

Aliyá felt her father's body twitch and thud to the ground. "Papá?" she shrieked, "Papá, answer me please! Papá, what's happening to you? Papá!?" She now had her hands on both of her father's shoulders, trying to force him still as he spasmed.

"Help!" she cried out. "Please, someone help. I think my Papá's having a heart attack."

It felt like forever before someone came to her aide. By that time, Oscar had curled up in a ball and was breathing heavily, but he'd stopped shaking at least. Someone touched Aliyá's shoulder and Paco Junior's voice said, "We need to get him out of here."

"I know," replied Aliyá. "I'm not the one that got us lost. We need to get him some air, get him away from this damned light."

Unseen by anyone else, young Paco unwrapped his scarf from his face, hung his sunglasses around his ears and cupped his hands around his eyes. He peeked through almost shut eyelids. "It's okay," he said, "I think I can see darkness up ahead. Here, let me carry your dad."

"Get away from him," Aliyá spat. "You don't have permission to touch me or any of my family members. I don't know what those hands will do. Don't think I've forgotten how weak you are either, how easily I fought you off me every time you tried to assault me!" She felt her father's body relax, his breathing settled into a sorrowful whimper. "Can you hear me, Papa?" she asked.

Oscar groaned.

19. Power

10th February 2048
Rusholme, Manchester

After the last election, when Minnie Brownlow had sat alone to watch Harry Lanker sweep to power, she'd been determined that the next time would be different. She spent that night at Dahlia's, with foraged snacks and homemade moonshine, in the company of others who cheered, laughed and sang together without the worry of waking husbands or kids.

At every seat that went to RASCAL, Neville, the delivery boy, would come over and offer Minnie his hands. She grabbed them with an enthusiasm that increased with each drink. By four a.m., they'd stopped even waiting for new seats to declare. For hour after hour, Minnie caressed the unfamiliar muscles of his back, enjoying the feel of Neville's fingers on the folds of her hips.

When Minnie left that morning, the sky was starting to brighten and all the street lights were off. She hardly noticed the drizzle as she walked tucked-up in Neville's arm, his hand on her shoulder pulling her close. When they got to the school at end of Welwyn Street, they held hands and gazed into each other's eyes.

"Thanks for walking me home," said Minnie. "I've really enjoyed tonight."

"Me too," said Neville. "I mean, I've fancied you for ages, Minnie, but tonight was really special."

Neville leaned his lips towards hers, but Minnie offered only her cheek. When he tried to look her in the eyes again she wouldn't meet his gaze. "I've got to go," she said, and shuffled off without a glance back.

Even if she didn't see him, Minnie Brownlow could feel Neville Jennings watching her all the way to the house at the far end of the road. Only when the door slammed closed did he slouch away, dragging the soles of his shoes on the pavement, hands in jacket pockets.

Minnie found the house as cold as always, she shivered in the draft as she shut the door.

And as soon as she'd done so a shout came from upstairs. "Is that you, Minnie?" asked her husband.

"Yeah."

Brian appeared at the top of the stairs. "I've had a dreadful night," he said. "The baby had me up three times and Naomi wet the bed because you weren't here. How am I supposed to get through the day now after such little sleep?"

"What do you mean 'get through the day'?" said Minnie. "What've you got to do that's so important? I've been out all night and I'm going to be shattered at work. He won you know."

"Yeah," said Brian. "I saw. I was going to look for a job, wasn't I? I was supposed to start this week. Well I can't now, I'll be too tired."

"Right," said Minnie, barging up the stairs. "Every day there's a new excuse, isn't there? Well, on your head be it, Brian Brownlow. Now, I have to get to work. You'll have to change Naomi's sheets. Run the bath and stick half a cup of bi-carb of soda in there, then leave them to soak. I'll sort it out after work. I'm already late so I've got to dash. Will you make sure Naomi gets to school on time?"

Brian nodded to his wife as she pushed past him. She picked her baby daughter from the cot and carried Ruth back down without waking her. Minnie wrapped her up in a shawl which she tied across her shoulder and headed out the door without saying goodbye. But when she did so, she found the drizzle had become torrential and she popped back inside for a waterproof which she fitted over two heads, making sure her baby had air.

Downing Street, London

Yielding a large umbrella, Samuel Dietrich walked along a wall down the side of Horse Guards' Parade. He turned a corner and stared into the garage, found the back door of his car open and a pair of yellow legs sticking out. "Hello," he said. "Can I help you?"

A man wormed himself out and stood with military deportment, his shocking blue eyes peering up from under the peak of a cap which matched his suit of lemon. "Morning Zachery," he said. "It's all done."

"Brigadier Atkins!" the driver exclaimed. "I wasn't expecting to find you here still. Is everything okay? Is it all wired up and ready to go?"

Francis Atkins nodded. "I was just making a last few checks," he said. "You know the story, same as always – if it ain't broke, don't fix it. The leads are attached to the back of the door handle. It's basically Oswald Kongolo all over again."

"Except that this is the Prime Minister of England and not a Congolese warlord. Not to mention something of a friend."

"Don't get emotional, Zack, don't let your vision get clouded. You've an important job to do today and you need to be at the peak of your abilities. You're a good man for doing this, you know."

"Good and bad has nothing to do with it," said the driver. "I'm PapCorp born and raised, just doing my job the same as you."

"I heard a rumour you're going to retire after this one."

The driver chuckled from his gut. "I need a break," he said, "that's for sure. I'll go away for a bit and consider my options. But I'll always be there if Lord Michael calls, you know me."

"I certainly do," said Francis, patting the driver's shoulder. "Now, like I was saying, there are a couple of leads on the back of the door handle. Just pass a finger over them and you're away. But remember, don't actually open the door, don't…"

"…break the integrity of the system. I know, Francis, I've done this often enough. Anyway, what are you doing dressed like that? Are you in the motorcade?"

"I figured the best way to keep an eye on things would be to go as an outrider in the security detail. That way I'll be on hand in case anything goes wrong. Now, are you ready?"

The driver arranged the black cap on his head, the white tie around his neck. He opened the door and got into the driver's seat, gripped the steering wheel with both hands and took a couple of breaths. "I'm ready as I'll ever be," he said, and slammed the car door closed.

An electric engine whirred the Rover P9 out of the garage, only for it to stop moments later outside the door to number 10. The driver gazed past a solitary tree, from whose branches rain dripped like tears. Through the gates to Whitehall he watched the crowds waving flags under their umbrellas, could see them chanting "Harry Lanker, Harry Lanker," even if he couldn't hear a peep.

When he looked back at the house, Prime Minister Lanker was standing on the step and waving to the crowds. The driver grabbed his umbrella from the passenger seat, got out and raced around to the back door, to hold it open for the Prime Minister.

When he met his driver, Harry Lanker was all smiles. "Morning Samuel," he said. "Did you manage a few hours' kip? It was a long way down from Bolsover, wasn't it?"

"I did, Harry, thanks for asking. How about yourself?"

"I don't need sleep, Samuel. I'm running on adrenaline as always. And today more than ever – Prime Minister with a majority of at least fifty. I knew it was a good idea to change election day to a Sunday, an 85 per cent turnout's almost unheard of. Now we're really going to show this country what for."

"It's been an incredible night," said the driver, feigning a smile. "Come on, let's get this done."

Police officers joined hands with their PapSec counterparts to work a gap through the umbrellas. Motorcycles zoomed through the gates of Downing Street, leaving trails of spray as they sped off towards Nelson's Column.

Harry Lanker stretched both his arms over the back seat. "There'll be no hanging on deals with champagne socialists this time around, Samuel," said the Prime Minister. "I still can't believe they brought down my government for trying to re-nationalise the hospitals. I mean, it was their party that bloody founded the health service. Still, we've shown them now, haven't we? The people of this country have told the world what they really want. With this number of RASCAL MPs, Samuel, we'll end homelessness in weeks. We'll make sure every person in the country has food on the table and clothes on their backs. The universal income will free the working man and woman from wage slavery, and bring in a new golden age of civic action and responsibility. Ah, Samuel, it's a heck of a job to prize this country from the mucky paws of aristocrats and undo the corruption of the past. But we've got five long years until the next election, and boy are we going to make this work. This is the moment, Sam. If not now, when? If not me, who? I'm this county's last hope."

"You certainly are that, Harry," said his driver, knives stabbing at his stomach.

"Aren't you behind me, Samuel?" asked the PM. "You're usually my biggest supporter. You should be happy but you're not. What's up?"

"Don't be daft, Harry, I'm over the moon like you are. It's just been a long night."

"That it has Samuel, that it has."

Rusholme

Minnie Brownlow removed her sodden poncho to reveal the cloth around her shoulder which held her infant daughter dry to her back. Even if it was early, the market was busy with shoppers and sellers and people wheeling deliveries in on trollies. A projection screen shone out against the dullness of the day, tracking the Prime Minister's progress around Trafalgar Square. But no one paid too much attention and the air buzzed with normality.

At the stall, Dahlia was already bagging up veggies and exchanging them for cardboard stamps. Minnie noticed Neville unloading groceries at the far end of the desk, but she felt too self-aware to say hello. Instead, she tightened the shawl around her baby and got straight to work. "Who's next?" she shouted.

PapPop Tower, Manchester

As head of PapPop, Zoltan O'Dillon's office was on the second floor of the tower which bore his division's name, but he never used the stairs. He never did any exercise, in fact, which was why his waistline had expanded with his chins. Despite being only thirty-seven, his boyish grin was long gone and bags hung dark under his drug-dulled eyes.

The lift dinged open and Zoltan made straight for his office, following the arrow which his PapDrive lenses superimposed yellow before him. He pulled up the leather armchair behind his desk and plonked himself into the seat. When he looked up, it was to find his assistant hovering at the door, the rosy-cheeked twenty-five-year-old with the toothy grin whom he'd recruited to replace Bernie the Earl.

"Ah, Jemima," said Zoltan O'Dillon. "Can you believe this shit? All the polls I had done said Harry Lanker was going to get absolutely battered, and now there he is on his way to meet the King with a majority of more than fifty!"

"Relax, Zoltan," said Jemima Kemal, heading for the drinks machine by the window. "Do you want a cup of tea?"

"I'd prefer a glass of Merlot and a line of coke."

"Of course you would, but that combination gets you into all sorts of trouble, doesn't it?"

"You're right as always, Jemima. That's why you're my Number One Lady. I will have that cup of tea. Have you seen Larry yet? I'm waiting for his update on the markets."

"Larry's not here," said Jemima, placing a mug of milky stew in front of her boss and taking a seat opposite him. "I haven't seen him all morning. But I can tell you what's going on, if you haven't already seen for yourself."

"I've seen the pound's tanking," he replied. "You can say what you want about Harry Lanker, but he's been a godsend for the PapPound."

"Yep," said Jemima. "I wouldn't be surprised to see it go past two-to-one today."

Central London

The Mall was a dripping reflection of what it'd been two and a half years previously. The rain was relentless against the limo's windshield, and although the dispersal system blew away the water, it meant that only a draggle of hardcore RASCALS were there to cheer on their Prime Minister. The umbrellas in most of their hands made applause impossible. But Harry Lanker didn't see much of it because he was fixated on the breaking news that flashed up along the bottom of his PapDrive specs.

When the Prime Minister swiped away the story with the back of his hand, he found they were already passing through cast-iron gates topped with gold leaf and his escort was peeling away around the front of Buckingham Palace. "Bloody markets," he said. "It's like we can't have an ounce of success without the national currency going into meltdown. If this goes on, it'll make all of our plans so much more expensive. A run on the pound, they're calling it."

Samuel Dietrich glanced into the mirror and nodded, but was unable to say a word.

Through an arch in the wall of sash windows, the Rover P9 reappeared in a courtyard of waterlogged gravel. Samuel Dietrich pulled an arc around a puddle that had formed like a lake in the middle, then stopped outside the North wing. He glanced in the rear view and saw the Prime Minister going for the door. "Just a sec," said the driver. "I'll get the brolly for you. And don't forget protocol."

Harry Lanker sat back in his seat, watched his driver scamper around the front of the car and unfurl an umbrella. He inhaled through his nostrils in thought. "Right," said the Prime Minister to himself. "Enough of this standing on bloody ceremony. This is a new dawn. Today we're going to do things a little differently." He reached for the door handle.

Samuel Dietrich was outside the PM's window, umbrella open. As his finger probed under the handle for the wires, his mind flicked to his wife, to how devastated this would've left her.

The last thing either man heard was the clicking of the latch. There was a flash, a blast that lifted the car on its suspension. It flung the door from its hinges and smashed the driver into a column of golden limestone.

Rusholme

Back at the market, people stopped what they were doing, chatter dropped to silence. Minnie grabbed the side of the desk. "What?" she stammered. "What, what just happened? Is Harry all right? Please say Harry Lanker's not..." She could feel her legs giving way below her. But before she fell, two taut arms caught her ribcage and held her upright. Minnie rotated herself in Neville's grasp and looked into his face which told her everything she feared. She grabbed hold of the man, buried her mouth in his chest and screamed.

PapPop Tower

Zoltan O'Dillon had been staring at his assistant as she read out a list of figures. He could just as easily have read them himself, but he liked the way her mouth moved, the way her chest expanded as she breathed.

The headline flashed up on the interface of Zoltan's PapDrive lenses and Jemima stopped talking. She'd seen the same news. He tapped a finger against the virtual headline, and when the pictures loaded they were showing the burning shell of a car in the courtyard of Buckingham Palace. He stared at the scenes, listening to the commentary in his ears. "... both the Prime Minister and his driver have been declared dead at the scene," Carolyn Hargreaves was saying.

"Have you seen this?" asked Zoltan.

"I'm just watching it," said Jemima. "Who do you think did it?"

"No idea. Maybe it was one of those RASCAL splinter groups who couldn't bear to see him take power. I wonder if my father knows what's going on. I should give him a call."

A swipe of his hand dragged the pictures away, a tap with his finger brought up his father's face. But the tone rang out in Zoltan's ears, and when asked if he'd like to leave a message all he said was "ring me now."

Buckingham Palace

On the pebble ground in the middle of Buckingham Palace, it felt like the whole world was swarming around the face of the North wing. There were drones dropping water on the flames, paramedics around the driver, ambulances, reporters, royal advisors, the Duke of Sussex, and all the PM's security detail.

All, at least, but one. Because Brigadier Francis Atkins had seen what he had to. He skirted the puddle to cross the courtyard, perched himself under the limestone lintel of the main door opposite, and tapped through the virtual interface of his PapDrive spectacles until Lord Michael O'Dillon's face popped up before him. A single tone rang through his ears and the image sprang to life.

"It's done, I see," said the CEO of PapCorp. "Another excellent job, Atkins. But what about that colleague of yours? The driver? The news is reporting he was killed in the blast. Is that true?"

"He's in a pretty bad way," said Francis Atkins, "but he's got PapMed's best looking after him now. I'm hoping against hope he'll pull through."

"I'm sure PapMed will do everything they can," said Lord Michael. "I've got my fingers crossed for him. He's a good man that Zachery Klein, PapCorp through and through, just like you and me. And as you well know, I like to ensure my men and women are well looked after. Does he have family we can send his reward to? In case he doesn't make it."

"That won't be necessary, sir," said Atkins. "As he put it, he was only doing his duty to PapCorp and Lord O'Dillon, they're what he considers his family. He grew up an orphan, but he's not exactly short of a few bob now. I have it on pretty good authority that he has his own little trading empire in central Africa."

"Yes," said Lord Michael, "I heard that story too. Now on the subject of jobs, Atkins. You remember how you always refuse my offers of promotions? Well, here's one you're simply not going to be able to turn down."

"I'm always prepared to hear you out, sir. You know that. And I'm always polite when I refuse."

"Well, listen, this one won't take you away from the action. If anything it'll bring you closer to it. You know Larry Pickering, don't you?"

"Your son's senior advisor, sir? I do know him, yes."

"Well something's about to happen that means I'm going to need him with me, something that means he's going to be more use by my side than at my son's. And I believe I've found the perfect replacement for the old man."

"Who's that, sir?"

"You, Atkins. You are my choice."

"But Lord O'Dillon, sir, that's quite a responsibility you're asking me to perform. I'm not a diplomat. I'm more into special operations, if you know what I mean."

"I've been watching you for years, Atkins," said O'Dillon. "And in all that time, you've taken everything we could throw at you, handled it with measured care and consistently come out with the right result for PapCorp. You were like a rock to me and Zoltan after Gariepdam, and you never let me thank you with anything other than a handshake and medals. It's precisely that kind of incorruptible stoicism and discretion I need around my son. That and your obvious tactical abilities. You've done this country a great service today, Francis Atkins, and you deserve the highest of rewards. Please, don't turn me down this time."

"And what does Zoltan say about this?"

"He'll be happy, let me assure you. You're one of the few people he actually respects."

"So he doesn't know?"

"Everything in good time, Francis. It was important we had this conversation first. My son's left me a dozen messages already but I'm determined to let him stew in his own juices for as long as I can. I certainly don't want to risk him doing something stupid to try and overshadow his old man, on today of all days. Now I take it you accept. The rate is thirty times your current wages."

Rusholme

It had been too much for anyone in the food exchange to watch the countless re-runs of Harry Lanker's assassination play out on every channel. So they tore down the projector screen, as well as all the banners they'd painted and hung with such care. The day dragged, and when finally the exchange closed up for the evening, Minnie Brownlow felt a tenth of the person she'd been when they'd arrived.

Minnie wrapped her waterproof over her shoulders and checked that baby Ruth was okay. She stepped outside and found it cold, dark, and drizzling. Water splashed onto the paving from cracks in the gutter. And from behind the waterfall stepped Neville Jennings.

"What are you doing here?" Minnie whispered, taking him by the arm and leading him under the lip of the roof.

"I've been waiting for you, Minnie. I can't stop thinking about you. You're like a ray of sunshine on this foulest of days."

"Aw, Neville," said Minnie, stroking his arm. "That's one of the nicest things anyone's ever said to me."

"Then kiss me, Minnie, and take away some of this pain."

Minnie stared up at the man, her heart thumping. In his eyes she saw a sadness that she longed to ameliorate. She reached up on tip toes, and although she only meant to give him a peck on the lips, she found it so difficult to pull herself away.

PapNews Studios, central Manchester

Although the Brigadier didn't know it, when Francis Atkins spoke to Lord Michael, PapCorp's CEO had been in the back of his limo between the construction site of the Zoltán Papp tower and the PapNews studios. He was there to address the nation, and while it was to be filmed by PapNews, his transmission would go out on every channel and all the newsfeeds.

With Union and PapCorp flags behind him, Lord O'Dillon spoke straight to the camera, his eyebrows turned down in sincerity. "Ladies and gentlemen of Britain," he said, "What we have witnessed today will live with us for many years. This will go down as one of the darkest days in our history. The assassination of a serving Prime Minister is almost unheard of in these isles, and the country has been placed on the highest possible security alert. As most British armed units remain deployed overseas, PapSec have stepped in to aid the work of both the army and the police, as they search for the culprits behind this most heinous of crimes. I can guarantee you all that we are doing everything we can to find those responsible, and when we do, justice will be swift and proportionate. At this time, we believe the culprits to be radicals from the Trotskyist wing of the RASCAL party."

O'Dillon took a sip of PapAqua before continuing. "Moments ago," he said, "I spoke to the King himself, to reassure him of his own security in light of today's events. The royal family are shaken after this morning but are physically unharmed and are safely ensconced in secure rooms, while PapSec specialists continue to search the Palace. We have witnessed today a breakdown in security at one of the most important moments in this country's history. Bearskin caps may look good for tourists, but the King's Guard have become rather more interested in posing for photos with pretty girls than doing their jobs. Which is why PapSec have agreed to take responsibility for security at airports and train stations, palaces and offices of state. The aim of these anarchists is clearly to decapitate the government and thrive in the chaos that ensues. But this is Britain, and here we refuse to let that happen."

Lord O'Dillon took a few more gulps from his PapAqua bottle before breaking the news to the nation. "His Majesty and I share many traits," he said, "not least the propensity to see the bigger picture. The King and I are both worried about the effects that today's events may have on global markets. Therefore, in order to bring stability to this country at our hour of greatest need, and to avoid the risk that a period of uncertainty would bring, His Majesty has asked me to take over the leadership of the country as emergency First Lord of the Treasury, until the time is right for new elections. Now, let us all share a moment of reflection."

Screens went black for white letters to fade in, saying,
'Harry Lanker, Prime Minister 1992 – 2048.
Samuel Dietrich, driver 2001 – 2048'.

In seconds, the words vanished behind a digitally waving Union flag and the drum roll to God Save the King.

Rusholme

Minnie tore herself away from Neville. She gazed up at him in fear, then scarpered off down Claremont Road without a word.

Thoughts of what had happened that day churned through her mind, and when Minnie looked at the houses they'd never seemed so scruffy, the road never so badly beaten up. By the time she got to Welwyn Street, the excitement of her encounter with another man had faded into worry and regret.

Minnie turned the latch and decided to tell her husband nothing. She stepped inside and thought their house felt colder than she could ever remember.

Six-year-old Naomi was wearing a coat and playing on the floor, Brian was sitting at his usual place on the sofa. "Isn't it great news!" he said.

"How can you say that?" said Minnie, hanging up her coat and untying the baby from her shoulder. "Don't you have any heart at all?"

"Not that news," said Brian. "I mean this news." He pointed to the screen, where a banner read 'Lord Michael O'Dillon made emergency First Lord of the Treasury.'

"What's First Lord of the Treasury?" she asked.

"It's another name for Prime Minister, apparently."

"What?" Minnie exclaimed. "What on earth is going on? He's not even an elected member of Parliament! How can he possibly be made Prime Minister? RASCAL won the election for goodness sake! Doesn't that count for anything?"

"They're saying it was probably a RASCAL splinter group what killed him."

"Why would a RASCAL group murder their own leader on the day he's elected? That makes no sense."

"Well, it's what they're saying."

"And has anyone thought to question Lord O'Dillon's role in all of this?"

"Are you saying Michael O'Dillon killed Harry Lanker?" Brian sneered. "That's ridiculous. Why would he do something like that? He's the most successful businessman in the world, and I for one can't think of a better man to be Prime Minister right now. I know you have something against him, Minnie, but you can't deny he knows how to run the show."

Minnie perched herself on the arm of the settee. "He's the CEO of PapCorp," she said, "the Lord Mayor of Manchester, and now Prime Minister. No wonder there's an unemployment crisis in this country. He can't possibly do all those jobs at the same time. There are massive conflicts of interest for a start."

"Lord Michael O'Dillon wins any conflict he find himself in," said Brian. "The man's a bloody genius. If anyone can keep all those balls flying, it's him."

"Right," said Minnie, glancing at their daughter playing on the floor. "Did you wash Naomi's sheets like I told you?"

"No," said Brian. "I didn't know how. I left them on her bed for you to sort out."

Minnie stared a moment at the side of her husband's face as he watched the screen. His puffy jowls and gormless gape suddenly repulsed her. She got up without a word and made for the stairs. It was only when the sheets were in the bathtub, water running from both taps, that she allowed her grief to take hold. She sat cross-legged on the bathroom tiles and wept into her hands.

20. Home

18th September 2059
Murcia

Even with the scarf around her eyes, when Aliyá Talavera heaved her father from under the sheeting she knew they were out by the darkness. She heard shouting, felt Oscar being lifted away and she collapsed face-up on the river bank. She tore off the shawl, blinked up at the lemon-tinged clouds and found the tears streaming down her cheeks were of relief and not regret.

Oscar barely knew where he was, let alone why all those hands were lifting him. When they laid him down it was on a plant-cracked road. Dolores knelt beside him to slip the scarf from his face and found it sopping in sweat.

The breeze blew cold against Oscar's forehead and up his nostrils. He blinked at the group of his friends peering down in concern and raised himself on his forearms.

"No, no, no, no," they all said at once.

"Just take your time," Dolores muttered. "You're safe now."

Oscar gazed at his wife, feeling a tear roll down his cheek. Another followed, and another. He curled himself into a ball and wept into his wife's bosom. The only words anyone could make out were, "sorry, sorry, sorry."

When at last Aliyá clambered up onto the roadway, she met the first sunrise of its kind; over the roofs to the west, the sky was lightening into an eerie shade of blue-yellow. She noticed the group gathered over her father and made her way over.

"Okay," she said. "Give him some air, he needs space to breathe."

"We're just concerned about him," said Carmen Hueso, moving away. "Is there anything we can do to help?"

"I don't think so," Aliyá replied, glancing at her parents' embrace. "We just have to get him home, that's all. It's a good job my Mamá has the key around her neck, because there was no way to carry our luggage and my father."

"I'll get your stuff," said Paco Junior. He looked to Aliyá but found her avoiding his gaze. So without another thought, he tied his shirt back around his face, climbed into the ditch and disappeared under the glowing sheet.

Blind Señor Rufián was the only one who didn't know what was happening. "Qué pasa?" he kept asking. "Qué pasa?" 'What's going on?'

"Your son's gone back to get the Talaveras' luggage," said Belén Molino.

"What?!" cried the elder Paco Rufián. "So we've lost our guide? It's going to take us long enough to get home as it is, without waiting for my Junior to get back. How's he even going to find a few bags under there?"

"Not a clue," said Chucho. "But I say we don't hang around. He could be hours yet. This is our city for goodness sake, I'm sure we can figure out where we are."

"I know where we are," said Dolores, cradling her husband's head in one hand and pointing towards a motorway slipway with the other. "I could swear this is junction seven of the MU30. We used to come off this exit every time we drove back from the beach. That's San Ginés on the other side. I say we go that way."

Aliyá would've loved to have carried her father home, but when they eventually got Oscar back on his feet she found she hadn't the strength. So, wrapped up in his jacket, a scarf around his neck and a woollen hat over his ears, Oscar leaned his gloved hands on the bare shoulders of Juanjo Cavernas and one of his boys while the other guided Paco Senior.

Even though the two men were carrying his weight, Oscar moved his feet as he walked. But while his mind was now clearing from the panic attack, a yellow mark had stained his soul.

They proceeded beneath a motorway bridge of concrete tiles fitted together like a jigsaw, where weeds worked through the gaps in between. Splashed atop the lot were declarations painted in Spanish over one side, English on the other, reading

'You are entering the Free City of Murcia. No property, no theft. No hierarchy, no violence.'

Beyond the bridge, triangular pylons dotted the scrubland on either side and cables joined every one, drooping over billboards that had bent and broken in the wind. To their right, over fields of thistles and thorn, where wild flowers sprouted white and yellow between scraps of plastic and strips of metal, the peaks of the Carrascoy floated like water colour lines above the haze of heated earth.

Carmen Hueso stopped and the others did likewise. "Dios mío!" she exclaimed, pointing at the eastern end of their sierra and crossing her heart. 'My God!' "Look at that, they've demolished the whole of El Valle. I hope they haven't destroyed the Sanctuary of Our Lady. Murcia would be nothing without the Fuensanta."

"All the springs in the province now belong to PapAqua," said Juanjo, "Even sacred ones. So any water Our Lady could find would be for them and them alone. We need a patron who'll provide from the sky now, not from the earth."

"Yes," said Carmen. "Now we need to talk directly to God."

The hill of the sanctuary still stood, it would transpire, towering close over the edge of the sheeting. But all the movements round about had cracked the foundations and reduced the monastery to a pile of stones, never to be rebuilt.

San Ginés had always been worn down. But after years of abandonment, trees had broken their enclosures, roots tore cracks along concrete pavements and up cement-fronted walls. Sun-blanched plaster, loosened by a decade of nearby construction, had dropped from the breeze blocks to leave bare patches. All along the road, squat dwellings were breaking apart; iron-barred windows and yellow-boarded doorways were no defence against the constant impacts of progress. And there was dust, everywhere, drifts of it against shopfront shutters, piles two storeys high in some corners.

Beyond the village, the houses grew further apart and the first front door appeared freed from its cladding. As they walked on, signs of life began sprouting up in parklands or empty lots. Over roundabouts and up embankments grew all number of plants and bushes, the earth below carefully mulched with grasses and leaves for the winter.

They passed a pruned lemon grove on their right, could see again the wall of the Carrascoy mountains illuminated sickly yellow against the brightening clouds. Oscar patted the bare backs of the two men supporting him. "Bueno, chicos," he said, 'Okay guys.' "Thanks for helping me but I've already been enough of a burden. I think I can walk on my own now."

"Are you sure?" asked Juanjo.

"You've all been very kind to me," he said. "Far too kind, really. I can't tell you how sorry I am that I caused you all that worry back there, especially you mee-khá. But I want to walk into my city on my own two legs."

Juanjo nodded to the boy on the other side of Oscar and they started inching away from the city's former mayor.

Oscar wobbled a moment. He felt suddenly more tired than ever he could remember and his legs gave way. The men caught him by the armpits and heaved him back upright.

Beside the orchard was the brick shell of a house, with never-filled windows and rebar sprouting from the roof. It stood behind a wooden fence and a rock-marked path that swirled between bushes and trees. In the garden, a grey-haired lady was picking the last fruits of a peach tree. She heard conversation, left her basket on the ground and trotted on down the garden path. She leaned against the gate and shouted in English. "Hello," she said. "Welcome to Free Murcia. What on earth has happened to you all?"

Aliyá gazed at the blank faces of her companions, realised only she could reply. "We had a difficult night," she said. "We got lost under the sheet, and it was very bright. We're almost home now so we need to keep going."

"Well, congratulations for getting this far," said the woman. "You're right, the city's not much further. And I think I've got something that could help that poor gentleman. Just a moment." The lady disappeared off into the bushes, and when she came back she was pushing a metal wheelbarrow. "I'd say this should hold him," she said. "I only fitted the wheel a couple of months ago so it should be strong enough.

"You mean we can borrow this?" asked Aliyá.

"Of course, if it'll help. I'll need it next week though, I want to make a start on the pruning. So if you could bring it back before then…"

"For sure," said Aliyá.

The lady watched Juanjo and his friend help Oscar into the galvanised bucket. "Have you come far?" she asked.

"From those mountains over there," said Aliyá, pointing back behind her. "We're coming home after many years in the Sierra de Carrascoy."

"Oh!" said the woman. "You're not the first to return."

"No," said Oscar from his seat. "But we are the last. There's no one left up there now."

"I hope everything's in order when you get home," said the lady. "There's been a lot of breaking in and squatting recently. But you have the right to your flat, not matter who or what you might find there. You may have to wait till the General Assembly next week, but you'll get everything back no problem, and in the state you left it. That's the agreement for anyone seeking refuge in Murcia."

"So why do you live in this house?" asked Aliyá, nodding at the unfinished shell.

"Because I didn't want to break in anywhere," the lady smiled, "and all the other places were locked. I've got a tent and blankets so I'm okay. It's nice and peaceful here, not like in the city."

They bade the lady thanks and farewell, then Juanjo took up the handles and weaved Oscar between the cracks in the paving. Aliyá and her mother walked one on either side. "Ves, mee-khá?" said Oscar. 'You see?' "I told you there'd be people here who speak English."

"Yes," Aliyá replied. "I just hope they haven't broken into our flat."

"Me too," said Dolores, fingering the key by her heart.

"That door has the best locks money could buy," said Oscar. "If anywhere's safe, our flat is."

As the group approached the city centre, Oscar flitted between wakefulness and dozing. The streets widened until Juanjo was zig-zagging him along a root-torn road laid out for four lanes of cars, which now hosted not a single one. The buildings grew taller as they went, the graffiti more profuse. Here, over the faded tags of yesteryear, were written slogans of today, all in the same white paint as under the motorway bridge. 'No Pasarán!' said some of the signs, in reference to a war long lost. 'No nos Papearán,' said others, using a word seemingly invented for modern Murcia. But most common were the slogans that read 'PapCorp Out,' 'La Ciudad Libre de Murcia' or its translation, 'The Free City'.

In a lucid moment, from his seat in the wheelbarrow, Oscar felt able to comment. "Que bueno," he said. "Wasn't it good of that lady to lend me her wheel? I feel like royalty in this thing. Like a Catholic king coming to reconquer my city."

"More like Quixote after losing a drunken duel," Chucho quipped. "Who ever heard of a king riding in a wheelbarrow?"

Oscar nodded. "I guess you're right," he said, staring through the yellowing leaves at a pair of cross-topped towers. He rotated his body towards his daughter. "I haven't thanked you, mee-khá," he said. "You saved my life back there. I'd have died if it wasn't for you."

"Don't say things like that," Aliyá replied. "I was just doing what anyone's daughter would've done. Now, try to rest."

Oscar relaxed back into his galvanised carriage and tried to close his eyes as his daughter suggested. But he found it impossible to look away from the streets and the memories they were unleashing.

The towers belonged to a church with a fine façade carved from stone the colour of peaches. If anything, an absence of cars and smoke meant it was cleaner than anyone remembered.

"I was named after that church," announced Carmen Hueso. "God be praised for preserving her so well."

"And we were married there," said Oscar, searching for his wife. "Do you remember?"

"How could I ever forget?" said Dolores, reaching for her husband's hand.

Opposite the church ran the iron railings of a park, where they saw people reaching through the twisted branches of fig trees. Others bent over patches of leaves, picking out produce or weeds. Two women strode past the group with wicker baskets on their heads, their skin shone like jet stone and they talked in a language of clicks and giggles. The group gawped at the exotic ladies, but they themselves didn't seem to notice the returning Murcianos.

After they'd passed the gardens, buildings closed in around the road and every single front door stood open. Above regularly spaced balconies, green rags of sunshades flapped in the wind beside horizontal tricolours of red-yellow-purple and rectangles split diagonally: half red, half black.

The rows of balconies stopped at a bridge, from whose ornate lamp posts hung those same flags of the Second Republic and Anarchism. Peeking over the tops of trees on the opposite bank was a pink triangle which held the clock of the city hall, the flag of the Spanish Second Republic flying from its apex. Behind it rose the cathedral tower like a chiselled-stone wedding cake; layers of arches stepped up to a dome topped off with a lantern and cross. Carmen crossed her heart and so did Aliyá; she felt so many emotions all at once but did her best to hide them.

"Help me up, mee-khá," said Oscar. "I've dreamed of this moment so many times, and it's almost just as I'd imagined. I need to walk from here."

"But Papá," said his daughter. "Remember what happened the last time?"

"Then help me," said Oscar. "I want to see if the Rio Segura is living up to its name."

Juanjo tipped the barrow upwards and Oscar collapsed into Aliyá's arms. He straightened himself on his daughter's shoulder, her arm clutching his waist, and he tested the ground. "I never knew you were so strong, mee-khá," he said. "I guess the climbing was some use after all."

Aliyá said nothing as she walked her father to the iron balustrade. He balanced both hands on the railings and looked out over the brick-lined channel, filled with reeds so high that a broken fin was all that was visible of the sardine statue cast in bronze many decades before. He sighed.

Central Murcia

From the matching stone plinths on the north bank of the bridge, it was a matter of minutes before the alleys of the old city enclosed them. In the shade of townhouses, more modernist than classical, the street buzzed with people like in Moorish times.

Aliyá had taken up Oscar's wheelbarrow, and he drifted off to sleep as she pushed him onwards. Dolores forged a way through the crowds for the makeshift chariot to follow. Before long they were at the glass-and-iron door to their building, hanging open like all the others. When they got inside they found the yellow PapSec shutter propped up under the stairs.

Mother and daughter glanced at each other. "Where did all those people come from?" asked Dolores. "It's like everyone under the sun's here. Isn't it exciting?"

"Maybe," Aliyá replied. "I was too worried about our flat to feel anything else. Do you think it's okay?"

"I guess we'll find out soon enough. You should wake your father."

Aliyá had to shake Oscar's shoulder several times before he prised his eyes open. When he did, a look of shock flashed over his face. "Dolores!' he called.

"I'm here, mi amor," she said. "You're quite safe. Do you know where we are?"

Oscar gazed around. "Are we home, Lola?" he asked. "Really home?"

"We just have to climb the stairs," she replied. "Do you think you're strong enough to do it?"

"It's only three flights," said Oscar. "With your help, I'm sure I can."

Aliyá perched the wheelbarrow under the stairs, beside the yellow panel, and the two women each took one of Oscar's arms. The family pushed themselves on to the first step.

The staircase wound itself up and around. Aliyá and Dolores helped Oscar to the first-floor corridor where they paused for breath. They saw that the mirror-image doors on either side had been broken open. On the second floor they found the same, and Dolores could take it no longer. As Aliyá held Oscar to catch his breath on the corridor, the mother of the family scampered up the final flight to check their own abode.

Dolores could see first their neighbours' door open, and felt a wave of relief at the sight of theirs still standing locked. She put a hand on the frame and repeated the prayer she'd recited almost a decade earlier. When she pulled her palm away she noticed the mark she'd left in the dust. She rubbed her hands clean, took the string from her neck and stared a moment at the little piece of metal in her hand. She could feel her emotions building, but she pushed back her shoulders and shook them away. When she put the key to the lock, she saw fingermarks all around it. The frame was chipped where someone had tried, and failed, to prise it open.

She rotated the key through the top lock then the middle. The bottom latch clicked and the door creaked open, releasing the smell of home just as she recalled, even if it was infested with the mustiness of a flat shut up for years. She stepped inside and left the key in a tray out of old-remembered habit. The first thing she noticed was the dust on every surface, especially in the corners. She was going for a broom when Aliyá called up from below. "Mamá!" she cried. "How is it?"

"It's fine," Dolores replied, dashing downstairs to take her husband's other arm and carry him up. "It's pretty dusty, but that just shows no one's been in."

As all three got into the flat, Dolores flicked the front door closed with her toe. Between her and Aliyá, they heaved Oscar around the bend in the landing, past the kitchen on the left and into the living room opposite. Three sofas were arranged in a U-shape, just as they'd been left. All were the same tanned leather and each was as dusty as the next. Dolores cleared away as much dirt as she could with a few swipes of her forearm, then puffed the dust out of a couple of cushions which she arranged for Oscar's head.

"You just rest," said Dolores. "Is there anything we can get you?"

"I'd love some water," he replied, his eyes closing.

"Okay," said Dolores, standing up beside their daughter. "I'll see what we can do."

In moments, Oscar was snoring. Dolores tapped her daughter's arm and beckoned her out to the kitchen. They found the fridge and freezer doors hanging open, the table covered with a red-and-white cloth and four chairs tucked in around it, all coated in a layer of orange-grey dirt. Dolores reached into the cupboard below the sink and retrieved a cloth, which she held to the tap and lifted the bar without thinking. Water spurted out and she stepped back in shock. "Have you seen this, Aliyá?" she asked.

Aliyá peered over her mother's shoulder. "It's not very clean," she said.

"Well if we let it run a bit, maybe it'll get better. Pass me some glasses out of that cupboard won't you, Ale? I'm going to do some washing up." Dolores let the mud of ages run through the system, and in a minute or so clean water was pumping out of the tap. She picked out a pint glass and ran it under the water, clearing the dust off with her fingers. Then she filled it to the rim and said, "Take this for your father."

"Don't you think you should boil it first?"

"How do you propose we do that?"

"I don't know," said Aliyá. "We could try the stove."

Dolores watched her daughter turn a plastic knob. The far-left plate took a moment to warm up, but soon it was glowing red under the glass. Aliyá grinned to her mother.

"I can't believe it!" said Dolores. "Running water and electricity. It's almost like the old days. Here, don't waste anything." She handed Aliyá a metal saucepan of water.

Aliyá placed the pot on the hotplate to boil, and stood back. "You know," she said, "until ten minutes ago, I think I'd completely forgotten my childhood. Now it's all coming back to me like a fairy tale. Do you remember the birthday parties we used to have?"

"I've never forgotten them."

"You never said."

"What would I say?" asked Dolores, placing a plate on the stainless-steel drying rack and going for the next. "Why would anyone have been interested in picking over the pieces of a lost world? I don't think I ever really thought we'd get back here. I'm not sure I even realise it now."

As the two women pondered a life which was already starting to feel more real than the last ten years, there was a ratter-tat-tat on the front door.

Aliyá looked in fright at her mother. "Do you think it's Paco with our bags?" she asked.

"It might be," said Dolores, "but my guess is he'll be a good while yet. Why don't you go and find out?"

"Can't you go?"

"I'm in the middle of this, Aliyá. And if it's a foreigner, I won't be able to say a word, will I? Better you do it."

Aliyá saw no option. She took a deep breath and tip-toed out of the kitchen, approaching the door as if it were a sleeping lioness. She got to the peephole, flicked it open and saw a man with blond dreadlocks knotted down to his waist, a copper beard spurting from his bronzed-pink cheeks. "Quién es?" she asked. 'Who is it?'

"Howzit!" the man replied in English. "I am your neighbour. I thought I'd come and introduce myself, to see if you need sugar or something like that."

"You're not Señor Ortega," said Aliyá.

"Um, no," he replied. "No, I'm not. But we're making good use of his flat until he comes back. We haven't destroyed anything, we've not even broken the locks. We have to be respectful of our hosts' property, it's one of the rules of living in Free Murcia."

Aliyá smiled at the idea of the Ortegas' flat being squatted, and she opened the door to find herself facing the flat chest of a man who must've been half a metre taller than she. His sky-blue eyes darted into hers and he smiled. "Hello," he said, "I'm Jaap De Waal." He stuck out a hand and Aliyá shook it.

"Aliyá Talavera," she said.

"It's a pleasure to meet you, Aliyá Talavera. Tell me this, how did you get in here? This door's tough as old boots, enough people have tried it."

"This is our flat," she replied. "My mother carried the key with her from the day we left. Do you mean people were trying to rob us?"

"No," Jaap chuckled, "They were just looking for a place to stay. It's a very sought-after area this, all the dissidents in Europe would like a flat in the centre of the 'o'."

"In the centre of the what?"

"The 'o'."

"What's Theo?"

Jaap smiled. "The 'Oh'," he repeated. "That's where we are."

"What are you saying?" Aliyá sneered. "This is Murcia."

The man smiled still wider. "Of course this is Murcia," said Jaap. "But it's also inside the 'o'. Don't you realise that?"

"No. Realise what?"

"Where we are."

"Why do you keep saying that?" asked Aliyá. "I know where I am."

"So you know you're inside an advert?"

Aliyá looked at the door frame, the walls of the hall. "It doesn't look like an advert to me," she said.

Jaap laughed out loud. "It's not meant to look like an advert to you. It's for the aliens."

"What?" she asked. "An advert for the aliens? What for?"

"For PapPop, of course. What else?"

"What's PapPop?"

Jaap stared in disbelief. "Are you serious?" he asked."You've really never heard of the world's favourite soft drink?"

Aliyá tutted. "Don't make fun of me," she said, and slammed the door in his face.

Her mother was still piling up plates when Aliyá came back into the kitchen. "Who was at the door, mee-khá?" asked Dolores.

"Our neighbour," Aliyá replied.

"Are the Ortegas here?"

"No, it was a guiri called Yap, or something. Apparently they picked the lock."

"I saw they'd had a go at ours too," said Dolores, smiling to herself.

"You know what he said, Mamá?"

"Tell me."

"He said the sheeting spells out the word PapPop."

"PapPop?" Dolores ran the word around her head, found it familiar but couldn't place it.

"It's the world's favourite soft drink," said Aliyá.

"Ah yes, of course. Why would they do that?"

"Because they can, I guess. They're calling it an advert for the aliens."

Dolores piled a plate on top of the others and turned to face Aliyá. "An advert for the aliens?" she said. "That's what old man Paco has been saying for years."

"Yes," said Aliyá. "That blind drunkard Paco Rufián knew what it was without even having to see it. Makes the rest of us seem like complete fools."

"I don't know," her mother pondered. "I still think it's a ridiculous idea. Take the water off the heat, will you? I think it's boiled for long enough now."

Jaap De Waal stood smirking at the Talaveras' door. He shook his head to himself, turned, and disappeared into the opposite flat, bolting the door behind him.

The Ortegas' place was a mirror image of the Talaveras', but this hallway was decorated with revolutionary paintings and slogans written on paper that they'd stuck to the walls. Along the floor, lengths of industrial cable trailed into the kitchen where, at a formica tabletop, sat a large man with a head the shape of a watermelon and a grey beard down to his bare nipples. It was like every millimetre of his skin was oozing sweat and he had a towel on his lap to dry his hands. He was holding the end of one of the cables, swiping a penknife over individual wires to cut their plastic sheathings into a neat pile on the table.

Jaap sat himself opposite and glanced at the mound of clippings. "I could watch you doing that all day, Reggie," he said. "There's nothing like seeing a master at work. I don't know you can be so precise, I'd be all over the place."

"Years of experience," Reggie chuckled. "What did you find next door?"

"Ah, bru," said Jaap. "You should see our new neighbour, man. She's real lekker."

"So why didn't you invite her over?"

"I did."

"And?"

"And she slammed the door in my face."

Reggie laughed from deep within his overhanging gut. "Well that's a good start!" he said.

"Have you noticed how the returning Murcianos never want to mix with us?"

"I'm sure they would if you learned some Spanish," said Reggie. "I guess they still kind of see it as their city. They must find it strange we're here, even though it's us that's made it inhabitable again. If we'd left it to them, we'd still be praying for rain to fall from the sky."

"Yep," said Jaap, watching Reggie shlish-shlash an inch of red plastic onto the pile. "How are you getting on?"

"I'm almost done," said Reggie. "I reckon we'll be able to go out and connect this lot tonight."

"Don't you think PapCorp mind us stealing their electricity?"

"If they were so concerned, they wouldn't have done such a piss-poor job of dismantling the city, would they? I mean, leaving all the pylons and substations intact. It didn't take a genius to figure out how to connect it all."

"And you don't think they'll notice?"

"They know we're here, Jaap, they must do. You've seen the patrol drones just like I have."

"Then why don't they clear us out?"

"Beats me," said Reggie Carson. "I guess we're just not that important. That or they're waiting for the right time."

As Oscar slept on the sofa, Aliyá and her mother cleaned the flat. They swept up countless dustpans of dirt, and without any idea of how to dispose of them they carried every one through the living room to pile it up on the concrete balcony until they could find out what they should do.

Aliyá was sweeping by the door when she heard it knock. She froze, staring at the latch. At a second knock, her mother shouted, "Aren't you going to get that?"

Aliyá could feel the tension building through her body, she breathed deep, her eyes wide. She reached for the handle and clicked it open to find Paco Junior outside with a pile of cases and baskets, a guitar strapped to his back.

The two old friends stood gawping at each other for a moment, then Paco picked up two suitcases and pushed by Aliyá into the hall. "Are you not going to talk to me at all then?" he asked.

"No," said Aliyá, "What is there to say?"

Paco slipped the guitar from his back. He brought in all the other bags before standing to face Aliyá. "I've got lots of things to say," he said, noticing her clamming up before he'd even begun. "I'm so sorry about last night. Is your father okay?"

"He's fine," said Aliyá. "No thanks to you."

"I said I'm sorry."

"How dare you turn up drunk and late? You put all our lives in danger. My father could've died. I'd never have forgiven you for that."

"But he didn't die, Aliyá," said Paco. "Both your parents are here safe with you and now I've even brought all your stuff. I can't tell you how sorry I am for what happened, for everything that's happened. Do you think you might forgive me one day?" He stretched his fingers towards her arm

Aliyá brushed his hand away. "I'll never forgive you, Paco," she said. "How could I? You abandoned me. You left me all alone on the sierra with no one to help or comfort me."

"I abandoned you?" Paco cried. "How can you even think that? You'd stopped speaking to me, if you remember. I wanted to stay, Aliyá, truly I did. But when you refused to see me, when you accused me of all those things I hadn't done. Well, I had to think of myself, didn't I?"

"And think of where you could get booze."

Paco stared a moment at Aliyá, then shook his head away. "I see you haven't changed then," he murmured.

"I see you haven't!" Aliyá responded, holding the door for him to leave.

But Paco wasn't done. "Why do you always see the worst in me?" he asked. "Why do you always put me down? It's been like this for as long as I can remember. Even before my mum died you were taking advantage of me, using me as a play thing and dropping me like a stone when you got bored."

"It's not my fault you fell in love with me, Paco. And it's not my fault you can't take it that I don't feel the same about you. I don't want to talk about what you did. Now, please leave."

Paco's head drooped, but he did as Aliyá insisted. She slammed the door closed without a goodbye or a thank you, then peered through the peephole to see him gazing forlornly at her. She watched him wipe his eyes on a sleeve and step away downstairs.

Aliyá only noticed she was crying when a tear dropped from her jaw. Her shoulders started shaking. She buried her face in her hands to stop herself squealing, darted straight past the living room and locked herself away in her room. She would cry till the morning.

21. Lies

6th November 2036
Whitby, North Yorkshire

Helen Humbolt arranged a final gingerbread man onto a plate, then stood back to admire the display. She'd never felt prouder than she did that day, sporting the white uniform and matching toque which one of the seamstresses in town had made in exchange for two dozen Eccles cakes. That same woman had woven the red thread over the chest of the apron, to spell out the name *'Four and Twenty Blackbirds'*. And Winston had painted those same four words above the plate-glass shop window where a sign declared 'Grand Opening Tonight!', on three sheets of A4.

Vincent squealed and Helen span around, to see her husband swinging their three-year-old by the arms. She grinned. "Be careful of the furniture," she said, heading back to the kitchen.

Winston Humbolt tossed their son into the air and caught him under the armpits. "Don't worry, Sugarplum," he said. "We'll be careful. And Vincent knows that if he breaks anything, he'll have to fix it. Don't you little man?"

Vincent looked up at his father. "I don't know how," he said.

"Then we'd better be extra careful," Winston smiled. "We don't want to wreck mummy's shop before it's even open."

Helen stepped back into the kitchen and checked the clock on the far wall. Half past four, it read. Just three and a half hours till opening time and she still had so much to do.

It felt to Helen Humbolt like she'd had time for little else over the past few months but work on this shop. There'd been the recipes to test and upscale, the loan to sort out, the equipment and furnishings to choose, the decorating, the adverts. And now, at last, opening day was upon them.

By the time the party started, the shop front was glowing in the night and rain was cascading down the window. Helen's parents were the first to arrive, with an uncle and her mum's two sisters. After them came a steady trickle, a few total strangers, many Helen had seen but never spoken to, some she knew well.

Melinda Spooner dinged the door open and strolled in with her Dave in tow. She barged her way to the counter that separated her old friend from the crowds. "This place looks great!" said Melinda. "And you're looking good."

"You too," Helen replied. "Here, have a curd tart."

Melinda turned her nose up. "Not for me," she said. "You know I have to think of my figure. I'm on the PapCare one a day diet. But you can try one if you want, Dave."

"Can I?" asked her husband. "Are you sure?"

"Of course," she replied. "Just this one mind, as it's Helen's special day. He's on the diet as well, you know. All PapTrans employees with a BMI over 26 are on it. It's meant to be super healthy."

Paul Broddle arrived soon afterwards. He worked his way inside brandishing four thick sticks of rhubarb, to find Helen in a frenzy of serving. But he soon caught her eye with his pink bouquet. "These are for you," he said.

"Oh, Paul!" said Helen. "How did you know? I've got a recipe for rhubarb and custard pie that I've been dying to try out. Where did you get them? It's a bit early still, isn't it?"

"First of the season," he replied. "I know a guy with a forcing shed in Rothwell. He's involved in building the case against PapHomes, the same as me in Whitby. I told him about you and he brought this lot over special for today. Are none of the others here yet?"

"Winston's here," she said, scanning the shop for her husband. "Somewhere…"

But she couldn't locate him, because at that moment Winston Humbolt was in the corner of the kitchen, behind the furthest oven. He had stretched his Xi-fan sheet to the size of a credit card and set the resolution as low as he could still to be able to read the message.

When Rebecca Kingston made her entrance, she was wearing lipstick the same crimson as her heels and a dress which splayed out over her hips to finish above her knees. She ignored Melinda and Dave as she waltzed past them to the counter. "Well, look at you!" she said to her oldest friend. "A proper little baker after all."

Helen beamed. "I'm so glad to see you," she said, glancing at the clock. "I guess it's time to start. Is Tariq here?"

"You mean Parjit."

"Oh yes, of course."

Rebecca stood aside to reveal a man in a bright orange turban, his beard a mesh of black.

"Blimey!" Helen declared. "I'd have hardly recognised you there."

Parjit smiled through his beard.

Rebecca watched her man grinning, then returned her gaze to Helen. "I feel the same way at times," she said. "It's like this new identity has given him a whole different personality. He tells me things he's done sometimes, and I'm not sure if he's making it up or if he really believes it."

Helen saw the uncertainty in her friend's look, but didn't have time to dwell on it. "Well, you're both here," she said, "that's the main thing. Let's have a chat later, I want to hear all the gossip. But I guess we need to get started." She glanced around the shop once more and found her husband now at her side. She smiled up at him, noticed the gantry where people sat and stood. "I was going to use that area as a stage," she said. "Are you sure it'll hold all those people?"

"Absolutely," said Winston. "I made it strong enough for twice that number. I guess that means you'll have to do your talk from down here."

"I guess you're right," said Helen. "Will you get everyone's attention?"

"Of course," said Winston, clapping his hands a few times. "Folks!" he shouted from the bottom of his belly. "We're all here today because of an extraordinary woman, someone I'm so proud to call my wife. This shop has been her life's ambition, and through her hard work she's made it a reality. I ask you all please to show your appreciation for Helen Humbolt, the master baker and owner of this fine establishment. Here's to her and her *Four and Twenty Blackbirds.*"

Everyone in the café clapped with all their might, even little Vincent joined in, despite being able to see nothing behind his grandparents' legs. And as they applauded, Winston strode out from behind the counter, grabbed Rebecca and her partner by the arms and led them towards Paul Broddle by the door. "So?" he said. "Are you ready?"

"Sure," said Rebecca. "As soon as Helen's given her speech, we'll be right with you."

"We can't wait," said Winston. "We have to go right now. Our man's only got a short window, he's got a boat waiting to get him out of the country this evening."

Rebecca blinked. "You're saying we have to leave before the place is even open? Winston, this is your wife's big day."

"I know," said Winston, "and I certainly wouldn't have planned things this way, but this is how it is. Now come on. Paul, you too. Let's go."

"I've told you I'm not coming," said Paul Broddle. "I'm going back to the picket after this."

"Fine," said Winston. "But there'll be trouble when RASCAL head office finds out, you mark my words." And with that, he, Rebecca and Parjit sneaked out the front door.

Helen was so touched by the warmth of the ovation that she didn't notice the others leave. When she spoke it was all she could do to stop her voice cracking. "Thank you, everyone," she said as the applause died down. "Really, thank you. I can't tell you how much all this means to me. I don't think I'll be able to speak for long, but there are just a couple of things I want to say. Those of you who know me will know that I've wanted to be a baker from the moment my grandmother showed me how to make apple strudel when I was five years-old. I've had so much help from so many people along the way, but none more than one man who's lifted this town almost as much as he's lifted me. Winston, without you, none of this would ever have happened. Its not always been easy, but I'm so grateful to be your wife. Now where are you?"

The crowd looked around but Winston wasn't there. "He left," said Paul Broddle. "He said it was urgent."

"Oh," Helen replied, pursing her face to hide her feelings. "Do you know where he went?"

"He didn't say," said Paul.

"Okay," said Helen. "Well, help yourselves to cakes and biscuits. There's plenty here, and I don't want to waste anything." And with that, she darted for the kitchen.

Winston's van was parked around the corner from the bakery, but it was Parjit Agarwal that opened it with a flick of his Xi-fan sheet, and it was he who took up the driver's position. Winston got in beside him as Rebecca slammed the rear door. She sat herself between the tools and scraps of wood, tucked her skirt between her legs, then looked up to see Fiona and Kyle perched opposite her.

"What did Helen say when you left?" asked Fiona.

"We didn't get to tell her," said Rebecca. "Apparently we're in too much of a hurry."

"That's why we didn't go in," said the Scottish woman.

"So then what?" asked Kyle. "Are you saying you did a Sandra Shaw on her?"

"Kyle!" said the two women at once.

"You can't say things like that," said Fiona. "Think of that poor girl's parents."

"It's what you did though, isn't it?" said Kyle. "You left the party early, never to be heard from again."

"We're only going up the coast," said Rebecca. "I for one very much plan to return."

Helen Humbolt didn't feel able to talk. She clattered through the kitchen, picking up trays and lobbing them into the sink. She was elbow-deep in washing-up foam when Paul Broddle looked in on her. "What are you doing that for?" he asked. "You should be out here, welcoming your guests."

Helen glanced up. "I can't go out there," she said. "What will people say? I can't tell where my husband is even on a day as important as this one."

"They're not here to see him," said Paul, "they're here for you." He gazed at the woman's mascara-stained eyes and saw his words had no effect. "I'm sure he didn't want to go," he continued. "But you know how dedicated he is to the cause."

"Yes," said Helen. "That's what you lot always say. He's more dedicated to that than he is to me and his son, that's for sure."

"He's also dedicated to you, Helen. I've never once seen him with another woman, and he's had plenty of chances. He loves you and Vincent very much, and just think how much he helped you with this place."

"Why are you defending him?" asked Helen. "Winston's had it in for you for as long as I've known him. You're too good for this, Paul Broddle."

Paul shrugged. "Thanks," he said. "Are you sure I can't help with the dishes?" He picked up a tea towel.

"That'd be nice," Helen sniffed. "But aren't you supposed to be going back up to the picket on the housing estate?"

"That can wait," said Broddle, picking up a tray and drying off the water with his cloth.

North York Moors

With no trees or bushes for windbreaks, the gusts off the North Sea buffeted the van along the clifftop. Driver and passengers watched the headlamps light two strips of the road ahead. After an achingly long silence, it was Fiona who was first to speak. "So, who are we meeting then?" she asked. "I've been wondering all week and now it's here, so no need for secrecy anymore, eh?"

"His name's Francesco," Parjit replied. "Winston and I met him at the RASCAL conference last summer."

"What is he?" asked Kyle. "Spanish?"

"He's an Italian anarchist," Winston replied. "Legend has it that his bombs have been used on every continent."

"You remember Oswald Kongolo?" Parjit added. "That was him."

Winston nodded.

"So he fought with the British Army?" asked Fiona. "Then how do you know we can we trust him?"

"He might've been a soldier once," said Parjit, "but now he's most certainly on our side."

"But how do you know?" asked Kyle. "You say he's an Italian anarchist who's been all over the world with the British Army. It doesn't make sense."

"They trust him at RASCAL," said Parjit. "That's all the proof I need."

"Who trusts him?" asked Kyle.

"I trust him," said Winston Humbolt. "Do you really think I'd go into this without doing my homework? I've found nothing on him but what I'd expect, so can we give this a rest? It's hard enough for Parjit to follow the road as it is, without you lot asking all these questions."

Whitby

Paul Broddle spoke as he dried. "It's important that people are picketing the streets," he was saying. "There's nothing that can beat a visual presence. But it's not the main arm of our strategy, of course. We've got some very good lawyers working with us. The government's deal with PapCorp to turn every publicly owned house and council estate into a PapHome is completely illegal. And there's evidence of bribery that could go all the way to the very top."

"Which is why no one knows about it," said Helen, handing Broddle a soapy tray. "If it involves powerful people, they claim it's a matter of national security and forbid anyone from talking about it. It's a good job we have people like Rebecca Kingston to report on these things."

"You're right there," said Paul. "But the *Star* could be in all sorts of trouble for going against that D-notice. I wouldn't be surprised if there's an attempt to shut them down because of it."

"They can try," said Helen, holding out another tray. "But the citizens of Whitby'll be ready."

Saltburn-by-the-Sea, North Yorkshire

When the van stopped and all piled out, it was onto a seaside car park. The bay windows of a pub sparkled against the raindrops and spray from the waves that crashed against the far side of a stone wall. Winston swiped the van locked and the others looked to him for their next move. But before he could say a word, a whistle came from over the road.

The group jerked their heads towards the base of a hillock. There, against the blue light of an arched doorway to a building that looked like an old chapel, stood the silhouette of a figure. He beckoned them over and vanished inside.

Rain and wind hit from all sides as the group trotted over with hoods pulled tight. Winston was the last into the hut. He shut out the weather behind an oak door, then looked up to find A-frame rafters casting undulating shadows over a corrugated ceiling. The only light came from the blue-white surface of a Xi-fan sheet, pulled to the size of a chess board in the middle of a table that dominated the single room. At the far end sat a man with blond hair and a Palestinian scarf around his neck, his eyes all the bluer in the electronic light.

"Good evening all of you," said the man in a plummy accent. "I'm glad you could make it. Gather round, please. I don't have a great deal of time. Now, how many are we?"

"Wait a minute," said Kyle. "I thought this guy was supposed to be Italian. He sounds like he's just stepped out of the gates of Eton."

"So what are you saying?" said Parjit. "An Italian can't speak posh?"

"An Italian anarchist supposedly wanted by the authorities?" said Fiona, "Who also used to be in the army? It doesn't exactly fill me with confidence."

"There are a lot of people that know him at RASCAL," said Parjit. "And you don't earn a reputation like his for nothing, do you?"

"Quite right," said Winston. "There are five of us here, Francesco."

"I can see that," replied the Italian. "I was expecting six."

"Broddle's got a strop on," said Parjit. "We should get started."

"Okay," said Francesco. He lifted a yellow shoebox onto the worktop and removed the lid, then picked up his Xi-fan sheet and shrunk it till he could hold it in the fingertips of one hand. He shone the blued light onto the jumble of pipes and cables within. "I'm going to show you how to make these bombs," he said.

"Why?" asked Kyle, "You've got one there. Isn't that enough?"

"Not even close," said Francesco.

"How many do you expect us to make?" asked Fiona.

"Oh, a hundred or so should probably do it."

"A hundred shoebox bombs?" cried Kyle. "What the hell are we attacking? A shoe factory?"

"Shoeboxes are inconspicuous," said Francesco, "easy to hide, easy to stack and easy to transport."

"One or two maybe," said Fiona, "not a hundred."

"That's why you're going to take your time over it," said Francesco. "And it's vital that you all do your bit."

"Do the risky bits, you mean," said Kyle. "This was supposed to be a radically democratic organisation. I thought we were going to decide together what we do. No one mentioned making hundreds of bombs."

"Its been decided democratically," said Winston. "Just not by us."

Fiona gawped. "And the committee have decided the target as well, I guess," she said.

Francesco and Winston glanced at each other. "It's the PapPop Tower," replied the Italian.

"You want us to blow up the PapPop tower?" exclaimed Kyle.

"That's the plan," said Winston. "And try to keep your voice down, we don't want the whole world hearing about it."

"Are you going to attack with everyone in it?" Kyle continued, more quietly. "Parjit, you're a doctor for goodness sake, not a murderer. Killing people is supposed to be against everything you stand for!"

"You call Zoltan O'Dillon a person?" said Parjit. "I call him a rat. After what he's done, I feel no pity for that man whatsoever. The guru teaches us to wield the sword and take life as the Lord chooses, and to please him. Killing Zoltan O'Dillon, and bringing down that horrendous tower, is a service, not murder."

"That's supposing those stories about him are even true," said Fiona.

"Which stories?" said Francesco.

"I don't know," she said. "Like South Africa."

"That one is true," the Italian asserted.

"And what makes you so sure?" asked Kyle.

"I just know things, okay?" said Francesco. "I know for certain that Zoltan O'Dillon committed genocide at a dam in South Africa. Just take my word for it. If anyone deserves blowing up, it's him. Now can we get on with this, please?"

"No we cannot just get on," said Kyle. "I feel lied to. I thought this was going to be an interesting exercise in direct action. But now you're talking about committing mass murder. I don't want my name to go down in history as the killer of anyone, not even Zoltan O'Dillon."

"Hey, Kyle, relax man," said Parjit. "We've all taken our oaths to do what is needed. And the target's the target, okay?"

"That's it," said Kyle, pulling his hood over his head. "I'm leaving."

"But what about the rain?" asked Fiona. "Can't you hear it?"

"I don't care about the rain," said Kyle. "I'm Yorkshire born and bred. I'll wait for you in the pub, but I'm not going to be party to some scheme that Winston Humbolt and his mate Francesco have dreamed up between them. I don't know, maybe the plan is that we build all these bombs in our homes so they can blow us all to smithereens any time they like."

"Don't be ridiculous!" said Rebecca. "This is Winston we're talking about, Winston Humbolt. The mastermind of Whitby's rejuvenation. I and my husband trust this man with our lives, and we will not hear you doubting him again. Don't you agree, Parjit?"

"A hundred per cent," said the doctor.

Kyle stood a moment and shook his head. "I'd expect nothing better from most of you," he said. "But you, Fiona. I thought you were more than this."

He turned for the door but Fiona pulled him back. "Don't go, Kyle," she said. "Please. I thought we were in this together, you and me."

"There is no you and me," said Kyle. "I wish there was, more than anything in the world. But you don't love me like I love you."

"What are you even talking about?" cried Fiona. Kyle reached for the door knob but she grabbed his shoulder with both hands and yanked him back into the room. "What makes you think you love me more than I love you?"

"I do," said Kyle, "it's obvious."

"Obvious to you maybe," Fiona replied.

Kyle blinked at his schoolboy crush. "What are you saying? You feel something for me too? You never said."

"Neither did you," said Fiona, gazing at Kyle with new eyes.

"So?" asked Winston. "Are you joining us after all?"

Kyle didn't know what to say.

"Come on," said Rebecca. "Get your coat off and get with the programme. We're about to do something extraordinary and you two need to be part of it. We're going to start the goddamned revolution! We'll be the catalyst for everything that follows. We're going to change the world and you're a bit upset because you thought it was going to be 'interesting'? Well boo-hoo. We're nothing more than cogs in this system and we will do what is needed of us, when it is needed of us. Now are you in, or are you going to pussy out?"

Kyle sighed. He gazed around everyone else before finally his eyes landed on Fiona's. She smiled at him, took his hand and nodded towards the table. Kyle shrugged. "Okay," he said. "I guess I'll stay." He loosened his hood and peered down at the shoe box to find Fiona still massaging her fingers against his.

Francesco nodded to himself. "Now, this might look complicated," he said. "But I can assure you, it isn't. The first thing I'm going to show you is the fuse." He held out two strips of cable. "Be very careful with these. Make sure these two wires never touch. This here is the stablest damned explosive you'll ever see, you can drop it from a plane and it won't go off. But connect these two wires, it doesn't matter if it's with a ring on your finger or the wheels of a train. Just make sure you're standing behind something hefty to deflect the blast. One of these may not look much, but it packs one hell of a punch. You'll find your boxes under the table. I'm going to show you how to set them up."

Francesco instructed the group to arrange the wires and cylinders. With his surgeon's dexterity, Parjit was the first to push his forward, completed.

"Jolly good, er, Parjit," said Francesco, peering inside. "Anyone'd think you've done this before."

"That's because I have," said Parjit, grinning through his beard. "Back when I was in the army, in Africa. I was a real dab hand at this sort of thing."

Rebecca looked at her partner, trying her best to hide the despair she felt. She put a hand on his wrist and spoke into his ear. "You were never in the army, Tariq," she whispered.

He stared back into her eyes. "I was," he whispered back. "And my name's not Tariq, that was just a disguise. I'm Parjit Agarwal, always have been. Please don't forget that. Now come on, everyone else has finished."

Whitby

Winston Humbolt dropped everyone home before returning to Raith Street. There were no lights on when he pulled up outside his house. But as he took off his shoes in the hallway he could make out a quiet tap-tap-tapping from the living room. He eased open the door and found his wife knitting frantically.

"So you've decided to come back then?" she said in the darkness.

"Helen, sugar," said Winston, flicking on the light to see his wife sitting at the dining table, beside a plate of crumbled cake slices. "This is my home. Of course I've come back."

"And where the hell did you disappear off to?" asked Helen, putting down her knitting. "One minute you were there, I asked you to get everyone's attention. And by the time I raised my glass in your honour, you'd gone. Not just you but Rebecca and Tariq or whatever he's called these days. What the hell were you doing?"

"I was doing my duty, if you must know. RASCAL HQ called me to rendezvous with an Italian anarchist."

"An Italian anarchist?" Helen screeched. "Do you think I was born yesterday?"

"You really do doubt my every word these days, don't you?" said Winston. "You know what, Helen, it's hard having morals and living by them. I made a commitment to you on our wedding day and I have never once broken that vow. But I also have strong beliefs, not least that a new world is possible if we can just blow away the old."

"Don't try your politics bullshit on me, Winston Humbolt!" said Helen, getting to her feet. "You have so many other priorities that never seem to include your son, and certainly not me! I've had enough of this charade you call a marriage."

"Helen, please, my Sugarplum fairy. You and Vincent are the most important people in my life. Let's talk about this."

"There's nothing to talk about!" Helen shouted, picking the plate of cake from the table and hurling it at her husband.

Winston dodged the dish and it shattered against the wall, smearing cream and icing down the wallpaper.

22. Growth

27th October 1961
Manchester, England

Attila Bacsik slapped his belly. "Köszönöm szépen az ebédet," he said. 'Thank you so much for lunch.' "It was almost like real goulash soup."

"It still wasn't spicy enough," said Gábor. "It's impossible to get strong paprika anywhere in England."

"The English don't like that sort of thing, do they?" said Attila. "Spicy food I mean. They prefer flavourless stodge."

Gábor grinned, held the front door open for his elder brother and they strolled out onto Oldham Road, doing up their jackets as they went. "You really should think about what I said," said the younger man. "If you come and live in my room, we'd be able to save up something instead of wasting so much on rent."

"I like it where I am," said Attila. "Since you moved out, I've got to sleep on my own for the first time in years. I might even bring a girl home some day."

"Since when have you been interested in girls?"

"I've always been interested in girls, Gábor. What are you implying?"

"Nothing, my brother."

Attila kicked the pavement with his boot. "If you're so desperate to save money," he said, "why don't you move back in with us?"

"You know I can't stay in the same flat as Zoltán and Nóra. I've nothing against him of course, I mean, he's why we're here, isn't he? From penniless refugees to foremen of our own factory in just five years. But her? I can't even bear to look at her."

But look at her he had to. Because as they crossed the road, they found Nóra Weissmann dancing along the opposite pavement, skipping over puddles and pirouetting towards the door under the Papp Beverages sign.

The young woman was so caught up in her jiving that she didn't notice the brothers, even though they arrived just behind her. She let the factory door swing closed and hung her woollen coat on a rack among all the others. In a sleeveless lemon dress which dropped to her knees, she bopped past machines and workers pulping ingredients, mixing and bottling what had fast become the North West's favourite drink.

At the far end of the factory, Nóra knocked once on the wood-and-glass panels and slid open a section of frosted glass. She peeked around a full-length curtain of blue and red splodges, to find Zoltán Papp picking a paper from his left, reading it, signing the corner, and depositing it in the out-tray to his right. Apart from the in and out boxes, the only things on the desktop were a marble pen stand, a bakelite telephone, a glass ashtray, a box of matches, and a half-eaten sandwich. "Hol voltál?" he asked, without looking up. 'Where've you been?'

"At the Plaza Ballroom," she replied, gyrating her heels and her hips. "You remember, I told you about the lunchtime dancing. You really should come one day, it's so much fun. This dance is called the twist."

"I've got way too many things to do for that sort of thing," said Zoltán, finally looking at the young woman. "There's so much to go through. You haven't found anything, have you?"

"Nothing," Nóra replied, sitting down in the chair opposite and lighting a cigarette. "I've been through all the quotes and every order, every receipt. All the numbers add up."

"Then where are they getting this money from?" asked Zoltán. "How could they afford to buy new houses out of the city when the books say they're earning the same salary as I am? I just don't get it."

A bell pierced the air and Zoltán's hand darted for the telephone. He picked up the receiver and found Éamon O'Dillon on the other end.

"Zoltán!" said Éamon. "Drop whatever you're doing. I need you here this minute."

"Why?" asked Zoltán. "Where are you?"

"I'm in Ardwick."

"Where's that?"

"Get the map out," said Éamon. "I'm on Tempest Street, just off the Ashton Old Road. In the Britannia Inn. Come straight here."

"Éamon, it's far too early to go drinking, I've got a whole afternoon's work to do."

"This is work, Zoltán. Vitally important work for the future of Papp Beverages Limited. Are you coming or what?"

"What is so vital for the future of the company?"

"We'll discuss it when you get here. The more you chatter on the phone, the longer you'll have to wait to find out."

Zoltán glanced at Nóra, at the clock on the wall that read two-thirty. "Okay," he said. "But I need to be back here at four by the latest." He hung up and got to his feet, picked a beige overcoat from a stand in the corner and slipped it onto the shoulders of his charcoal suit. "Na," he said. 'Right,' "apparently I need to go to a place called Ardwick for some vital business."

"Do you need some help?" asked Nóra.

Zoltán thought for a moment. "Okay," he said. "I guess you can read the map. And it'd be good to have some backup."

By now, Zoltán Papp had his own company car, a sky-blue Morris Mini-Minor van with 'Papp Beverages Ltd' stamped in black over the side-panels. He kept it around the back of the train sheds, and used it very rarely, which is why he found it covered in soot. Zoltán had a rag ready to clear the windows, and when both were seated inside, Nóra with a map on her knees, he pulled out the choke lever and turned the key. The engine started immediately.

Past row on row of houses they drove, around the brick embankment to Ancoats Goods station, under chimneys spewing black into the clouds. But Nóra wasn't looking at the scenery. Glancing only occasionally at the map, she was more taken with the tension in Zoltán's face. "Just stand your ground," she said. "Whatever they say, you're in the right."

"I know," he replied. "You don't need to tell me."

"It makes me think of a poem," said Nóra, clearing her throat.

"If born a man, then be a man, Strong, brave and true as steel!
Then trust that neither man nor fate can crush you 'neath their heel..."

"All right," said Zoltán. "There's no need to quote Petőfi at me. It's all very well being a man, but with those two I never know what they might do."

"Just don't let them take advantage of you," said Nóra. "We're in England now, where they have laws. And they're doing something wrong for sure. We just need to keep looking and we'll find it."

"I don't know," said Zoltán. "All I can think is that, if they're bringing me here to kill me, I want you to make sure you're safe. Don't try to be brave or anything."

"Zoltán, stop being so melodramatic! They're not going to kill us! We'll be in a public place so loads of people will see us. In fact, we're nearly there. It's the second left after the Sunday School."

They passed the public wash house and turned into a maze of terraces. The car wheels juddered against the cobbles and a boy in short trousers and ankle socks stopped rolling a tyre along the road to watch the car pull past.

Ardwick, Manchester

Like every house around, the Britannia Inn was a working-class place built of sooted brick. The only sign that this building was different was the name of the pub stamped on boards above the first floor, and the carved oak doorways which might once have been rather fine but were now smoke-stained and flaking like everything else.

They found Éamon O'Dillon propping up the bar, wearing a double-breasted pin-striped suit with a black-dotted pink handkerchief spouting from the breast pocket. Beside his half-drunk pint was a mustard-coloured Fedora hat with a brown ribbon tied around it. An air of cologne hung around him and mixed with the tobacco smoke.

Éamon was engrossed in a newspaper, and only looked up when Zoltán called his name. O'Dillon folded up his *Daily Herald* and showed off the front page. "You seen this?" he said. "Looks like your Ruskie mates are at it again."

"What's going on?" asked Nóra.

"Commie tanks at Checkpoint Charlie," said Éamon, "that's what's going on. You have to wonder where they'll stop. First Hungary, now Berlin. They'll be on our doorsteps before you know it. If they're not already here, that is, infiltrating the unions and persuading them out on strike. Now come on, there's something I want to show you." Éamon downed the frothless remains of his beer, slammed the glass on the bar and got to his feet, slanting his hat over his left eyebrow.

The Hungarians followed Éamon's lead and they walked three-abreast down the side of a fan-windowed factory, opposite a line of blackened-brick terraces whose front doors led straight out onto the street. Most hung open, and women with scarves around their heads and woollen stockings on their legs stood chatting or bending over scrubbing the front step. A black girl in a white dress and ribbons in her hair skipped and hopped over a chalk-drawn game of hopscotch, while a white boy in shorts was swinging himself around a lamp post on a rope.

"Now then, Zoli," said Éamon, putting an arm around the Hungarian's shoulder. "Did I tell you about the Moore's Stores deal?"

"Who?" asked Zoltán.

"The owners of Burgons and Seymour Mead. They've got shops all over the north west. I approached them last year but they were sceptical about changing suppliers. Then after they and their customers saw our advert on Granada Television, they were straight onto me for a trial order."

"That's good news," said Zoltán, without emotion.

"Damned right it is!" said Éamon. "When you combine that with the Berni Inn contracts, and the success of Blue Moon of Kentucky Burger. I mean, we're on a roll."

Zoltán nodded. "That's great," he said. "But why did you have to bring me here? You could have told me all this in the office."

"Do you remember the summer?" asked Éamon. "Do you remember how crazy it got at the factory?"

"How can I forget?" said Zoltán.

"Well, we're going to be even more pushed next year," said Éamon, "what with all these new orders. How do you think you'll cope?"

"We'll be okay," said Zoltán. "In spite of everything, we didn't miss a single delivery this last summer. We're already stockpiling for the next season, and we learned so much that next time must be easier."

"That's something we need to make sure of," said Éamon, leading Zoltán and Nóra around the corner of the factory to find Callum O'Dillon towering over a group of kids, all admiring a sports car. Its space-age lines and dull-gold finish were quite alien against the age-dulled hovels of Ardwick.

The younger O'Dillon, in his drainpipe suit and thin black tie, his hair piled up into a neat quiff, looked more suited to Carnaby Street than the back alleys of Manchester. When he saw the three approaching, he shouted, "I'm just making sure these kids keep their mucky paws off your wheels."

"They'd better not lay a finger on her," said Éamon. "I might well be employing their fathers or mothers soon enough, and they wouldn't want to go prejudicing nothing now, would they?"

The crowd of boys and girls shook their heads and stared at the floor.

Callum pushed himself free to greet the others. He shook the men by the hand but didn't even acknowledge Nóra. When he spoke it was like she wasn't there.

"What do you think?" asked Callum. "Have you ever seen a car as beautiful as that?"

"It looks expensive," said Zoltán.

"You can't put a price on quality," said Éamon. "And she goes like a dream. I've not had her two months, but I've been out to the Stretford by-pass almost every day. Got to 118 mile an hour a few weeks back, during that dry spell. That's my record so far, but I reckon she'll go past one-twenty."

"And what happened to the Rover?" asked Nóra.

"It was slow and smelly," said Éamon to Zoltán. "Stuck in the last decade. I need something to show we're a company for the 1960s, and what better than with a Jaguar E-type? They're already calling it the car of the century."

"What she means," said Zoltán, "is how can you afford it? We're supposed to be earning the same money, you and me. Yet I'm stuck in a Mini-Minor van while you've got the latest sports car and a new house. I just don't understand how it's possible."

"It's something my bank manager calls creative accounting," Éamon muttered. "Anyway, never mind that. Haven't you seen where we are?" He pointed at the sign at the top of the brick factory, declaring 'Chester's, brewers of quality.'

"Do you bring me here for a pub crawl?" asked Zoltán. "I don't got time for this, Éamon. I got real work to do. And there's not a chance in hell I'm ever touching that Chester's Mild again. I was confused for days the last time."

"I remember that," said Callum. "Made a proper Chester's Case of you, it did."

"This isn't a pub," said Éamon. "This is the brewery. Or, at least, it was. Now it's the new home of PapPop."

"What!?" Zoltán exclaimed.

Éamon laid an arm around the Hungarian's shoulder. "Chester's just got took over by Threlfall's of Liverpool," he said, "and they've moved all their brewing over Salford way. Now, there was talk of them offering this place to Stafford's or Arthur Edge. But I managed to get in here first, thanks to my contacts, and, well, here we are. The new home of PapPop. This place has its own power supply and everything, so even if the unions do manage to close the country down, we'll still be able to get our drink to the thirsty masses. Come on, let's go inside."

"Wait a minute," said Zoltán. "What do you mean the new home of PapPop? What did you do?"

"Come inside and have a look," said Callum.

"No."

"All right," said Éamon. "Then stay here and argue in the street in front of all these kids. Have it your way."

Zoltán glanced at the gang of boys and girls staring at them. He looked at Nóra, saw his resignation reflected in her expression, and shrugged.

Éamon undid the padlock at the bottom of the shutter and clattered it upwards. As the other three followed him inside, they found the brewery had the chill of empty brick, the organic ring of fermentation. "Isn't it magnificent?" said Éamon. "Our very own brewing palace."

"And what about all this machinery?" asked Nóra, scraping a finger over a copper tub and inspecting the dust.

'That's all included," said Éamon. "We've bought the place lock, stock and barrel. That includes a dozen Karrier Bantam delivery trucks and even a couple of horses with carts. The entire manufactory. I mean, quite a lot of it is pre-war, but it all still works. And with the Bacsik brothers around I'm sure they'll have it up and running in no time."

"Attila and Gábor are rushed off their feet," said Zoltán. "They don't have time for to set up some new factory for the O'Dillons."

"Then we'll get Meadowcroft's men in to do it," said Callum, "Maybe get in a few new foremen. I don't understand what's up, you should be happy. You complained all last summer about how mad it was trying to keep up with orders, and we don't want to face that same problem again now, do we? This factory has ten times the capacity, so we've got room to expand. And we've got it at an absolute steal."

"I don't care who you steal it from!" Zoltán screamed. "Or however you get it. You cannot make these decisions without ask me, I'm the majority shareholder! Baszd meg!"

"Hey, Zoltán," said Callum. "Don't get your Hungarian knickers in a twist. We're just trying to do what's best for Papp Beverages."

"You're trying do the best for the O'Dillons, more like!" shouted Zoltán. "Despite all the new order, we still no making no profit. Yet now you find the money to buy new factory as well your new houses and luxury car."

"What you trying to say?" said Callum, squaring up to the Hungarian.

"I'm trying to say I don't trust you," said Zoltán. "You pair is getting rich while we in the factory don't even earn enough to pay for two council flat. Is not right. I certain you taking money from every deal we do."

"What you implying?" asked Callum. "That us two's on the take? I'll have your guts for garters, I will." He clenched his fist.

But a hand on Callum's shoulder stopped the young O'Dillon. "Don't give him what he wants," said Éamon. "He's trying to provoke us."

The men stared each other out, which left it to Nóra to break the impasse. "The way I see it," she said, "you need Zoltán a lot more than he needs you. PapPop is his drink, but distributors are everywhere. If you don't like how we run this business, you're welcome to step away and leave Zoltán to get on with it as he wishes."

"Exactly," said Papp. "And I do not wish to change factory. It took two year of hard work to get things how we want them, and I am not prepared to do that all again."

"Well it's not really up to you," said Callum. "We've already done the deal."

"Then you had better go and un-do it!" Zoltán Papp screamed. "I am the majority shareholder of this company, I am the only person who can make these kind of decisions. But you two always think you know better. Well you don't! I am sure you think you both very clever for stealing from company, buying yourselves the sports cars and the mansions and taking the clients for all-afternoon lunches, while I do all hard work. But I know you are cheating me, and I will catch you. Just you see if I do not!" Zoltán yanked at Nóra's arm and pulled her out of the door.

The O'Dillons watched them go. "By gum, Éamon," said Callum. "He were coming on a bit much, weren't he?"

"Hell hath no fury like a Hungarian's scorn," Éamon replied, fumbling for his pipe. "What the bloody hell are we going to do about this, my brother? He can't keep this company back. It's expand or die, he has to understand that."

"Ay, it's coming to summat when some immigrant is telling a man how to run his own business."

"We need to come up with a plan."

"You're right there," said Callum. "Pint?"

"Ay, pint. But let's not stick around here. Let's head closer to home."

"The Volunteer?"

"All right," Éamon wheezed. "The Volunteer it is."

Zoltán Papp made straight for his blue Mini-Minor, fiddled with the lock and slammed the door behind him. He grabbed the steering wheel in anger, fuming through his nostrils.

Nóra knocked on the passenger window and Zoltán lifted the knob to let her in. They exchanged a single glance, and as soon as she shut the door he sped away as fast as he could. Zoltán didn't see the miniature football that a group of boys and girls were kicking across the road. And when it popped under his wheels he thought for a moment that he'd burst a tyre. But the kids shouting after him told a different story, and he span rubber to escape onto Chancery Lane.

They were back on Oldham Road when finally Zoltán spoke. They could see their ornate house block, the potato warehouses behind which steam engines added their smoke to the winter gloom, the Papp Beverages sign shining out. "I just can't believe those guys," he said. "How can they make a decision like that without consulting me?"

"I know," said Nóra. "But you stood up to them. I thought you were great in there, actually."

"They're not finished with me yet," said Papp. "I just don't know what they're going to try next."

"Come on, Zoltán, relax. What's the worse they can do?" Nóra saw his expression was unchanged. "Maybe I should speak to someone. A lawyer maybe."

"Do you know any lawyers?"

"Of course I do. Half the old men that go to the synagogue are lawyers. I'm sure one of them would give us some advice. But just try to remember, Zoltán, you're an important man now. The O'Dillons can't just get rid of you, people know who you are. You're the face of PapPop, the talisman for a new England – one where people prefer jukeboxes and American negro music to a pint of warm beer. You know what all the girls drink when they're shaking their hips and trying to impress the boys? PapPop is what. Even the O'Dillons must realise that they need you, as much as they may not like it. And when we find the evidence that they've been stealing from us, we'll have the company to ourselves."

Sale, Cheshire

The Volunteer Hotel was a testament to late-Victorian bravado, all bay windows and half-timbered rooflets, topped with a rounded tower that wouldn't have looked out of place in a water park. The brothers parked one sports car behind another, right outside the front door.

Inside, the air was a fog of tobacco smoke. Callum sat himself in a red-leather sofa behind a round table and lit a cigarette. He watched his brother pay for two pints and carry them over, foam dropping over the edge and splashing onto the pile carpet. Éamon set one glass before Callum, one at the seat opposite, and sucked the spume from his thumb as he sat down.

"What're we going to do about all this?" asked Callum. "I reckon they're on to us."

"Him and his Eastern-bloc broad can look all they like," said Éamon. "They won't find nowt. We've got the best accountants in the North West for a reason, you know."

"Yeah, but what if he does?"

"Callum..."

"I'm serious, Éamon. If he finds evidence we've been skimming off all those deals, he could get us sent down for years. He knows the situation. If we go down, he gets the whole company. I've been behind bars once and I have no intention of going back. We have to start making plans."

"You might be right, Callum, but what can we do? We can't exactly buy him out, can we?"

"You should've let me give him a fourpenny one," said the younger O'Dillon. "Cheeking us like that. It's getting out of hand."

"It is that, my brother. We're not going to persuade that dirty Hun to part with his drink for all the tea in China, but violence won't help us. We're going to have to be a bit clever about how we go about this."

"What you got in mind?"

"I don't know," said Éamon. "I guess we could try and renegotiate our roles."

"He won't go for that either, will he? We need summat more drastic."

"Aye," said Éamon. "Can you think of owt?"

"I don't know," said Callum, supping from his ale. "That's why we're here, in't it? Why don't we just do him in and lob his body into the Ship Canal?"

"Oh aye, right. And who will the finger of justice point to as the most likely culprit. Thee and me, Callum, that's who. No, if we're going to do this, we have to be a bit clever about it. Maybe we could get him abducted or something. Sell him and his mates to the Soviets or the Hungarians or summat like that."

"You know what," said Callum, "I know a guy, a Union man. We met in Strangeways but he's out now and all. Was involved with some of them what brought Yuri Gagarin to Manchester."

"Oh yeah? You reckon he's got contacts?"

"Sure to," said Callum. "but that still don't solve our problem, do it? If he just vanishes like that, someone's bound to notice. He's got a public presence these days, I mean, we've helped him become the face of PapPop."

"Celebrity's temporary," said Éamon. "But I intend PapPop to be around for some time yet, with an O'Dillon in charge."

Callum supped his beer. "Then we have to do something about that little circle of his," he said. "Divide and conquer, you know, like Napoleon. We could start stirring things up between him and his fancy piece, start rumours he's been shagging around behind her back. Summat like that."

"Him and Nóra?" Éamon pondered. "Na, they're thick as thieves, them two. But them brothers on the other hand, well..."

"I heard the younger one had a thing with Zoltán's bird," said Callum. "That's why he don't live with them no more. He's about my age, you know. A mouthy little so-and-so. But if I make friends with him, show him a good time around town, well then maybe..."

"Do that," said Éamon. "But we also need to come up with a plan about what to do with Papp."

"I'm sure we'll sort something out," said Callum, getting to his feet. "What you having? Same again?"

23. Pressure

16th July 2061
Rusholme

When Ruth Brownlow awoke that morning, it was to the twittering of birds and sunlight gleaming through the curtains. She leaned over the side of her bed to pick up her old laptop, prised it open and began the start-up process.

This was not the easy task it once had been; Ruth's computer, as with all such devices, had fallen victim to the many bugs sent out around the time their software makers collapsed and found their way under PapCorp's wing. But Ruth had learned all she knew from this ancient computer, she felt an affinity with it, which is how she was able to install an operating system that by-passed infected parts of the hard-drive and allowed her to use it for basic but untraceable tasks, such as reading the dark web or email.

It took an hour or so of tampering to get to her mail shell. When at last it opened, Ruth found only one message. And it wasn't the one she wanted. 'Undelivered:' it read. 'Email to Naomi Humbolt not permitted due to security infringement. Please try again from a PapDrive or other PapNet-approved device.'

"Damn!" Ruth cursed, slamming the screen closed. "I really thought I'd got through that time." She reached into the bedside drawer and scrabbled around for a yellow credit card. She turned over its plain faces in her fingers and rolled out of bed.

When Ruth came downstairs, she was in a black sleeveless t-shirt and a purple skirt. Her hair was cropped so it stood on end without her needing to brush it. On the bottom stair she sat to tie the laces of her black boots. "I'm going then," she shouted.

"But you haven't had breakfast," said her mother, drying her hands on a tea-towel as she came out of the kitchen.

"I'm meeting Nao for lunch, aren't I? You know what that Pap-crap's like for filling you up."

"Have you heard from her, then?" asked Minnie.

"Nope," Ruth replied, "my email bounced again."

"Then what are you going to do?"

"What choice do I have? I have to go, don't I?"

"But what if she's forgotten?"

"It's a chance I'm going to have to take," said the fourteen-year-old, getting to her booted feet. "My card's down to the last entry, and if I don't get it renewed there'll be no way to get back in the Bio-dome. Seeing as how I can't even message her anymore, that means we'll have lost our last way of contacting her. You see, I'm going to have to go."

Minnie Brownlow shook her head, glanced through into the living room where a bottle of wine stood uncorked on the mantelshelf. "I don't know," she said. "She only lives in Didsbury, not even three miles away. But it's like we don't exist anymore. Imagine getting married but being too embarrassed to even tell your family."

"I'll ask her to contact you," said Ruth. "Like I do every time. But you know what she's like."

"I know," said Minnie, trying to hide her sadness.

Ruth hugged her mother, clicked open the door. "Bye then dad," she called.

Brian poked his head around the top of the stairs. "Are you off then?" he asked. "Don't forget to tell your sister we're always here if she needs us."

"I will," said Ruth, closing the door behind her.

In the year and a half since Naomi won PapStar, Brian Brownlow had changed dramatically. He now worked in the gardens with the others, and had lost so much weight that he moved better than he had in decades. He took a couple of steps downwards, untroubled by his knee. But then he saw his wife at the bottom of the stairs and blinked away from her, turned, and stormed back up without a word.

"Brian!" Minnie shouted. "Come on, don't be like this. Let's talk."

He answered by slamming the bedroom door shut.

Murcia city, Spain

Oscar Talavera was sweating. The yellow sheeting above his head was glowing through the scarf and his brain, sending him dizzy. He knew he had to keep going, but he didn't know how. His heart was pounding like something dreadful was about to happen. He called his wife's name but she didn't answer. Then the panic started and his chest tightened. He collapsed onto the dry streambed.

But instead of hitting the rocky floor, his eyes blinked open and he found himself in his old bedroom in Murcia, where his wife was stroking his clammy forehead.

"It's okay, mi amor," said Dolores. "It was just another nightmare."

Oscar rubbed his eyes with the balls of his hands and rolled away into a ball. It always took him a good few moments to reconcile his dreams with reality.

In a high-cut-off pair of jeans and over-large t-shirt, Aliyá Talavera was biting her nails over the kitchen table when the door knocked. She scraped the chair back, dashed to open it, and found Jaap smiling down on her. "Breakfast's ready," he said.

Aliyá pulled the door closed without a word, her parents knew where she'd be. She trotted after the man's blond dreadlocks into the opposite flat. In the kitchen they found Reggie Carson wearing only an apron and a pair of shorts, sweat dripping down his back. He stood over a frying pan, scrambling eggs on a blue flame.

Jaap and Aliyá sat down, each at a plate dressed with a slice of bread and a wedge of tomato.

Reggie turned off the cooker, carried the pan to the table and served up dollops of yellow onto every dish. He sat down and tucked straight in. "So, have you thought any more about tonight?" he asked as he chewed.

"I don't know," Aliyá replied, picking up a bit of egg in her fingers. "It seems very dangerous to me. I'm not a violent person." She plopped the food onto her tongue and swallowed.

"You won't hurt anyone," said Jaap, "Those trains are unmanned. And it's on the very end of the 'o' so there'll be no one else around. We've got our viewing platform, haven't we Reggie?"

"That we do," Reggie confirmed. "We'll be as safe as houses up there. It's not really violence, if no one gets hurt. You should look at it as a public service."

"Why?" asked Aliyá. "Just because it allows us to steal gas?"

"That and much more," said Reggie.

Jaap chuckled. "With a bit of luck we might even find weapons one of these days," he said. "So, what do you think? Are you coming?"

"I still don't know," said Aliyá, picking up her toast. "I'll think about it."

The Zoltán Papp Tower, Manchester

Halfway up the world's tallest tower, some seven thousand feet above Manchester, Zoltan O'Dillon sat at the end of a long oval table. He was scrolling through animated war scenes on his PapDrive, until an icon flashed at the bottom of his vision and told him his senior advisor had just entered the boardroom. He flicked the button and the digital layers vanished, to leave Francis Atkins standing before him, his hair a wispy grey but his eyes as blue as ever.

"Francis," said Zoltan. "Is that junior advisor of mine in yet? What's her name? Sarah, is it? Or Claire?"

"It's Mary, sir. And no she isn't."

"For Papp's sake," Zoltan sighed. "What is it with these girls? It's like they all have something wrong with them. How hard is it to turn up to work on time? I mean, you and I manage it every day of the week."

"Indeed we do, sir. Most days at least."

"You're always here, Francis, that's the main thing. Bring back Jemima Kemal, that's what I say. Now, what's up?"

Francis sat himself in the chair opposite his boss. "Do you remember Sandra Shaw?" he asked.

"Wasn't she that 1960s' singer who didn't wear any shoes?"

"Close, but no. She was a young woman who disappeared twenty-six years ago. In London, on the night you received your Victoria Cross."

Zoltan O'Dillon leaned forward on his elbows, placed his chin on his fists. "And?" he asked.

"And the body's turned up," said Francis. "PapAid workers in the Chilterns came across a shallow grave as they were building an extension to the migrant camp there. The corpse is in a bit of a state, as you can imagine, but there's still enough of it to take DNA samples. And there've been a couple of positive identifications."

"Is that so?" asked Zoltan. "And who did they identify?"

"Well sir, one of them is Bernie Douglas-FitzAllan, the Earl of Angus. And the other, I'm afraid, is you."

"So?"

"So, you're suspected of rape and murder."

"And what do you expect me to do about that?"

"Well, I um. I thought you should know."

"Listen Francis," said Zoltan. "I admire you as a soldier, and you're invaluable as my right-hand man. But I do wish you'd show a bit more tactical nous sometimes, be a bit more Larry Pickering. Now, how do you know this information? Who else knows?"

"The investigation is being carried out by PapSec, sir, on behalf of the Crown. Apart from the lab staff, I'd say there are just a couple of PapAid technicians, as well as the three PapSec Community Crime Prevention Officers who attended the scene."

"Well? Are they good people? Will they be able to keep quiet or will we have to do a Sandra Shaw on them?"

Francis Atkins inhaled at his boss's choice of humour. "No sir," he said, poker-faced. "I don't think it'll come to that. There are a good many ways to convince them to keep schtum. I'm sure murder won't be necessary."

"Excellent, then I'll leave it in your capable hands, Francis."

"But Zoltan. What about the family?"

"What family?"

"The girl's family, the Shaws."

"Who cares about them?"

"Well, they'll want to know what happened. Remember all those appeals on the news?"

"Come on, Francis," Zoltan sneered, "stop being dim. What do the family matter? We're talking about my career here, basically the most important career of any person in human history. And we both know that all that's not going up in smoke because of some little indiscretion I committed decades ago. You do understand that, don't you Atkins?"

"Crystal clear," said Francis. "But I think you should remember that we're talking about rape and murder here. I'd hardly call that a little indiscretion."

Zoltan O'Dillon slapped his palms flat on the table and stared out his advisor. "Well, I would," he said. "Now on to more important matters. What on earth is going on in the 'o'?"

Rusholme

Even half a mile away, Ruth Brownlow could see the security wall the moment she turned onto Yew Tree Road. It towered yellow over the two-storey terraces, the Bio-dome ceiling arched away from its top and glinted in the sun.

As Ruth approached the wall, a turnstile slid open. It shut behind as she entered, leaving her in a completely dark space. She stepped forward a couple of paces and a yellow square appeared in the far wall. She took the card from her back pocket, held it inside the void and the wall flashed with the PapSec logo.

A metallic voice rang through the blackness. "No destination has been programmed onto this card," it said. "Please remember you can register your destination from the comfort of your own home by using your choice of PapDrive devices. You can also log in through our PapNet portal."

"You can't unless you're a subscriber," said Ruth. "There's no other way to get through to PapNet these days. And believe me, I've tried."

"Please state your destination," the wall interrupted.

"I'm going to the Atom Complex to meet my sister."

"What is the purpose of this visit?"

"Like I just said, I'm going to meet my sister, if she remembers. Do you hear me?"

"This is your final entrance pass to the Manchester Bio-dome Complex," said the voice. "Remember to top up your pass at any PapMart or other PapCorp-affiliated retailer before you leave. Alternatively, all PapDrive implants now come with unlimited access to any Bio-dome in the country, and are currently available for the special price of 999 PapPounds 99."

The yellow square flashed three times, and when Ruth removed the card the wall itself moved aside. She stepped into the Bio-dome, found the conditioned air rubbed up her nostrils and she shivered. "Mum's right about these places," she said to herself. "You can't even get inside without being bombarded by adverts."

It took Ruth Brownlow an hour to get to the Atom Complex, along a route she knew all too well. Because while her sister had become a major popstar, whose last five singles had all gone straight to number one on the PapCharts, she was very much a creature of habit. The only place Naomi seemed to eat, at least with Ruth, was at PapBurger. And always at the same restaurant in an 'electron' of the Atom Complex.

There was no sign of Naomi when Ruth arrived. So she sat herself down on the worn-brick floor, dangled her feet into the dried-out canal basin, and waited.

Murcia City

Jaap and Aliyá left the flat together and walked a couple of minutes to the head of Murcia's old bridge where their strides slowed to a halt. Jaap looked at Aliyá's feet. "Are you sure you don't want to wear those shoes I made for you?"

"No," said Aliyá. "I don't like them. They're so artificial, and make me feel constrained."

"Well, you should wear them on the bike, if you come tonight."

"I haven't ridden a bicycle in years, Jaap. Not since I was about twelve."

"It's not something you forget though, is it? You really should come. I'd love you to see what we do."

"I don't know," said Aliyá. "I'm still not really sure about Reggie."

"How do you mean?" asked Jaap. "He's the most trustworthy person I know. He's got me out of some pretty dicey situations."

"Like Marseille?"

"For example."

"Yeah, I remember you saying about that. But I'm still not sure. Tell me something to persuade me. How did you meet him?"

"I never told you that?" asked Jaap. "Are you sure? Well look, I'll tell you after, when we've had lunch."

"Tell me now."

"We're supposed to be going off to work," Jaap chuckled. "You're going down the river to pick vegetables, and I'm going to the highway to do some digging."

"I don't want to go to the garden. I'm coming with you."

"Really?"

"Sure," Aliyá shrugged," why not? This is a free city, isn't it? So go on, tell me where you met Reggie."

Jaap stared at the young woman, smiled to himself and set off alongside her. Past the marketplace they strolled, where people came and went from an arched doorway so tall as almost to kiss the roof. "You know about me leaving South Africa," said Jaap.

"After your parents were murdered and you had to run away?"

"That's it. Although it wasn't just my parents, of course."

"No."

"Right," said Jaap. "Well, I don't know how long I walked before I got to the jungle. It felt like forever at the time. I'd heard a lot about it, everyone had told me it was real dangerous. But when you've seen your entire community mown down by bullets and burned in front of your eight-year-old eyes, well, it gives danger a different perspective."

"So Reggie was in the jungle?" Aliyá asked. "Is that where you found him?"

"I didn't find him," said Jaap, "his men found me. Reggie was a bit of a personality in those parts. There'd been a warlord that everyone hated, and Reggie had killed him. He was a hero to the locals. Even though he wasn't born in Africa, they took him as one of their own. He had a kind of empire going at that time. When I got taken to him, he was sitting on a throne carved from the trunk of a gum tree."

"And that's how you came to Europe?"

"Exactly. I mean, a few years later that is. There's only so much time you can spend in a place where pretty much everything wants to take a bite out of you. Reggie organised an aeroplane which didn't even need a runway, it just came and picked up a hundred or so of us, dropped us off in Milan and, well, you know most of the rest."

"How you had to fight your way out and ended up in the Marseille Commune? Yeah, you've told me. But you said you were a hundred people. What happened to the others?"

"We lost them on the way. Only about twenty of us got out of Milan without being captured or killed, and I think it was only me and Reggie that managed to escape Marseille."

"So you trust him then?"

"With my life."

"You know he's the first black man I've ever met?" said Aliyá, staring at her toes. "What I find amazing is he's just like you and me, basically."

Jaap laughed so hard that he had to stop walking. He rested his hands on his hips, glanced at Aliyá and burst out laughing once more.

"Hey," she said, slapping his arm. "Stop making fun of me."

"Oh come on, Al, you deserve it when you say things like that. Of course Reggie's just like us, he's a human being you know." Jaap looked at Aliyá and saw the offence in her eyes. "Come on, don't get upset, please. Look, we're getting to the defences."

Sure enough, through the palm trees, the roadway ended under a highway bridge which had been filled up with earth and fortified with lengths of crash barrier.

"There are so many people here," said Aliyá. "What are they all doing?"

"They're digging trenches around our side of the motorway," said Jaap. "This way, when PapSec finally attack, we'll have at least one continuous line of defence. We'll build a second one too, if there's time. But first we've got to finish this. It's a good spot; in most places we have a natural wall of tarmac to hide behind, and we'll have a clear sight of the oncoming enemy."

"So do you think we're going to get attacked?" asked Aliyá.

"It's only a matter of time," said Jaap. "But this won't be like you remember. Before, you just gave up. This time we're going to make them fight for every centimetre of our city. We're going to show them what people can do if they're organised."

Aliyá stopped to reach for Jaap's hand. "You know what's amazing about you?" she said. "That despite everything, even though you've lived your entire life on the run and you've seen such dreadful things, you're always so positive." She worked her fingers around the South African's and stared up at him in admiration.

Atom Complex, Bio-dome 4, Manchester

Ruth waited for hours under the hovering yellow spheres of the Atom Complex. She watched every car intently, wondering if maybe her sister had changed vehicle again. But even though a few pulled up at her spot, Naomi emerged from none of them.

There was only so long she could wait, but the problem of how she would arrange to see her sister again kept Ruth under those orbs until the Pap-yellow surfaces were shining out against the darkening Bio-dome sky. When she left, she trudged towards Rusholme with her hands in her skirt pockets, her mind churning.

She followed the path she always trod, balanced on narrow kerbs and waited for gaps in the lanes of traffic before she could dash across the highways. Ruth rounded the back of the PapUniversity and paused at a four-way junction. She waited ages for a break in the cars, but none appeared. So she changed her mind and her destination and skipped up along the kerb to her left rather than going straight on home.

Murcia

As the morning turned to afternoon, with the sun beating on their heads, the workers by the motorway put down their tools and headed home for lunch. Aliyá left her pick next to Jaap's, and they walked back down the off-ramp, towards the shade of trees and apartment blocks. Down one side of the street, looking over a park and the river opposite, five floors of ripped awnings flapped like flags. And lying in one of the doorways was a mass of cloth. Aliyá slowed to take a look, as did Jaap beside her. She walked up to the rags and prodded them with her finger. They shook to life and a head appeared.

"Paco?" said Aliyá. "Estás bien?" 'Are you okay?'

Paco Junior gazed up at Aliyá with faraway eyes. "Coño," he slurred. "What are you doing here?"

"We were just walking past when we saw you lying there," said Aliyá. "Are you okay? What have you taken?"

But Paco was concentrating on the tall blondman behind her. "Is that your guiri boyfriend then?" he asked in English. "I always thought you were a lesbian."

Aliyá shook her head. "You're an idiot, Paco," she said. "You should go home. Where are you living these days?"

"I don't have a home."

"Don't be ridiculous, everyone has a home. There are a few thousand people living in a city built for half a million. You have your choice of homes, it's not like it was in the sierra. Where's your father living?"

"I don't have a home and I don't need one," said Paco. "I'm perfectly capable of looking after myself."

"Hey, bru," said Jaap. "You're obviously not capable of looking after yourself, are you? If you were, you wouldn't be lying in the street drunk out of your face. Now get the fuck up and go home so my girlfriend and I can enjoy our walk."

"Listen, you dreadlocked hippie!" slurred Paco Junior. "You need to remember whose city you are in. You're a guest here. You don't even speak Spanish. So don't come here and tell me how I should live, okay?" And with that, Paco Junior clambered to his feet and staggered off towards the river.

"That's not the first time I've had words with that guy," said Jaap. "He looks like a real waster."

"He's had a hard life," said Aliyá, turning her face away to hide the tears rolling down her cheeks.

But Jaap couldn't miss her expression nor the tension he saw in her shoulders. "What's up, Aliyá?" he asked.

"It doesn't matter."

"It matters to me when you cry."

Aliyá smiled up through her tears. "Paco was my closest friend," she said. "But he fell in love with me and I didn't feel the same for him. It drove him to drink, like you saw. And to many worse things."

"Oh, shame. Did something happen between you two?"

"No, I mean. He tried. It's complicated. Can we talk about something else?"

"Sure, like what?"

"I don't know, tell me something completely different. Take me away from here. Say something about the world. Tell me about PapCorp."

"PapCorp?" asked Jaap, striding out between the poplars. "Really?"

Aliyá nodded.

"Okay, well you know PapPop of course."

"I know the name," said Aliyá. "And I know PapAqua."

"Sure," Jaap replied. "The drinks were where it started. But things are a lot more complicated than just that. Have you ever heard of the Omsk Accord?"

"No, never. What is it?"

"That was the solution to the last great crisis," he said. "To split the world into 'spheres of influence', they called it. The five biggest companies would get to dominate or share markets dictated by the Accord. There was the American company Spokane, the Russian Beztalneft, Xi-fan from China, Gooda Industries from India and PapCorp from England. The idea was that these national champions would only be allowed to compete in certain places, while other markets would be protected. It was doomed from the beginning, of course. The Russians were the first to go, their borders were just too long and they got attacked on all sides at once. Spokane Inc lasted until the 2030s before it was responsible for little more than a handful of Confederate States. PapCorp took over most of Spokane, and Xi-fan followed a few years ago. Which means it's PapCorp and the Indians left, but Gooda Industries are dwarfs in comparison."

"I never knew any of that," said Aliyá, staring at the ground. "Carmen Hueso barely mentioned anything recent in our history lessons and there was no internet up in the mountains."

"The internet's full of lies," Jaap replied, conceit ringing through his words.

"Then how do you know all this?"

"I've talked to a lot of people, but I got most of it from Reggie. He's a real mine of information. Knows things that no one else's ever mentioned."

"And that's why you know how to attack PapCorp?"

"You mean knowledge is power?" he smiled. "I guess so. I really want you to come tonight, Aliyá. To help us give that stinking company a bloody nose."

"You want me to go on a bike ride somewhere with two foreign men that I barely know?"

"You know me," Jaap responded.

"I do," said Aliyá, gazing into Jaap's eyes. "I'd be a good guerrilla, I think. I've lived in the mountains for years, I can survive anything. I can climb, carry things, swim. Now I just need a bit of military training and I'll be ready to take them all on."

"So you'll come then?"

Aliyá shrugged. "Yes," she said. "Why not? It should be fun."

Manchester

Ruth soon came to a road far too wide to cross, so she did as she'd done the whole way and hopped along the single-slab kerb. But after a mile or so of this, the PapWay split off into ramps which wove themselves into a four-storey stack of motorway. On the lowest level, as she kept going, a tunnel closed in around her and the little pavement vanished into a glowing-yellow wall.

With traffic speeding by inches from her feet, it didn't take long before she heard sirens come to a stop just behind her. "Do not turn around," a voice crackled. "Remain exactly where you are. This is PapSec Highway Patrol, and you are under arrest for trespassing on the PapWay. My colleague will now search you for weapons and other contraband. Do not try to run or we will shoot."

Ruth did exactly as she was told. She'd never pictured herself in a situation like this, especially not alone, and she had no idea what would happen next. All she knew was she didn't want to be shot. She could feel her knees shaking but didn't dare look down at them.

A pair of yellow gloves grabbed Ruth's ankles and worked quickly up her thighs. The officer forced his hands up her skirt, between her legs, over her hips and yanked at her adolescent breasts. Ruth shrieked, tried to twitch away but the officer shouted, "stay still!" He turned to his colleague and said, "I think a full cavity search may be in order."

"Very good," said another man from behind Ruth. He grabbed her shoulders and span her around to face a pair of glaring headlights. "I.D." he demanded.

24. Pop

16th July 2061
Murcia City

Aliyá Talavera was lying on the furthest sofa from the living room balcony, listening to her father pick out a mournful fado from the guitar on his lap. He didn't stop when the door knocked, nor when his daughter jumped up from the opposite couch. But when she clicked the latch open, Oscar spoke before she did. "Is that you, Jaap?" he shouted.

Jaap smiled down at Aliyá but called to her father. "Yes, Mr Talavera."

"Then come inside and say hello, won't you?"

Aliyá shrugged and led him into the living room. At the sight of Jaap's dreadlocks poking around the door, Señor Talavera grinned. "That was a good jam session we had the other night," said Oscar. "Don't you want to get your guitar out and play for a while? You could invite your mate Reggie. Those car-tyre sandals he made for us are brilliant and I'd like to say thank you in person."

"I'd love to," said Jaap, "but we'll have to do it another day, I'm afraid. We have plans for this evening."

"¿Á dónde vais?" asked Dolores from the third couch. 'Where are you going?'

"We're going out, Mamá." Aliyá replied. "We're going to see the 'o'."

"What for?" asked Dolores. "What are you planning?"

Aliyá looked at Jaap but saw he'd understood nothing. "I can't tell you, but you'll find out soon enough."

"What's that supposed to mean?" asked Dolores.

"It means we're taking the fight to the enemy," Aliyá replied. "I don't want to just sit around like before and wait for them to throw us out. When they come for us the next time, we'll be prepared."

"So you're going to attack the 'o'?"

"Not exactly."

"Then what?" asked Dolores. "I'm not letting you leave this flat till you tell me."

"I'm doing this whether you approve or not," said Aliyá.

"It's not about me," her mother responded. "Under whose authority are you acting? This was never discussed at the General Assembly."

Aliya didn't know. She translated the question for Jaap to respond. "Anarcho-syndicalism is non-hierarchical," he replied. "We don't need anyone's permission. But people know us as the Murcia Defence Collective."

Aliyá translated for her mother.

"I don't care what you call yourselves," said Dolores. "You can use whatever name you like. This is our city, your father's the mayor, for goodness sake! And the rule is that these decisions can only be made by the whole General Assembly."

"That's not the rule anymore, Mamá," said Aliyá. "We're not in the Carrascoy now and Papá's role is purely ceremonial."

"Your mother's just concerned about you," said Oscar. "You're the light of our lives and we couldn't bear to see anything happen to you. So be careful, okay?"

Aliyá hugged her father but her mother wouldn't meet her gaze. "I just don't know how it's got to this," said Dolores. "It's like I don't know you anymore. These foreigners have changed you."

"They've changed me for the better," said Aliyá, kissing her mother's cheek. She turned to Jaap, nodded, and followed the South African out to find Reggie.

Dolores heard the door slam and three locks click in turn. "I wish you'd stand up to her," she said. "You of all people should respect the General Assembly."

"Lola, mi amor," said Oscar. "I think she's old enough to make her own decisions now, don't you?"

"I'm not talking about that. They're planning another act of violence without consulting anyone."

"They don't think like us, these kids," said Oscar. "All those years we spent developing direct democracy mean nothing to them. They respect no one's opinions but their own, not even the wishes of the General Assembly count now. We might be living back in Murcia, Lola, but this isn't our city anymore."

Manchester

With nothing to see but the yellow interior walls of the PapSec patrol car, Ruth Brownlow closed her eyes and focussed on her breathing. She found herself whimpering, her knees shaking, butterflies scraping her stomach.

The journey lasted less than ten minutes, but to Ruth it felt a whole lot longer. When they stopped and her door lifted open, it revealed the two officers standing camouflaged against the all-yellow walls of a parking garage. They escorted her into a lift, whose doors closed and shot them upwards so fast that it made her stomach churn. It was all Ruth could do to keep herself standing, she was so scared at the thought of where she might be heading. The lift gave no clues, it was the same plain yellow as the car and security walls, with no buttons or screen – at least none that were visible to Ruth. So she had no idea they'd stopped at the thirty-second floor, didn't know where the officers were leading her down non-descript yellow passageways. They halted beside a section of wall no different from any other. One of the officers whirled his hand and they waited, Ruth now visibly shaking. When the door finally slid open, it revealed a man in a dinner jacket on the other side.

Ruth had never felt so relieved to see Vincent Humbolt, his scalp was as shiny as it appeared on TV, his grin familiarly toothful. "Ruth?" he asked. "What in Papp's name have you done now?"

"We found her walking down the side of the PapWay," said one of the officers. "Her access card gave this as her contact address, so we're just returning her. As she has no previous record, and given her contacts, we're going to overlook this incidence of trespassing. But we advise her to be careful in future, and she's going to need to get her card renewed. This one's run out."

The officers shook Vincent's hand when they left, with thanks for being famous and nice to them.

Ruth stepped into the flat and found herself in a same-yellow box-room with a staircase up the far wall and a doorway below it. It was from there that her sister emerged, in a black dress that hugged her ankles and her hips before finishing at a line under her armpits. Her blonde hair was piled up to reveal diamond earrings that matched the necklace around her bare collar, which glittered like the implants in her eyes. "Ruthie?" she asked. "What's the matter? What're you doing here?"

"We were supposed to meet for lunch."

"Lunch?" said Naomi. "But that was hours ago. Where've you been?"

"I waited for you at the Atom till it got dark," said Ruth. "Then I was walking home when I realised I wouldn't have any way to see you again. So I thought I'd come and find you."

"Down the PapWay," Vincent added. "No wonder PapSec picked you up."

"Next time, send me a message," said Naomi, "and I'll come and collect you."

"I did," said Ruth. "It didn't get through."

"Come on, Ruthie," said her sister, "you're a whizz at computers. Surely you can send me an email."

"I can't. I tried so many ways but PapNet blocked them all."

"Then I need to get you a PapDrive fitted," said Naomi. "We can go tomorrow. You can see me any time when you've got your implants done. We'll get you a room here. You can design it yourself using this great new app I got for the house. I guess you can't even see the Turkish wallpaper and flagstones, can you?"

Ruth shook her head. To her, every surface was the same glowing yellow.

"Come on," said Naomi, "we're having a dinner party. All the guests are here, so you've timed it perfectly. We have room for one more, don't we Vincent?"

"I guess so," Vincent responded. "But don't you think she should get changed first, or do you want our friends to meet your sister looking like that?

Zoltán Papp Tower, Manchester

A sunset projected through Zoltan O'Dillon's implants, reds and ambers streaking across the virtual windows of his office, their reflections shimmering off the dome-humped surface below. A beep in his ear and flashing letters along the bottom of his interface told him that his two advisors were waiting. He flicked his hand and a section of wall slid away to reveal Francis Atkins standing beside a young blonde woman in pig tails and a short denim skirt.

Zoltan O'Dillon wiggled his fingers and a second chair appeared on the other side of his desk; the worker who carried it in was augmented out of their vision.

When his two advisors were seated, the young woman began. "We've been looking at our options," said Mary, "for how to clear the 'o'. Obviously, the terrorist attacks are helping our publicity effort, so we're pretty sure of being able to sway global opinion in our favour. It's just a question of finding the legal way to do it."

"What you don't realise," Zoltan sneered, "is that, ten years ago, when you were still at school, we went over this. Just cut their water off, that's what we did last time."

"You have to remember," said Francis, "that they're significantly more prepared and self-sustaining than before. They've bypassed PapAqua's blocks and now control the water themselves. They grow what they eat and they steal what they don't have from PapTrans trains or convoys."

"What more legal justification do you need?" asked Zoltan. "If they're not stealing from PapAqua they're stealing from PapTrans. I say send in PapSec and show them who's in charge."

"I'd urge caution," said Francis. "We don't want this situation to repeat itself again in ten years' time, so we have to do it right. We're building an international consensus. We'll get the UN resolution and then we'll go in."

"I thought you were a man of action, Francis," said O'Dillon. "I didn't expect to find you sitting on the fence like this. It's almost like you're not with me."

"I'm with you 100 per cent," said Francis, "being a soldier isn't just about action, it's about taking the right action at the right time. We're not there yet, but we will be soon enough."

"I keep thinking," said Mary. "They're not really doing any harm, are they? If PapTrans stop sending convoys and trains through the 'o', they'll have nothing of ours to attack. Why can't we just leave them? I mean, we're building refugee camps for millions in this country, at a cost of who-knows how much. So why are we so intent on clearing somewhere thousands of miles away?"

Zoltan O'Dillon shook his head, inhaling through his nostrils. "I can't believe this," he said, "not only do you come in late, without even a word of an apology. Now you're questioning long-established PapCorp policy without knowing anything about it!"

"I'm sorry for being late," said Mary. "I was here till after two this morning and I slept through my alarm."

"That's no excuse," said Zoltan O'Dillon. "I don't care how late you stay, I need you here first thing, every day. Like Francis. As punishment, I'm going to dock half your wages for this month."

"But..."

"Look, you're lucky I don't just sack you. If you want to argue, I suggest you do it with someone else. I'm a very busy and important man, and I don't have time for all this. Now Francis, have you sorted out this morning's issue?"

Francis Atkins nodded. "It's all done," he said.

Murcia

Along a concrete promenade, beside a route of reeds covering the trickle that remained of the Segura river, Jaap De Waal was riding with his fingers on his scalp, worked into the dreadlocks. Using his thighs to steer, he weaved his bicycle past cavorting couples and families out for a stroll.

It was that time of the evening when the light of the advert overwhelmed the last of the day. In the lemon twilight, Jaap glanced over his shoulder to see Aliyá and Reggie struggling behind him.

"Come on!" he shouted, "put some effort in."

"I'm trying," Aliyá shouted back. "I haven't ridden a bike for years."

"And some of us aren't as young and agile as you," said Reggie.

Jaap stopped to wait, and by the time the others got to him they were deep in conversation.

"So what else have you blown up?" Aliyá was asking.

"Oh, this and that," said Reggie. "There've been a few bridges, a couple of PapTrans trucks, the odd car. But we're not blowing up the train, we're blowing up the track underneath it. The plan is to derail it."

"Right," Aliyá said, considering his words. "Look, I understand why we're digging trenches, to be prepared for when they attack. But what's the point of derailing their trains? Surely all we're doing is provoking them."

"We're taking the fight to them," Reggie responded. "They'll attack us sooner or later, no matter what we do. And we have to be ready for that. Those trains carry all sorts of supplies and come straight through our city. It's like they want us to rob them."

"Maybe that's why we never find any weapons," said Jaap, now riding at Reggie's shoulder. "We're hardly going to be able to fight PapSec with slings and stones, are we?"

"You can do a lot of damage with a well-directed slingshot," said Reggie.

"Not against bombs or machine guns, you can't," Jaap replied.

"We might get lucky," said Reggie. "You never know. Maybe tonight we'll get our first cache."

"Maybe," said Jaap. "I was telling Aliyá earlier about when we met. You were the greatest gun runner in central Africa. But you've not even been able to find us a single pistol."

"In case you need reminding," said Reggie, "I've not been in Africa for years. We're here in the middle of a PapCorp ring, so it's not like I can just click my fingers and magic up some field artillery now, is it? But believe you me, I'm doing everything I can and I'm quite sure we'll have what we need when the time is right."

"Fine," said Jaap, "if you say so. Now could you two just try to go a bit faster? I'm getting bored of waiting."

Aliyá glanced at Reggie and found him smiling at her. She grinned back and chuckled to herself.

Didsbury Bio-dome, Manchester

It was half an hour before the Brownlow sisters were ready. When they entered the living room, Ruth was decked out in a black dress which a woman in a yellow bodysuit had tacked up to fit on demand. They found a room full of guests in suits and dresses. More all-yellow women squirmed in between them, filling glasses and plates, but no one seemed to notice.

Among the jackets and ball gowns, one man stood alone in khaki overalls. His skin was the colour of milk chocolate, his hair a mop of curls. He noticed the new arrivals and shuffled over to them. "Hello," he said. "I didn't think we were expecting anyone else."

"We weren't," said Naomi. "This is my little sister, Ruth."

"Hello Ruth," he said. "I'm Benjamin Humbolt, your brother-in-law, I guess. I didn't see you at the wedding." He stretched out a hand in greeting.

Before Ruth could respond, Vincent slapped his younger brother on the back. "Watch out for this one," he said, "She bites. And I dare say she's carrying something. She's one of the tin hat brigade."

Benjamin chuckled. "Then again," he said, "according to you, I'm also a conspiracy theorist, aren't I? Basically anyone outside the Manchester-PapCorp bubble is mad, according to you lot." He turned to Ruth. "What they don't understand is that the real world goes on regardless of whether or not it's in the *Herald* or on the Humbolt Hour. Despite what they keep repeating, PapCorp isn't some kind of benign entity cast out into the world to do good, let me tell you that."

"So you don't work for them?" asked Ruth.

"I work for them," said Benjamin. "We all work for them, one way or another. There's no one else, is there? I'm a PapNews correspondent embedded with PapSec Fourth Airborne."

"Haven't you just been in Africa?" asked Naomi.

"I've been in the Middle East," Benjamin replied, "just got back a couple of days ago and I'm already itching to get out of the Bio-dome. I hate the way you're never sure what's real and what isn't, and the fake air makes my nose itch."

Ruth giggled. "I know what you mean," she said.

"Speak for yourselves," said Naomi. "When you've lived outside for as long as I have, you get to appreciate the purity of the Bio-dome air."

"Only because all the pollution ends up in Rusholme," said Ruth. "You know how it gets sometimes."

Naomi hummed a response, then turned to the room and clapped her hands. "If you'd like to sit down," she announced. "Let's make a start with dinner."

Yellow-clad servants rolled out a table big enough for all. Sat between her sister and Benjamin Humbolt, Ruth thought herself a halfling at the dinner party. Half guest, half servant, she was the only one at the table who could see the PapMaids. But while she sat with the others in their finery, Ruth missed most of the conversation as they shared animations or jokes through their PapDrives.

When the starters had been cleared and there was a lull in the conversation, Ruth tapped her sister's forearm. "You should see dad," she said, "he's like a new man. He must've lost eight stone since you last saw him. He's even working. They really miss you, you know."

"Yes," said Naomi, fingering a wine glass that magically refilled. "What do you think of my dress? It's by this Mexican designer, Gasparo De La Rey. He's the latest thing, you know, all the top celebrities are wearing his work."

"Nao," said her sister, "please don't change the subject. I haven't finished."

Naomi sighed. "It's just nothing ever changes in Rusholme, Ruthie," she said. "I know dad's doing well. You told me last time."

"Maybe," said Ruth. "But I didn't tell you that mum's been having an affair."

Naomi had her glass at her lips, but put it back down without taking a sip. "Sorry?" she said, now looking at her sister. "What did you just say?"

"Mum's been having an affair," Ruth responded.

"Who with?"

"Neville Jennings from the gardens."

"No way!" said Naomi. "How long has that been going on?"

"Ages, Nao. A decade at least. She even had an abortion, and no one ever knew."

"I can't believe it," said Naomi. "Mum and Neville Jennings… Oh wow, suddenly so many things make sense. He was always around her, you know. And she touched him all the time. Err, how horrible is that? How's dad coping?"

"They're not speaking, let's put it that way. It's a good job he finally has some mates, otherwise he'd be completely on his own. He misses you more than anyone, you know."

Naomi nodded, downed her glass of wine and it refilled itself. Ruth looked up at the servant holding the bottle and nodded in thanks. But the woman in the all-yellow overalls wasn't waiting for a response, and she vanished off to the corner to await her next order. When Ruth tried to continue the conversation, she found Naomi laughing at a skit on her PapDrive, joking with the ham-faced gentleman on the far side of the table.

Murcia

Prickly weeds invaded the paving, leaving just a sliver of asphalt for the three to cycle single file, Reggie at the front, Aliyá then Jaap. Out of the city centre, the air was sweet with citrus from the groves of oranges and lemons. Bats swooped between the trees to feed off the insects that filled the night with their chirping. Between the orchards, the group passed two-storey houses and bungalows with bent-in-the-middle roofs and flaking-plaster walls. On the opposite side of the path, the railway embankment rose up under a mesh of lilac, yellow, and red flowers.

The path widened to a road, which had baked under the sun until the tarmac split. Their bicycle wheels wobbled as they followed the track up over a bridge of cracking concrete and rusted railings. They paused a moment to see the railway split into a delta of lines on the far side, before it vanished into an oblong tunnel under the luminescent sheeting.

This was the closest Aliyá had been to the 'o' since they'd dragged Oscar out more than a year before. She squinted over its flat extent, and when she blinked away the yellow imprint remained on her retina. She looked for the boys and found they were already rolling down the far side of the flyover.

When Aliyá caught up with the others, they were waiting with their bikes by a siding. "So, what we're going to do," Reggie explained, "is lay the device under one of the lines and watch it all from the bridge up there." He wiped his head with a handkerchief, knelt down to open up a hole already clipped out of the fence, then led the others onto the patterned tiles of a platform.

Aliyá looked over the mesh of rails. "How do we know which one the train will come along?" she asked.

"Because I've done my homework," Reggie replied. "I've been out here for weeks, stalking the place out. The PapTrans Express passes at 21:35 every evening, and is precisely six kilometres long, meaning if we stop it here it'll reach all the way back to the city and give everyone a feast at PapCorp's expense."

Aliyá spied a camera on the corner of a hut, looking over the tracks. "Shouldn't we cover our faces?" she asked. "They might see us."

"It's a bit late for that," said Jaap. "If they're watching, it won't just be here. They could just as easily have tracked us the whole way."

"Try not to worry about it," said Reggie. "They want you to feel intimidated, that's how they work the world over. If you're scared of being caught, you shouldn't be out here. But we're quite safe, I'm sure of it. Come on. Don't you want to lay the bomb? My hands are too sweaty." He pulled a box from his backpack and held it out to Aliyá.

"What's that?" she asked.

"This is it," said Reggie. "This is the device."

"Where did you get it?"

"I made it."

"What?" asked Aliyá. "The shoebox?"

"Oh, no," said Reggie, "that I found in the storeroom of an old shop on the Gran Via. Look!"

He opened the lid and showed her the mass of wires and tubing. "I've never yet known one of these to fail. It's simple but effective. And as it's your first time, I just thought you might like to do it yourself."

Fear flashed over Aliyá's face as she considered her response. "Okay," she said in the end, and accepted the box in both hands.

Reggie kept a cable in either hand. "This is the switch," he explained. "Whatever you do, make sure these two wires never touch. When you pass a conductor between them, it triggers what's inside. It's very sensitive, you could even make the connection with your finger."

"Or a train wheel," added Jaap.

"Exactly," Reggie continued. "You just need to make a little space in the stones, slide the box under and keep the two wires separate. Then comes the only delicate part. You have to remove the tape from one wire at a time and attach them to the track, making sure they don't touch any part of the metal. Then we just have to wait for the train to connect the circuit, and 'ping'."

Didsbury Bio-dome

After dinner, most of the guests went off into town to continue their revelling with others, which meant, by the end of the night, only four remained at the Humbolts' flat in Didsbury: the two sisters, Ruth and Naomi, and the brothers Vincent and Benjamin.

Ruth got to her feet and held out her access card to Naomi.

"Could you recharge this?" she asked. "I'll need it for the next time I visit."

"Are you leaving?" asked Naomi. "I thought you were going to stay. I was planning on taking you to get your PapDrive done tomorrow. We won't even have to leave the building, there's a place that does it on the seventh floor."

"No, Nao," said Ruth, "stop it. I don't want one."

"You'll never have to worry about getting into the Bio-domes again," said the older sister.

"Please, Naomi. I don't like those things. They make me dizzy. And I find it weird that you and your friends can see things that aren't really there, but don't know what's right in front of you."

"Well, suit yourself," said Naomi. "Are you sure I can't get a bed made up for you? I've got an app that does it automatically."

"Benjamin's offered to give me a lift back to Rusholme," said Ruth. "I'm going with him."

"Oh," said Naomi. "Come on, the least you can do is stay over."

"I can't, Nao. I don't want to leave mum and dad alone with each other, I'm not sure what might happen if I do. You really should come and visit you know, they miss you very much."

Naomi nodded. "Okay," she said. "Maybe one day. But before that, let's set a date now so next time we don't have to go through all this rigmarole."

It took a while for Naomi to go through her diary, to find a few hours for her sister. She found she could spare none for her parents for at least the next six months.

With the date recorded on Naomi's PapDrive calendar, Ruth and Benjamin shot down the lift to the loading bay, to find a PapAuto taxi waiting like a big bubble of yellow paint. It cracked open and they piled into the driverless pod which closed as they sat themselves inside. Benjamin wiggled his fingers and the car sped away, not that Ruth saw any of the route beyond the padded interior.

"I'm sorry about my brother," said Benjamin. "He can be a real arse sometimes."

"He's a famous man," said Ruth. "I guess he can do whatever he likes."

"That's certainly what he thinks."

Ruth smiled. "He seemed very closed up when I asked about your family," she said. "Was that really a problem?"

"That's how he is," said Benjamin. "Vincent trusts very few people. It's understandable really, Freud would have a field day with him. He knew my father, you see. Not like me. The swine disappeared two months before I was born, never to be heard of again."

"So your mother raised you?"

"She did until I was five, then she had a nervous breakdown so we were basically raised in a PapKids' Home."

"Oh, I'm sorry to hear that," said Ruth. "That must've been very difficult for you."

"It really wasn't that bad, you know," said Benjamin. "We always seemed to have nicer rooms than the other boys and no one ever abused either of us. It was like we had a guardian angel looking after us. And then, yeah, we both got jobs with PapNews. They knew Vincent by the time I finished my degree, so I basically had the pick of any work I liked."

"And you chose to be a war reporter?"

"Well, yeah. It seemed like a chance to travel. I just never imagined I'd have to see so many places destroyed. It's my job to file reports on PapSec activities, although by the time any of my work gets on air it's been redacted so much that it's nothing more than propaganda. I've seen some things, believe you me. I've seen what lengths PapCorp will go to get what they want, and it's scary."

"Do you think that's what they'll do in the 'o'?" asked Ruth.

"In the what?" Benjamin replied.

"In the 'o' of the PapPop ad for the aliens. Surely you know there are people living there."

"Yes, I know," said Benjamin. "I was just surprised you did."

"You see," said Ruth. "The dark web isn't always wrong. What'll happen to them, do you think?"

"The same as PapCorp do everywhere," Benjamin replied. "They'll wait till the time is right, then they'll send in PapSec to go house-to-house and clear the entire city. Same thing they've done from Marseille to Mecca. The communes hold out for a day at most, before falling to the worst kind of defeat you can possibly imagine. There are some real thugs in PapSec."

Murcia

The rail line ran dead straight out of Murcia. So, from their lookout on the bridge, the three could see the train's triangle of headlights for miles. The engine glided through the night, approaching them apparently ever faster until it passed beneath with a whirr, dissecting the delta of railway sidings beyond.

The silence broke, not with a ping but an enormous blast. The front car lifted into the air as momentum took it forward, then crashed to the floor and jack-knifed onto its side, to screech and scrape along the tracks. Wagons piled up behind the engine and ground the train to a halt. But just as the screeching was easing up, there was a second bang, much closer this time. The bridge shook.

"Shit!" shouted Reggie. "Quick! Run! One of the carriages has hit the stanchion."

But as the two men scarpered, the chunk of concrete on which Aliyá was standing cracked and dropped onto the carriages below.

Reggie and Jaap heard the crash and looked back to find their friend gone. "Aliyá!" they cried in tandem.

They heard no response.

Jaap started towards the hole but Reggie pulled him back.

"It's too dangerous," he said, pointing downwards. "We have to get down there. If the rest of the bridge collapses on her, she's really done for."

"You're right," said Jaap, racing for the edge of the road. He climbed the crash barrier, hurtled himself down the bank and towards the piled-up wagons.

But before he reached the first set of tracks, a voice from above stopped him. "Where are you going?" shouted Aliyá.

Jaap and Reggie gazed up to see the young woman dangling from a steel girder on her fingertips.

"Will you help me down?" she asked, shuffling her weight along the underside of the bridge. She jumped into Jaap's arms, said, "thanks," and planted a wet kiss on his cheek. "That was so exciting!" she exclaimed. "When are we doing it again?"

25. The Ides of March

15th March 1962
Manchester, England

As long as they were boxed in between the trucks and buses and factories of Stretford, the cars of all three Papp Beverages directors stayed together. But after the roundabout at Kickety Brook, the O'Dillons were away in their sports cars, up the pristine overtaking lane of the M62.

In his Mini-van, Zoltán Papp tootled along in their wake. Nóra Weissman sat in the passenger seat while Attila Bacsik was crouched away in the back. The men were both wearing the best suits they owned, Nóra had bought a new beige dress. And on their chests all three wore a little rosette, a three-coloured ribbon of red, white and green.

"This is the only reason they wanted to go this way," said Zoltán. "So they can have a race and leave us behind. That's them in a nutshell, basically. All they're ever interested in is showing off and making a fool out of me."

Nóra placed her hand on Zoltán's thigh. "It's only a matter of time," she said. "We have the evidence that shows we're paying 15 per cent more than market rate for pretty much everything we buy. As soon as our lawyers find a witness or two, we'll have a real case."

"I don't know," said Zoltán. "The O'Dillons have a lot of mates who are happy to help cover their tracks."

"As long as they also get their slice," said Nóra. "But we'll get there. As soon as we find that one supplier who'll go public, we've got them."

"That's easier said than done," said Zoltán, brushing her hand away. "I wish I'd never got involved with that pair. I never know what they're up to. I mean, why the hell are we going to Southport? Today of all days? Why couldn't we have done this in Manchester?"

"They're putting on a party for us," said Nóra. "It's going to be fun. The Kingsway Club's famous."

"And I get the feeling they're planning a bit of a surprise," said Attila. "Gábor's been acting strangely around me for a while. He's keeping something quiet, I can read him like a book."

"Something bad?" asked Zoltán.

"I don't think so," Attila replied. "He's been smiling a lot. My guess is it's got to do with Callum."

"So you think they're up to something?" Zoltán continued. "Gábor and Callum O'Dillon have become very friendly all of a sudden."

"The only thing that pair of rascals are capable of getting up to," said Nóra, "is dancing the creep with young girls at the Plaza."

"I know Callum's been teaching him a bit of English," said Attila, "and they've been to a few concerts together. But I don't think the friendship goes any further than that."

"Well, I don't like it," said Zoltán. "And I still don't see why we have to go all the way to Southport to celebrate the fifteenth of March. We could just as easily have done it at the Hungarian club in Chorlton. And I don't like the idea of Gábor and the O'Dillons plotting behind my back."

Nóra laughed. "Do you always have to think the worst of people?" she said. "I mean, I think the plan is to use this for some free publicity. I know there's been a lot of talk about the band that's playing. They were on the radio last week. They sound lively, should be good to dance to."

"Oh no!" said Zoltán. "Will I have to dance as well? I'd have preferred to have stayed back in Manchester."

Nóra tutted. "That's just the answer I'd expect from you," she said. "I wish, for once in your life, you would lighten up and have some fun."

"I can't help worrying," said Zoltán, "it's in my nature. I've never liked dancing, and with the O'Dillons, well, you just never know what they'll do."

Worsley, Lancashire

The motorway ended as abruptly as it began. Éamon O'Dillon pulled his off-gold Jaguar to the side of the roundabout, to wait for Callum then Zoltán. Drizzle splattered the windscreen.

The three Hungarians were five minutes behind the others, but when they got to the roundabout, the O'Dillons were ready. When they set off again, it was back into old England; after the speed of the motorway, it felt like they were crawling past the drystone walls and leafless forests.

"Wasn't that brilliant?" Éamon O'Dillon said to his wife.

"I'm glad we're back on normal roads," said Doreen. "It's like some kind of mania comes over you when you're on that bypass."

"It's my own personal racetrack," Éamon declared. "I know every single curve of that motorway, and I've not yet met a car what can beat me."

"Aye," said his wife. "You keep going like that, you'll end up like James Dean with your beloved motor wrapped round a lamp post, and you in the middle of it."

"Don't you worry, my petal," said Éamon. "I'm always completely in control of my motor. And I do enough miles in her, especially as I'm still searching for a new factory site. I lost a lot of face when Zoltán bloody vetoed the last one."

"I remember. Any news?"

"I'm still working on the Globe Works in Salford. The place's been sat vacant since Grove and Whitnalls got took over. It's not that easy though as no one at Greenall Whitley's is a lodge man, not even in the Warrington branch. But I'm still hopeful it'll be a track worth pursuing."

"If anyone can persuade them," said Mrs O'Dillon, "it's you, Éamon."

Approaching Skelmersdale, Lancashire

It took the three cars an age to get through Wigan, but when at last they were free of the industrial air they could almost taste the seaside approaching. In Callum's royal blue MG, wind rattled against the joins in the cloth roof, gusting through the gaps. Even though the heater gauge was pushed up to maximum, both Callum in the driver's seat and Gábor Bacsik alongside him were well wrapped up in coats and woollen hats.

"Is it always this cold in March?" asked Gábor.

"Not normally," Callum replied. "They're saying this one might be the coldest on record."

Gábor gazed out at a snow-covered fields. "I guess the fifteenth of March was never summertime in Hungary, neither," he muttered to himself.

Callum reached into the glove compartment and pulled out a packet of gum. He offered a stick to Gábor, who unwrapped the silver foil before plopping it into his mouth.

"Something up?" asked Callum.

"I just thinking," said Gábor. "Are you sure this is right thing to do?"

"Of course it is," said Callum. "You've been putting other people first for far too long now. You need to start taking yoursen into account."

"But is my brother."

"Your brother, what's deserted you in the middle of a foreign city. It's him what's chose to live with your ex rather than doing the loyal thing and moving in with you. You don't owe him nowt, Gábor. It's like I always say, look after number one, and number one will look after you."

"Is true," said Gábor. "You right. I just wishing it is not like this."

"Well it is," said Callum, chewing on his gum. "Now come on, we're going to have a good night tonight. You looking forward to the band?"

"I guess," said Gábor, "Who it is?"

"We saw them last month at the Oasis. You liked them a lot at the time."

"We go so many concert lately," said Gábor. "Is difficult for remember the detail."

"I know what you mean," said Callum. "Despite you telling me a hundred times, I'm still struggling with that name. What was it again? Sow-bodge mode-yar?"

"Close," Gábor replied, "Is So-bod mod-jar."

"So-bod mod-jar," Callum repeated.

"That's it."

"So-bod mod-jar," Callum said again. "And you're sure that means 'Free Hungarian'?"

"Exactly."

"And these things?" he asked, tugging at the tricolour ribbon on his coat.

"They for celebrate the revolution against Austria."

"Oh," Callum replied. "A glorious victory, was it?"

"No," Gábor sighed. "Was finish in one year, our national poet die in last battle. For next twenty year they shit on us very bad."

"Great," Callum chuckled. "That's quite a thing to celebrate!"

Southport, Lancashire

The cawing of gulls and salt in the air announced the sea long before they got to the shore. On their way into town, the three-car cavalcade rolled down wide streets with lamp posts painted white on red bases. Trees, still bare from winter, stood in the front patch of every orange-brick townhouse.

"This takes me back," said Doreen O'Dillon. "Remember when we used come up Southport for us holidays? I kind of liked it, you know."

"No you didn't!" said her husband. "You always complained about there being too many people on the beach 'specially when the sun was out. You could hardly move some days."

"Aye," said Doreen, "but Spain's going the same way, isn't it?"

"We'll not be mixing with the plebs in Benidorm no more, my love."

"No. I guess not. We just have to spend a whole day flying to get there. Not exactly somewhere for the weekend, is it?"

"It'll be worth it though, won't it? Having us very own island. Just think of it, Dors. You'll have your own private beach where you'll never have to worry about no one seeing you. You'll be able to get your knockers out any time you like."

Doreen slapped her husband's knee. "That's typical of you," she said. "You do something lovely, like buying us an island, and then ruin it by getting all sexual."

"It weren't meant to be romantic," said Éamon. "It's a business investment and it were going cheap."

"Little wonder," said Doreen. "I mean, who'd buy a place called Mosquito Island?"

"It's named after the Miskito Indians," said Éamon. "that's why they spell it with a 'k'."

"Oh ay right, who told you that? The salesman?"

"It's not important who told me," said her husband. "It's all part of the plan. Us having our own getaway, for any such times as we may need it, is just a happy coincidence."

"The mystical 'plan'," said Doreen, "I'm wondering when exactly you'll tell me what that is."

"You'll find out soon enough, my love. You'll find out soon enough."

Their hotel was a palatial affair of all-white curves and bays, towers and faux-gothic windows. They parked all three cars, one beside the other, facing a low stone wall and the promenade. Through the bare branches of the park beyond, the beach went on forever before a distant sea merged into the churning grey sky.

When everyone was out, Éamon glanced at the gold face of his watch. "Right," he said. "We've got about ten minutes to check-in, drop us bags off, use the loo and get out. I told Mr Jameson we'd meet at seven and I don't intend on being late."

And with that, he picked up his briefcase and swaggered towards a quarter-globe awning, where a man in a black suit was waiting to open the door.

Éamon O'Dillon made sure he was first for the facilities; he didn't even wait for his wife. So, while all the others were still queuing for the lavatory or doing up their hair, he was marching past the façade of their hotel.

On the next corner stood an art-deco building with a flat roof and horizontal grooves in the brickwork. Around the side, a queue of people waited under a covered walkway of little canvas domes. But filling the doorway was a large man in a morning suit, his thinning hair combed over with grease. His nose was pox-marked and bulbous, his belly rotund. He popped the cigar from his mouth and greeted Éamon with a firm but sweaty handshake. "Mr O'Dillon, I presume," said the man, in the sing-song Welsh of the valleys. "You said you'd be here at seven on the dot, so I thought I'd pop down and see if you'd be as good as your word. Now, are you on your own? I was expecting a group of you. Where are the Hungarians?"

"They'll be down in a mo," said Éamon. "They've got to share a toilet you see. But I told 'em I weren't waiting around for no one, as I had an important meeting with Mr Jameson. Like I said on the phone, there's nothing you need know about a man but that he be punctual and have a firm handshake."

"Well, it's good of you to be so considerate," said Mr Jameson, his chin wobbling as he spoke. "You know, it's not often you meet good honest folk like you these days. I had this young lad come for an interview the other day, wanted to be a doorman at my place in Port Talbot, he did. I tell you this as straight as I look at you, he was half an hour late, he was. Come in mumbling something about the buses. Had his shirt out and his hair all over the place. Just weren't right, it weren't. So I said to him, I said 'look you, you can't come here for an interview looking like that. This is a classy establishment I run, and I have no time for scruffiness or tardiness.' And you know what he did? He shrugged his shoulders and walked out with his hands in his pockets, without even a sorry or a thank you for my time. I tell you, the youth of today. They've got absolutely no respect."

"I know what you mean," said Éamon. "Those what ain't fought, that is…"

"Oh don't get me started on the war," said Mr Jameson. "I mean, I wouldn't wish it on anyone, you know. Signed up young, I did, underage like. I mean, things weren't going good in 1917 and everyone was expected to do their bit. But I regretted it the moment I got to basic training, and out in the trenches, well, it was like hell out there, I tell you. Wouldn't wish it on nobody, I wouldn't. But it teaches you discipline, it certainly does that, Mr O'Dillon. Discipline and respect. It was that or die at Passchendaele."

Mr Jameson gabbered on for a good few minutes, as Doreen and Callum turned up with Gábor right behind them. The other three Hungarians came not long after, and Éamon touched Mr Jameson's arm so he stopped talking long enough for the older O'Dillon to say, "This is him. Zoltán Papp, meet Mr Jameson, the biggest casino mogul in Britain."

"It's a bloody pleasure to meet you, Zoltán Papp," said Mr Jameson, grabbing the Hungarian's hand and pumping his loose grip. "And I take it these are your countryfolk. I'm not sure I've ever met real Hungarians before. I mean, I've seen that Zsa Zsa Gabor of course. She's a real stunner, isn't she? And that Ferenc Puskás. Blimey, he can play a bit. But real Hungarians in the skin, I can't say I've ever actually had the pleasure. And now here are four of you all in one go, here to celebrate your national holiday with us in the Kingsway Club. Well it's a real honour, I tell you that for nothing. I thought we'd give you fifteen minutes before the band comes on, to do your bit. Do you know what you're going to say?"

"Who?" asked Zoltán. "Me?"

"Of course you, boyo!" Mr Jameson boomed. "You're the guest of honour, you and your PapPop. My grandkids say to me every time I come up north, they say 'bring me back a PapPop, grandpa.' We had the golfers from the Open here last year, get all the latest popular music ensembles in from Liverpool, but do they care? Not a jot! For my grandkids, your PapPop's the biggest thing around. Now you look a little nervous, why don't you have a drink before you go on? Settle your nerves a bit. Come on, follow me."

Despite the queue around the block, Mr Jameson ushered the guests past the doormen. Through the lobby and up the stairs, he led them into a large room with wood-plank walls and tinsel hanging from the ceiling. Amid a fog of tobacco smoke, conical lamps illuminated green baize tables where men and women sat or stood in all their fineries. They puffed on cigarettes, laying piles of chips on letters and numbers, on the roll of the dice, the drop of the ball. Against the wall, a one-armed bandit pinged out a cascade of coins.

Mr Jameson reached into his jacket and produced a handful of chips. "Now you share these out between yous," he said, dropping the plastic counters into Éamon's upheld palms. "Come downstairs just before a quarter to eight and that way we'll keep on time. Until then, gentlemen and ladies, please feel free to enjoy yourselves. The bar's in the next room. Just tell them you're with the Hungarians and you can have what you want."

Zoltán, Nóra and Attila stood gazing around the room. A man in a dickie bow walked past, carrying a plate of wooden toothpicks stuck into chunks of fruit. Attila helped himself to one and plopped it into his mouth. "Cubes of pineapple on sticks," he said as he chewed. "I wish my colleagues at the locomotive factory on Csepel could see me now. My brother would love this. Have you seen where he went? Don't you think he's acting a bit weird?" He scanned the room but couldn't see Gábor, and neither could any of the others.

That's because the younger Bacsik was sitting at a felt tablecloth on the far side of the room, already sipping from a cocktail glass. The coiffured croupier was dealing cards with the end of a large wooden spatula. And Callum O'Dillon was leaning on Gábor's shoulder, whispering instructions on when and what to play.

But Zoltán Papp had other concerns. "What did he mean I have to give a speech?" he asked. "I hate talking in public, especially in a foreign language. What on earth am I going to say?"

"It'll be fine," said Nóra. "Just say thanks to everyone for liking your drink, and to all the people in England who've helped you along the way. I'll come up with you if you like."

"Yes," said Zoltán. "I'd like that. So what do we do until then?"

"He said it's a free bar," said Nóra.

"Then let's get something to drink," said Attila.

"Do you think they'll have wine and soda water?" asked Zoltán. "I'd love a large fröccs."

"Let's find out," said Attila. "Come on."

They followed the man's broad shoulders, through the gaggle of gamblers and into a room off to the side.

They were waiting in the crowd to get served when Zoltán received a hefty slap on the back. "Ow bist, Zoli?" boomed Henry Gritton. "I've been waiting for you to arrive."

"Hello Mr Gritton," said Zoltán. "Mrs Gritton, it's lovely to see you both. What are you drinking?"

"Just PapPop," said Marjorie. "Henry just doesn't do well on alcohol."

"Nonsense," Henry chuckled, "if there's one thing a belly like this gives you, it's a capacity for ale."

Attila handed out the drinks, including a watery wine for Zoltán and a PapPop for his girlfriend. Mrs Gritton glanced at the young woman. "Is that you, Nóra?" she asked.

"Yes it's me," Nóra replied. "Hello, Mrs Gritton."

"You've really grown up since you were at the farm," she said. "I'd have hardly recognised you. And I see you're not drinking alcohol." She stared at the young Hungarian, saw the flush in Nóra's cheeks, the bump at her belly, and understood.

But Henry hadn't noticed. "The farm's not been the same since you lot left," he boomed. "Now it's just work again, the same old chores, day in, day out. Not like when you were there. Then we were on to something. Still, I guess you're doing what you have to do to keep the wheels turning. We could never have put on an event like this in Clun. Do you remember when I came up with the name, PapPop?"

"When who came up with the name?" interjected his wife.

Zoltán flashed a smile at the woman, but her husband continued. "I read in the paper that you were opening an orphanage," said Henry. "That's a bit different for you, isn't it?"

"I'm not opening it," said Zoltán. "I'm stopping it from closing. The nuns that run the place asked if some of their kids could come for a tour of the factory, and when I saw how thin they were, the rags they dressed in, I offered what I could."

"Good on you," said Marjorie. "I wish there were more…"

Mrs Gritton was in the middle of the sentence when a cloud of pipe smoke engulfed Zoltán's head and a hand at his elbow pulled him away. "I was just having a word with the band," said Éamon O'Dillon. "Four young lads from Liverpool, they seem nice fellas. They're all big fans of PapPop, that's for sure. Won't you come over and say hello?"

As quarter to eight rolled around, Nóra and Zoltán waited in the wings of the stage. Éamon and Callum O'Dillon stood close by, but the four had exchanged barely a word since they'd arrived. And all now were listening to Mr Jameson announce them on stage.

"People love my stories," the Welshman was saying. "I've been told many times I could talk for Wales. But I'm afraid I can't witter on too long tonight, because we've got a great band coming up shortly; I'm not the only one predicting they might be the next big thing. But before then we have some very special guests indeed."

Mr Jameson reached under the lectern for a bottle of PapPop, which he lifted to the stage lights. "I'm sure you all know what this is," he said. "The latest craze sweeping the North West. One I very much hope will soon also make its way to Wales and the rest of the country. And I'm delighted to tell you all that the inventor of this fine drink is here with us tonight. Him and his friends have come here to celebrate a great and important date in their country's history. But I'm going to let them tell you all about that. Because, ladies and gentlemen, I present you here tonight at the Kingsway Club in Southport, the inventor of the greatest drink in the world, Zoltán Papp!"

Zoltán stepped onto the stage, gazed into the spotlights and had to shield his eyes from the brightness. He felt Nóra wrap her fingers around his to guide him, could hear so many people applauding and whistling. But he could see none of them beyond the glare.

Nóra let go of his hand at the wooden lectern. Zoltán looked to her for guidance, and she nodded towards the chromium microphone.

Zoltán took a step forward and coughed. "I'd like to thank everybody here," he said. "Everybody in England for the kind welcome we receive like refugees and for the support you have given us all. Thank you for making PapPop a success."

He stepped away from the podium and Nóra mouthed "ez az?" 'Is that it?'

Zoltán nodded, so Nóra took his place at the mic. "My dear friend Zoltán's English still fails him at times," she explained, "Especially on occasions such as this. But like he said, we're all so grateful for the support the English people have given us. You've made us all very welcome in this country, and you've made Zoltán's PapPop into the fastest growing business in Manchester. Now, I'd like to tell you a little bit about why today is important for us as Hungarians. On the fifteenth of March 1848, the citizens of Pest met in the city's central square to demand an end to Austrian repression. Thousands of patriots rose up against the enemy. On that day, our national poet Sándor Petőfi read out a poem which is now one of the most important verses in the oppressed Hungarian culture and language."

She gripped both sides of the podium and chanted into the mic.

"*Talpra magyar, hí a haza!*
Itt az idő, most vagy soha!"
'On your feet Hungarian, the homeland's calling!
This is the time, it's now or never!'

The Nemzeti dal is six stanzas long, and Nóra recited them all from memory. But while the crowd admired her passion, none but the handful of Hungarians understood a word she said.

People talked louder and louder through the performance, and the applause at the end was more of relief than appreciation.

Mr Jameson had been an entertainer all his life, and after watching the young woman lose the room, he barged her out of the limelight at the first opportunity. "Now, without further ado," he announced, "let me hand you over to Mr Papp's business partners, the O'Dillon brothers, who have a very special announcement to make."

The brothers strode up to the mic and stared into the spotlights. The elder of the two spoke first. "We live in dark times," Éamon declared. "It feels like every day a new story comes out about the Soviet Union and their push westward. The communists are constantly finding new ways to threaten our way of life, whether it's with tanks in Berlin or infiltrating the unions in this country. Against this red tide, many fear to tread. But we have here a shining example of people who said no to Stalin's band of reds, and tried to put a halt to their advance. We have with us today four Hungarian freedom fighters, and me and my brother are delighted to be business partners with one in particular, Mr Zoltán Papp."

The brothers clapped their hands and the crowd did likewise, there were even a few hoots and whistles from the back. When the ovation died down, Callum stepped up to the mic. "Now, we know today's important for Zoltán and his friends," he said. "That's why I'm wearing this ribbon, to celebrate Hungary's national day. And me and my brother, well we were thinking, we'd like to mark this day as well, to show our business partner how much we appreciate him. So we got on to our friends at J&J Vickers of London, the makers of Cossack Vodka. And with their help, we've invented a new drink to add to our range. Based on the refreshing taste of

PapPop, with just enough Hungarian vodka to give it a kick, we are launching a new drink here tonight. We know that our success is all thanks to people like you, people who always choose PapPop. Which is why, with the kind agreement of Mr Jameson, and for tonight only, you can have as many of these new drinks as you like. On the house."

The crowd roared, clapped their hands and started to head for the bars. "But before you all disappear," Callum shouted, "I need to tell you the name!" The chattering faded away and people turned back to the stage. "We've decided to name this drink in honour of our founder, Zoltán Papp. It's not an easy word, but I'm sure we'll all get used to it soon enough. I'm reliably informed that it means Free Hungarian in their language. The name of this drink is So-bod mod- jar!"

The audience muttered among themselves and Callum hollered into the mic until feedback whistled through the speakers. "Say it with me!" he demanded, pumping the air with his fist. "So-bod mod-jar, So-bod mod-jar, So-bod mod-jar..."

As the crowd were caught up in a most un-English of chanting, Zoltán Papp was fuming in the wings. "What the cock is this all about?" he asked. "This is the last straw. Now they've gone and launched a drink behind my back."

"They've named a drink in your honour," said Nóra. "I think that's a lovely thing to do."

"Well, I don't," said Zoltán. "Vodka isn't Hungarian, it's a whoring Russian drink. And where did he learn the pronunciation? I bet Gábor's got something to do with this..."

When the band came on, they were wearing black turtle-necks and leather jackets, their hair flopped over fringes like mops. They took a few minutes to set up, but a couple of guitar strums were enough to get Nóra on her feet at the edge of the auditorium. "Come on," she said. "Let's dance."

"Really?" said Zoltán. "Do I have to? Why don't you go and I'll watch you?"

"Because I want to dance with you, stupid!" she replied, grabbing his wrist and pulling him onto the dance floor. She took his hands in hers, led him into the middle where she started kicking her feet in time to the beat and nodded at Zoltán to do likewise.

Callum O'Dillon had come off stage triumphant, everyone he passed wanted to pat him on the back. When eventually he found Gábor, the Hungarian was hanging around the back of the hall. He hugged his new friend. "Wasn't that great?" Callum asked. "They got the pronunciation pretty good at the end, don't you think?"

"Sure," Gábor replied, staring over the dance floor.

Callum followed his gaze and saw Nóra and Zoltán dancing together. "You want her, don't you?" he whispered. "Think how much it burns seeing that bourgeois arsehole touching up your woman."

"You're right," said Gábor. "Like you say, that fella been keeping me back since I help him out from Hungary."

"Well, you won't have long to wait," said Callum. "I'll give you the signal."

"Okay," said Gábor. "Where's my brother?"

"Don't you worry about him," said Callum. "He's already been taken care of…"

It took six songs of jiving for Zoltán to forget himself on the dance floor. As he waited for the next number, Nóra kissed him on the fold of his neck. "I have to go to the w.c." she said. "You'll wait for me here, won't you?"

"Of course," said Zoltán, kissing her forehead. "I'll be right here. I might even dance a bit on my own."

Callum O'Dillon watched the young woman work her way through the crowds. "Now's your chance," he said, pushing Gábor forwards. "This might be the only time he's alone. Go and do your thing."

"All right," said Gábor, finishing his PapPop and leaving the bottle on a table. "It's now or never, I guess."

Gábor pushed through the dancers and made straight for Zoltán Papp. "Gyere velem," he said. 'Come with me,' "I've got a surprise for you."

"I've had enough surprises for one day," Zoltán responded. "Did you come up with the name Szabad Magyar?"

Gábor beamed. "I certainly did," he said. "And that's not the only thing I've done for you today. Come on, come and have a look."

"I'll just wait for Nóra," Zoltán replied. "I'm sure she'll want to see it too."

"She's already there," said Gábor. "She's in on the whole thing. You know what a good liar she is. She knew about the Szabad Magyar for ages, but I bet you couldn't tell. Come on, follow me. It's in the car park."

When Nóra stepped back onto the dance floor, she stood under the chandelier where she'd been with Zoltán not five minutes previously. But as she looked around in ever more anxious glances, she found he was nowhere to be seen. She realised she was all alone, that she recognised no one there. She ran around the hall, searching every face until she found Henry Gritton slouched on a sofa. "Have you seen Zoltán?" she asked, breathlessly.

"I think he went out the back with Gábor," said Marjorie.

"Thanks," Nóra replied. "Is your husband okay?"

"He's never been able to handle his drink," said Marjorie. "Whenever we go out, he thinks he'll be fine. Then he has two or three glasses and always ends up like this. It was that new Sow-bodge mode-yaar of yours that did it. He only had two, but he put them away like PapPop. Well he'll be paying for it in the morning, let me tell you that."

Gábor Bacsik led Zoltán out of the side door, into an unlit parking lot. "So what is it you want to show me?" asked Papp.

But Gábor had gone. From behind a brick wall appeared a group of men in half-egg helmets and black uniforms. Two of them grabbed an arm each and forced Zoltán to the ground. One covered his mouth with a leather glove while the other pulled back his hair for Callum O'Dillon to glare into his face.

"It didn't have to be like this," said Callum, spitting into Zoltán's eyes. "If you'd been willing to negotiate, we could've bought you out ten times over. But instead, all you've done is hold us back the whole way and plot to have me and my brother arrested. I know what you wanted, you stinking turd."

Zoltán struggled, worming around on the dirt floor. The glove vanished from his mouth, but before he could shout a word, Callum's shoe cracked against his cheek. As Papp reeled, the young O'Dillon searched through his pockets for his wallet and his keys.

Nóra found Gábor waiting by the door. "You shouldn't go back there," he said. "Not now."

"Why not?" asked Nóra. "Do you know where Zoltán is?"

"Yes. That's why I'm saying don't go there. Stay with me, Nóra. I'll take you back to Manchester and we can live together. I'm going to save up for you to do a course at Manchester Polytechnic, like you always talked about."

"Manchester Poly?" Nóra sneered. "I want to study literature, not typing! But you're probably too thick to understand the difference. Now, where is Zoltán?" She barged past her ex-lover, into the forecourt out back. There she found large men in police uniforms dragging a man with a bag over his head towards a black van. "Zoltán!" she shouted, "What's happening?"

"Nóra!" Papp yelled from within his cloth hood. "Menjél ki!" 'Run away!'

Nóra saw Gábor guarding the door and took a look at the large men surrounding her. She charged towards the least agile, ducked under their arms and ran out into the night.

Struggle all he might, Zoltán Papp was unable to stop his captors from lobbing him into the back of the van. As he lay on the floor, bewildered and lost, he heard Callum say, "look at this Gábor. Isn't it a wonderful sight?"

Zoltán tried to get up and run towards the voices. "És te, Gábor!?" he shouted. 'And you?' But that was all he could do before the rear doors clunked locked. Zoltán Papp heard the engine start, the squeal of wheels on tarmac, and he fell back onto the van floor. "Stop!" he shouted. "Stop this now! You can't do this to me. You've made a mistake! I'm the inventor of PapPop, and this is England, where there are laws! This is our day, they've just named a drink after me! I'm the Szabad Magyar for goodness sake! I'm Zoltán Papp!"

"Tudják, ki vagy," a familiar voice growled. 'They know who you are.' "That's why you're here."

"Attila?" asked Zoltán. "Is that you? What's happening?"

"Yes, it's me," said the man. "And I think it's obvious what's happening, isn't it?"

"For you, maybe," Papp replied. "I've got a bag over my head."

"So have I," said Attila. "But you don't need to see to realise what's going on. We're being kidnapped, we've been betrayed."

"Kidnapped? Betrayed? Who by?"

"By your business partners, of course."

"And your brother," said Zoltán, as he realised what was happening. "My God! What do they want with us? Why have the police arrested us?"

"They're not police," Attila replied. "They're Hungarians. They sounded like ÁVOs to me."

"But how can the ÁVO be in England?" asked Zoltán. "This isn't right. Let me out!" He banged on the side of the van.

The moment the back door had closed, Gábor vanished off into the night shouting "I have to find Nóra!"

He never would find her. That night she vanished so completely that it would take generations to discover where she went. The young Bacsik would return to the Kingsway Club hours later, dejected and alone.

Callum and Éamon watched the van scoot away; the younger brother sucked on a cigarette, the older wheezed on his pipe. Callum fumbled in his jacket pocket and produced a set of keys. "Here," he said. "You'd better take these."

"What for?" asked Éamon.

"Well, if no one turns up to pay his bill, the hotel are going to get suspicious, aren't they? Get in there in the morning and pack up his stuff. Tell them he urgently had to go back to work or something like that. Make sure you tip them well, so as no one asks any questions. Gábor's going to drive the Mini back to Manchester in the morning. You got me?"

"Bloody hell, Callum!" said Éamon. "Who died and made you king?"

8th April 1962
Clun

Henry Gritton liked his toast with a thick layer of marmalade and a healthy serving of butter. He took great pleasure in spreading out the homemade cream, and was always meticulous in making sure it didn't contaminate the marmalade spoon. He crunched a bite from a slice, turned the page of his Sunday newspaper and found an article headed 'PapPop founder retires'.

He read on without noticing the blob of marmalade splatter into his lap. 'With the proceeds he's made from PapPop,' read the article, 'Zoltán Papp has bought his own island!

According to a statement released by the company, Mr Papp has left Papp Beverages Ltd. He is retiring to Moskito Island, in the British Virgin Islands, with his friends Nóra Weissmann and Attila Bacsik. There, they will be reunited with their families from Hungary, and will get to live out their days in peace. The *News of the World* wish them all the best for the future. The company is now being run by local Manchester businessmen Éamon & Callum O'Dillon.'

"Hey, Marjorie," called Henry. "Have you seen this?"

"What's that?" she asked, coming out of the pantry with hands full of turnips.

"Zoltán's retired," said Henry.

"What?" asked Marjorie. "Retired? That doesn't seem likely. All he ever wanted to do was make that drink of his."

"I know, but look what it says here."

Marjorie read the article. "Well I never," she said. "I guess you're right, wouldn't be in the paper otherwise, would it? It would've been nice of him to say goodbye though, don't you think?"

"Yep," said Henry, folding up the newspaper. "That's just what I was thinking."

26. Truth

9th December 2037
Whitby

Rain cascaded from the guttering atop whitewashed ends of terraces, off the edge of Helen Humbolt's umbrella and into streams on the pavement. The streetlights were off – they barely came on at all these days. But through the early morning darkness, Helen was already hurrying her four-year-old son along by the wrist.

Even though Rebecca and Parjit lived just a few minutes' walk from the Humbolts, Helen could count the number of times she'd been there on the fingers of one hand. It'd been almost twelve months since her previous visit, to drop around last year's Christmas card. But today she wasn't going to exchange pleasantries.

When she got to the house, Helen barged through the gate and hammered on the front door. Despite the hour, a light flashed on in the upstairs window and footsteps were soon pattering down stairs. The spyhole flashed and the door swung open.

"Helen?" said Rebecca, pulling tight her dressing gown. "It's not even six a.m. What on earth is the matter?"

"Is he here?" asked Helen.

"Is who here?"

"Winston. Is he here?"

"No," said Rebecca, "why should he be? Come inside, it's pouring with rain."

Helen did as her friend insisted. "I'm sorry for waking you," she said, leaving her umbrella in the porch and wiping her feet on the mat.

"It's okay," Rebecca replied. "Parjit's on night shift and I never sleep well when he's not here. What's the matter? Are you crying?"

Helen wiped her face with her sleeve. "I just don't know what to do," she said. "He went out in the early hours, when he thought I was asleep, and he hasn't been home since, even though he knew he was supposed to take Vincent this morning. So I was wondering…"

Rebecca shook her head. "Sorry Hells," she said. "He's not here."

"Do you promise?"

"Of course," said Rebecca. "I would tell you that, you know."

Helen nodded. "I guess so," she said. "I've got used to him vanishing off without a word, he does it so often these days. The only time I can normally trust him is when he says he'll look after our son. I really don't know what's got into him, it's like he's turned into someone I don't know, like all this stuff is taking him over. Whenever I ask, all he says is that we'll all be safe. All three of us." She undid her coat and unveiled her pregnant belly.

"Oh, Helen!" said Rebecca. "Congratulations! I didn't know."

Helen tutted. "Winston didn't mention it?" she asked.

"No…" said Rebecca. "We've had a lot going on of late. Things are about to get interesting. But you look about ready to drop. How far gone are you?"

"Seven months," said Helen. "Would you believe it? We had sex once in like two years. One romantic night to celebrate our wedding anniversary, and this happened."

"I see," said Rebecca.

Helen dragged Vincent around in front of her. "Listen, I'm already massively late opening up the shop," she said. "Do you think you could take this one to school?"

"Of course," said Rebecca. "It's not like I have much else to do these days, not since they issued me with that gagging order and closed down the *Star*." She opened the door to the living room.

"That was dreadful," said Helen, peering in to see a pile of yellow shoeboxes arranged against the far wall. "What've you got there?" she asked. "Are you selling shoes now or something?"

Rebecca giggled. "No," she said. "They're not shoes."

"Then what are they?" asked Helen.

"I'm not sure I'm allowed to tell you. Winston's sworn us to secrecy."

Helen blinked at her friend. "Is it safe?"

"Basically."

"What do you mean 'basically'? Is it okay to leave my son here?"

"Sure it is," said Rebecca. "That's what we've been preparing. It's all set up but it's perfectly safe, we haven't attached the batteries or the fuses yet."

"You mean they're what? Bombs?"

Rebecca put a finger to her lips and nodded. "We don't use those kinds of words," she said. "You never know who might be listening. But you needn't worry about Vincent, he'll be fine." She turned her attention to the four-year-old. "Would you like some breakfast?" she asked. "I'll make pancakes if you want."

It was always dark when Helen got to her bakery, at that strange hour when the shopfront Christmas lights were off down Bellevue Terrace. She found the lock without looking, opened the glass-panel door and inhaled. For a moment, the blend of old baking and pine furniture took away her worries. She flicked on the lights, headed behind the counter and disappeared off into the kitchen.

She opened at eight as always, she had regulars to serve, even though by then her products were still in the oven or sitting on trays to cool. A queue soon formed, people took up tables on the ground floor and the gantry, eating their cakes and sipping their coffee as they browsed their various-sized Xi-fan sheets.

At just past nine, a pair of PapSec Community Crime Prevention Officers entered the shop and pushed straight to the front of the queue. "Mrs Humbolt," the shorter of the men demanded. "I'm going to have to ask you to come with us."

"What for?" asked Helen, counting out change into an old lady's hand before continuing. "I can't go anywhere right now. I'm alone here today, Stacy's having the day off and my husband's gone awol. I've got customers almost queuing out of the door as it is. Now, who's next?"

"I'm serious, Mrs Humbolt," said the officer. "I can see you're busy but we have a job to do. You're going to want to come with us. We have your son."

That got Helen's attention. She put down the currant bun she was serving. "What do you mean you've got my son?" she asked. "Where is he? Is he okay?"

"He's perfectly well, ma'am. Thanks to PapSec that is. We caught him playing on the floor just feet from a hundred kilos of high explosives."

"Oh," said Helen. "Rebecca said he'd be safe. Is he hurt? What's happened? Does this have something to do with my Winston?"

"Ma'am, your son is perfectly fine. Will you please accompany us to the station?" She glanced at the queue of customers. "Am I under arrest?" she asked.

"Not at all," said the taller officer. "We just want you to collect your son."

"Okay," she said. "Then shut the door and turn the sign to closed. I'm going to serve all these people as quick as I can."

"Can we help?" asked the shorter PapSec man. Helen shrugged. "That'd be great," she said.

In the back of the PapSec patrol car, Helen Humbolt watched lights blinking the outlines of reindeer and stars. From behind rain-streaked windows, she saw the flat-towered church on Flowergate; the dinky old alms-houses; the backs of St Hilda's and St John's; the front of the train station which now advertised its owners as 'PapTrans'.

They parked up opposite the hospital, where cranes were swinging together sections of yellow tower and the sign at the entrance read 'PapMed Whitby'. PapSec had their headquarters in a brand new building opposite, where the North Yorkshire Police had once been.

Helen followed the men across a walkway over a waterless moat and through a revolving door. They went straight on past a reception desk and the lightning-like PapSec logo, down a corridor of concrete walls and flickering neon lights. After passing countless steel doors on either side, they stopped before one on the right. The shorter officer tapped at his Xi-fan sheet and the locks clicked open in turn.

Inside, the walls were the same bare grey as the corridor, a strip glowed identically from the ceiling. In the middle of the room was a metal desk with a chair on either side. The officers marched on in but Helen held back. "Where's my son?" she asked. "You said he'd be here. What's going on?"

"Your son is safely in the building," said the shorter officer, "we'll bring him to you when you're ready."

"I'm ready now."

The man responded by pulling out the chair closest to them. "Take a seat," he said.

"No," Helen replied.

"Please," said the officer. "Make yourself comfortable. You're not in trouble, you know."

Helen Humbolt glared at the young man. "Then tell me what's going on," she demanded.

But before either officer could answer, in walked a slight man in a yellow dress uniform. A shock of blond hair stuck out from under his peaked cap and he carried a cup of coffee in either hand. He smiled as he strode past the other three, placed one paper mug on the far side of the desk and the other before Helen's seat. He pulled up the far chair and sat down, nodded to the two officers and they left the room. He pulled a Xi-fan sheet from his breast pocket and tapped the screen until the door swung locked behind them. "It's better we're not disturbed," he said, gesturing towards the seat opposite. "Please."

Helen thought a moment before sitting down, but sit down she did. She looked at her cup of steaming brown, then into the sky-blue eyes of the man opposite.

"Milk with three sugars," the man declared, in a voice straight out of public school. "Just as you like it, Helen. You don't mind me calling you Helen, do you? I feel like we know each other so well."

"You can call me Mrs Humbolt," Helen replied. "I've never seen you before in my life."

"No," said the man. "Of course you haven't. It's just, I know so much about you."

"Do you?" asked Helen. "Where from?"

"Listen, Mrs Humbolt, there's something you need to know about your husband."

"Why? What've you done to him?"

The man smiled. "We haven't done anything to him, he's quite safe."

"I don't believe you. I want to see him. And I want you to bring me my son so I can go back to work."

"We'll bring you little Vincent in good time," the man replied. "But I'm afraid Winston Humbolt no longer exists."

"But you just said he was safe."

"He is."

"You talk in riddles," said Helen. "Will you just be straight with me and tell me what's going on?"

"My name is Brigadier Francis Atkins," said the man. "And I'm in charge of various PapSec special operations. Which is how I know the man you know as Winston Humbolt. He's one of us."

"What are you saying? That Winston works for PapSec?"

"Precisely."

"Since when?"

"Pretty much since he was born. He was raised at the Zoltán Papp Memorial Orphanage, after all."

"So all the time I've known him?"

"Sure. How do you think you were able to give birth in a PapMed clinic, and have your bank loan postponed while you took maternity leave?"

"We're with the District Bank," said Helen. "What's that got to do with PapCorp?"

"The District Bank is a front for PapBank. Has been for decades."

"Oh," said Helen. "I didn't know that."

"Not many people do," Francis Atkins replied.

"So you're telling me he's a spy?" asked Helen, quite calmly. "And you've been watching me for years?"

"Not really you, Mrs Humbolt. You're what we call a Collateral Intrusion."

"What on earth does that mean?"

"It's the term we use for innocent people affected by PapSec's operations. I'm afraid the man you knew as Winston Humbolt went a bit over the line with you, but we are prepared to make you a handsome offer. He's a good man and he feels very strongly for you."

"You think you can just buy me off?"

Francis smiled, pinched the opposite corners of his Xi-fan sheet and pulled it to the size of a letter. He laid it on the table, clicked a couple of icons and a document appeared. He swivelled his index finger over the sheet's surface and dragged it around for Helen to read. "This is our proposal," he said.

Helen glanced at the first page. "What's this?" she asked. "Some kind of gagging order?"

"It's a wide-ranging contract including a generous refinancing package for your bakery, a half-mile exclusivity clause for baked goods in Whitby town centre and PapMed care for life, for you and your boys. Not just that though, because PapCorp will ensure they get the best education money can buy. When it's time, your boys will get grants to go to university and study whatever they wish. We'll even find them decent jobs and set them up for life."

"I only have one boy," said Helen.

"Not for long," said the Brigadier.

"So you even know the sex of my unborn child?"

The man nodded. "His sex and his name," he said. "He's going to be called Benjamin. It's Winston's wish."

"But Winston doesn't exist!"

Francis Atkins grinned. "The man's still alive," he said, "still working for PapSec. He's just not going by the name Winston Humbolt anymore."

"Then what's his real name?"

The Brigadier shook his head. "That's something you can never know," he replied. "I'm afraid one of the conditions of our agreement will be that you're never allowed to search for your husband, and that you can never speak about what happened."

"Then I can't agree to this," said Helen, pushing away the Xi-fan sheet. "This is illegal."

"Let's not get into the legalities of the past, Mrs Humbolt. We're here to discuss the present and the future."

"I should go to the police," said Helen. "The real police, I mean. You people should be punished for what you've done."

"I would strongly advise against that," said the Brigadier.

"Would you now? Well I want to speak to someone from RASCAL, I want a lawyer."

"Mrs Humbolt, please. I know this is a lot to take in, but let's try to be civil about it. After this incident, I wouldn't be surprised if RASCAL disappears from Yorkshire completely. Paul Broddle's been arrested as the ringleader."

"But he had nothing to do with it!" Helen screamed. "When I'm called to court, I'll testify on his behalf. Poor man, Winston had it in for him from the start, and now I know why. He's been set up, he never would've been involved in anything like this."

"There, I'm afraid, you're wrong. Mr Broddle was found with the same explosives as at three other properties, including the house of your friends Rebecca Kingston and Tariq Emami. Along with Fiona McIntyre and Kyle Clarke, they're being charged under the Justice and Security Act 2013, and are therefore outside regular judicial proceedings. You can forget your day in court, Mrs Humbolt. In fact, you can forget about everything if you go public. If you choose to reject this agreement, you'll lose your house, your business, your family and your reputation. You may well end up being tried for treason in a special tribunal, like your friends, and be sentenced to 30 years' hard labour without parole. We'll have your sons taken away and raised in a PapKids Home, and you'll never see them again. Believe me, we can make your life hell in many different ways. But if you accept. Well, then you'll get to return to normality, to raise your sons and run your own business, just as you've always wanted. The one condition is your silence."

"So if I sign this contract, will I get Vincent back?"

"The moment the ink is dry, virtually speaking, your son will be returned to you and you'll be free to leave."

"Why?" asked Helen. "What's the catch? I still don't get why you're doing this. You could frame me just as easily as Paul Broddle."

"We're not in the business of framing anyone," Francis Atkins chuckled. "Your husband is one of Lord Michael's most trusted servants. We know you're not exactly PapCorp's biggest fan, we have years of you on record saying so. But we know you're not an extremist either. You just want what's best for your family, and we understand that. PapCorp is also like a family, you know. And you're one of us. More so than you could imagine."

"Just because the father of my children is a PapCorp stooge, doesn't make me part of the Pap family."

"I'm not talking about that," said the Brigadier. "Do you have any idea who your grandmother was?"

"She was a German Jew. What's that got to do with anything?"

"She was Jewish," the man explained, "and she did have a German name."

"Noreen Whitman's not very German."

"Her name was Nóra Weissmann, you know her by the anglicised version. We believe that your grandmother was the woman who fled Hungary in 1956 alongside Zoltán Papp. When he retired from PapCorp and left the country, he left his pregnant girlfriend here. She fled Manchester and went into hiding, never to be found during her lifetime. We're virtually certain that your grandmother was that woman. Which is what I mean when I say Vincent and his baby brother are the nearest you can get to PapCorp's own children. They're more than likely Zoltán Papp's great grandkids. So we'll see them right, don't you worry."

"What absolute tosh!" said Helen. "One minute you're telling me my entire life's been a lie, and now you're claiming I'm Zoltán Papp's granddaughter? Let me tell you this, Vincent and this unborn child are mine and mine alone. PapCorp cannot touch them."

"On the contrary," said Francis Atkins. "PapCorp are providing your medical care, as we've done all along. Do you really want to risk giving birth in a public hospital? Child mortality rates in those places are almost medieval and the nearest one's in Leeds. Agree to this and you'll get the best medical care money can buy, here in Whitby. Not to mention all the other benefits I've mentioned. It'll be like returning to normality, only with a secure financial footing."

Helen stared at the page for a good while before she spoke again. "You know," she said at last. "It's like suddenly everything makes sense. I knew something was going on, and I'd been dreading the moment I'd find out what it was. I thought he'd been having it off with Rebecca or Fiona, but instead he was planning to betray them. I thought maybe he was involved in the mob or something, that I'd come home one day and find his headless body on the sitting room floor." She shrugged her shoulders. "I guess things could've been worse," she said. "He always said he'd make sure we were safe, so I guess this was what he was talking about. Give me a pen or whatever it is I need to sign his thing, and let me get back to work."

"Just press every page with your index finger," said Francis, relaxing back into his chair. "And Vincent will be right with us."

Rusholme

Brian Brownlow, fifteen-years-old, had run the eight miles back from training to his parents' house on Welwyn Street. But he was barely out of breath when he pushed open the front door. The warmth of the living room hit him as he entered, and when he took off his training shoes he also removed his red jumper. "What's for tea?" he asked, stepping inside.

His mother tutted. "Oh Brian," she said, "you've got mud on your socks. And now I'm going to have to clean the carpet."

"Oh," said Brian, rolling off his football socks. "I'm sorry about that, mum. Do you want me to help clean up?"

"Don't you worry," said his mother, "I'd rather do it myself. You have a sit down, I bet you've had a hard day."

"I scored five goals," said Brian. "They're talking about moving me up to play with the under seventeens."

"Oh, well done! Then you deserve a rest. Go on, take a seat. Put a blanket under you, mind. I don't want you getting mud all over the chairs as well."

Brian did as his mother said and glanced at the screen to see a seaside town and lines of PapSec vans. "What's all this?" he asked.

"It's been on all day," said his mother. "Another gang of radical terrorists been found out. Apparently they had enough explosives to blow up half of Manchester. They were plotting to assassinate Zoltan O'Dillon. Thankfully, PapSec got there in time. The news is saying they've arrested half the local RASCAL party, including the Parliamentary candidate. He was in charge of it all. Another was the editor of a newspaper that got closed down for telling lies about Lord Michael, his dad. Hang them, I say. Traitors they are, the lot of them. Prison'd be too good for those bastards."

27. Exile Again

2nd April 2063
Murcia

Even though the sun was yet to breach the horizon, the omnipotent lemon glow of the 'o' lit the streets of Murcia. People thronged through the alleyways and boulevards, but their chants of excitement were drowned out under the chiming of what felt like every church bell in the city.

Aliyá, Jaap and Reggie Carson rode their bicycles between the pedestrians and the piles of furniture on every corner, there ready to be moved into barricades at the shortest notice. Despite the car-tyre sandals, which even Aliyá now wore, the bottles, sacks and ammunition dangling from the belts of their patched-up cargo pants made the three of them look every bit revolutionary soldiers. It was an image only compounded by the metal whistle around Reggie's neck and the rifle at Jaap's shoulder.

Over the old bridge they went, past the church of Carmen and the gardens that shared her name. But no one today was working the vegetable patches, because what seemed like the whole city was out walking, skipping, marching down the boulevard. People carried flags of the Second Republic, banners with the word Pap crossed out in black. Some held their friends' shoulders or bottles of alcohol, singing or chanting as they went. Aliyá and the men passed a group of teenagers, arms around shoulders, chanting, "No pasarán! No pasarán!" 'They will not pass! They will not pass!"

Ahead, a wall of bricks and sandbags blocked the roadway and the crowds bunched as they squeezed onto a footbridge. When their turn came, Reggie, Jaap and Aliyá swung the bike frames onto their shoulders and shuffled over the train tracks, up the steps which swayed under the weight of so many.

Aliyá Talavera glanced at Jaap. "Isn't it brilliant?" she said. "I've never felt an atmosphere like this. It reminds me of that poem 'blessed it was to be alive that morn, but to be young was very heaven'."

Jaap smiled down at her. "Aren't you nervous?" he asked.

"Not at all," Aliyá replied. "I've never felt better. Why? Are you? I thought you'd done this sort of thing before."

"Nothing quite like this," said Jaap.

Reggie slapped the younger man's dreadlocks. "You'll be great," he boomed. "I can feel it. We're really going to show them who's boss today."

"So you're not scared?" asked Aliyá.

"I'm running on adrenaline, like you," said Reggie, between breaths. "When you've seen as much action as me, you get used to it in a strange way. But there's still nothing like the thrill of the build-up."

"And you never got hurt?" Aliyá enquired.

"Sure, I've been injured," said Reggie. "I've died more than once."

"How can you have died?" asked Aliyá. "You're right there."

"Magic!" said Reggie, panting heavier as he reached the top of the walkway.

"Don't make fun of me..." Aliyá's thoughts trailed off as she too got to the top step and had her first sight over the city. The sky to the south was alive with aircraft, that swooped and swirled before a mountain range which glowed yellow and vanished at an artificial cut-out. "I've never seen so many drones," she said.

"They're not all drones," said Reggie. "Some of those aircraft are Nordenfelt troop carriers. Do you see the parachutes with people on the end? We're going to have quite a battle on our hands today."

"How are we ever going to fight against that?" said Jaap.

"Just follow the plan," Reggie replied.

"It'll be tough without weapons," said Jaap.

"We have weapons," said Reggie.

"Yes, sorry," Jaap sneered, "I forgot. A few hundred old MX75s with four bullets each. I can imagine we'll make a great show with them."

"We wouldn't even have that if it weren't for Aliyá."

"That was just luck," she responded.

"You make your own luck in this world," said Reggie. "But you were like a charm – every train we attacked with you brought ever greater rewards. Between you and our defensive plan, I'd say we're ready to put up a good fight."

On the other side of the tracks, the mass of people started to thin out as they took up their assigned positions. Back on their bikes, the three cycled on only a few more blocks, then swung themselves into the last alleyway before a stack of refrigerators, washing machines, tables and sofas completely blocked the main road. On the pile, people were climbing to take up their positions and defend the line.

The barricades had been placed to seal off the route, to lead the invaders down narrow alleys decorated with a strategic pattern of shoe boxes. Aliyá, Jaap and Reggie slowed to wind through them, before leaving their bikes propped up against a rust-closed shutter below a sign that told of once being a hairdressers'. Then they darted inside an open doorway and hurtled themselves upstairs.

Reggie was some way behind the younger two when they got to the fourth floor.

"It all feels so well-planned," Aliyá said to Jaap. "We're really going to fight PapCorp. It's like I've been waiting for this moment all my life!" She flung her arms around the man's waist and stretched up to peck his neck with her lips.

But Jaap pushed her away and refused her gaze.

"What is it?" said Aliyá.

"Nothing," said Jaap. "I'm just nervous."

"But you've faced PapCorp before."

"And every defeat was worse than the last," said Jaap. "I can't stop thinking about all those times, in Milan and Marseille just like at Gareipdam. I guess at least this time we're taking the attack to them, we're prepared and everything, but…"

At this moment, Reggie finally got to the top of the stairs. He was panting, sweat was pouring from his brow. "Why didn't you go in?" he wheezed. Seeing his younger companions shrug, Reggie turned the handle, barged the door with his shoulder and it swung open.

They found themselves in a single-room flat without furniture. Only one door led off it, to the balcony beside the window under which stood a row of glass bottles filled with clear liquid and rags stuffed into the necks.

Aliyá eyed the bottles. "Is this all there is?" she asked.

"That's all we need," Reggie replied. "Just enough to block off the alleyway and give us time to attack."

"And hope they step on a shoebox bomb? I was dreading hitting one with a bike tyre." Jaap and Reggie glanced at each other and shrugged. "You shouldn't have worried," said Reggie. "Most of them are filled with stones."

"What's the point in that?" asked Aliyá.

"It's designed to slow them down," said Jaap, peeking around the curtain at the empty street below. "If they have to stop to defuse all those boxes, they'll be like sitting ducks for us to pick off."

"But didn't you say bullets wouldn't work?"

Reggie smiled. "It's nice to know you were listening," he said. "I'm not sure about the bullets, it's been a long time since I had any contact with PapSec. But I do know they've been working on defensive forcefields for decades. I'd be surprised if these metal bullets have any impact at all."

Aliya pulled a slingshot from a trouser-side pocket. "Which is what these are for," she smiled.

"Exactly," said Reggie. "Nothing metallic can penetrate PapSec's defensive forcefield. But we have stones and glass and fire."

Aliyá nodded. "So what do we do now?" she asked. "Shouldn't we prepare something?"

"Everything's ready," said Reggie. "Now we just have to wait. Take a seat, it's better not to move around too much in case someone spots us. Jaap will tell us when he sees anything."

Aliyá shrugged. She took a couple of strides towards Reggie and sat down on the floorboards beside him, crossing her legs and balancing her elbows on her knees. Off in the distance, she could hear the clatter of gunfire and cracks of explosions.

"Why aren't we on the front line?" asked Aliyá. "It sounds like they need everyone they can out there."

"Because this is our station," said Reggie. "Far enough forward to help take the attack to the enemy, and close enough to the bridge for us to lead the organisation of the railway defences."

Aliya fingered the slingshot, jangling the stones in the leather pouch at her waist. "And you think stones will really work?" she asked.

"Sure," Reggie responded. "A bombardment on an armed car will create such a racket that they'll be unable to concentrate, and a well-placed rock to one of those helmets will knock out their circuits and leave the soldiers blind and deaf."

"But do you honestly think we'll be able to overpower an army with tanks, cannons and aircraft?" Aliyá glanced at Reggie and saw she wasn't going to get a reply. She pondered the situation for a moment before changing the subject. "I was wondering," she said. "What did you mean you've died more than once? Were you being serious?"

"I've had many lives," Reggie responded. "Too many for one lifetime, if truth be told."

"So you never got injured?"

"Oh, I've been injured," said Reggie. "Sometimes very seriously. I've not always been so careful, you see. My worst injuries were all self-inflicted."

"Then you didn't fight?"

Reggie turned his eyes to Aliyá's, and she felt him baring his soul. "I've been at war my whole life," he said. "Even when it looked like I was at peace, I was fighting. Even when I didn't want to be. To me, death has been a means of escape. It can be very useful being dead, you know. You can get up to all sorts of things that living people cannot."

"Like what?" asked Aliyá.

Reggie smiled. "Like all sorts of things," he said. "I wouldn't be here if I was alive, for instance." He relaxed the back of his bald head onto the wall, closed his eyes and started moving his mouth like he was counting or praying.

"I don't understand," said Aliyá. But when she saw there'd be no answer, she too sat back against the painted-plaster wall and fiddled with her slingshot.

Reggie was nursing a terrible but familiar weight in his stomach, and he felt he'd already let out too much. So he kept his eyes closed, his face blank, and listened to the advancing crackles and bangs.

They could feel the guns approach long before one turned into their alleyway. Aliyá had no idea how long they'd been waiting, but by the time the vibrations shook the walls, the sun was shining yellow through the curtains and she'd bitten off most of her fingernails.

She and Reggie had been watching Jaap for ages before he turned and nodded to them. They got up on the signal, grabbed a couple of bottles each and crept out onto the balcony. Aliyá crouched behind the plate-metal wall and turned to face Reggie who'd done likewise. He pulled a lighter from his pocket, clicked the flint and lit the rag of a bottle which he leaned towards Aliyá for her to light her own. Fuses burning, they waited for what felt like an age. Aliyá's heart pulsated through her whole body. Then Reggie said, "now!" and they tossed the bombs over the wall. Smash, smash, bang!

Jaap came out from behind the curtain with a rifle at his shoulder, his eye in the sights like a hunter. He took aim at one of the soldiers, fired, and went for another, then relaxed the barrel of his rifle. "The bullets have no effect," he said. "I guess you were right about that forcefield. And I think they've seen us." He nodded at the gun turret jerking into alignment at the end of the road. "We have to get out of here!" he yelled. "They're going to shoot!"

The South African charged off the balcony with Reggie and Aliyá close behind. She glanced at the base of the wall and paused. "What about all these bombs?" she asked.

"Take some with you if you want," said Jaap. "But we have to go this instant!"

Aliyá gathered up four bottles in one arm and dashed after the men. She got to the stairwell, grabbed the railing with her free hand and bounded downstairs. She'd got down one floor when the shell hit the building. The floor shook and plaster dropped from the walls and the ceiling. A second later, there was an even bigger explosion as the petrol bombs ignited. Flames tore through the door and robbed away the air like a hurricane. Aliyá didn't pause to look up, Jaap and Reggie were already around the corner below. She glanced at the bottles in her arms and bounded after them two steps at a time.

When she got to the foyer, Aliyá still hadn't caught up with the men. She didn't see where they ran from the door, and as she opened it she hesitated a moment to take in the scene.

There was now rubble everywhere. Torn concrete blocks and bent metal bars littered the roadway. There were fires like puddles of flame. Around the robotic gun at the end of the block swarmed soldiers in all-yellow body suits and spherical lemon helmets.

Aliyá's caught her breath. Now was her chance. She put down all the bottles but one, which she tipped towards a flaming puddle. The rag caught and Aliyá threw the bottle as hard as she could. It exploded some metres away, throwing blazing petrol over the first two soldiers, who screamed into their helmets and ran away. "Siiiii!" Aliyá screamed. She picked up another bottle and threw that one too "that was for all my friends you've killed! This one's for Juanjo's house!" She lobbed another, and another. "And that's for my childhood, which you stole!"

It was only when she had no petrol bombs left that Aliyá noticed the wall of fire she'd created. The heat hit her cheeks and she turned to run from the drones that were hovering over the flames.

But as she did so, Aliyá found her way blocked with a familiar form. "Paco?" she asked. "What are you doing here?"

"They're advancing faster than anyone imagined," Paco Junior replied. "I heard you shouting and I came to find you." He glanced upwards. "You have to take cover!"

Paco jumped at Aliyá. He tripped her up and fell on top of her.

"What are you doing?" Aliyá shouted. "Are you drunk? Get off me!"

"I always loved you!" Paco shouted above the drone of swooping rotors. "I've only ever wanted to make you happy and safe."

Then the firing started. Remote-targeted bullets ripped into Paco's back. Aliyá felt the life shudder out of the man with every hit, until blood splattered from his mouth and all of his weight pushed down on her chest.

Her breath stuttered. Her heart pounded adrenaline. She heard the drones whirring away and someone lifted Paco's body from hers. She scrunched up her eyes, took a breath and muttered a prayer to herself, "nuestro señor…"

But instead of the gunshots she expected, there was a tug at her shoulder and an, "Are you okay?"

She opened her eyes, found Jaap staring down at her. "I," she stuttered, "I think so…"

"Then get up, we need to get back behind the railway line."

Aliyá staggered to her feet and chased after Jaap. Around the corner she ran, saw Reggie with the bikes and she slumped against a brick wall. She closed her eyes and inhaled, feeling her hands shaking in shock.

Reggie took one look at the blood dripping from the young woman's face, neck, and t-shirt. "Good God, Aliyá!" he said. "What happened? Are you okay?"

"Yes," she replied. "I think so. This isn't my blood."

"Oh, well done!"

Aliyá shook her head away and Jaap took hold of her arm.

"We have to go," he said, placing the handlebars of her bike into her hands.

She blinked up into Jaap's sky-blue eyes, saw the waves of black smoke obscuring the heavens, and jumped onto the saddle. Aliyá pedalled with all she had, clutching the handlebars so tight that her hands stopped shaking. But her heart still fluttered with relief and regret as much as fear at the explosions and the whirring rotors, the barrages of shots and the screams of pain. She rode straight and didn't look back.

Aliyá only slowed down a few metres from the footbridge. There, lingering behind a tree, she spotted her former teacher.

"Señora Hueso?" she said, pulling to a halt. "It's dangerous here, you should go back home."

"And wait to be captured?" said Carmen Hueso. "No thank you. I'm going to attack."

"You can't attack," said Aliyá. "You don't have a weapon."

Carmen wobbled a moment on her feet and unbuttoned her jacket. She pulled it open to flash a mesh of wires and tubes. "I have this," she said, fastening her coat again.

"But…" said Aliyá. "But you'll kill yourself!"

"Not just myself," said Carmen. "I intend to take as many of the invaders as I can with me. If anyone can afford to put their body on the line, it's an old widow like me. What do I have to live for now? Three forced removals is too much for any lifetime, especially at my age. But you youngsters, you've got your whole lives ahead of you. This will give you time to get away. You stay safe and free, Aliyá Talavera. Don't let them lock you up and take away your spirit. Now, go on, go. Save yourself."

Old Señora Hueso turned from the railway and hobbled towards what remained of the barricade, where all-yellow PapSec soldiers were spewing through the gaps that'd been blasted through the piles of household furniture.

Aliyá caught up with the men halfway up the footbridge, as Reggie puffed and panted and all were carrying bicycles on their shoulders. She was expecting the flash of light that lit up the street, and held on tightly to the handrail. When the blast hit, it shook the metal structure but nobody fell.

Aliyá's calmness surprised even herself. She felt more lucid than ever as she muttered a prayer for old lady Hueso. But if her thoughts were clear, her drooping mouth told of the despair that ravaged through her belly and her tearless eyes.

Reggie noticed Aliyá's face. "Mourn them later," he panted. "We need to get behind that wall."

"I know," said Aliyá. "That's now pretty much our last line of defence before they get into the old city." Reggie nodded, but Aliyá wasn't finished. "Where did Señora Hueso get the bomb from?" she asked.

Reggie shook his head. "It doesn't matter," he said.

"It does matter," said Aliyá. "Did you two make Carmen Hueso a suicide vest? She was my teacher, you know."

"I know," said Reggie. "She told us that all the time."

"She was very insistent," Jaap added.

Aliyá shook her head away but didn't reply. She found she hadn't the words for this situation, and certainly not ones in English.

On the other side of the railway bridge, Reggie parked his bike up against a crumbling concrete wall. Jaap and Aliyá did the same, then turned to the steps like Reggie did, directing people left and right to man the barricade.

"Take up your positions!" Jaap shouted. "Be ready to engage."

"But don't attack until you get the signal," Reggie added.

After some minutes of pointing, Reggie turned to the other two. "I think it's time we got into position," he said, "now that I've finally caught my breath. People seem to know what to do."

They found a spot at the wall not fifty paces away. Jaap and Reggie were tall enough to see over, but Aliyá had to climb up on the sandbags to get a look at the other side. She saw PapSec soldiers pouring down every street towards them. They gathered across from the railway tracks, in an unbroken line some ten fighters deep.

Jaap glanced at the few defenders along the wall. "My God," he said. "We haven't got a chance."

"We have to do what we can," said Aliyá. "Hold out for as long as possible."

"And what do we do when they defeat us?" said Jaap.

"We go home," said Aliyá. "What else can we do? I have to try and defend my parents."

"That's what we agreed," said Reggie. "If we get split up for any reason, we rendezvous back at the Talaveras' flat..." A buzzing of overhead rotors drew away Reggie's attention. He glanced over his shoulder, yelled, "Take cover!" and ducked down just as the first wave of attack drones sprayed shot all over the far side of the wall.

Reggie Carson listened intently to the attacks, counting the time intervals between each one. But it was too much for Jaap to take. He unstrapped the rifle from his back and put it to his shoulder.

Reggie pulled down the barrel. "If it didn't work on people," he said, "it won't work on drones. And don't attack till I give the word." He saw he had the attention of those around him and cleared his throat. "Listen folks," said Reggie. "I would hope that in the years we've known each other, that we've developed a kind of mutual trust. From now on, it's going to be very important that you heed my orders. As you've all seen this morning, we're not playing battle games now, this is the real thing. The only way to defend this city is to hold this wall. And we'll only make a difference if we all attack as one."

Reggie removed a slingshot from his back pocket, put his whistle to his lips and blew. "Take arms," he shouted. Other whistles sounded down the line and the order got repeated. Reggie Carson waited for the next attack to pass over, then blew on his whistle again. "Take aim!" he ordered, standing to face the onslaught. The defenders stood on command, swinging slings above their heads as Reggie'd taught them, waiting for the command of "Fuego!" 'Fire!'

Most of the pebbles dropped harmlessly to the ground, but Reggie's and Aliyá's weren't the only ones that flew like bullets. One hit the drone at the apex of a v, smashed into the rotors and sent the tiny helicopter veering into the path of the next in line. That one hit the next, and they collided like flying dominoes, sending half a dozen smashing onto the train tracks.

"Great shot!" yelled Aliyá. "That showed them!"

Even as Reggie smiled, there was a distance in his look. "There are plenty more to come," he said.

But as they waited, the next drone attack just didn't seem to arrive. Reggie peered over the wall. "Oh shit!" he blurted. "They're advancing!" He blew on his whistle again. "Take aim," he commanded.

This time, Jaap aimed his rifle.

"Fuego!" Reggie shouted.

Shots and stones rang out, but the PapSec line just kept getting closer.

"Fuego!" Reggie yelled again.

Aliyá let out screams and sprays of pebbles, which crashed into the advancing army but didn't seem to have any effect.

When Jaap ducked behind the wall, Aliyá did likewise. "Do you want my bullets?" she asked.

"There's no point, is there? They don't make any difference."

The clacketty clack of rifle shot soon died away as all the defenders ran out of ammunition. There was a moment of quiet, a pause long enough for someone to shout "No pasarán!" Then the storm broke all around them. Remote-guided missiles blasted holes in the concrete and brickwork.

A mortar shell exploded behind the wall, far enough away that they were out of range of the shrapnel burst. But the arms and legs flying bloodied through the air were clear for all to see.

Jaap fell to the floor.

Aliyá saw him drop and she crouched down beside him. "Are you hurt?" she asked.

The South African lifted his face to Aliyá's, but found he was shaking so much that he was unable to speak. There was another blast, a bit closer this time, and Jaap collapsed into Aliyá's arms. Suddenly he was eight-years-old again. "Mamma!" he yelled. "Mamma!"

Hugging her blubbering boyfriend, Aliyá assessed the scene. "Hey," she said. "Have you seen Reggie?"

Jaap shook his head but didn't look up.

People were rushing from the wall, more every second. Aliyá stroked Jaap's cheek. "I can't see him anywhere," she said. "And we're going to be completely isolated here. If we don't move back this instant we'll be surrounded by PapSec."

"But we're supposed to hold the line," said Jaap. "And what about Reggie?"

"He'll meet us at the flat, like he said," Aliyá replied. "The line's already disappeared, there's nothing left to hold. Now come on. Run!"

They dashed doubled-over from the railway defences, to the cover of the wall where they'd left their bikes. Seeing Reggie's gone, they grabbed their own and pedalled for all their legs could carry them.

Aliyá and Jaap sped past so many others, all with terror strewn through their faces, none daring to look back. Nobody stopped to arrange the final barricades, knowing they'd be useless. Drones tracked the retreat, but they weren't dropping bombs or bullets. Instead they carried speakers that spoke to the crowds in a synchronised mixture of English and Spanish.

"This action is being undertaken in accordance with UN Resolution 10-42," they announced. "All resistance is illegal under international law. Give yourselves up to PapSec soldiers and you will be peacefully relocated. Do not resist. Resistance will be met by force. Surrender in peace and you will be allowed to live." It repeated in Spanish, and then English, and Spanish again, all the way back to the Talaveras' flat.

When they got inside, Aliyá and Jaap dumped their bikes in the hallway and sprinted up the three flights of stairs. Aliyá undid every latch in turn, and on the inside she locked them again the same way. Then the pair darted into the living room, to find Oscar playing his guitar, Dolores standing at the window.

Aliyá knew just what her mother's reaction would be when she caught sight of her. "Dios mío," Dolores declared. "What happened? Where are you injured?"

"I'm not injured," said Aliyá, "This isn't my blood. Is he here?"

"Is who here?" Dolores replied.

"Reggie. Have you seen him?"

"No," said Oscar, putting down his guitar. "Why? What happened? Wasn't he with you?"

"He just vanished," said Aliyá. "One moment he was there, the next he'd gone."

"Well, he's not here yet," said Oscar. "He's probably off blowing up a bridge or something, you know what he's like. Now what happened to you?"

Aliyá went to reply but the words stuck in her throat.

"Whatever happened," said Dolores, "you need to get clean and changed," She caught a glimpse of Jaap's face. "And what about him? He looks like he's seen a ghost."

Aliyá glanced at Jaap. "It got a bit scary out there. The bombs were too close and I think it reminded him of his childhood." She tugged his sleeve and spoke in English. "Jaap, why don't you sit down?"

"I don't want to sit down," Jaap replied. "How can I sit down at a time like this? I don't even see why we're here. We should make a run for it while we can."

"Because this was where we agreed to meet," said Aliyá. "We can't go anywhere until Reggie turns up."

"He might as well be lying dead in a ditch, for all we know," said Jaap. "It's ridiculous to think we're waiting for a dead man. Every second that goes by, we're putting our lives in ever more danger. If we'd kept going on the bikes, we could be at the 'o' by now."

"You think they've killed Reggie?" said Aliyá. "I really doubt that. My dad was just saying he's probably off blowing up a bridge or something. Like Reggie told us, he's been in these situations before. He's got more lives than a cat. He'll know what to do."

"Then where is he?" Jaap whined. "Every minute we spend in this flat is a minute lost. We have to make a move this instant. I've got a bad feeling about all this."

"You hear what they're saying," said Oscar. "That we will all be peacefully relocated if we don't resist."

"I don't trust a word PapCorp say," Jaap replied. "How did we ever think we'd beat them? What chance did we have when our opponent owns the world and everything in it? We need to get out while we can."

"And where do you suggest we go?" asked Aliyá. "All the villages around here are empty, and I doubt they'll let us back into the Carrascoy. Anyway, what makes you think they'll find us? There are hundreds of thousands of apartments in this city. Why do you think they're going to come straight to this one? We have time. We just have to figure out what we're going to do."

"All right," said Jaap. "But let's do something. We still have a few Molotov cocktails in my flat, let's go and get them, just in case."

"Jaap!" Aliyá shouted. "Calm down, for goodness sake. If we attack them now, it's provocation and they'll just kill us all. We've put up our fight, and now have to wait here to see what happens, there's nothing else we can do. Now, will you please sit down? I have to get changed."

Benjamin Humbolt had witnessed many scenes in his time as a PapNews war correspondent, from devastating bombing raids to relentless tank assaults. But the thing he hated most was going house-to-house, pulling out the enemy and using that as an excuse for whatever the PapSec soldiers so desired.

In the stairwell between the second and third floors, Benjamin glanced up at a dozen fully armed PapSec troops in their seamless yellow helmets with rifles at the ready. The only two men whose faces he could see were at the front of the section, near the door. One was the commanding officer of the mission, Sergeant Tompkins, whose yellow beret did little to hide the clumps of baldness in his blond hair. It was he that addressed the squad. "It could get a bit hairy in here," he said. "According to our intel, this is one of the nerve centres of the resistance. Don't touch anything, you never know what might be booby trapped. And follow my orders to the letter."

The man he was with looked like a rebel fighter, with a slingshot in his back pocket and a whistle around his neck. But it was he who was unlocking the door.

When Jaap and the Talaveras heard the key in the locks, they knew it could only have been Reggie. But their hopes collapsed when the door crashed open.

"This is PapSec Fourth Airborne!" Sergeant Tompkins shouted. "Everyone in this flat is ordered to show themselves immediately. Come out with your hands in the air. Don't try anything or we will shoot."

Panic flashed across Oscar's face, but he replied with all the calmness he could muster. "Okay," he shouted. "We're coming now. There are four of us. We're coming with our hands up. I am the elected mayor of this city, and I claim diplomatic immunity for myself and my family." He did as instructed, marched out of the living room and around the kink in the corridor.

Dolores followed, but Jaap held Aliyá back by the wrist. "Whatever happens," he said. "I want you to know that I love you more than I've ever loved anyone in the whole world. Have you got that?"

Aliyá slapped her lover's chest. "Don't be silly," she said. "What do you think's going to happen? I've been through this before, you know. We'll be fine." She reached up to peck his cheek with her lips, turned on the toes of her sandals, put her hands above her head and followed her parents into the corridor. She stopped at the sight of half a dozen large men down either wall, wearing all-yellow skin suits and same-coloured helmets. In the middle stood a thin man, tall, his pencil-line lips and pointy nose visible under a yellow beret.

Jaap was the last to join the group. When he came around the corner with his hands up, the officer shouted "that's him!" and the two nearest soldiers took an arm each.

"What are you doing?" said Aliyá. "He came peacefully. You're supposed to let him go."

"That doesn't apply to this one," said the officer. "Jaap De Waal, you have been sentenced to death by firing squad, which we will perform immediately outside." The two officers yanked him towards the door while a third covered his head in a sack.

"Stop it!" Aliyá shouted. "You can't do that! He came peacefully!" She ran at the officer, grabbed him around the throat and dug her fingers into his neck. Four PapSec soldiers came to his aid. They prised Aliyá's hands from their Sergeant and forced her down in an armlock, pushing her face towards the parquet floor.

Just before they forced a bag over her head, Aliyá noticed a familiar form at the door. "Reggie!" she yelled, "Reggie, help! Reggie!"

Then her voice was muffled inside a cloth bag and she was forced back to her feet. Aliyá struggled against the men holding her wrists and kicked out at whatever she could. She shouted, screamed, cursed in English and Spanish. But to no avail.

Reggie saw what was happening but didn't try to stop it. Outside in the corridor, he glanced at the man with floppy black hair and olive-smooth skin, wearing a vest emblazoned with 'PapNews' and 'Press'. "You're Benjamin Humbolt, aren't you?" he asked.

"I am," Benjamin replied. "Who's asking?"

"That's not important," Reggie responded, pulling the journalist up the last couple of stairs and towards the flat opposite. "Listen, son," whispered Reggie. "You need to take better care of your mother. She's an old lady now and she's only ever had your best interests at heart. Without my food packages, she'd probably have starved years ago. It's not her fault what's happened. When you're back in England, go and see her, she'd like that. She's going into hospital next week and she could do with some support. And get that good-for-nothing brother of yours to go too." He nodded towards the open door. "Now brace yourself," he said. "This isn't going to be pleasant."

Benjamin looked over to see a gaggle of PapSec soldiers heaving out two rebels with bags over their heads. Behind them stood an older couple in shock and in tears. He looked back to find the man had vanished. "But…" he stammered to no one.

The section set off with Tompkins at the rear, and Benjamin skipped down the stairs to join him. "Who was the man that led us here?" he asked.

"Who?" said the officer. "The big bald black fella? Don't you know who that is?"

"Nope."

"That's Zachery Klein," said Tompkins. "He's one of PapSec's finest men. You never quite know where he'll turn up, but as soon as he does you know to follow him. The man's an absolute legend. So much so, I thought he was dead. But that's the PapCorp rumour mill for you, you never can tell what's true and what isn't."

Credits

This novel contains excerpts from a number of verses, as credited below:

Chapter 1

Excerpt from the poem *'Sípja régi babonának'* (*The whistle of old superstitions*) by Endre Ady. Translated by Hanna Hámori and Adam R. Mathews, 2018.

Chapter 5

Final lines of the poem *'In valleys of springs of rivers'* by A.E. Housman, from *A Shropshire Lad*, first published 1896.

Chapter 9

Excerpt from the song *'Hard-headed woman'*, written by Claude Demetrius and released by Elvis Presley in January 1958 through Gladys Music.

Chapter 16

From *'Dirty Old Town'* by Ewan MacColl, written in 1949 and first performed in 1952.

Chapter 18

From the song *'Big Yellow Taxi'* written, composed, and originally recorded by Joni Mitchell in 1970.

Chapter 22

From the final stanza of the poem *'Ha férfi vagy, légy férfi'* (*If born a man, then be a man*) by Sándor Petőfi, translated by William N. Loew and published in English by Paul O. D'Esterhazy, New York, 1881.

Chapter 25

The first lines of Hungary's *'Nemzeti Dal'* (National Poem) written by Sándor Petőfi in 1848, translated by László Kőrössy, 2004, and adapted by Adam R. Mathews, 2018.